Praise for *Blackchurch Furnace*

"*Blackchurch Furnace* is one of the most amazing books I've ever read. It reads like an underworld testament, groaning with ghost histories, clanking and burning with all the shuffling grandeur of its subject, Cincinnati. It's haunting, it's furious, it's beautiful, it's a book only Nathan Singer could have written. He's the kind of writer who'll just destroy you, in all the right ways."

—Benjamin Whitmer, author of *Pike* and *Cry Father*

"Similar to author Victor LaValle (*The Ecstatic*, *Slapboxing with Jesus* and *Big Machine*), Nathan Singer is an urban wordsmith that blisters the pages with a language only he can scribe. *Blackchurch Furnace* is an apocalyptic head-scratching mystery laced with hip-hop, Louisiana metal, 9/11, Afghanistan and Iraq. Characters scour to L.A. and back to where the story is rooted amongst the struggling class of Ohio with Gothic saviors, saints and prophets searching to redefine what was once moral and just. This book is loud, comical, witty, and comes with a soprano-shriek that screams 'fucking read me!'"

—Frank Bill, author of *Crimes in Southern Indiana* and *Donnybrook*

"Reading Nathan Singer's *Blackchurch Furnace* is like coming across a lost book of the Bible, equal parts profound and profane. Singer's work has beauty and brutality in a balance no other writer can match. *Blackchurch Furnace* is a brilliant story of loss and struggle, pushed by an unrelenting momentum and characters of such power, such precision, that their impact will leave a sacred mark on the devout reader."

—Steve Weddle, author of
Country Hardball

"*Blackchurch Furnace* is a relentless, visceral, and black-humored ride through America's alternately pious and depraved id. It turns a keen and tender eye to bars, churches, porn mansions, and boiler rooms. Singer has managed a finger-trap of a story that weaves together realism and apocalypse, heavy metal and children's books, redemption and the lack thereof."

—Tyler McMahon, author of
How the Mistakes Were Made

Diane,
We all live happily ever after!

BLACKCHURCH FURNACE

OTHER BOOKS BY NATHAN SINGER

A Prayer for Dawn
Chasing the Wolf
In the Light of You
Transorbital
The Song in the Squall

NATHAN SINGER

BLACKCHURCH FURNACE

Down & Out Books
3959 Van Dyke Rd, Ste. 265
Lutz, FL 33558
www.DownAndOutBooks.com

Cover design by Inabsolute

ISBN: 1-946502-18-9
ISBN-13: 978-1-946502-18-6

This book is dedicated to Benjamin Michael LeRoy.
Straight-up fuckin' stardust, son.

CONTENTS

OLD TESTAMENT

Psalms....................3
....................27

Ecclesiastes....................5

Exodus....................63

BLACKCHURCH FURNACE....................189

for Inanna's daughter (with notes)....................317

Apocrypha....................329

PROLOGUE PART 1

MIN, AGE 14..."QUE SERA SERA"

Exhibiting the titular wisdom, like Tituba at a witch burning, MeShayle stood pointing fingers at other dead-ringers and hangers-on. She lived on her own, where Countee Cullen met Geezer Butler for pagan prayers and H-bomb bass tone. She lived on her own. Alone, where lost poets guzzle Jack and go deaf from thrash and blind from dirt crank (and there are no *old* brothers here).

There'd never be a blast beat without Art Blakey. Street corner rhymin' set to tin cans rolling down an alley. And it just ain't loud enough. This just ain't loud enough. TURN THIS FUCKER UP.

MeShayle was a no-nonsense baller, ya heard. Played the streets like a violin, like a Shaolin, her body was the temple where the lonesome and the loathsome came to worship. Worshipping as they came. Her thighs the gateway to the garden. *Or so she kept 'em figuring,* triggering hot-spot guilt rides when suburbanite suitn'tie albino cockroaches come to town for conventions and a taste for the unconventional. To go to town on a lil sista who's been down here before. Fever producer, tension reducer, she's a street walking medic holding the world's oldest cure-all. Keepin' a steady beat blasting—

"This all you got?"

And she fourteen years old.

"You cain't fade me!!!"

Did I mention that she fourteen?

She fourteen years old
and she ain't never owned a pair of roller skates.

MeShayle ain't never been to a school dance. Never had a first date or bum-rushed a show. Ain't ne'er gonna crush on nobody her own age. Her peers are zombies, wash-outs and ain'never-beens—young enough to know better, too old to care. Rocking a tune at the edge of the world…And it's flat, ya heard. Flat.

The tune, the world, the rock, the edge—

It's flat, ya heard? It's flat, ya feel me.

Feel me. You feel me?

It's flat. *Turn it up.*

She ain't got no delusions that it ain't all flat and dry like a drought-choked wheat field in July. Whores burn like witches out here. Burn like fading stars. Like little Black girls in an Alabama church basement.

(MeShayle, my bail, someday won't you play your very own song? Trés bien ensemble.)

But for now, here, in 2001, whatever will be will be. She just fittin' to let 'em all burn. And keep a driving beat on old trash cans and thrash a hunk of old furnace and rusted drain pipe and scream at the night—

"This all you got? This all you got!?!! You ain't fadin' me! This ain't loud!!! It ain't loud at all. This ain't LOUD enough, ya heard!?!! TURN THIS FUCKER UP!"

Letters to Eva

Reminiscing on the dawn of the apocalypse. Year one. You remember, right, the floods that year that drowned the Big Easy and ravaged the mighty Mississip? You remember the all-out war in the holy dust pit and the children of Abraham massacring each other over sand and the love of a merciful god? Remember all that? Those were the days, huh? Simpler times. F'real. I was living then as I am now in a one-room efficiency in an old Catholic church. It wasn't a church by the time I moved in. Archdiocese sold it cheap to a neighborhood slumlord. That's my luck, y'heard. I am only the third tenant ever. I gotta bounce soon, though, cuz I'm taunting fate up in here.

Kinda crazy living in a converted church. Cuz it still *looks* like a church, knamsayin? It's got all the regular church shit, but none of it's holy anymore. I guess. No more crucifix on the wall, just a pale shadow of a cross in the paint left behind. Where the confessional used to be is now a storage closet. In what was once the sacristy I found a half-filled wine rack. Cheap, screw-cap Rosé. The blood of Christ, $11.95 a jug. Amen. I drink it late at night in the parking lot behind the abandoned orphanage. Some nights, if you're quiet enough… and sufficiently tore up, you can hear the ghost whispers of long-gone sinners echoing faintly through the hall, begging forgiveness for they trespasses. Sins of the mind. Of the heart. Sins of the flesh. And they all *boring as hell.*

On the corner of Blackstone and Churchwalk is where we live. The lullaby of a twelve-gauge. Forgotten, bloody, on the last page. A lost riddle in a bullet night, and we ambling, dexterous, down a sidewalk of dull and forgettable secrets. Alleys littered with wreckage lead to the cage door. To the stage door. To the tabernacle. And the raked stage is breaking straight through to the cellar floor, bleeding through a river of black. Cellar door leading to a river of black. Flowing to the mouth of the hell-blasting furnace. Screaming, rattling, wailing, clattering. And we all feed the furnace in this Blackchurch. On the corner of Blackstone and Churchwalk where we live.

I make my living, such as it is, flipping boxes on an assembly line at a factory that makes plastic bottles. Every bit as big ballin' as it sounds. Cuz nothing says *true playa* like wearing goggles and earplugs at 2 a.m. surrounded by Northern hilljacks with Confederate flags on they belt buckles. Bitch-ass crackers can't even pronounce my name.

"Deanntry, go'n wrap that skid."

"It's D'antre, mothafucka!"

"That's what I said: Deanntry."

"DEE! ON! TRAY! D'antre!"

"I'll jus' call yah Philips. Philips, go'n wrap that skid."

Ain't so bad, though, really. The machines keep a straight beat going, so I just spend my time on the line following the rhythm and working out my words. It's not like I need to think too much doing that shit. Got some rough characters working this factory, and that's good to me. Always looking for characters. One time back, while I was doing a stretch at County, some little chicken-n-dumplins-lookin housewife who worked here just up-ended one night and shot some other bitch right in the throat. No words went down or provocation that anyone could see, she just pulled a snub-nose out of her purse and started popping. Just standing there in line at the punch clock. I can see how that could happen. And a coupla years before that one of the forklift drivers got brought down in a hail of cop gunfire outside a house he'd just set fire to. Right on the outskirts of downtown Cincinnati. Course there was a woman involved, ya heard? I don't normally take up for the police, but the cat was one of them neo-nazi skinheaded motherfuckers, and he shot a homeboy of mine who lived in that house. So fuck his bald ass. Word.

Rent's cheap in the Church, and that's what I'm all about right now. I'm just biding my time, you know, until my shit gets worked out. I've been MCing in this town since high school, and I've had some success with the mic. Rocked a few crowds in my day. Back in the day. Way back, at this point. Before I went to the pen. And then I went back. And then I went back again. But I'm out now and I'm putting the pen to paper this time, you feel me? I'm published, son. Believe that. When my daughter was little I wrote a book for her called *Princess Africa Jones.* Maybe you heard of it. I doubt it. But it got picked up by Hedgehog Press in 2002, and to date I've made one hundred forty-seven dollars and sixty-two cents in royalties. Pimp. That's probably the end of the line, though, cuz it got remaindered a year later when Hedgehog done got bought out. I haven't so much as heard from my agent in 572 days and thirteen hours. I don't even know if he's still my agent any more. Maybe I should call him. Maybe he dead.

My baby girl's mad teenagerish these days, and she and her mama done moved away to Wisconsin. *Word. Wisconsin.* Now look...I can understand being born Black in Wisconsin, and all right, you got people there, so you stay. You can't help it really. But to be Black...and *move* to Wisconsin? Did I miss something? Tijuana, my baby's mama, is a dancer of the exotic variety, and I know she making her daily bread with that...but come on now. They ain't got no decent strip joints in Chicago or Detroit? I guess they pay top dollar for a naked Black ass up in the land of cheese. Makes sense. Last I heard TJ done got pretty fat...I'm sure she still fine as fuck. Always was.

Make some noooooise, fellas! Don't you wish YOU were in Tijuana right now?

And my baby Dameka, she at that age, you know. When she was tiny, I was her hero. Her whole world, you feel me. Even when I was locked up I could do no wrong. But she don't want to know about me these days. What can you do? That little book I wrote for her as a baby don't mean much now. And she ain't impressed that her daddy used to kick it with The Pharcyde. She ain't fazed that her daddy's crew opened up for The X Clan. *Who The X Clan?* Just some corny-ass old shit. She's all about that capitalist money rap that rules the game these days. The fake thugs. Rims and furs and too many gold. *The red the black and the green? That shit don't look nice on me, Daddy.*

So here I am back living in Madisonville, on the Blackchurch side. Day Jah fuckin' Voo. Thought for sure I'd have at least be moved out of Cincinnati by now. Or even Ohio. But nope. Not only am I still in Cincinnati, I'm right back in the same hood I stayed at coming up. Now it's really just me, though. Most of my relations are dead or moved away. Most of my cats coming up are all in the ground or locked up or gone. And the few left over are just shells anymore. If I'm about chilling with ghosts I'll just stay up in this haunted-ass church. So that's just what I do. Drinking free wine, puffing a blunt or two, eating jalapeno salsa, and jerking off to *Steel Magnolias.* Daryl Hannah, son, what? She got that lazy, sleepy *fuck me* look in her eyes that's real good to me. You ain't got to judge. (And people will say, D, why not that mermaid movie instead where you can see her titties? Cuz I ain't into fish, kid. Y'all got me fucked up.)

Anymore I'm just chillin' in the wake of the apocalypse.

I guess it all started when I got some mail that wasn't mine. It was addressed to some woman named Eva, no last name given, in Canton, Ohio. RETURN TO SENDER. The return address was a nameless P.O. Box in Tennessee, but right there was that big yellow forwarding label with *my* address as plain as day. Figured it was a screw up at the post office. And I suppose the neighborly thing to do would be to walk on over there, step over the homeless people, bob and weave through the crackheads, wait nine years in line—*fuck that.* I threw it away and thought no more about it.

Until the next week when I got another one. Same deal—Eva, RETURN TO SENDER, P.O. Box, yellow label forwarded to Blackstone St. And I threw that one away. Next week I got another and said, Hell with this. Shit shows up at my crib it's my shit to read, know what I'm saying?

This is what the letter said:

Dear Eva,

Hope you're well. Haven't heard from you in a while, so I thought I'd drop you a line and say howdy. I'm living with Dino and Chip these days. Yes, they're still with Lynne and Margie. Everyone sends their love. Some good news, my headaches are a lot less frequent now. Still having that eye thing, but I'm coping. Everybody's cool and actually mellow, if you can believe that. Dino's eased up on a lot of the old "Indian rights" stuff these days, and isn't so much giving me and Chip the business about "Your ancestors destroyed my people and took their land" blah blahbity blah. I'm sure it's only temporary, though. You know how he is. Crazy red bastard.

You'll be happy to know I'm seeing a doctor about the anger issues. A specialist. I think I'm making a lot of progress. It's hard with that retarded jackass still in office, but I'm making my personal peace. One day at a time, right? So there it is.

Dino and I are laying asphalt full time now, plus making some scratch on the side...but I probably shouldn't go into that *in detail. THEY're likely reading my mail. I know they're tapping the phones.*

I was thinking about the baby the other day. The first one. Do you realize if he (or she) had lived he'd be ten years old today? It's kind of weird to think about what could have been. Guess all you can do is play the hand God deals you and pray for the best. Well, that's all.

Talk to you soon I hope. Give my best to Micki and Jason and your mom.

All My Love,
A

Just a bunch of jibber jabber to me, so I pitched it. Another came the next week and I didn't even open it. Out to the trash it went. Then another came. And then another…

Proper Care and Maintenance

Doorbell jangled me out of bed around nine-twenty-nine. My apartment is on the second floor, where the church offices used to be. I stumbled on down the stairs and opened the door to find this pasty looking white dude in navy blue coveralls sniffing and blinking back a weekday morning hangover.

"Help you?"

"Are you D'antre Philips?"

"Yup."

"Will Fanon." His eyes and nose screamed 'Alcoholic!' Blood-spotted red. On his left hand he wore a black leather glove. On just the one hand.

"'Sup."

"Your landlord hired me to come service your unit."

"Say what now?"

"Your furnace. Says it makes some horrible noise and clicks on and off real sporadic-like."

"Yeah. Come on in."

"Name's Will Fanon," he said again.

"Good to meet ya. It's down this way. Watch your step. This basement is crazy."

I grabbed a flashlight from the hall closet and led him down into the church cellar—which sorta has the vibe of an eighteenth-century prison. Dirt floor, stone walls, old broken pews and church brik-a-brak sinking into wet earth. The crumbling foundation has let an ever-present river of mud furrow itself a pathway through the floor.

"Well," Will Fanon said, "this certainly ain't too pleasant down here. Looks like a good place for a murder."

"Folks *have* been murdered down here, actually. Upstairs too."

"In this neighborhood I believe it," he replied.

"Every other tenant that has rented the crib upstairs done either killed or got killed by a loved one. That's why I live alone, ya heard?"

"Any other problems with the machine besides the noise?"

"Well, it's either arctic-ass cold up in this piece, or so hot your skin melts off. Even three floors up. Out in the church proper the stage floor is warpin' cuz it's right over the furnace."

"You'll have to talk to somebody else about that. I just deal with pressure boilers and furnace units."

"Well, here it is. Watch y'head." I flipped the bolt lock on the broken wooden door to the furnace room. Creaked as it opened. Will held a quick breath at the sight of the thing.

"Man alive," he gasped. "Is she ever a beauty." Just looked like a big nasty hunk of scrap metal and aluminum tubes to me. But he obviously saw something more there. Way more, apparently. "Great model. Great year. She'll blast for a hundred years yet. You're a lucky man, Mr. Philips."

"Yeah, it's a charmed life I live."

He proceeded to poke his head around the various shafts and pipes, whistling and nodding in approval, but periodically clenching his teeth and shuddering in what I took to be withdraw. "You know, on the boiler end, they're replacing these old models with what's called an Ohio Special." *Twitch.*

"Is that right."

Don't be havin' no delirium tremens 'til you leave out this bitch, goddamn it.

"Requires no operator at all. Blasphemy. No good will come of that. Mark my words, Mr. Philips."

"Call me D'antre."

With his one good hand he popped off a metal plate and began messing with this coil and that switch. I heard a scratch-and-scurry sound down the cavern a ways. I aimed my flashlight around the cellar. *Fuckin' rats.* 'Bout shit when I saw a bunch of giant, rotting papier maché faces along the south wall, probably from a play or something. *Mental note: don't never come down here drunk or blunted.* Over one of the heads, *The Castle of River Sam* was painted on the back wall. Figured it was the name of the play the decaying faces were from. (I was mistaken.)

"There's no major problems with this unit, D'antre. It just needs a little love."

"Aw'ight. Say brah, what happened to your hand?"

He stopped and stepped out to engage me directly, just as serious as a razor at your nuts.

"I got arrogant. And prideful. I love my boilers and they love me. But they won't be taken for granted. Now I know. My heart has been humbled."

Oooooookaaaay...

And back to work he went, mopping the sweat from his forehead, even though it was plenty cool down there.

"Yeah, this is a wonderful piece of work," he said. "Wish I had both hands, but you know what they say. If wishes were beggars we'd all have a free ride."

???

"Hey man, this gonna take long?"

A resonant slam of metal and a few echoy clicks, and he dusted his bare hand against his coveralls.

"That's all, folks. Should purr like a JAP on payday."

"JAP on payday. That's a new one."

As I led him back up the half-broken steps he started in with, "You live in Blackchurch a long time, D'antre?"

"Well, I was born in Madisonville, and I grew up on the Blackchurch side. I've spent most of my life either in...or near...greater Cincinnati. So yeah, more or less. But I moved into *this* place a minute ago."

"A minute ago?"

"Well, not literally a minute. What about you?"

"We've been here ten years, or there 'bouts. It's okay, I suppose. I'm not really too comfortable being surrounded by

Blacks, though. No offense."

"Um. Aw'ight. None taken I guess."

Least he's honest.

As we got to the foyer by the front door I saw him hesitate to leave.

"These bullet holes?" he asked referring to the poor putty job on the door.

"Yup."

"Figger'd." *Twitch.*

There's really no missing a DT shake if you know what it is when you see it. *Hmmmm...let me see now. Bet ole Mr. Fanon here's got a whole day of calls up ahead of him and no chance to take a little nip. Gonna be a looooong day, ain't it Mista Alki White Man. Hurts, don't it. HURTS!* I had a half a mind to just chuck him on out the door and let his withdraw-sufferin', Black-fearin' ass sweat it out...but what can I say. I got a big heart, knahmean?

"Say, uh, Will, right?"

"Yessir."

"If you got a minute, you want a beer before you go?" And his red eyes lit right up. "Oh wait. I ain't got no beer. How about a cup of wine?"

"Wine?"

"Don't worry, I ain't gay. It's church wine. Came with the church."

"Wouldn't say no to a sip or too."

Course you wouldn't.

So at 10:29 a.m. I poured us both two jumbo-sized plastic cups of Rosé. Fine breakfast.

"Here's to ya," I said. He raised his cup and nodded thanks.

"So what do you do with yourself, D'antre?"

"Well...I write. I plot hostile takeover. I struggle to maintain my tenuous grip on reality. Not much."

"Yeah, I heard from your landlord yer a writer."

"For all intents and purposes."

"I ain't much for books or reading or any of that stuff. But I would like to write a book someday."

"Yeah? And what would that be about?"

"It would be partly an operations manual for high pressure boilers. And partly a Bible."

"A Bible?"

"Partly."

"Like the King James?"

"No, my own Bible. Entirely my own. Even got a title already."

"Lay it on me, slick."

"*For Proper Care and Maintenance of Ancient and Angry Gods.*"

"Word."

"If you doubt the holy power of pressure boilers let me take you sometime to see what's churning deep underground beneath University Hospital. *Massive* boiler. Three stories large. Red hot coals. Conveyor belts. Multiple operators on hand day and night 365 days a year. That baby runs the sterilizers, the incubators, everything in the entire hospital. It gives *life*...and can just as easily deliver death. We boiler operators are mad fools. But we keep your world alive. And we pay a heavy price sometimes."

He looked at his gloved-hand and guzzled a mouthful of wine. I saw his eyes relax for the first time, and the jittering eased away.

"Why do it?" I asked.

"Because...I have felt the touch of God."

"Haw preach'em now," I said, and poured him another full cup.

"You got kids, D'antre?"

"Daughter. Don't see her much. She and her moms hit the open road some years ago."

"Moms? As in she's got more than one?"

"Uh...no."

"Okay. So you got rid of the kid AND the woman? Jackpot!"

I should have felt mad, maybe, but I didn't.

"Yeah...well...I was aw'ight with seein' her mama go, anyhow."

"I'm shocked my wife don't leave," he said. *No shit.* "I got a son myself. Goes to college up at Ohio State."

"Good for him."

"He's a goddamn toad."

"Oh yeah?"

"Nothin' but a rotten, ungrateful little punk growing up," he said, shaking his head in well-rehearsed disgust. "You understand. Angry at the world. But now he's all big and smart with his college learning. Thinks he's better than me...*little self-righteous creep*...on the rare occasion we actually talk it's all...I don't know..."

"That's hard, man."

"I had two boys, actually. Once. The little one, well... *Christ*...I loved that boy. But he died."

"I'm sorry to hear that."

"Thanks. The other one, peh. *He's* the one that's had to *live.* Least he left. Good riddance."

"What's your problem with him?"

"I just don't need to be preached at by some snot-nosed liberal know-it-all. I'd call him out for a faggot, but he's got himself a wife now, so there goes that theory. I really only see him 'bout once a year, but he manages to ruin everything any time he's down here. Every year come Christmas time I gotta hear 'bout how I'm wrong about every goddamn thing under the sun, and I gotta spend my entire Christmas—or...what do you people call it...Swanzea? Quasi?"

"Kwanzaa?"

"Yeah, I gotta spend my entire Kwanzaa hearing about how I'm a bigot, or I'm a sexist, or I'm a zeeno, phobo, whatinhellever."

"That must make for a tough Kwanzaa."

"Does it ever."

"But then...he still your son, knahmsayin?"

"He's a fuckin' toad." Will raised his cup and said, "To our babies. And the goddamn monsters they become." I raised my cup as well, and couldn't help for the moment but to think about my own Mama.

Princess Whatever

Got another letter to Eva, and was just about to pitch it when I noticed she had a last name now. And I noticed that it was post-marked Sept. 15, 2001. *Damn, what's up with the postal service?*

Dear Eva,

Happy Anniversary. I know you remembered because you always do. Did you do something fun? I hope so. Me and the boys went out and saw a band play. Not for the anniversary, just to get out of the apartment. They're called Stigmata Dog and they are shit-hot. Really amazing. I don't know if you're still into metal at all, but if you are, definitely check them out. Great, sludgy NOLA-metal but original as all get-out. I'd have to say they are my new favorite band. They are going to be playing Doom Fest in Northern Ohio sometime soon. We're definitely going to go.

Everything's cool here. I'm now seeing the doctor twice a week and it's really helping me a lot. I'm a lot better than I used to be and I really think I've turned a corner. I don't sleep or eat very much anymore, but it's not because of anything bad, I just realized that I don't need to. I'm focused on streamlining my life these days. No fluff, just the essentials. I bought a new van. It's a '65 VW bus, mint. I think you'd really like it if you saw it.

All in all I have to say I'm a million times happier these days and I'm seeing much much clearer now the government did 9/11 and I've got a job interview next Tuesday there are nazis marching in the street outside CIA are tapping my telephone I saw your old piano teacher the last time I was in Memphis she said hi eva please help me and she said I hope shes still practicing her scales Im choking help me please theres a recorder in my head and they are stealing my thoughts I met some cool people down at the vfw a hooker in dallas implanted it there when I was sleeping everyone is really kind to me there the army are always watching me they know I know about what they did to us in iraq Ive joined a darts league at the vfw and they are going to kill us all were aiming for the championship the bushes are nazis they stole the country I hope we win eva youll always be special to me

Well, I guess that's all. Tell Jason and Micki congrats on the bun in the oven. I saw them a couple of weeks ago, but they didn't see me. Micki's as big as a horse barn! Oh, one last thing: if you still have my dad's deer head in storage I'd like to get that back at some point. No rush, though. Thanks.

Sleep tight, Evangeline. I'll see you in my dreams.

Your loving,
A

ps Dino and Margie overdosed on sleeping pills last night. We had to rush them to the hospital. They're fine now. Said it was an accident, but I know better.

Decided not to throw any more of these away.

ringringringring

"Hay-luh?"

"This is a collect call from—" "—D'antre—" *"To accept these charges press 1. To refuse press 2."*

And then a million years went by.

"*This is a collect call from—*"

"Dameka Shaniqua Philips, you BEST be accepting these charges!"

beep

"Thank you."

"Hey Daddy."

"Girl, you lost your goddamn mind?"

"Sorry Daddy, but Mama been on my ass 'bout playin' on the phone."

"A call from your father is NOT playin' on the phone!"

"I know. I'm sorry. Why don't you hit me on my cell?"

"Cuz your cell is for emergencies only. Right? RIGHT?"

"Yeah." I could practically hear her eyes rolling. "So wussup, Daddy? How your new book comin'?"

"It's aw'ight. It's actually a satire on religion, but prolly won't nobody see that 'til close to the end."

"How 'bout that other one? The one that's out. That *Princess* whatever."

"Nev'mind. I'm callin' 'bout your birthday, Boo. Right around the corner, is it not?"

"Uh huh. Well, in December. But yeah."

"The big one-four."

"Yep."

"I was thinkin' 'bout rollin' up there to see you."

"Yeah? Really?"

"Would you like that?"

"Umm...yeah! Course I would."

"Why you pause? You ain't wanna see me?"

"I ain't pause. I'd love to see you, of course."

"You is your mama's daughter, no doubt."

"I'm for serious!"

"Aw'ight then."

"So...uh...where you gonna stay at?"

"I'll get a hotel room. What difference does that make?"

Just then I heard a man's voice somewhere in the background.

"It's my daddy," Dameka told the voice, barely covering the mouthpiece. More yak yak yak. "Yeah, fool, my *real* daddy."

"Oh snap!" I heard the voice say, and then some more muffled nonsense.

"Who that?" I asked.

"Daddy, Ramon wanna holla at you."

"Who the fuck is Ramon?"

"Helluh? This D'antre Philips?"

"Yeah."

"You used to be Daddy Molotov, right? Of *Tha Bomb Droppas*?"

"Used to be. Who this?"

"Aw YEAH, son! I bought yo' first single when it came out. WAAAAaaay back in the day, son. That shit was deep, you know?"

"Glad you liked it."

"*Straight Clockin'*. HA HAAAAAAAAAA! You still keep up with DJ Mao Mao and MC Keyz?"

"We talk from time to time."

"Yeah that shit was NICE, ai'ight? I bumped that for a minute back when. Why you ever fall off, dog?"

"Man, can I talk at my daughter right quick?"

"Aw snap, son. She done lef' out already. Color guard try-outs, you know."

"Muthafuck."

"But you comin' up for her party, right?"

"Party?"

"Me and TJ goin' all out for this girl birthday, right? It's gonna be off the chain, son. We'd be honored to have you here as our guest. You being Meka's biological an' all."

"Uh—"

"Shit. I got another call comin' in, brotha. Yo' ex-wife ringin' from the club. But I'll tell her you called, ai'ight? And we'll see you up in here in a minute. Cool. Peace, nigga."

"Yeah. Peace."

A WORD FROM THE PROPHET

Working the late shift leaves me with way more idle daytime than is probably healthy for me. I can't write when the sun is up, and I've never been much on hobbies, so I picked up a twenty-hour-a-week position shelving books and whatnot at the local library. Normally they hire high school kids to do that, but since the Madisonville Branch is so small they never bothered. Library's a five-minute walk from the crib, so it affords me a stroll down Churchwalk and past all my old haunts. I must be a glutton for punishment. *I fought Suchand-such over there. I fucked [insert name here] in that parking lot.* I pass by a new joint that's not open yet, but sure to be off the hook once it is. Rakeem's Funky Chicken. "Smoked Barbecue and Roadhouse Blues" (I don't know what makes a blues "roadhouse" or not, but it sounds hip). The eponymous Rakeem is my old partner coming up Rakeem Hollis. I'm proud as hell of the cat, even though we don't really talk much anymore. Keem was the only other brotha I've ever known who shared my taste for OPM. (For some reason the fruit of the poppy ain't too large in the hood. Who can figure these things.) We actually did time together some years ago. But when Keem gave up bangin' and thuggin' he did it because God "touched" him, or some shit. Sounds dirty to me. He had one of them big Saint Paul-ish revelations, y'heard, talking 'bout "I've been saved."

Me, I just got wise, got some knowledge, gave it up. Because Keem's all high on Jesus these days, I really don't have a lot in common with him. I just don't trip like that. Still got love for him, though. Raise up my forty and a "long life to him." Can't wait to eat some of that barbecue.

It's funny to me, the whole religion thing. I mean, I was raised on the Bible just like everybody else. But how can otherwise perfectly smart people not see some flaming bullshit when it's burning right in front of they faces? I mean, who really thinks a card trick is real magic? And yet, them same people will believe that there used to be a time of talking snakes and talking bushes and oceans splitting apart to accommodate a bunch of Jews. And shit. The average motherfucker walking down the street these days can diagnose schizophrenia on the spot, but won't recognize it in they "saints." Fucking crazy. Word.

Ain't nothing more hilarious to me than the Mary story, though. Here we got one of the biggest religions of all time sparked by the quick thinking...and well-justified lies...of an abused and desperate girl. Every time I hear about some little homegirl in the Middle East or somewhere being "honorably" stabbed, stoned, beheaded or otherwise carved the hell up by her family and/or community for her lack of *purity*, for fornicating, or getting divorced or getting raped, I always think, "Damn. Is it too late to bust out the ole 'Mary defense' again? Or is it too soon?" I mean yeah, it's kinda been done. But there's that whole "Second Coming" thing y'all got up your sleeve. Call me selfish, but if it comes down to a choice of me getting stoned to death, or perping like I'm suddenly a vessel of the Lord and it's the end of days, it ain't gonna take but a hot second for you to hear this nigga screaming from the rooftops, "A miracle! A miracle! Praise his holy name!"

And people be saying, "Aw D, you can't say that. You saying little Mary made up the whole virgin-birth-son-of-God thing to get out of being killed for infidelity...thus sparking the whole Christian Church and whatnot?" I'm saying raped by angels...raped by drunken sheep-herders...and a stoning's on the line? Then mum's the word, Bob's your uncle, and the Lord Jehovah's your father, little man. Ya heard? Stick to the goddamn script. F'real.

This is the shit I be thinking on in lieu of having a life.

On my way down Churchwalk I also have to pass Lumpton's Grocery—first place I ever held up. I was fourteen. The gun was plastic. Didn't even look real. It was orange. Old Man Lumpton (who was younger at the time than I am now) snatched it out of my hand and knocked me upside the head with it.

"D'antre Philips, is you the dumbest boy what ever lived?"

"I'll hafta get back to you on that, sir."

"How you gonna try to rob a store that's right around the corner from your own damn house?"

"Short getaway?"

"Boy, I used to date your mama! You know I'm fittin' to call her up right now. Your daddy and me was good friends coming up! Good thing he done passed on, or he'd skin your little black ass alive. Then fall right over dead of shame, damn your soul."

Lumpton's kids run the place now. Lumpton himself is buried not too far from my father's grave. Probably telling on me for all eternity. Mama is buried in Kentucky for some reason. Never did find out why. Don't really care, I guess.

First thing I do when I get to the library is turn on the microfiche reader. There hasn't been any microfiche in Madisonville for fifteen years, and no one has *ever* used the fucking thing, but I gotta turn it on every day, then turn it off every night at closing time. Does give me an audience with the one and only Petey Wheatstraw, though, and that makes it all worth it. Old Petey spends his entire day every day the library is open at the table next to the microfiche machine. Petey is your standard issue *crazy homeless guy*...on the surface anyway. He ain't took a bath or changed his clothes in four decades, and he smells like roadkill boiled in throw-up. Pretty much keeps quiet and all to himself and most folks around here think he's a drunk. I happen to know that he's never touched a drop of liquor in his life, but Pete is just fine with everyone thinking wrong of him. He prefers to be left alone, knamsayin? Petey Wheatstraw doesn't talk to *nobody*...but he talks to me. Maybe because I'm a writer. Maybe it's because I know his secret. Maybe both. Like I said, he spends every possible moment in the library sitting at that table in the far corner. Drawing. Endlessly drawing page after page. What he's drawing, if anyone ever cared to notice, are blueprints for luxury homes and office buildings. Shit is off the hook.

See, back in the '60s Peter James Wellson, "Wheatstraw" to his friends, was a hot young architect fresh out of the Design, Architecture, Art, and Planning program (DAAP) at the University of Cincinnati. Job offers were pouring in and he and his fine new bride Olivia were getting set to move to Seattle and live happily ever after when...well, do I even gotta finish this story? They found out old girl done caught the deadly C. It filled up her brain, spine, lungs, stomach. When Petey lost Olivia, he lost it all. His mind included. His mind most of all. Only thing that lingered on was his talent. But with nowhere to put it, all that talent could do was haunt him like a vicious old ghost. Still does to this day. For whatever reason, I think Petey sees me as a kindred spirit. But most I ever get from him is crazy talk.

"Young D Philips. How is your mama?"

"My mama dead, Petey, and you know this."

"Tell her I said hello."

"Will do."

"The wildest ride is for the man *inside* the horse."

"Man, that don't relate to nothin'."

"The shepherd is the king AFTER the flood," he said, pointing at me and winking. "That's you."

"After the flood, yup."

"All your Christian neighbors are jacking off to kiddie porn."

"I'll keep that in mind."

Just the week before he informed me that—

"All your neighbors' kids are jacking off to Christian porn."

"Good lookin' out," I say.

And he just smiles and winks, tapping the side of his nose. *And that's how we do.*

I must say, though, I enjoy working at the library. I like being around the books, and I'm thinking that old library's got spooks haunting it just like the church I stay at. The only thing that gets me down is when I find myself shelving a copy of *Princess Africa Jones.* Worse than that is checking it out for somebody, knahmsayin? Even though pretty much everybody in this neighborhood knows who I am, not one person has ever noticed that my name is on the book. *Don't matter no how.* And I can't even say why it eats at me. But it does.

Blue Ida Was There

Everybody knew her. Knew that voice. Knew her name. Miss Ida, queen of the voodoo blues. *Stop on in for a drink and some fried shrimp with cheese and feel grease fires catch in your soul.* With her smoke charred, whiskey scarred, wail-callous'd pipes she'd send crowds into fits one number in. *Jes' be makin' good'n sho' y'conscience is inna clear 'fore she done brung out I Put a Spell on You…you jes' might not ever see the sun rise again.*

Blue Ida, Miss Nodding, in her time, like a spider, a Black widow, done had herself lotsa babies. And like spiderlets they all left the nest. Some were artists too, ya heard. Some went suit-straight. Some came on back to play in Momma's band. You understand. But Lakeisha went wrong all the way. She fell in with a dude with a hot car and a pipe and she got burned on all three, you feel me. Dropped a bassinet on Blue Ida's door one morning with a note, *"Here Momma, Bye Momma, Sorry Momma,"* and she was gone gone gone forever gone, like a rumor proven false, leavin' a lingering half-truth behind.

But that baby, oh lord, that baby girl…

Everybody called that baby MIN.

MeShayle

Ida

Nodding

Ya heard.

Everybody loved that baby Min. Bright-eyed and gorgeous and a ticklish little giggle that'd melt you like butter on a steaming biscuit. *Pass 'at chile on down thisaway*, and she was snuggled and sugared up on down the line. That girl. That beautiful dark-eyed baby girl. Lemme tell ya li'l story 'bout Minnie tha Smoocher...

One time when she was four she skinned her knee on the curb and there was so many sugars to make her feel better couldn't nothing hurt too bad for too long ever.

Sometimes all the love was Just. Too. Much.

Nineteen Hundred and Ninety Three

and little Min, age of six, got a present that birthday she can't recall

but somehow she'll never forget.

Grammama, Miss Ida, had herself a boyfriend back when. Name of Edgar. Mista Edgar. "Uncle" Edgar, to some. Uncle Edgar had a present to give. A joke to tell. A trick to play. "You wanna see a trick, little girl?" Uncle Edgar was the favoritest favorite of all.

Lil MeShayle, baby Min, six years old, stood in the laundry room stationary tub waiting with a tap of her heel for her big, secret birthday surprise.

"You ever seen a dragon, Min? This here's a dragon. You grab its neck and pull real nice, well, it just might spit fire, it might." Or it might just spit all rude-like. It was a fine and funny trick and Min she laughed and laughed—

"Do it again," she demanded clapping her hands. "Wake it back up."

"Not today. But you gotta keep our game a secret now, you hear?"

She did.

"Cross your heart."

She did.

"Swear to Jesus."

She did.

"Now give Uncle Edgar a kiss."

But secrets don't keep and Grammama just had to hear all about tiny dragons in the laundry room and the messes they make. "Just don't tell Uncle Edgar I told shhhhhhhh."

Everybody knew her. Knew that voice. Knew her name. Miss Ida, queen of the voodoo blues. With her smoke charred, whiskey scarred, wail-callous'd pipes she sent a chill through the bayou when she let out that scream.

And from then on MeShayle never saw ol' "Uncle" Edgar again.

"He had to go, honey-chile. Leave out far away, hear? And he ain't never coming back here no more."

Nobody ever told Min just where Uncle Edgar done gone to. But even swear-on-the-Bible secrets don't keep forever, ya heard. When Miss Ida's boys—Min's *real* uncles—got the call, they didn't back-talk or disobey. A long sharp knife will send a tiny dragon flying...and gasoline and a match will send a tricky "uncle" on his way.

Don't Even Trip

ringringringring

"Tijuana Smalls."

"What's good, girl."

"Oh. Hey D. How you feelin'."

"Good in the hood, baby."

"That's good. Whatchoo need?"

"Damn! Aw'ight. Well, you know. Just thought I'd holla. No thing. I just wanna maybe know why the mother of my only child—"

"—far as you know."

"—why the mother of *my only child* can't call a brotha back concerning his baby birthday party."

"So you really comin', huh?"

"Hell yeah I'm comin'. I talked at your boy…Whatsitcalled. Ramon."

"Oh yeah, I know 'bout ALL that shit a'ight. Got his ass ALL excited. 'I done talked to Molotov! I done talked to Molotov!' You'da thought he done holla'd at Vince Neil or somethin'."

"What? Who Vince Neil?"

"Ugh. Vince Neil, D! Lead singer of Motley Crue?! Don't you know nothin' 'bout music?"

(It is my experience that, on the logic tip, talking to a stripper about music is up there with sticking your dick in a door hinge. Her perception of it will be based entirely upon what she hears at the club, and more importantly what "works." What gets dollars rollin'. I'm convinced that there could be a hillbilly song called "Let's All Rape Aunt Jemima with a Broomstick" and TJ would dance to it if it put bills in her garter. And then she'd tell me it's a nice cut. "The words are busted, but I like that washtub bass.")

"So anyway, what's up with the no call back?"

"You want me to be honest?"

"I'm not sure."

"I don't think...I don't think I *ever* want to talk to you no more, D, cuz...I think it'll just depress me."

"What the fuck that mean?"

"Cuz I know how you do. And nigga...it's sad."

"Huh. Yeah. Aw'ight, tell me how I do."

"Oh you don't think Imma 'bout to get third-eye right about now."

"I can't wait."

"Lessee...I'll bet since the last time I holla'd you done got yourself a new apartment, am I correct? Cuz you got kicked the fuck out the last. I'll bet it's a ratty little shit-ass dump in Over-The Rhine, or Avondale, or Mad-ville...ooooo yeah, I'll BET it's in Blackchurch f'sho. And you prolly spendin' yo' days workin' some job you be hatin', BECAUSE you hate it, cuz you need that pain like you need the money, and it give you time for reminiscin' on how good you had it back when you was ballin' and all the shit you done *fucked up*. So you smoke five packs of Camels a day, even though your own mama done died of emphysema, sometimes rewardin' yourself with a Swisher and Dragon's Blood...as if you done somethin' that *earned* a reward...and spend your free time at the library readin' some dumb old books don't nobody else care about, sit around your funky-ass apartment writin' some corny shit ain't nobody ever gonna wanna read, wishin' you was still nineteen. Oh...and I bet you still writin' rhymes...cuz ERR'BODY know there ain't no problem for a thirty-four-year-old rapper who ain't never had a hit and was never signed to a decent label to break back into the game. No problem. No trouble at all."

I let her catch her breath and prepare for the truth and knowledge I was 'bout to unleash.

"Pfffffft. You...please. Girl...you WAY off."

"F'real."

"Couldn't be MORE wrong. I ain't smoked no cigarettes in over eight months. Except for last Tuesday, but that was just three."

"Uh huh."

"And I ain't even writin' raps these days. I got a whole nother flow now."

"You gonna break my baby's heart?"

"WHAT?"

"You gonna break my baby's heart? Again?"

"You…you trippin'."

"I tell her you goin' be here, and you'll BE here? You goin' be here FOR her? Cuz to me, she better off without you. But she think she *need* you, D'antre, no matter what she say."

"What…what she say?"

"Don't you break my baby's heart, nigga. I ain't playin'."

"She my baby too. Aw'ight?! She *my baby* too."

Big long pause. I'd heard that silence a million times before. That's what TJ does when she's trying not to cry. I spent our whole time together trying to figure out how to make those silent pauses disappear. I failed.

"Ohhhhh…D'antre Philips…D'antre Philips…you know I still love you, right?"

I don't even know what I know anymore.

"Yeah?"

"Even though you don't deserve it."

"Yeah."

So where'd we go wrong? We fucked around on each other…

"You don't deserve *nobody's* love."

And then we fucked each other over…

"That's cold-hearted."

And then we fucked everything up.

"Am I lyin'?"

"Nuh."

For a minute, though…she was my all-there-is. *My Inanna…*

"I'm just sayin' it real." And I heard her choke a little bit.

"I love you, D. I really really do."

She was my whole world.

"I love you too, Boo."

Soon and Very Soon... or A Bomb in Jerusalem

My Dearest Eva,

It is the end of the line darling. There is just no point in carrying on this charade any longer. I quit my job at the factory. I have not slept or eaten in days. Could be weeks. Could be months for all I know. It is all the same to me now. And it is all over. Dino and Margie kicked it off. Set the idea in motion. It is how we are all feeling. I know. Dino and I have worked it all out. It is the end of the line. The pigs done won Eva. The nazis done taken over America. For good. I cannot live carrying this disease around any more. I cannot carry this poison around. I cant carry the things I carry. Do you know how it feels to be the only person who knows the truth? They poisoned us Eva. It is not just crazy talk. It is not combat fatigue. I am not crazy. You saw the babies. OUR babies. Why would THAT happen? I have seen the files. I have seen the photographs. I done seen what that stuff does. My government poisoned me. And they done it to millions of people. On purpose. We have known each other since we were in grade school Eva. Since I pulled your hair in second grade and you colored on my shirt with magic markers. You know I have spent my whole life believing in just three things. Three things and three things only. God. Family. and the USA. ALL THREE HAVE TURNED THEIR BACKS ON ME. It is the end of the line. The girls dont know yet. And Chip does not know. But I am sure they will go along with it. They have to. There is no other way. Critical mass. We are going to that big music festival in

Northern Ohio. Point of no return. Then poof. All gone. So long. Last hurrah. Hurray. Good bye. Blaze of glory. Shock and awe. Fire and brimstone. Screwtape and Wormwood. Dead rotten cold and gone.

Sleep tight Evangeline. I'll be there in your dreams.
Your loving,
Anton

ringringringring

"Speak."

"D'antre?"

"Uhhh...yeah..."

"Did I wake you up?"

"Sorta, but it's aw'ight. Who this?"

"It's Will Fanon. The boiler operator."

"Oh. Hey. Whass up, Will."

"Not much of nuthin'. Just wanted to check and see how that little honey is pumpin' for ya." And with that I had to take a moment to ponder the delicate intricacies of the universe. And scratch my nuts. "The furnace, partner," he said interrupting. "Howz it working?"

"Oh. Yeah, it's doin' real good."

"No more problems or nothing? Cuz I can come back over and look at it if you like."

"Nuh, I'm cool. Heat comes on. Air comes on. Muhfucka's right with it so far as I can tell. But it does still make those crazy-ass noises. Bangin' and kinda wailin' and shit. But it's old, I know that. Plus, it's haunted."

"Hmmmm...noises, huh. That shouldn't be."

"Like I said, I can hang with it."

"Yeah, but I don't see why that would happen. Are you sure that them noises ain't just all in your head?"

"Uh, no I ain't for sure of that actually."

It was a late shift night that night and the phone call from Will Fanon kicked off the morning way earlier than I would have liked. Ya heard. But there wasn't no sense in trying to force my way back into Sleepville, so I rolled up out of bed with the intention of doing something constructive. Thus I proceeded to burn a fat blunt and dismantle the church's security alarm. *We try to make a diff'rence, knamsayin?* I've always hated that corny motherfucking alarm. Jostle the front door too hard and this stupid loud robot voice starts screaming *Intruder! Intruder!* Figured one of these days the police will get called and I'll end up getting popped right in my own house. The invisible robot had to die. Landlord didn't install it to protect my black ass anyhow. Shit's only there to keep the crackheads from breaking into the church proper and setting up a squat. *Not no more it ain't.*

That good deed done I headed out into the gray Blackchurch afternoon for a pack of grape Swishers and some pretzel Combos. *Just the essentials, knahmean?*

Stepping out of the corner market I pulled out the pack of Marlboros I'd just bought. I hate Marlboros, so I bought them figuring I wouldn't want to smoke them. *Logic, baby. Logic!* Four little girls all in cornrows played double-dutch by the gate of the tow lot. Someone had spray-painted *Follow River Sam* across the cement wall. Two baseheads carried a futon mattress up Blackstone Street. Lotus-style on the bus stop bench sat Petey Wheatstraw nodding his head to the double-dutch rhymes flowing fast and free.

"I see yo' hiney / All black and shiny / Better hide it / Fo' I bite it..."

"What do you say, Petey?" I said, throwing him the peace sign and dropping the pack of cigarettes back in the sack unopened.

"Spare a trash bag, young brother?" He asked. *Just never can tell with that guy.*

"Aw'ight," I said, rooting around through my groceries.

"'Syuh lucky day, ol' son." I popped open a box of extra-large Hefty Cinch Sacks and peeled him one. He proceeded to rip three holes in it and slide it over his head and stick his arms through. I stared at him for a few long moments, a little blunted yet from the lingering effects of my breakfast smoke.

"*Po' Frankenstein / Is it his dick or his breaf'? / Cuz every ho he fucked / he done fucked her to deaf'!*"

"It's gonna rain," Petey said, by way of explanation.

"Word."

"Wordy word word. Wordiddy word. All your jack-off neighbors are kidding 'round with Christ and porn. Ask Margaret."

"See now, my man, I think I done figger'd this out. You just say that kinda mess when you want people to go away. Am I right?"

"All your porn is jacking 'round kids and neighbor Christ."

"I'll take that as a *Yes.*"

"All your Christ is jacking porn from round neighbor's kids." He said winking and tapping his nose.

"I feel you, dog. I'm out. Church." And away I went.

"*Myyyyyyy sista Suzie / She a floozy / Sucka mouf an' drippy coozie / Beat her / punch her / gank her purse / Watch that hooka cry an' curse / Oh! / Oh! / Take it slow / Muthafucka here we go / Eat a pussy / suck a dick / Bitch-ass niggas make me sick!*"

"Hey Young D!" He called out.

"Yeah? Wussup?"

"Porn kids all jack off Christ, neighbor."

"Good news."

"You'll see the girl soon."

And I locked up still and cold as a bank vault.

"What? Huh? What you say? You mean my daughter? See my daughter soon?"

But he was already shuffling away muttering, "soony soon soon." *How the fuck does he know about Dameka?* I thought.

"*Abraham Lincoln was a good ol' man / He jumped out the window with his dick in his hand / Sayin' 'Hey muthafuckas /*

do my duty / Pull down yo' pants and gimme some booty / When I die / Bury me / Hang my balls on the cherry tree / When they ripe / take a bite / Don't they taste like dynamite—BOOM BOOM!'"

My walk back takes me past The Soul Lounge, so I stopped in there for a quick bit of internal lubrication. The Soul Lounge is my confessional, ya heard. I say shit and think shit in there I don't otherwise. I'm also not a big vodka drinker, but I order Screwdrivers whenever I'm in there. For the vitamins, knahmean. Gotsta keep up with my health.

I smoked one of the Marlboros and gave the rest away. One word to describe the vibe inside the Lounge: *dank*. There are airborne pollutants in that joint that are older than I am. *Love it.*

Dontell, the cat tending bar, is a fatally addicted news junkie, so the bar TV is always set to twenty-four-hour-up-to-the-minute-your-first-look-news-you-can-trust-information-when-you-need-it. Nobody ever seems to mind. Dontell and I are usually the only ones watching it. Everyone else is too busy turning the whites of they eyes a deeper shade of custard yellow. This particular day's breaking story was all about another marketplace bombing in Jerusalem.

"Dontell," I said, "I can't lie, dog, this shit keeps me up at night. This Israel business. Jews, Palestinians, what the fuck, ya heard?"

"Who you rootin' fo', young brotha?" some fossil puffing away on my cigarettes asked, as if it were the Super Bowl or something.

"I ain't rootin' for nobody. I gots mad hate for the idea of ANYONE gettin' bombed and blown the fuck up, knahmean? But my heart's wit the Palestinians."

"Why's that, D?" Dontell asked.

"Cuz...cuz they niggas."

Some of the old brothers chuckled to themselves.

"I gots niggas of my own to worry 'bout," Dontell said. "I start worryin' 'bout every nigga on the planet I'd die of worry.

So far as I'm concerned the whole world is Palestine."

The whole world is Palestine...

Back at the crib there was a message waiting for me on the answering machine from the operations manager of a major chain bookstore that shall remain nameless. Said his name was Scotty, calling from some store in Columbus, talking *somethin-orother* about *Princess Africa Jones.* The quickness in which I called him back betrayed my cool on the real.

"This is Scotty. How may I help you today?"

"Uh...hi, Scott. This is D'antre Philips. You called?"

"I did! Hello, Mr. Philips! Super to talk with you!"

"Um, yeah. Super likewise. What can I do for ya?"

"Well, let's put it this way. You can do a LOT for me, how's that? And that lot would be if you could come up for a visit."

"You mean...like a in-store? A signing?"

"I sure do!"

"For *Princess Africa Jones*?"

"The one and only!"

"Uh, not to shit in your dinner, Scott, but that book was remaindered a couple years ago. I don't think it's currently in print."

"Hmmm...really? That's not what our warehouse records say."

"Do they say anything about me shittin' in your dinner?"

"Hold on, let me check. Nope. So what do you say? We'd be thrilled to have you."

"Well..."

"Do you know a young gal by the name of MeShayle Nodding?"

"I do not."

"She's one of our booksellers, and we just love her to pieces, and she is VERY insistent about you coming up for an in-store. She has promised me that she will personally get a crowd of book buyers in here if she has to drag them in by hand. Ha ha ha! Can't say no to that, now can you?"

"No, I don't s'pose I can. When do you want me there?"
"Soony soon soon!"

The Oscar Letters

Writer's block. It happens...although usually not to me. But I found myself staring at my notebook and I had nothing to burn onto the pages. *Nothin'.* So for the first time in a coupla years anyway, I dug out the rest of the red brick I done bought the last time I was in County, crushed it up into the last of my shake and rolled it all into a flowery joint. Now before you go trippin', or thinkin' I am, recognize that red rock is NOT OPM. It ain't. I think it's just incense mixed with catnip. But sprinkled over cannabis like Sweet N' Low, it takes me there real nice. And it actually makes me *more* clear thinking. No lie. (If you want OPM for real, it's gotta be a hard chunk of black. *For real.* But remember, once you go black you never go back.)

But anyway...

It had been a while since I'd gotten a letter to Eva, and given the tone of the last one I figured that it really would be the last. And I was right. Sorta. Couple of days before I made the sojourn up to Columbus there it was in my mailbox. Same handwriting. Same P.O. Box return address. But...no yellow forwarding label this time. And unlike the rest of them it was not addressed to Evangeline Poole. It was addressed to one Oscar Pederson Montgomery. *What the fuck?!* My address, postmarked just three days prior, Oscar Pederson Montgomery. Here is the letter in its entirety:

Sorry for the mail. Sorry in advance for everything. See you soon.

Anton

And so I headed on up North wondering who's been up in my business, who's got an eye on me, who's been inside my head.

Daffodil Junction

"Mr. Philips I presume! Welcome to _________ Books!"

I ain't gonna lie to you, I was a little high. With traffic I had figured on a three or more hour drive, but I actually made it in a little under two. In other words, I was somewhere early for a change, ya heard. So I stopped in at a Friendly's, burned one out in the parking lot, and had myself a little key lime pie. Walking in the store I was feeling pretty good, but then the hazy, piss-yellow cast of the store's lights colliding with the earth tone color scheme of the walls instantly made my teeth hurt.

"Thank you. You must be Scotty."

"I must be. We are just thrilled to have you here."

"The thrill is all mine. So where you want me at?"

"Well, thought we might do something special tonight if you don't mind." *Great.* "Normally we have 'Jammy-Time Tales' about now. In about twenty-nine minutes, actually. Kids come to the store in their pajamas—we call them the *Jammy Club*, they get such a kick out of that—and one of our booksellers usually reads the little ones a story."

"Yeah?"

"Often a new release, you understand."

"Sure."

"Buuuuuut, since you're here, which is totally exciting, we thought it'd be super if you could read 'em *Princess Africa Jones*!"

"Oh."

"Sound good?"

"Um."

"The kids will just flip for you. I know it."

"Jammy-Time Tales?" I asked as I scanned the length and breadth of the entire store clockin' the clientele.

"Yep!"

"Scott...can I ask you a question?"

"You bet!"

"Any Black people ever come to this thing?"

"Nope!"

Surprise surprise. My eyes may have been red and heavy, but they had not lied to me.

"Any people of color at all? Mexicans even?"

"Not so far. Not for story time, anyway. Just regular shopping, sure. Absolutely."

"Cuz the thing is...*Princess Africa Jones* is set in a urban environment. The story is geared toward young African-American girls. For the most part. That's kinda the target audience."

"I see." He bit his lip, deep in thought, tapping his cheek with his index finger. "Well," he continued finally, "maybe we'll get lucky!"

"Yeah."

"Can I get you something from the café? On the house, as they say."

"Aw'ight. I'll just get a cup of coffee, if that's cool."

"Sure thing. Would you like a pomegranate latte? Perhaps a sunburst macchiato? The yerba mate is popular this time of year. They just added a ginseng-flavored decaf if that sounds good at all, or my personal fave *Espresso Fantasmagoria.*"

"Uh, just a coffee and I'll be straight."

"Hmmm. Okay then...hot or iced?"

"Coffee, man. Just coffee." I could tell by his furrowed brow that this was not an adequate answer. "You know. Cuppa joe." *Nothin'.* "Hot."

"Hot cup of joe it is. Now you just go on and make yourself comfortable over in Kiddy Korner, and I'll have one of the part-timers bring you your drink on the double."

"Thanks, dog. 'Preciate it. Much love."

"Umm...uh...okay then. Thank *you.*"

So there I sat on a large plastic patchwork block waiting for the Kiddy Korner Klub to arrive. On display, like a fourth grade science project that had been built with no parental assistance. For twenty-seven of the longest minutes there ever was. On a small table off to the side were set brand-new display copies of my book, just waiting to be signed and/or purchased. Most of the folks walking by hurried past, avoiding possible eye contact at all costs. The rest tossed me a meager, closed-lipped smile and a pity wave. The "coffee" said part-timer brought me tasted exactly like liquefied sweet potato pie with caramel drippings. *Not bad I guess.* Then sure enough, top of the hour, there they were all sitting in a half-circle, in they "jammies," eyes glued to me. All eight of them. Eight boys. All white. All (I was told) from a gated community called *Daffodil Junction (*formerly *Sleepy Hollow).* Three, I was told (unsolicited), lived on Ichabod Lane.

"Princess Africa Jones stopped in the library one day, that one day, the day her wish came true. She stopped in the library most days after school, so it made sense that she'd stop in that day.

'How are you today, Princess Africa Jones?' I asked as she walked by.

'I have important business in Egypt, and on Alpha Centauri, and a kerzillion wonderful places,' she replied in a hurry.

'Well you'd best to scurry and get to it then,' I said. 'It's really that simple.'"

The kids seemed to like the story, though. They clapped at the end. I was given eight hugs total. One boy's moms quietly slipped me her cell phone number and whispered, "*Papa Bear goes on long business trips.*" I was asked if there would be more books starring Princess Africa Jones...

"Princess Africa Jones headed home with her head held high. High in the clouds: which is a mighty fine place for a head to be. She headed home to Sixth Street where the other

girls might have laughed, and the other kids may very well have pointed, and all the grown-ups could very possibly have clucked their tongues and shook their heads and said, "What is wrong with that Princess Africa Jones?" But Princess Africa Jones paid them no mind."

...I lied and said "yes."

One kid asked if he could feel my hair. I said, "Why not." So then they all had to. No shame to the game. Five books in all were bought (one by an employee). Scotty called it a "Great success."

As I packed up my two ballpoint pens and one felt-tip, getting ready to make the two-hour drive back home, a young, sour-faced sista whom I had not seen all night came lurching up on me.

"Mista Philips?"

"Yup. And *you* got to be MeShayle."

"How you know?"

"Call it a wild guess."

"I'm glad you came."

"Yeah. Me too."

"Long drive I guess, huh. I mean for a one-shot signing. I mean..." she stared at her shoes, kicking her left heel into the carpet.

"So MeShayle, you the one who got me up in here, huh? Whass it all about?"

"Well...er...hey check it. I'm off in fifteen. There's this place across the street stays open 'til two. You any hungry?"

"Uh...could eat sump'n."

"Cool. I want you to have dinner with me. My treat."

Here you go, D. A real good test to see just how stupid you really are.

"Huh. Hmm. Thass nice of you but...how old are you, girl?"

"Nigga please," she snapped, hand on her hip. "First off, I'm eighteen. Second off, don't even sweat me. I just want to talk, ai'ight?"

I tried not to laugh.

"Aw'ight then. But I gotta get home, knahmsayin, and iss a bit of a haul. Could I get a raincheck?"

"You gonna wanna talk to me."

"Why's that?"

"Cuz *I am* Princess Africa Jones."

I ordered a nine-ounce New York strip medium-rare, potato wedges, Caesar salad no croutons extra anchovies on the side, and a Sam Adams. She ordered the exact same thing. I didn't ask why. I also didn't ask how she was able to order a beer and not get carded when *I was*. Some shit's just a mystery.

"I like this place a real lot," she said.

"Yeah, it's good."

"Thursday nights they have a crab special and fifty cent Bloody Marys."

"So you come here often?"

"What's that supposed to mean?"

I had to pause for a moment and wonder how else I could have possibly meant it.

"So let's hear it, girl."

"Hear what?"

"How, or in what capacity are you or did you become Princess Africa Jones?"

"What, that's it? No chittin' or chattin', just right on it?"

"Okay...let's talk about somethin' else first."

"Forget it."

"Hey, I'm easy, y'heard?"

She took a long pull off her Sam Adams. Finally,

"Your dude picked me up one evening, coupla years ago. It was winter. Paid me for the whole night, and I modelled them pictures for him."

"Yeah?"

I didn't like the sound of that at all.

"Or most of 'em. You can tell that some of them are by a different artist. I can tell any ol' way."

"Yeah, it was originally meant to be a chapter book. Juvenile fiction. But the publisher wanted me to scale it down into a easy reader. Maximize on the pictures. But they needed more cuz Jeff...I still don't know if it was a good move or not. ANYWAY...Paid you for the whole night, huh." I started to get a prickly itch on the back of my neck, and I kinda wished I'd never made the trip at all.

I'd never asked old son about the illustrations. I assumed the girl he drew was just from his imagination. But looking at her then, I could see that it was the same girl. Three or four years older, sure, but goddamn if it wasn't her right off the page and in the flesh.

"Yeah. I liked that job a *real* lot."

"My boy Jeff...the artist...picked you up...where?"

"Not too far from here."

"I see. And...well...so you was jus' out and about and he saw you and—"

"I used to fuck for money," she said, answering the question I was too much of a chump to ask. She said it so casually I thought maybe she'd said something else...

"How...how long ago was this?"

...No I didn't. I heard her loud and clear.

"Don't start preachin', cuz you ain't my fatha and n'er is anybody else. I'm fine with myself, ai'ight? Just fine. And besides, I don't even do it no more. But I would if I had to, cuz the money was good and it weren't real hard to do. Let me start at the beginning..."

...I used to stay with my grammama down in Louisiana. She raised me up cuz my mama couldn't handle me and she done run off with some dude who I don't know if he was my daddy or not. Me and Grammama stayed at different places early on. She had family and friends everywhere and we was always surrounded by people that loved us. My earliest memory is in Baton Rouge when I was real tiny, but we moved to Jefferson Parish when I was three or four. My uncle Boz, Grammama's second oldest boy, he play'd a naaaasty horn and he and his band owned they own house in Metairie. They ain't

mind Boz's momma and baby niece moving in cuz, well, his momma was Blue Ida. THE Blue Ida. 'Fore too long them boys was Grammama's backup band.

"I heard of Boz Nodding."

"For real?"

"Trumpet player. Course. He dead, right?"

She dropped her fork into her Caesar salad, chipping the frozen glass bowl.

"He *is*?! Uncle Boz is DEAD?!"

Aaaaaaaagh. Goddamn it, D'antre.

"Shit. I'm sorry. Fuck. But yeah. Hurricane Katrina. They all drowned in they rehearsal pad. It was on the news."

She hung her head low for a moment. Then, "Well anyway…"

…Grammama had been saving up for a long time and she finally opened up her own club and restaurant in the French Quarter. We stayed in an apartment upstairs from the club. That was the funnest time ever in the world! I ain't really go to school a real lot back then, but I helped in the restaurant cleaning tables when I was even so small as six. We'd open up for lunchtime just serving po' boys and gumbo. But come dinner it was the whooooole spread. All kindsa bands from all over the South would play there, from gospel groups to old drum and bugle bands to loud screaming n' growling rock bands, and I loved it all and so did Grammama, dancing and cheering louder than anybody. But what had people coming from ALL over was Grammama her own self. When she sang she could scare you to death, or make you laugh so hard, or she make people want to fuck right then and there. Course I ain't know that *then. When it was late she'd make me go to bed and send one of the girls up with me to make sure I got scrubbed up and straight to sleep. But I could hear that music coming up from downstairs and it just fill me with the devil. So I'd sneak on down behind the bar and watch Grammama sing. Sometime she'd see me and bust me in front of the whole crowd. But she ain't never got mad. She just say, 'Y'all turn round and say hey to my precious baby girl!' And the whole crowd would go*

'Hey baby girl!' or 'Whatcha say, Skinny Minnie!' That's what e'rybody call'ded me. Or just Min. I get so embarrassed by it, but I loved it every time. I was so happy in them days. Bad shit happened too, though…bad…

"Like what?"

"Nev' mind."

…I was thirteen when Grammama died. Broke-hearted onna REAL. I didn't know what I was gonna do or how I was gonna go on without her. Lotsa my kin and friends of the family offered to take me in, but I decided I wanted to be with my mama. 'Last we heard,' folks said, 'Lakeisha is all the way up in Columbus, Ohio!' As if that was the other side of the Earth. But my mind was done made up. Uncle Boz, rest his soul, hunted her down for me calling half the United States, and arranged it that I'd come up. First time they done spoke in over fifteen years. He founded out she was clean and sober and in a steady marriage and it'd be good for me to come, so then e'rybody was relieved. He gave me some money and I rode the Greyhound up here to stay with Mama. Without Grammama around, all our kin done drifted apart, moving all over the country, and I didn't keep up with nobody. Phone numbers, addresses, nothin'. I was so sure Mama would be good to me that I ain't need nobody else. Well…here's what I found in Columbus: Mama weren't using drugs no more and she was living clean and right, no doubt. She done gave up her pills and pipe and filthy, sinful ways so she could better praise and serve The Lord. Hate to say it…but I woulda preferred she stayed a crack fiend instead. Her "steady" husband was gone by the time I got there, done run off with another man from they church. Takin' it up the booty for Jesus, I guess. And all that was left going on for Keisha was God God God God. And more God. With some God on the side for garnish. I'd come straight home from school and we'd pray. We'd pray 'fore dinner and *after. We be praying every night for forgiveness. 'Oh Lord have mercy on my wicked daughter and teach her the path of righteousness.' All that shit. She'd make me 'pologize to God for every little thing I did and even shit I ain't*

even done. She'd make me pray and say I was sorry so much I'd start crying, and then she'd get the belt. 'Cryin' when you talk to God!?' SMACK! 'That PROVES you a sinner!' SMACK! 'Get the devil behind you, child!' SMACK SMACK SMACK! I told her one day I wish'ded she'd just smoke a rock and suck a cock and forget the praying for one goddamn night, and that's when she put me out. For good. No test. No lesson. No I'm sorry. No nother chance. Just git on out. 'And don't never come back you evil little suchandsuch.'

"You ever think of trying to get back to New Orleans?"

"Course I did. That was my goal from the first. Raise up some dollars and catch the next bus outta town. But 'fore long my situation got good to me. Kinda. And something in my head was warning me; don't go back down there."

"Good thing, huh."

"You know."

"Buy you a drink?"

"Something with a umbrella."

I fell in with some girls from 'round the way. They'd get me into the clubs and said I could stay up in they apartment so long as I wanted. It was cool. They was nice. Fucked up, but nice. After while, though, I had to start payin' in on rent. I was scared at first, sure I was. But it wudn't really no big thing after a while. Ain't like I hadn't seen that shit my whole life down south. Some of them girls had it bad with the drugs. But not me. I ain't never got with drugs and I ain't never got with Jesus, cuz I seen with my own eyes how that shit'll fuck you up. Hoin's just a job to me. Payin' the bills, f'sho. I ain't never had no pimp or nothing neither. Some the girls I stayed with, they share half they money with they punkass pimp boyfriends. By the way, all that shit you see in movies with pimps livin' large and big ballin' is some BULLSHIT. Every pimp I ever done met ain't nothing but a bodyguard-slash-driver. And a PUNK. ASS. Well anyway I ain't need one. I got my feet and a bus pass.

"I've known some pimps in my day."

"Was they large?"

"Nuh. They were bitches."

"HELL-o."

"Still, you could have got beat or raped out there." Father in me kickin' in, knahmean? "Or robbed. Or killed. That's dangerous shit, girl."

"Yeah, but I didn't. Just got lucky I guess. But I got out of it after like just a year and a half. Thank you for the drink, by the way. It's real good. What is it?"

"Singapore Sling. Drink it slow."

Tell you the truth, I really liked walking round in the city at night by myself. Most times I'd make my money pretty early and spend the rest of the night just walkin' and thinkin'. I be thinking of Grammama and her songs and I'd sing to myself. Keepin' a beat, you know. I got a natural knack for percussion, everybody say so, and I'd find myself bangin' away on a trash can or old sheet metal singin' them songs I remember comin' up. Not just the songs Grammama sang neither. I be singing that crazy metal stuff—"My fingers trace the exit woooooounds by graveyard light!" HA HA! Or spirituals or old blues—"When mah heart is filled wit sorrow/ and mah eyes is filled wit tears/ Lawd I jus' cain't keep from cryin' sometime!" I 'member all of it.

"I like that."

"Thank you. I'll be here all week. Be sure to tip your waitress."

There's this record shop I like a real lot downtown and one afternoon I'm in there just lookin'...cuz I couldn't really buy nothin' nohow. I see these two white college kids, a guy and a girl, and they real...whatchoo call it...alternative looking. He kinda shaggy and got tattoos every which way, she gots a ring through her nose. That sorta thang. I noticed her first. Kind of a big girl. Not fat really, but you know. Full bodied. And I be thinking, Damn, that girl really fine. Not that I swing that way. Well maybe I do, who tha fuck knows. But I notice her and I'm thinkin' she got her thing going on, and he ai'ight too in his way. I see they buyin' up all kindsa CDs, just stacks you know, and they keep talkin' 'bout 'NOLA.' 'NOLA metal,'

'NOLA this,' 'NOLA that,' and I shout out to 'em, Hey! Whatchall know 'bout New Orleans music? So we start conversating. Turns out a lot of the music I know from down south as just, you know, part of my life, Mikal got on record and CD and alla that. They even heard of Grammama's club! Marsia said she went there during Jazz Fest back when she's in high school. We talked forever 'bout every little thing. They done took me to dinner, then back to they place afterward. They apartment was FULL of people. Just a crazy mix. Next day we hung out all day, and the day after that. Next thing you know we together ALLA TIME. Not just the three of us, but a bunch of us. They whole circle of friends. Then, blink your eye, and I'm living there too! And I done lef' alla my ho friends and club friends behind without a call. It's a small place, Mike and Marsia's, and kinda crowded. But it's okay. Always different people coming and going. And all different KINDS of people. It's off the chain. And they all sooooo cool. Some of 'em OSU students like Marsia and Mikal, but not all. The people I live with now: Mike, Marsia, Sharisse, Craig, Chen, Dalton, and Brenna, we tight...although these days it's just been Me, Mikal, Marsia, Chen and Dalton. And Chen and Dalton 'bout to take a trip to see Chen's folks...first time since he come out gay to them. But there'll be more people stayin' up in there soon I'm sure.

"You tell them you a hooker?" I was more surprised by the question falling out of my mouth than she was. She wasn't even fazed.

"I prefer 'ho,' actually. I ain't shamed. But I don't like the white version: whore. I hate that word. Sounds devilish. And I REALLY hate prostitute. EVERYBODY a fuckin' prostitute. You is. I saw it tonight."

"Girl, you ain't never lie." We laughed. "I like the word whore, myself. It's got teeth to it, knahmean?"

"Whatever, nigga. That's just the writer in you talkin'."

Mikal's a writer too. Or he tryin' to be. He writin' a book right now, but won't let nobody look at it 'til it's finished. He owns a million books. I think every book that's been wrote in

English he gots somewhere. And he always tryin' to get e'rybody to go through his records and books and alla that. And we ALL do, for real. I know I do. Yeah, they know I was hoing for a living, don't none of them judge me. Believe this, some of them done WAY worser than I done. But I wanted to get out of it and do something that's new. So e'rybody say they gonna help me get a different job. We find a ad for ______ Books lookin' for people. Sounded good to me. Thing is, you gotta take a book test as part of your application. We cook up some lies about my education and job experience, and e'rybody help me to study for the test. Readin' and quizzin'. Readin' and quizzin'. Well one day, what do I find in Mikal's collection—

"*Princess Africa Jones.*"

"And I'm like, 'Awwwwwwwwwww shit! That's me! THAT'S ME!' We all just bugged out! Mikal say that he knew of you cuz y'all come from the same neighborhood in Cincinnati. That's why he done bought the book. They ain't got kids."

"Um...I don't know no white boy from the hood named Mikal. Or I don't r'member one anyway."

"Well he know you. He be playin' your old CD and e'rything."

"Huh."

"Maybe you could help him out with his book once he finish it."

"Maybe..."

The joint finally threw us out at 2:29 a.m. We ended up walking and talking, wandering around the suburban streets by the strip mall until five. And sure enough she'd periodically stop to tap out a beat on a signpost and sing a few bars of something or other. I don't know if she even knew that she was doing it.

"MeShayle, I—"

"Call me Min."

"Aw'ight, Min. I gotta ask you a question, and I hope it don't make you mad, but it's been biting at me all night. When my partner Jeff picked you up to do those illustrations for the book...did he...I mean did anything else..."

"He ain't fuck me."

"Ah."

"It never even come up, to tell the truth. I never saw that job as a trick. He ain't neither, obviously. He said I should put it on a job application someday. So I did."

"And it was good for ya?"

"Got the job, didn't I?"

I felt the huge rock I'd been carrying on my back all night turn into a cotton ball and blow away. I know I had no personal business being bothered by the idea that my partner would have done something with this little sista when she's fourteen. It isn't my concern. But it did bother me. She a Black Queen, knahmsayin, ho or no ho. And when she told me that it was all on the up and up, everything was all good again.

"That's interesting," is all I said.

"Yeah, I wudn't even f'sho he got into pussy at all anyway." We laughed. "But he had his daughter with him, so I guess he musta got into one at least once."

I dropped her off outside her friends Mikal and Marsia's crib just as the sun was peeking up.

"You wanna come up? Mikal would bug out to see you."

"Nah."

I gave her my phone number, my address, my email address (which I never check, but promised I would start), and told her to keep in touch.

"You ever in the Nati, drop on in."

"I will. Thank you, Mista Philips."

"Come on now: D'antre."

"Ai'ght, D'antre."

"Aw'ight, Skinny Minnie."

As I drove on back home I couldn't help but remember what Petey Wheatstraw had said:
"You'll see the girl soon."

You'll see the girl soon...

On the Corner of Blackstone and Churchwalk

Coming off I-71 into Mad-ville I dropped in at the Sunny Mart. NOT to buy cigarettes. I wanted to prove to myself that I could drive that whole way and not need one when I got home. I bought a cheese danish instead, which is no kinda substitute. I didn't even want it. Walking out I spotted Petey Wheatstraw, still in the garbage bag I gave him, hanging out with Loraina the Tweak and some other old bum in a wheel chair.

"Wussup, Petey," I said. He whistled some sort of greeting and shook his hands in the air. "Aw'ight," I said, heading toward my car.

But then I stopped short...and I'm not sure exactly why. "You know what," I said, "Fuck this." As soon as I turned around Loraina darted off.

"It's late!" she screamed as she disappeared down Stewart Ave.

The two elderly hobos looked up at me with wide staring eyes as I advanced on them.

"You," I said to the bum on wheels, "roll."

"Don't nobody tell ME to roll, nigga!" He shouted loudly. "PO-lice don't tell me to roll! NASA don't tell me to roll! I decide when I roll! IMMA roll!" And away he went.

"I want to talk at you a minute, old man," I said to Petey. He whistled a chirpy, questioning ascending pitch, like that one Marx brother. The mute one. I was angry. Irritable. Old Petey Wheatstraw hadn't done nothing wrong to me, or anyone, but my head wasn't screwed on straight, and mess was leaking out. “Thass what I’m talkin’ ’bout,” I continued. “I’m callin’ you out, ol’ son. Ya heard? This is an *act.* This crazy actin’. It ain’t even a good act. Iss like some dumb shit from a movie you saw.” He whistled a “sad” *whah-whah,* and flipped me off. “Why you doin’ this?! You uh edj’cated man, Peter. *You are an educated man.* A brilliant man. I know yo’ girl died, and thass hard, son. Hard. I’m sure it is. But that was forty fuckin’ years ago, knahmsayin? Most of these old cats out here can’t help theyselves. They sick or they hooked or both. Or shell shocked. Or all three. But you ain’t GOT to be homeless, son! You don’t *have* to. Why don’t you get a purpose? Goddamn, I shouldn’t have even called you by your first name: Mr. Wellson. Sir. You lost yo’ lady before I was even a seed in my father’s ballsack. Sir. Every mothafucka in this town, fuck, this whole COUNTRY should tip they hat when you walk by. Mr. Wellson sir.”

He stared at me long, but not hard. Then he cracked his knuckles and flicked at his temples as if he was drawing up a vein. Finally he said,

“I like cheese danish.”

I handed it to him. He shoved the entire roll into his mouth and gobbled it down in one thick gulp. After he’d swallowed thoroughly, he very deliberately wiped the vanilla glaze from his beard and the corners of his cracked lips. “I have a purpose, Young D. I most certainly do.”

“I’m listenin’.”

“I am,” he enunciated, very clearly and considered, “a conduit of The Lord.”

“F’real,” I said, exasperated. “Yeeeeeeeah…” Not mad at *him*, actually, but disappointed in myself. For expecting something more. “Yeah, that make sense, aw’ight.”

“I thought it might,” he said quite pleased.

“That explains all that Jesus porno shit you be talkin’.”

He smiled wide. “I didn’t say anything about Jesus, my friend. Jesus was just a man. A rabble rouser. Just a man fighting and losing the class war. I am a conduit of *The Lord.*”

“You a…what do they call it…a oracle.”

"That sounds good. I should get a business card."

"So...you tellin' me...you actually *are* crazy."

"A wink's as good as a nod." Then he winked and whistled. "I'm not homeless either, young man. The Blackchurch is my home."

"Yeah. Aw'ight. Thass real poetical and shit. I gotta go."

"Not *Blackchurch* like this," he said, waving his hands indicating the neighborhood. "THE Blackchurch. The one. On the corner of Blackstone and Churchwalk. Where *we* live."

I felt the skin on my back prickle, and a cold chill shoot through my ribcage.

"Huh? Wha? What you mean? MY church? I mean, the place I stay at?"

"That'd be the one."

"You live there?"

"I do sure enough." And that's just how he said it. *Sure enough.*

"Fo'...for how long?"

"Since long before you dismantled that sensor alarm. Thank you, by the way."

"But..."

"Since before you moved in. I wasn't there when old Rosa pushed her husband Miguel down the basement stairs, but I was there for the *second* murder. The second tenants, the ones right before you. I was there when that white soldier girl killed her lover. I didn't know until it was too late. I didn't know until she opened fire through the front door."

"Does my landlord know this?" I instantly felt like a simp for asking that, and Pete gave me a look that said the feeling was justified. "Well, why ain't you never say nothin'? Us being house mates, or church mates or some shit."

"It's more than just me, D'antre."

"What?"

"There are quite a few of us."

"Us who? Bums?"

He laughed and clapped his hands.

"Bums. A rush of bums. We all followed River Sam."

???

"So," I went on, hoping he wasn't about to derail into one of his gibberish jags, "y'all..."

"Do you hear voices, young man?"

"Yeah..." I mumbled, not really listening. Trying to make sense of it all.

"In your head?"

"Used to. Back when I was dumpin' a lot of shit into my dome. Gets cluttered up there. Noisy. With static...voices...But now..."

"Now..."

"They...are in *the church.* I hear them at night. Out loud."

"What do you hear?"

"Talkin' faint, and it ain't *to me.* Confessin' and prayin'. Wailin' and moanin'. But! Now I know it's just y'all squawkin-ass derelicts down there!"

"No. Ha ha. No, it isn't. We never make a sound. Not a peep. Not a whisper. Never even set off the alarm. Not once."

"But—"

"But we hear it too. We hear the wailing. The rattling. The *chunk* and *boom.*"

"The furnace."

"She'll blast a hundred years yet."

"So...then what are y'all doin' up in there?"

"Preparing the way of The Lord."

"Huh."

"Or so I hope."

"So...this is, what, the end of the world? Cool. I can see that."

"Don't think of it as the end. Think of it as—"

"Don't fuckin' say *a new beginning.*"

"A new beginning."

"*That's SO whack.*"

"New beginning."

"Is that from The Bible?"

"Hell if I know."

"Word."

"You just got back from Columbus, yes?"
"How you—" *Never mind.* "Yeah. I did."
"You saw the girl."
"I...Yeah. Yeah, I saw *a* girl."
"They are on their way."

When I got home to the corner of Blackstone and Churchwalk there was an envelope waiting in the mailbox. Addressed to Oscar Pederson Montgomery. It read:

D'antre,
Sit tight. We are on our way.
Anton

Prologue Part 2

1996

I was sitting at the bar at Blue Ida's having a Maker's on the rocks working out the set list for the night, when this creature fell out of the sky and landed on the barstool next to me.

"You're Sheldon Ackerlin," she said. It wasn't a question. It wasn't surprised realization. It was simply a statement of fact.

"I couldn't agree more."

I was happy at least to be called by my actual name and not SHELLAC, as I'd been dubbed by the underground metal press. There's already a *band* called that, apparently. And anyway, it's a dumbfuck stage name. I would've never picked it for myself.

"Good crowd tonight," she said.

"About average for us."

Before I go on, I should say that I didn't know she was a *she* at the time. But I figured chances were good that this person was either a rather boyish woman, or a real faggoty teenage boy. Fifty-fifty odds.

"I just drove all the way from San Pedro, California," she said.

"Yeah? What for?"

"To give you some advice."

"This should be good."

I'd been offered plenty of counsel during my (relatively brief) tenure in the music world up to that point: some of it sage, some of it stupid, some of it just plain old peculiar...

"You should fire your lead singer and replace him with me."

...But, strangely enough, this was a first for that particular suggestion.

"Is that right?"

"Yep. He's crap." She waved to the girl tending bar,

and a shot of something clear immediately slid down in front of her. "Hmmmm. No, he's not crap. He's good." In a flash before my eyes the shot disappeared down her throat and the empty glass went flying. The barmaid caught it in the air non-non-plussed and went about her business. "But really, he's just another Phil Anselmo-wannabe, and the metal world is crawling with vocalists like that right now." She gave a bit of shudder as the alcohol hit her system, and she wiped her tattooed hand across her lips. "There are worse things for sure... but *your* music needs something more than that."

"And that something is you?"

"It is."

"You can't be fuckin' serious."

"Oh, I'm pretty sure I can be."

I thought, *This has got to be a gag. Is it my birthday or something and I forgot?* I have, in fact, forgotten my birthday before.

"My name's Pearl Harbor," she continued.

"Huh." *Cres and Pierre have got to be behind this.*

"My real name is Katsumi. Katsumi Yoshimoto."

"But you go by Pearl Harbor," I said, deciding to play along. "Tasteful." She smiled. "Sounds pretty punk. Are you a punk singer? Cuz we're not a punk band."

"Ohhhhh really?" she replied in mock shock. "Shucks. Cuz, you know, I just drove all the way from Southern California to Louisiana to join your band. I guess I probably should have found out what music you play before I did that. Boy am I ever embarrassed."

"I'm just saying."

I really hoped Pearl Harbor was a woman, because I sure as fuck wasn't having some teenage punk rock drag queen singing for Stigmata Dog. Hold on. I'm getting way ahead of myself.

"I happen to know," she continued, "that your singer Bradley is getting burned out playing this...*experimental avant garde doom metal* or whatever somebody would call your music. Also, he's playing bass for Mimecrusher now, and his heart's more into that than Stigmata Dog these days. You, Shel, are well aware of this and have been entertaining the notion of taking over all the vocal duties yourself. And that's killer, cuz you've got a hella-cool voice, BUT…that would severely hamper your ability to focus on your guitar playing to a degree in which you would be satisfied." *Have to admit, this creature has done its homework.* "What you need is a co-vocalist/frontperson whose voice will play dynamically with yours. I think you'll agree when you hear me that my voice is the perfect complement to yours."

"Uh huh…"

"Cuz you've got that cool, low-register croon and guttural growl thing going on. My voice is pretty high. I can go from a soft lilt to a pretty nasty scream, if I do say so myself."

"No need to get modest at this point."

"Indeed."

"Well, you know," I said, getting caught up in the idea way more than I had any business being, "You seem all right. I wouldn't mind jamming with you sometime. Maybe next week. I'll give you the address of our practice space and—"

"No way, man."

"What?"

"I'm ready now."

"What do you mean?"

"I'm ready to play. Right this moment."

"Uhh…we've got a gig tonight. In about twenty-nine minutes to be exact."

"Yeah. EXACTLY. So let's rock. I know all your songs."

"You mean you know all four on the EP."

"No, I know ALL your songs. To the note. To the beat. Anything you've ever played live I can do. I don't wanna jam next week or tomorrow. I wanna play with you tonight." Crickets. "I'm totally serious." I was dumbstruck. "*Hey*!" she shouted, shaking her fist in their air. "*This is what the people say! A new way! A trial by fi-yaaaah!* That's Testament."

"Yeah, I know."

I was impressed simply by the sheer boldness of it all. Even if she sucked—*and how could she not?*—my curiosity had gotten the best of me.

It wasn't hard to convince Bradley to sit out the set and get drunk at the bar instead. His cut from the house was still secure. Pierre and Cres were a little surprised, though.

"What the hell is that?" Cres asked as we met for sound check. "Where did it come from, and what is it doing on our stage?"

"This is Pearl," I said. "She's gonna sing with us tonight."

"Whoooooo!" Bradley hollered from the bar, a fat girl on each arm. "We want the Dog! We want the Dog!"

"Hello New Orleans!" Pearl Harbor shouted into the mic, one foot on the monitor. "We are Stigmata Dog from Baton Roooooouge!!!"

Silence.

Complete, dead, pin-drop silence. The crowd, rowdy and drunk up to that point, stared at us, mouths agape. They looked collectively at Pearl, then they looked at Bradley sitting on his stool at the bar. Then they looked back at us on stage. After a few seconds someone laughed. I think somebody else coughed. Bradley threw up the horns and yelled, "YEEAAAAAH!" banging his head to nothing at all. Ms. Harbor looked over at me and grinned. I shrugged, and slammed the first F# power chord on my guitar and we kicked into *Squeal My Name in Prison,* a fan favorite (though, admittedly, not one of mine. At least, it hadn't been). Pearl let out the most horrifying screech I'd ever heard, and we dug the fuck in. Stalking the stage like a rabid Doberman, rolling her eyes up 'til they were naught but pale white crescent moons, and spitting out noises that were thoroughly inhuman, this little wisp of a girl instantly morphed into the sickest, hardest, raging-est metal demon in the room. And the competition was definitely stiff that night. After a few more moments of blinking disbelief, the crowd found itself grinding right along with us, completely caught up, screaming and banging their heads to our lysergic riffs and lumbering rhythms. The nastiest sludge pit I had ever witnessed opened up and churned like human magma right in front of the stage. I looked over at Pierre beating his bass so hard both hands were bleeding, then back at Cres abusing the skins like he hadn't since two days before never, and I thought, *Goddamn. We're on to something here.* Sliding seamlessly from a soulful warble into ethereal moan to gut-wrenching shriek, Pearl brought my songs somewhere they had never been. She *owned* this house. WE owned it. And I knew we had a good thing going when I saw Blue Ida herself swinging her ample hips and shaking her salt-and-pepper dreads.

"G'head, baby!" she shouted. "Let 'em have it now!" Pearl blew her a kiss then in one fluid motion jacked

some douchesack in the bridge of his nose with the mic.

Fucker should have kept his hands to himself.

"This one's for you, Ida!" I shouted as we broke into the down-tuned chug of *This Whole Side of Town,* a throwback from our earlier, bluesier, swamp metal days.

"*I'VE COME TO WATCH THE FIRE LIGHT / IN YOUR EYES FLICKER, FADE AND DIE!*" Pearl and I sang in unison. *"I'VE COME TO WATCH YOU FADE AWAY AND DIIIIIIIE*!" Our voices gelled like we'd been playing together for decades

...instead of the fifty minutes it had actually been.

End of the set we were all awash in sweat. "I wanna thank you all for raging with us tonight!" Pearl shouted, and was answered with a great roar of approval. "We got one more song to play. But before that, I wanna introduce these motherfuckers to ya. To my left raping the four-string for your amusement and delight is the man, the legend, The Champ: Pierre DuChamp!" Cheers and whistles. "Behind us, blasting holes in the earth, is none other than the lovely and talented Cres Lafonde!" Cres being the token "pretty boy" of the group (relatively speaking) always got the biggest scream from the ladies, and that night was no exception. "And last but most definitely not least, give it up for the wizard of sub-sonic sludge Shel Ackerlin!" Loud hollers and "Fuck yeah!"s. A couple of people shouted "SHELLAAAAAC!" and I mentally flipped them off.

"But who the hell are *you*?" somebody yelled to Pearl. She didn't answer. Cres, Pierre and I all looked at each other and smiled.

Good question, cuz'n. You'll know her name soon enough.

I'm not actually from Louisiana. I not really from anywhere, to tell the truth, except a lime green VW bus called *Cholly*. My folks were hippies tie-dyed-in-the-wool, and I spent my entire childhood on the road. I guess you would say we were poor. Dirt poor in fact. But really we lived beyond the economic spectrum. We were dead broke, but never wanted for a thing. And I never really lost my taste for living that way, even after Dad cashed in his check and Mom and I parted ways. Longest stretch I ever did in one place up to that time was two and a half years in high school in Baton Rouge. That's where I met Cres and Pierre, and we started jamming. We were a lot more Slayer-ish back then. I hit the highway again not long after graduation, but I kept in constant contact with those guys.

A year or so later, toting nothing but my guitar and one small duffel, I returned. They had by then bought a shack down in the bayou, equal parts crash-and-rehearsal pad. I moved into that sweltering, bug-infested hovel with them and their Rottweiler Cerberus, that poor beast cursed with chronic hot spots on his front paws that he would constantly lick open into bleeding sores. Thus the birth (and the naming) of Stigmata Dog.

It has been suggested by a few doctors that I may have been born with some...what would you call it...*peculiarity* pertaining to my inner ear. Several tests have indicated that I am able to hear pitches and frequencies that most other people cannot—"Like a Monarch butterfly sees beyond the color spectrum," is how one specialist put it. I don't know if it's true for Monarchs or for me, but having had nothing else to compare it to I had to take their word on it. (That's all changed now, of course. Everything's changed now, since all Hell broke loose. Since the end of the world. Everything's different in the wake of the apocalypse, and I KNOW now that I hear things not everyone can hear). But even back when everything was relatively fine, I knew I was different. That probably explains, at least in part, why my music sounds the way it does.

The NOLA metal scene is one of the best in the world. New Orleans music across the board is pretty much untouchable. Even if I weren't a musician I'd want to live where I could hear these artists play all the time. Early on our sound was more consistent with the rest of the scene down there, but we were never part of "the boys club." All the guys in almost all of the other bands in town have known each other since the dawn of forever, and they all play in each other's groups. Like I said, it's a great scene, but very incestuous. Stigmata Dog have always gotten the respect of our peers, but we were kept at an arm's length as well. That's fine with me. I prefer it that way. And as our sound evolved, the more isolated we became. The last straw as far as that went was the uncanny arrival of Pearl. When she came into our lives nothing was ever the same again.

1997

“Hey! Ain’t you that cunt ’at calls herself Pearl Harbor?”

(I can’t remember at which club this took place, but I believe it was in Alabama somewhere.)

Pearl looked up from her cran and vodka and smiled sweetly. “I am that cunt, yes.”

“Listen up here and listen good...you fuckin’...goddamn... my grandfather was blowed up in Saipan by Tojo’s goons, hear?”

“Yeah? Huh. How about that. My grandfather died in an internment camp in Arizona. I feel so close to you right now. Wanna make out?”

“I oughta break yer yellow fuckin’ neck, bitch.”

“Come on. Give us a cuddle.”

Dumbass actually threw a punch at her. She ducked and I nut-slugged him just as Cres smashed a pool stick right across his back. A couple of more quick thumps and he didn’t get up off the floor. His friends came and scooped him up, apologized for bothering us, and dragged his bleeding husk back to their table. We bought them a round of drinks and went on to play a crushing set. I think Pearl ended up fucking the guy after the show. And all was right with the universe. Pretty standard night for Stigmata Dog.

PEARL:

I’d been playing in bands since I was fifteen...around the same time I started smoking, as luck would have it. From coast to coast and a good bit right smack in the middle, I have shredded my throat in groups all across the US of A. I’ve played all kinds of music too, but for some reason I feel most at home with metal and scum punk. Mostly metal. But either way I stand out like a hard on at swim practice, and I guess I really like it that way.

By this time we were starting to garner a bit of attention from underground record labels. We'd had a handshake agreement with Sisyphus Records after our first EP and we ended up inking a two-record contract with them (it was down to either them or a company called Big Pile of Corpses. Ultimately it was a question of possible upward momentum. I stand by the decision). Sisyphus were very excited by the addition of Pearl and wanted us to re-track the first EP using her voice. I refused, saying I wanted people to be able hear our evolution as a band from recording to recording. That seemed important at the time. Funny how I couldn't give a flaming hot fuck about that sort of thing now.

"You ever ride the horse, Shel?"

It must have been three-thirty in the morning, and Pearl and I were up working on new material for the album. The four of us, plus Cerberus and Pierre's on-again-off-again girlfriend Sally, had moved into better, but still modest, digs in East Baton Rouge Parish. We were actually working on lyrics at the time, which was interesting as a collaborative effort. My approach has always be fairly clinical: what works for the song is what I write. Period. Pearl, conversely, has this rather stream-of-consciousness method to writing (and thinking), which often yields complete nonsense...sometimes, though, it's brilliant nonsense. That mix is what makes us click. Before long I'd even started writing down the bullshit she would mutter in her sleep, and use it in compositions. More on that later.

"I assume you mean heroin, right?"

"Indeed."

"Meh. I'm more of a whiskey/weed/Darvocet kind of guy myself."

"I hear ya, dude. Me too, for the most part. Not Darvocet, though. But I try to do every illegal drug at least twice a year. Just to keep things interesting. I'm not even a big junk fan, to tell the truth. I don't like that sluggish feeling. Plus it's hard to turn off the noise machine," she said, tapping her forehead. "But I do push off every once in a very blue moon."

In the relatively short time I'd known Pearl by then I had already come to the conclusion that, barring air travel, she would do pretty much *anything.* She went an entire week getting a brand new tattoo every single day. Big pieces too, on her spine, on her throat and shoulders. And she would fuck pretty much anybody—men, women, ugly people, people she hated, didn't matter. With a fifth of rum she'd wash down pills some random stranger handed her

...then be fine the next day, drinking cinnamon tea and greeting the rest of us poor, hungover sacks with a "Good morning, sleepyheads!" So it came as no surprise to me that she'd periodically shoot H just for the hell of it. What did surprise me (although it really shouldn't have) was when she said:

"Of course, I have to admit, I do shoot up more when Penn's around."

"Penn who?"

"Penny DeVour. You know of him?"

Okay...you find me one male touring musician who has never heard of Penny DeVour. For those of you fortunate enough to be in the dark on the subject, Penny DeVour is the creator of some of the most wretched, despicable pornography ever captured on tape, film, or digital video. Now, I like porn as much as the next guitar player, don't get me wrong. But I must say that I draw the line somewhere. And that somewhere is WAY earlier than when Penny DeVour enters the picture. Not only do I not find his shit arousing, I find it revolting, and anyone who would beat off to that stuff is no friend of mine (except, of course, for the people who do beat off to it who *are* friends of mine). Most well-known for the *STOP! IT HURTS!* series (up to volume seventy-two by now I believe), he's also fairly infamous for the four-hour gonzo extravaganza *Penny's*

Arcade. The scene from that which stands out in my memory is the last minute or so of a nine-way gangbang that appears to take place in an actual pig sty—Our young starlet has just been put through the business by eight large (and rather disgustingly overweight) men in rubber pig masks, and she is now drenched in all of their jism. Bruises are already starting to arise on her legs and shoulders. She flings her soaking wet hair out of her face, and says with a grin and a twinkle, "I'm ready for my close up, Mr. DeVour!" Everyone, cast and crew, laughs like hell. At which point the camera zooms in on her and we hear the voice of Mr. DeVour say, "Sandi, tell us about the first time your father raped your anus." Blood drains from the girl's face, her bottom lip begins to quiver, and then Cut To Black. The End.

By '97, however, DeVour had "gone legit." He'd directed a handful of low-budget, straight-to-video horror flicks, and had made a pretty damn good name for himself directing music clips for hip hop artists, as well as quite a few flavor-of-the-week bubbly pop confections. Hard to believe the parents of those girls would let that guy anywhere near their daughters, but hey. What price fame, right?

"Of course I know of Penny DeVour. You *know* him?"

"Yeah," Pearl chuckled. "He's my husband."

PEARL:

Penny and I met one stupid night at The Whisky. Some disgraceful, shit band was playing. Whatever they were called… they had that one sorta-hit "I Like It How You Lick It." I don't know why I was even there. He was friends with the band. I didn't know who he was. He didn't really look all that good to me, and he's quite a bit older. It worked out somehow. He was actually there with some other chick that night, but he went home with me. Sorry about your luck, sugar-pie. We got married a couple of months later in a complete chemical haze. I remember we were heading to Nevada, but I think we only made it as far as Baker.

Like any reasonable person would upon hearing the above news, I proceeded to wake the entire house and alert them to this new found nugget of information. After a bit of hooting and carrying on, we all agreed that we should pick three songs from the new collection, record, mix, and master them, and send them off to Pearl's estranged husband in California to see if he would shoot a video for us. Well…we weren't *all* in agreement. But Pearl's lone nay vote was soundly defeated.

Pearl and Penny DeVour were technically still married, but they hadn't actually lived together in over a year and a half, and hadn't spoken in four months. But she said they were still on "good terms," whatever those are. When asked about her own extra-marital behavior of late she said that they had an "open relationship." Made no difference to me one way or the other. I just wanted the goddamn video, and I figured with dude at the helm we might actually get some play.

PEARL:

I know I'm not the prettiest woman in the world. But apparently I make for a fairly attractive adolescent boy. And what I've come to discover is that EVERYONE wants to screw adolescent boys (except, I suppose, some adolescent girls). People of all stripes want to climb all over me naked because they get the thrill of screwing a lithe young gent without being busted as a queer or a child molester or both. My pussy is the doorway out of jail. Everyone wins a free pass through heaven's lips.

I called our man at Sisyphus Records first thing the next morning and told him about the Penny DeVour thing. They were psyched. "Keep playing out," they said. "Get those songs sharp!" So we were on stage somewhere pretty much every night from then on. Studio time was booked. Shit was HAPPENING.

* * *

PEARL:

Understand that I loved those guys. I will always love them. Cres, Shel, Pierre, they are the only band I would ever drive for days on end to audition for, and they are my family. Forever. Take that however you will. (I do have an actual brother. Dave is his name…who knows where he is in the universe). But sometimes I just needed to get away from them. So one night I drove the hour to Blue Ida's on my own. I knew someone would be playing, but I didn't know who. I didn't really care, as long as it wasn't us. I was a little disappointed when I walked in and saw a piano on the stage instead of amps and a drum kit. But whatever. I took a table by myself, lit up a smoke, ordered some beer-battered shrimp and tequila. Some people recognized me, but none approached. Good.

"Granmama!" a little girl protested somewhere behind the bar. "I wanna see the music!"

"Chile, you best be gittin' up them steps," Ida announced. "It is late an' you got school! G'on now, git!"

"C'mon, baby girl, I'll take you on up," said another female voice.

Grumpy little footsteps clomped away. I had to laugh a bit. Blue Ida's is as good a school as any other, I'd say.

Eventually a long-haired, barefoot white girl in a peasant skirt and suede jacket mosied up onto the stage, giggled a nervous hello, and sat at the piano. A ginger too. I've always liked gingers.

I could tell her fingers were cold, because the first few chords she struck were brittle and stiff. It was kind of embarrass sing to hear. A few passes through and they did warm up. But then…she sang. With a voice like a feather against a crystalline bell. I could feel her singing inside me. Annalee Silver. Her music…so simple and plain. Like her. And beautiful. Like her. Wow…just wow…

My music, OUR music, the music I've always loved, is so cluttered and hectic. So seemingly chaotic (though actually it is rigidly plotted out). That's what I like about it. Before that night I would have assumed that listening to some hippie chicky plinkle plinkle on piano keys singing winsome melodies about loneliness and rainy mornings and letting go of someone who's wrong for you would have put me straight to sleep. But she didn't.

I found myself wrapping her voice around me like a lover's arms. That night she sang to me about parts of myself I didn't know were there. Parts of me I was sure I had killed off. But I hadn't. I saw her there, a small, simple girl alone in a universe that is cold and brutal. Like me. She didn't match it cut for cut, punch for punch like I do, though. She didn't need to. I saw her walking through a glass-littered world in bare feet. Like I do. But not *like me, because she was soft and clean where I am hard and polluted—and happily so. Somehow she remained uncut. Unbloodied. There was…a purity there.*

I didn't say a word to the guys about her when I got back home. And I saw her live three times before I ever told them about her (or had the nerve to speak to her). I considered never telling them. Keep her my secret. But that would be cruel. And I'm not a cruel woman, after all.

The first round of studio sessions were, well, what can I say. They were *fucking awesome.* The vibe was right, and because we were only recording the three songs, we didn't feel molested by the clock. We took our time, tinkering with shit, dicking around with the microphones. We discovered that, although she has no formal training as it were, Pearl is able to pull some mighty interesting sounds out of a pump organ and a mandolin. Did that have a place in Stigmata Dog? *It does now.*

It was then that I started to get obsessed with the idea of the music of "empty" space. Anyone will tell you proper acoustics are essential to capturing a solid recording or delivering a live performance. But that's not what I'm talking about. It's *much* more than that. A space itself will actually have its own pitch and rhythm. Sometimes its own harmonies. The rest of the band got into the idea as well, and we set about scouring the outlying area for killer tones and where they "lived." Cres made a discovery and decided that we needed to record his drum tracks outside, in a cemetery, in between two mausolea. He was right; it was the best possible tone. Needless to say I told the engineer to ditch the digital, we're recording everything reel-to-reel. Artificial ambient sound irked the shit out of me back then anyway (and within my present state, it makes me physically ill). I felt sure that one of those three cuts would be our ticket to the big show. I still don't think I was wrong.

It was at one of these sessions, as Pierre was finishing up a few bass punches, when Pearl asked us, in an uncharacteristiccally nervous fashion, "You guys wanna go hear something really different?"

That question will hook me every time.

So we hoofed on over to a sleepy little downstairs café not but a couple of blocks from the studio to check out a solo artist named Annalee Silver. We were four of maybe eighteen people in the joint, although it probably couldn't have held much more than thirty.

"I just can't shake this broad's music," Pearl said. It had gotten to her. Deep. We were curious, to say the least.

Twenty-nine minutes after we arrived the girl came out on stage, smiled awkwardly, sat down at the baby grand, and mumbled something that I guess was a joke because a couple of people in the back chuckled. Whatever it was I couldn't decipher it. *Hmm.* I was pretty skeptical that this was going to be worth my time. As it turned out, my doubts were way off base.

"*Although I hope to never see you again / that doesn't mean that I don't miss you every single day...*"

She was, I have to say, every bit as good as Pearl claimed (not too hard on the eyes either, I might add). We all thought so, although perhaps the material may have grabbed Pearl a little closer to the chest than the rest of us.

"*Can't walk...can't walk a straight line / Not even in my*

mind / But sometimes I can still still feel you dancing, babe..."

It wasn't mind-blowing by any means, but very well done. Simple, lyrical, and most of all *honest.* Annalee's music—kinda jazzy, kinda folksy—struck me as having a joyful quality to it, even though a lot of the subject matter was melancholy. It is weird for me to even write that shit, because I don't usually think about music in those terms. But hell, it's a wide canvas. If we all painted the same stuff the picture would be a giant, boring wash of suck, wouldn't it?

After her set was complete, as is our custom, we bought her a drink and had it sent over to her. I believe it was a glass of *Chateau Le Thys.* Seemed appropriate. Much to our surprise, instead of running off screaming or calling the cops, she walked right on over to our table.

"Holy jeezus!" she said in a faint Jersey-girl pitch that I hadn't anticipated. "Stigmata Dog at my show? Ha ha! Wow!"

"Great set," Pierre said. "We really loved it."

"You have an amazing voice," Pearl and I said in unison (further proof of our gradual morph into one being).

"God, thank yous so much. That means a lot to me. Yous guys rock so hard! When I came out on stage tonight and saw the four of yous sitting there I thought, 'Aw jeez! Are they here to beat me up or something?'"

We all laughed.

"Nah, we won't do that," Cres said. "But if you're looking for some players to ugly-up your next album, we work cheap."

"I will take that into consideration!"

And so our unlikely—but genuine—mutual admiration society was founded. Sometimes I still think back and laugh, remembering being on stage and looking out at all the screaming grind freaks acting like our music was sending them into violent convulsions...and there Annalee would be, right up front and to the side, eyes closed, swaying gently back and forth as if our music DIDN'T sound like a woolly mammoth being gang-raped to death by a pack of hyenas on Angel Dust. She was a sweet girl that way.

1998

PEARL:

I'm what is known as a "nelipot." I'd never been big on shoes anyway...or clothes for that matter. But by the time I got to Louisiana I was barefoot for good. Some would think, you see some artist walking around in bare feet and it's because of some hippie crap about "being closer to the earth" and "feeling Mother Nature under your toes" or some rubbish (that's something Annalee would say for sure). But that's not the case for me. I'm a metal nelipot. Being in my bare feet all the time is just part of strengthing my warrior spirit. Building callouses. Body and soul. No more hiding behind the protections that modern life offer. I'll walk over jagged rocks, scorching asphalt, snow and ice, hot tar, bent nails, anything. Many a night I've pulled bloody shards of glass out of the soles of my feet. But broken glass doesn't even cut me anymore. NOTHING cuts me anymore.

"Shel?" Pearl asked. "You ever have nightmares?"

This was a common line of discussion with us.

"All the time."

"About car crashes?"

"What? Yeah, sometimes."

"Is there a tractor trailer and a blue van involved?"

"What are you getting at?"

"I think all musicians have nightmares about car accidents."

"That and spiders," I said. "I hate spiders."

I wasn't really going to get into this conversation with her.

She was free to tell me whatever she wanted, but...I'm a closed man. By design. My dreams belong to me. I don't really do the sharing thing.

"You're always writing songs about spiders," she said.

"Because I fuckin' hate them."

"Yeah. Webs are cool, though."

For the record, I did dream about car crashes (and sometimes tractor trailers and blues vans were involved). I would dream about violence that I am powerless to stop. Still do. People choke, and people fall, and people are stabbed, and ripped apart by robot arms, just beyond my reach. Beyond my ability to help. I am powerless to stop it. And that's really all that I dream about. I hate sleep.

"So tell me, Pearl, what is all that shit you're always muttering about in your sleep?"

"Fuck should I know. I can't hear it."

"I'm going to start recording you."

"What?"

"The world," I said in my bosso Heston voice, "and all contained therein, is naught but raw materials for my art. You are no exception."

"Don't do *that*!"

"Do what?"

"Record me in my sleep."

"Well then I'm going to write down everything you say."

"That's cool."

"Of course, that would be easier to do if you didn't get up and pace around when you do it."

"I do that?"

"Yup."

"Is it freaky?"

"Some of it."

"Is it about Penny?"

"Not that I can tell. Do you think it's some hang-up you have about him manifesting itself in your dreams?"

"No," she said. "And that's a gay way to put it, by the way."

"What a second," I said. "You did say something really fucked up recently that might have been about him."

"Oh Christ..." she put her face in her hands. "What was it?"

"I couldn't decipher it at first, it was kinda gurgly. Like Linda Blair-style."

"What was it?"

"*I will find you. And I will make you love me. And then I will destroy us both.*"

"Oh, that's not me," she said, waving it off. Only Pearl could casually dismiss something that sinister. And then, quietly, as if to herself she said, "I wonder if it's Anton."

"Who's Anton?"

"Yeah..."

"Pearl." I whistled. "Over here. Who's Anton?"

"Shel...there's something...you should probably know about me."

That's hilarious.

"I imagine there's quite a bit I should probably know about you. But go ahead."

"I...hear voices."

"Eh?"

"I hear voices in my head. Sometimes. Not all the time, very seldom, but..."

"Okay?"

"But I'm not schizophrenic, though."

"Pearl, if you hear voices in your head, that is literally schizophrenia."

"It's not, though. Not for me."

"Ah. Well...that's good."

"It's *totally* good."

For some reason, I believed her. I believed that she wasn't schizophrenic. I guess, really, because I *wanted* to believe her. I didn't want to think that any of the things she had said to me up to that point had been untrue. That she was living in some sort of delusion cloud...

"Have you always heard them? Like since you were a kid?"

...because that would make me think that maybe she didn't really know Penny DeVour and we had no shot at the video and all of this had been a total dirtfuck.

"No, not at all. And most of the time it's just one—"

"*Anton.*"

"And it's only when—"

"Let me guess. Only when you're smacked out."

"How'd you know?"

"Call me Criswell. So does this Anton tell you to do things?"

"Not really. He, it, whatever, mostly talks to himself. He's an angry voice."

"Are there *others*?"

"Yes, but he's the main one. There's a female voice too, but I actually think that *is* me. You think I'm nuts, don't you."

"Yeah...but no more than I did yesterday."

PEARL:

I started hearing Anton the first time I shot up. Gravelly and hickish, he/it muttered something about murdering the president. I don't remember which president that was, but it was probably the first Bush. Most of the time the voice didn't speak to me, it was like I was listening in. Sometimes there were *other voices too. Sometimes there still are. I remember the first time Anton said directly, "Pearl. I'm yer biggest fan," I thought Okay, if this is just me talking to myself, my ego is now officially licking its own clit.*

Once we finished mastering the three songs for the DeVour sampler, we packaged it up and sent it off to him. Pearl said she called and left several voicemail messages, but he did not call back.

"I think he'll probably like it," Pearl said. "He seemed to dig you guys all right back in the Bradley days. At least the stuff I forced him to listen to. Over and over."

"But...do you think he'll do the video?" Pierre asked, like a kid listening for that ice cream truck jingle.

She shrugged. "Never can tell with that guy. Might *not* do it just to spite me."

Not wanting to sit around staring at the phone, we went back into the studio and got cracking on the rest of the LP. Annalee Silver was hanging around a lot by that time, and soon became a constant in our tight little inner circle. She was very welcome there. I believe Cres had a thing for her from the get-go, and it may have been mutual, but some boyfriend in Connecticut was a significant—though thoroughly invisible—presence. So "just friends" became the official policy with Annalee. As for Annalee herself, I personally think she had it bad for Pearl, as did most people (which baffles me to this day. Sorry, Pearl). At the very least she had an *intimate admiration* for her, if nothing deeper. But like I said, "just friends." If you listen closely to our disc you can hear Annalee sing a really chilling, dissonant harmony with Pearl on four songs. She appears on the album uncredited (although I don't know why), and I'd wager most people assume it's Pearl double tracking. But nope. They were both live in the booth together. I can't listen to those four songs today because they make me too depressed, remembering what a good time that was back then. Truth be told, I can't listen to ANY of the music Stigmata Dog recorded anymore. I've just lost too fucking much.

It was around this time that I started having a reoccurring dream I just couldn't shake. *I'm in a motel room with a bunch of guys I don't recognize. There's booze, there's coke, everyone's wearing the same baseball jersey. I'm stumbling around in a whiskey drunk, everything's silent and scratchy, like old Super-8 film. I see a bunch of guys are gathered around one of the beds cheering and whooping. I move in closer and see that they've got a young Black girl naked, pinned to the bed at her wrists and ankles. They're taking turns on her, one by one, fliping her back to stomach and back again. I'm shocked and sickened and furious. I yell at them to let her up, but it's a silent film. Nobody hears me. I try to grab them off of her, but my arms float weak and light in the air like helium balloons. I look at the other bed and see that there's money laid out in a loose pile. I look back at the first bed and they're doing her two at a time. I look down at myself and I'm as hard and stiff as a rifle barrel.*

And then I wake up.

At the time, it was just a dream. I didn't know what it meant...swear to god...

Word was leaking out to the underground press about our album in process (a song or two just happened to leak out as well. Funny that). Buzz was buzzing and keys were tap-tapping (and the collective readership of seventy-five people awaited news with baited breath). We began to get calls at the house for interviews, and we decided through a unanimous vote that Pearl should be the sole spokesperson. Several rags had initially asked to speak with me, but I declined, claiming I wanted to retain "an air of mystery." That was, of course, hot bullshit on a long stick. I just didn't feel like yakking about the same stuff over and over.

Pearl did a great job, though, liberally mixing the cold, hard facts and truthful anecdotes with whimsical flights of fancy and flat-out fuckin' lies. Lying to the metal press is a time-honored tradition, and it ultimately doesn't matter what you say, it's how badly you sucker them. There were times when she was *unintentially* hilarious, though, and those were probably my favorite. When asked the old yawner about "influences," she'd rattle off the usual litany of badass metal babes, along with a few male vocalists as ringers like Iggy Pop and/or Mike Patton. But then she would say—

"I also take great inspiration from old-time female performers like Marlene Dietrich. I would argue that she was metal as hell in her own way. She drank like a man, cursed like a man, smoked like a man, fucked like a man, but on stage she was a pure-class dame."

Good riff, and I heard her give it nearly verbatim several times, sometimes switching it up with Greta Garbo or Bessie Smith (with the latter she also added "fought like a man.") Made me laugh every time, because although I know Pearl is deep into Bessie, I'd put money on her having no clue who Garbo or Dietrich are, beyond their names.

We had just started mastering the final mixes when Pearl got this email—

My dearest Katsumi,

Got the disc. Your band is phenomenal. I would be honored to shoot your video. Don't worry about the money. Am I coming to NOLA or are you coming to LA? Let me know. I eagerly await your reply.

All of my love and more,

Penn

ps I miss you

And then we all lost our minds.

1999

"Do mine eyes see before me Beatmaster Cres Lafonde? Good to meet ya, bud."

Handshake.

"Welcome to Loozie-anna, Mr. DeVour."

"And Pierre The Champ. It is my honor." Handshake.

"Glad you could come down, sir."

"Dudes, please," said Penny DeVour. "Enough with the sir and mister shit. Call me Penn. By the way, my great-grandparents were French, and I'm positive I've got Cajun in my blood. I hope, before I leave, you might consider me an honorary coonass."

"Membership pending," said Pierre with a wink. DeVour laughed uproariously and slapped him on the back.

"Fair enough, fair enough. Ah ha!" he said looking over to me and extending the glad hand. "And this must be SHELLAC himself!"

I just nodded and shook his hand. "Glad to know ya, cuz'n."

First impressions? Meh. Pretty much what I expected. Mid-to-late forties. Short, black, beatnik hair with speckles of white. Insanely toned, gym'd-out physique under tight black polo and slacks. Man-made, oxygen-bleached smile. Leather-belt-tan complexion. In so many ways *That Guy*. It would have been interesting to have met him at the *start* of his career for a compare/contrast: to have met the scabby, volatile, speed-ball-jacked pervert shooting his first basement-quality spank videos with terrified teenage runaways and a stolen camera. The guy who actually made porno as debased, depraved, degrading and defiling as the Christian pisspants always fantasized (and hoped) that it was.

This man, however, who showed up in Baton Rouge with his skeleton crew and personal assistant to shoot our music video was *in sales*. He could have been selling tires or soybeans or double-vaginal-double-anal. In the market it's all the same product…and I guess, right then, I realized that *we were too.* I was happy he was there, but in that moment I realized why Pearl was ambivalent. And she had plenty of other reasons of her own. Still…pretty goddamn cool for us, no?

"Hey Pearl," DeVour said, dropping at least a bit of the act for a moment. "How've you been, sweetheart?"

"Never better, Penn. You look great."

Then he kissed her, which was fine, but it went on for an uncomfortably long time, and I wondered if this was indicative of how the whole shoot was going to go.

In the days and weeks leading up to DeVour's arrival I had noticed a tangible difference in Pearl. Not necessarily anything I could describe, or even say was positive or negative. She just had a different vibe about her. Well…there was the packet of syringes that I found in the back of the freezer. But then I saw them in the trash later, broken and unused. There was also the marked increase in the frequency and intensity of her somnambulistic soliloquies that were really getting interesting (incidentally, I plan to write an opera someday called *Somnambulistic Soliloquies*. Should be a blockbuster).

"And how is *this* these days?" DeVour said to Pearl gently caressing her temple with his index finger.

"Very quiet," she lied.

"I wouldn't think that, listening to your music of late," he said with a Cheshire grin. We all chuckled. "Clover wanted me to say hey and that she misses you."

"Is she still with Spitfire?"

"We should talk later."

***

PEARL:

I don't really have much to say about that period. The video shoot and whatnot. It was all right. That's all.

I know it's been said before, but it really can't be said enough; making videos is fucking *cheesy*. DeVour's "concept" for the clip was to have us playing on the banks and boat docks of various swamps. Sometimes the guys and I would be faking along to playback, sometimes we'd just stand there looking hardcore. The really lame shit was pretending to play along to a sped-up version of the song so when they cut it later at normal speed it'd look like we were in slo-mo, but still perfectly in sync. It actually looked pretty bad-ass in the final product, but pretending to play along to your own composition as if it were recorded by a bunch of jacked up castrati is a bit humbling.

We spent a good portion of the first week driving around to different locales trying to find the "evilest" looking swamps. DeVour finally settled on Cypress Brake and Switch Canyon Slash, although I'm not really sure why. They're not tremendously evil as swamps go, but what do I know (incidentally, there's a local band called Switch Canyon Slash. Check them out if you can). We had friends who lived in nearby Walker, so that was cool anyway.

The highlight of that part was a shot of Pearl crawling out of the dark water screaming, crazy, and naked, like some sort of genderless Asian swamp thing. She must have done it for three straight hours. I fell asleep at one point, woke up, and they were still trying to capture the perfect take. That's dedication.

I figured the nudity would be an issue, but once the thing was edited only her pussy got blackbarred. DeVour liked the idea of showing her tits (such as they are) and getting away with it. Sure enough, when the clip finally made air no mention was made of the clandestine nipple shots. Either the broadcasters thought Pearl was a guy, or they just didn't give a shit.

By the way, the song we chose for the video is called *Eyes Melt*. It has nothing to do with swamps or naked, mud-covered fish women. I wish it did.

All told it ended up being a good time. And worth it...I think. The Louisiana shoot (principal photography?) was a little over a week and a half. Plotting, location scouting, and all of that had taken about the same. During that time Cres, Pierre and I hit it off really well with DeVour's crew: camera guy Monroe, Monroe's lady and sound tech Tina, and Katt, DeVour's all-purpose assistant. We hung out and got high with them while Pearl and her husband were off alone. I didn't see much of Pearl or DeVour that month. It was odd. Like I said before, she seemed like a different person with him around.

DeVour was nothing but cool to me, and by and large he came across as an all-right fellow. I was a bit taken aback by how randomly hostile he was to right hand man Katt. He'd say things like:

"Well, I think that take was pretty good, despite Katt's raging incompetence."

Or

"I'm glad to see Katt managed to keep from shitting all over the floor. Kudos to you, lad."

No one said anything about it, however, and Katt didn't seem to mind. I certainly wasn't going to make issue of it.

Whatever. Show business. None of my concern.

It was decided (though not by me) that the *denouement* of the clip should be the Pearl-beast slithering like a gator into the water at Cypress Brake, then reemerging from the briny deep onto the shores of Venice Beach. I think, although I'm not sure, that the concept behind the concept was that Stigmata Dog had arrived to wreak havoc upon LA, and the unsuspecting California halfwits were not prepared for the awesome destructive power of the Dog. Or something. I didn't quite get it. But no matter. Of course, this would require a trip to the City of Angels.

***

"There aren't enough drugs in the world to get me on a goddamn airplane to LA," Pearl said emphatically. "Trust me, I've done them all."

So DeVour and his people went on ahead and we decided to make a mini-tour out of the drive. Sisyphus tossed us a couple of bones and called it a "tour budget." We called Bradley and Annalee to come along for company and general assistance.

"Aw, naw cuz'n," Bradley said. "LA gives me herpes."

"Fuckin' A!" said Annalee. "I'd love to roll with yous guys!"

We plotted our route and away we went. Annalee booked herself a couple of small venue gigs for after-shows and a few of our off-nights. I accompanied her on acoustic guitar for those sets. It was a cool change o' pace. All the shows went respectably well, if I do say so myself.

Normally, because our "tour budget" could not be written without quotation marks around it, we would forgo lodging in favor of a system we called *paying the rent.* How it worked was: one person (on a rotating basis) slept in the van with the gear, while everyone else was on their own to find a local to bed down with after the show. (Come to think of it, this doesn't really qualify as a "system.") I actually preferred my turn in the van, simply because I was paranoid about the safety of my guitars.

However, we didn't think that arrangement was appropriate with Annalee along for the ride, so we all chipped in for a single motel room in every town (and I slept nearest the window with one ear toward the van outside). It was actually a lot of fun. Kind of like summer camp (...I suppose. I never went to summer camp). And it was cool to have Pearl temporarily back to "normal," such as that was, sans Penny DeVour. I think it was good for her to have Annalee along too. It was good for all of us. Nobody got laid and nobody minded. LA was calling after all, and we were almost there.

All in all we clocked 1,672 miles, played six shows total, drank our collective weight in Irish whisky and cheap vodka, and rolled into Los Angeles at three-twenty-seven on a Friday morning. Once there Pearl wasn't quite sure where exactly we were supposed to go, and we couldn't reach DeVour on his cellphone.

"There's nobody I know in this town that I really wanna call on right now," Pearl said. No explanation why. We opted to not press the issue.

Just for the hell of it we decided to park the van up in Hollywood Hills and try to snag some shut-eye until sunrise. That lasted all of twelve minutes when we found the van surrounded by the LAPD flashing red and blue. Weapons drawn, bullhorns shouting—

"What the hell are you doing camped out in front of these people's houses?!"

Good sense somehow reared its head and Annalee was elected to speak on our behalf.

"Yous guys should know the score here," Annalee said to the cops in her sweet yet practical way. "The five of us just rolled into this fine city from South Jesus, just outside of Nowheresville, and we are without a place to be until one-thirty in the p.m. today. Now, yous could make us leave, and we could drive aimlessly around your town, bleary-eyed and half-dead, until the sun comes up. We *could* do that. OR...you could just let us sleep here and we won't bother anybody and all will be right with the world."

Believe it or not, it actually worked. They turned off their rollers and drove away. *Pigs. Who can figure 'em.*

Not wanting to tempt fate, we opted to leave the Hills and find somewhere else to crash.

We settled on the parking lot of a little touristy crap hole called the *Hollywood Celebrity Hotel,* off Sunset right around the corner from Grauman's Chinese Theatre.

"Maybe we should see if they've got a room available," Pierre suggested.

"They don't," said Pearl. "Money on it."

Pierre decided to check anyway, and returned less than a minute later.

"She's right," he said. "Not a single room to be had. Kinda biblical in its own way."

So we hunkered down for a power snooze in the van before the morning sunlight cooked us all alive.

"Goodnight, ladies," said Pierre.

"Goodnight, John-boy," said Annalee.

"Goodnight light and the red balloon," I said.

"Goodnight sweetheart, well, it's time to go," said Pearl.

"Goodnight...uh...fuck, I can't think of one," sighed Cres. "I hate you all."

"Seriously?" I said. "No *Goodnight Irene*? The Leadbelly classic? Pshh. And you call yourself a Southern man."

"I'm not a...word guy," Cres protested. "I just know how to play them hoes, you know what I'm sayin'?" Crickets and tumbleweeds. "Let's just get some sleep."

Just as we were drifting off, the van began to rock back and forth. I peeked out the passenger-side window to see this pop-collared fuckstick nailing an old, peroxide-scorched whore against the side of our vehicle, her squishy, fishnetted thighs wrapped awkwardly around his waist. She didn't even bother to fake a moan or feign any enthusiasm. I was too tired and disinterested to interrupt, so I simply let the movement rock me to sleep.

"You ever get homesick for this place?" Cres asked Pearl.

"Eh," Pearl shrugged. "A little."

We half-slept until eleven-thirty or so when the heat inside the van finally rendered the atmosphere sufficiently intolerable.

"It's probably safe to go to Penn's," Pearl sighed, stretching.

"So where're we headed?" I asked.

"Pacific Palisades," she replied. "He's either at the office in the village or at the house up on Vance. I'm guessing the house, but it's pointless to call before two."

"Vance?" I said. "Isn't that pretty close to here?"

"Eh, close is a relative concept."

"Why couldn't we just have gone there as soon as we came to town?" Pierre asked the question we were all wondering. "Dude is expecting us, right?"

"Look," Pearl said emphatically, "I'm married to the motherfucker. If I say it's a bad idea to drop in on him at four in the morning just trust that I'm being straight with you."

And with that we were off.

Penny DeVour's pad was like nothing Annalee or the male portion of Stigmata Dog had ever seen. It probably wasn't that spectacular compared to plenty of others in the area, but suffice it to say it was over our collective station. We had to struggle a bit to maintain some level of hep and not come off like the goddamn Clampetts.

"Nice place," Annalee said as we piled out of the van and caught our first eyefull of the canyon view.

"It better be, for ten grand a fuckin' month," Pearl snorted.

"You left *this* to go live in a damp hovel in Baton Rouge with a bunch of drunk, broke-dick headbangers?" Cres asked.

"No," Pearl said, "I left *San Pedro* to join my favoritest band in the world." She clearly did not want to play along. "You guys will like it here. They call this style Country French."

And just at that moment the oak front door flew open, and a very thin blonde in a *very* small bikini came flying out of the house, tits abounce, screaming in a pitch just slightly low enough to be heard by human ears.

"PEEEEEEEEEEEEEARL BABYYYYYYYYY!!!" She threw her arms around Pearl, still squealing. "It's so good to see youuuuuuuuuuuuuuuuuuu!!!"

"Hey, sweet thing!" Pearl said to the wet, nearly naked

banshee, returning the embrace. "Guys, come here. You gotta meet—"

"We know who she is!" Pierre exclaimed, losing all pretense of cool. "Pleasure to meet you, Miss Honey! We've seen *all* your movies."

Dude...Pierre...seriously...

I wanted to crawl into the van and gore myself to death with a pair of dull pliers.

He was right, though. We did know who she was. Her name was Clover Honey. And we had seen at least *several* of her cinematic efforts, if not all of them. There were, after all, quite a few. But telling a porn star that you really admire her work doesn't quite seem to carry the same complimentary air that it might for some other purveyor of the creative arts. At least that's what I thought at first. But upon later consideration, if someone told me that they periodically rubbed one out to the sound of my guitar, I'd be nothing but flattered. And apparently that's how Clover Honey felt as well.

"Awww, thank y'all so much!" she replied. *Well I'll be goddamned. A southern belle.* "The pleasure is all mine. It usually is," she giggled. "Why don't y'all come in! Take a load off yer feet! Imma run'n' dry off and meet y'all in a jiff." I had never realized before that Clover Honey had a down-south twang. But then again, I probably wasn't paying adequate attention to the dialogue.

The inside of the place was much classier than I would have guessed of a scumbag like DeVour: pecan hardwood floors, mahogany beamed ceilings, tasteful middle-eastern décor.

"The dungeon and torture racks are downstairs," Pearl said, apparently reading my mind.

"Hey Pearl," a male voice hollered lazily from down the hall.

"Joey, get your ass out here and give me a hug," Pearl demanded.

Out shambled what looked like an extra from a Stray Cats video, replete with greasy doo-wop do, and cigarette pack rolled up in his T-shirt sleeve. He gave Pearl a quick squeeze and patted her ass, then proceeded directly to the wet bar for a Pabst Blue Ribbon. Motherfucker was *in character.*

"Howdy kids," Bowser slurred. "You lads are...uh...Stigmatized Dog, right?" He cracked the tab and downed half the beer in a single drink. "I heard your demo. Cool. Cool stuff. I don't really get it...but I *get it,* you know?"

"Joey's a writer," Pearl said. *How about that.*

"Penny should be here any minute," Clover Honey said walking back in wearing tight, cut-off jeans and a towel around her tanned shoulders. "Y'all want a drink?"

The one called Joey proceeded to pull out several bottles of Wild Turkey and Absolut.

"I think we'll be just fine here," said Cres with a grin.

We small-talked with Pony Boy and Blondie for about twenty-nine minutes until Penny DeVour came bursting in through the front door and immediately began ticking off the agenda. He barely acknowledged us with his eyes.

"Hey, glad you guys are here. Katt's on his way with the van. He's picking up Monroe and the camera in Frogtown, and we'll be ready to roll. We're gonna take Pearl down to Venice and shoot this thing guerilla. I didn't bother to secure a permit. Provided Katt doesn't completely piss the bed and ruin everything like he normally does, we should be done in less than an hour. The rest of you stigmata dogs are welcome to come with us, but I suspect that you'd probably rather hit Amoeba Records." *You suspect correctly.* "We can grab a bite after that, and then we're headed to The Whisky. I've secured the stage for four hours, so we can bag some live shots. Not a lot of time, but I think it'll be enough."

"We've got a gig at The Whisky tonight?" Cres asked. I think we all got a jolt of excitement from the notion. It was to be short lived.

"No offense, my man," DeVour said, "but I don't know if you guys are enough of a name draw around here just yet. We can't risk a half-empty house. Not tonight. I put out a call for extras, so we should have it well packed."

"Are you paying the audience?" I asked, a hint of embarrassment slipping through my voice.

"Hand jobs and bong hits," DeVour replied with a shrug.

"Nice."

"It'll be pretty much just like the swamp shots in NOLA. We'll try different angles with the playback at different speeds."

"Well..." Cres said, "Couldn't we just play it live?"

"If I had a budget for more cameras, sure," DeVour said. "But we've just got a short window of time for this thing, and every moment's gotta count. It's gotta be in sync, spot on. Sorry, folks. This shit ain't glamorous. I hope nobody has lead you astray."

"Yous guys, it'll be great," Annalee said. "It's gonna be *bad-ass.*" She danced a bit in excitement. "I'm gonna go with Pearl for the beach thing, if that's okay."

Pearl's face lit up. I'd wager she probably would have liked all of us to go, but sorry. They don't have record shops like Amoeba in Louisiana, even in the *Vieux Carré.*

"Sure," DeVour said with a shrug. "There's room."

So as half the assembled headed off to Venice Beach, international erotic film sensation Clover Honey volunteered to babysit the remaining seventy-five percent of Stigmata Dog for a couple of hours (her fella Soda Pop opting to stay behind, alas). I thought at first that this was above and beyond the call of duty on Ms. Honey's part. Certainly she had better things to do with her time (...or perhaps not). But her motivations became baldly manifest as soon as we stepped onto Sunset Blvd.

Dorks of every stripe instantly began to swarm and flock, seemingly from nowhere, begging for photos, autographs, and county-fair-style kisses on the cheek. And Clover was all-too happy to oblige. It was her clear intention to get noticed and approached, hardly subtle, and the pleasure she received from the attention was palpable. Which was little but a curiosity to

Cres, Pierre, and me. We were never wired for that sort of thing, and were more than a bit baffled by those who are. She'd occasionally say something to the throng of acne-scarred wankers like, "Y'all wanna see the real talent in the room, this here's Stigmata Dog. They're gonna be HUGE! They RAWK!" and so on. Nice of her, I suppose. But unnecessary. And fruitless. These guys were really only interested in a chance to be close to her, and maybe a shot of a butterfly tat titty flash to show off for the rubes back home.

Interestingly enough, the only place no one paid Clover Honey any mind was at Amoeba Music. Someone did, however, recognize *us. What are the odds?* A heavy-set Mexican kid in a Lakers jersey just happened to be buying a copy of our EP at the moment we walked in, and came running up to us chattering something about how his cousin serving life for aggravated manslaughter turned him on to us. Or something. I didn't quite follow it. But whatever, we were grateful for the purchase. And yes, we signed it for him. We also told him about the video shoot, and he said he'd be there. *Stigmata Dog: spreading a little joy everywhere we go.*

I picked up some obscure Japanese imports. Cres bought "The Best of Jelly Roll Morton" and I thought, *You couldn't pick that up back home, cuz'n?* Hey, it was his money. Clover Honey snagged some Cramps record on vinyl, apparently for Joey ("I prefer Dangerous Toys," she said. *Fair enough*). She went about trying really hard to flirt with the counter clerk, but to no avail. I don't think people who work on Sunset get too star-struck, especially over stars better known for anilingus than Academy Awards. Plus, I thought I was picking up a bit of a gay vibe from that kid, so maybe that was the problem. You can't win 'em all.

The more time we spent with Clover, the more I liked her… and the less attractive she seemed. Her generosity and courtesy felt genuine to me. It wasn't a put-on or a show. It also felt just a bit needy. She struck me as the kind of girl who could actually fall in love on a porn set. I don't know, maybe it was all an act. If so, kudos to her. I bought it. I did like her, in a sad sort of way.

The entire crux of her conversational MO revolved around name-dropping someone (usually someone marginally famous and/or porn related), and then gushing, vaguely, about what a wonderful person he or she was.

"He's just a gem!" "Oh, I hope y'all get to meet _____ while you're here. She has such a beautiful spirit." "What a complete darling." "A total class act." "Just a doll." Et cetera.

I would find this to be a pattern throughout the majority of the people we met that weekend. Someone would walk up to me, ask me if I knew So-and-so, I'd say no, and they would proceed to shower said person with glowing, yet oddly non-specific, praise. It got to the point where I would just lie and exclaim, "I sure do! God, what an absolute sweetheart!" They would agree enthusiastically, and then walk away satisfied. To this day I don't know if this is a Southern California thing, a porno thing, or simply a quirk particular to this group of people. I asked Pearl about it, and she just laughed and rolled her eyes.

Pearl called Clover Honey's cellphone around 4 p.m. to tell us that the shoot went well, but they weren't going to be able to meet up for dinner because she and DeVour had to go "see a friend." *Indeed.* She said to meet up with them at The Whisky exactly at seven.

So the four of us grabbed some In N Out burgers, a six-pack of Corona, and headed to the beach. I'm not really a beach kinda guy, but no matter. It was rather hilarious because there were a lot of family-types frolicking about at this particular location, and I could tell that many of the fathers (and a number of mothers as well) recognized Clover...but no one approached us. *Come on, folks. Don't be shy.*

With a few hours to kill we did the requisite running about on Sunset. We invaded the Scientology museum just for a goof, intent on stealing something, but the creepy, hive-like atmosphere and the nauseatingly friendly "tour guides" sent us awkwardly on our way empty-handed.

We tried and failed to get into Capitol Records, and ended up giving the gate guard our demo.

"Hope you dig it, cuz'n," we said, knowing that's as far as it would ever go. For some odd reason I was really hoping he would actually listen to it. Not so he'd pass it along to his bosses, just so he heard it. I'm all about building the fan base one at a time.

All in all I'm cool with LA, I guess. But for some reason it feels like it has no center. Like a whole lot of random crap happening next to other random crap. Who knows...

Finally it was time for the shoot.

Clover dropped us off, said she'd meet us later back at DeVour's pad, and we headed on inside.

Katt and Monroe were already there setting up when we arrived. Tina and Annalee arrived shortly thereafter, thankfully.

"Free drinks at the bar for band and crew all night!" Katt announced. "Don't ask questions, just roll."

"You got it, bro," said Cres. We would definitely be taking advantage.

Pierre and I never used cordless systems, and since we weren't really going to be playing live we simply plugged our respective cables into the jacks on our guitars and stuffed the loose ends into our pockets. Cres set up his drums in record time (no tuning necessary), and we stood there on stage like potted plants, not knowing what else to do.

Tina brought us up a round of snakebite shots (one part Jack Daniels, one part tequila, ten drops of Tabasco sauce). We slammed them, and Tina went and got us some more (I guess there's really not a lot for a sound tech to do on a video shoot. At least not this one).

We were told that the extras were gathering outside, and it

looked like a decent crowd. In all the years I've been a performing musician, I've never once gotten stage fright. I don't even get antsy right before show time. But this one instance when we weren't actually going to be playing a single live note, I was a knot of nervous tension.

"Ready?" Annalee asked, kicking off her sandals and plopping down on the edge of the stage. Pierre and I removed our axes and sat with her. Cres came out from behind the kit and joined us on the floor.

"Born to do it," Pierre said, throwing up the devil horns.

"I don't know why everybody bad mouths lip-syncing," Cres said, deadpan. "It really is a fine art."

"The shoot at Venice Beach was so bitchin'!" Annalee said, nearly spilling her wine in the process. "God, I don't know how Pearl walks around this town in bare feet. It's rough enough back in NOLA and Baton Rouge, but here

...everything's broken here."

"Warrior spirit," Cres, Pierre, and I all said in unison.

"Whatevs," Annalee replied. "Man, isn't this the most exciting thing to ever happen in all of human existence!"

"Literally THE most," said Pierre.

"I'm so happy for yous guys. Who woulda thought, huh? I can't wait to say *I knew them when*!"

"Riiiight," I said. "Annalee, I predict, within the year, you're gonna be on a major label and we'll never see you again." (I was half right, anyway.)

"Wrong," she replied. "Nuh uh. I mean, the label thing, that'd be tits. But we're gonna stick together, dudes. We gotta do an LP together. I'm totally serious about that." We clinked glasses on the idea. Good as a contract, as far as I'm concerned.

Finally Pearl and DeVour arrived, appearing tremendously calm and collected, sedate even, with a mob of enthusiastic rockers trailing behind them. Most of them were young Chicano headbangers rocking Brujeria and Sepultura T-shirts.

But some of them were simply folks from the neighborhood, several pushing—or over—fifty. Katt went about rounding up the olds, positioning them at the back of the crowd, and handing out a few ballcaps and ridiculous looking costume-shop 'metal' wigs to cover up the offending gray hair.

DeVour gathered the band up center stage for a huddle.

"You dogs ready to rock out with your cocks out?" he asked (and it sounded like a genuine question).

"I left my cock in El Segundo," Pearl said dryly. "*I got tah git it / Got-got to git it.*" It was an eerily accurate Q-Tip impersonation. *Chick's a treasure trove of hidden talents.*

"So it goes," said DeVour. "You wanna stage dive, Anna Banana? It'd be a killer shot."

"Aw jeez," Annalee replied. "No way, man. I'm too chicken."

"Suit yourself," DeVour said. "Well, we're going to have a number of stage divers, so don't be surprised when they jump up there, guys. I really want to make this part look like a late eighties thrash video."

"We shoulda got white high-tops and bullet belts," Pierre said.

"Maybe next time. All right then, assume your positions. We're going to get the lighting scheme worked out, and we'll be ready to roll tape in less than ten." He gave Pearl a quick smooch and headed over to conspire with Monroe and Tina. Annalee gave us all hugs and hopped down into the crowd.

The opening drumbeat began to pound on the overhead speakers in normal time, and the "audience" started to move. The lights went down and commenced building along with the rhythm, preparing to come alive when the song kicked in proper. I decided this would be my only chance to do a Townshend-esque windmill with my arm, as our music is a bit too tight for that sort of showboating normally. *Golden opportunity, I hear ya knockin'.* 3-2-1 and BOOM! The place went bonkers. Pearl instantly flew around the stage like a pinball gone loco. Although her mic wasn't on, I could hear her screaming out the words as if this were a real show. People began flying off the front of the stage and I got the notion, as ridiculous as it felt to do it, that this was going to show up amazing on the final print. *It was fun, man. It was fuckin' fun.*

Four and a half hours later, I never wanted to hear *Eyes Melt* again for as long as I walked the earth (in fact I've never played it live since). DeVour said something about checking a gate and "that's a wrap" and everyone cheered and clapped. DeVour hopped up on stage, high-fived the lads, man-hugged me, and whispered in my ear, "Party at my place."

It's happening. It's really fuckin' happening...

Some hours later, back at the DeVour Estate, I awoke in an unfamiliar bedroom half knotted in a leopard-skin blanket. I peeled a lovely young fluffer named Amber Chestnut from me, and she murmured and rolled over, never stirring. My head spun, and my mouth tasted like I'd been licking out an aquarium.

I guzzled the warm backwash out of a near-empty bottle of Rumple Minze to cut the taste. *Fuckin' balls, that's even* worse. I sat at the edge of the bed trying to remember anything of note about the party. I also tried to remember how exactly I got my pants off with my boots still on. Chalking it up to a mystery destined to remain unsolved, I got dressed and headed on outside for some fresh air.

It was nearing daybreak, but still pitch black out. I had assumed there would have been people raging straight on until sunrise and beyond, like the parties back home. But the house was unnervingly quiet...as if folks had locked themselves away on purpose.

Out by the pool I found the air not tremendously fresh, but it would have to do. I thought about the day we'd had and wondered what was next. Would the video get us noticed?

Would it even get played? Would we get to tour Europe? Or South America? Or Japan? Maybe we'd be the next big thing and all of that...which I know as well as anybody you shouldn't even ponder, lest you jinx it and queer the deal. But I felt like I had earned a little flight of fancy.

I turned to go back inside, just as the glass doors slid open and Penny DeVour came stumbling out, pointing a full-size UZI Carbine directly at my face.

And silence.

For a moment all I saw was the black of the gun and the shimmering whites of his eyes, ripped and jagged with red spiderwebs.

"Um...hey, Penn."

"Oh hey, Shel."

His eyelids fluttered and his teeth were clenched hard. Not in anger or fear, but absently, as if by habit.

"Just me out here," I said calmly.

"I see. Nice night, huh?"

He did not lower the weapon even the slightest bit.

"Yep." I stared at the black nozzle pointed right at my forehead, and I wondered, if it were to spray me, would I feel anything? Or would the world just go dark. I tapped my front pocket, hoping that maybe I had grabbed my butterfly knife out of my gig bag and forgotten about it, *as if a butterfly knife would protect me from a fucking UZI.* "Um, er, um...so how do you think the shoot went tonight?" *Don't say "shoot," dumbass.*

"Oh, real good. Real good. Yeah. I think you are gonna like the bit we taped at Venice Beach too. Totally freaked out a family of tourists. Heh. Got some great spontaneous reaction shots."

"Good. Good. Glad to hear it."

"Yeah, I think you're really gonna be pleased with the clip. Your label too. I don't want to speak too soon, but this might really do something big for you."

"That'd be great. Thanks a lot. I mean that."

"Glad to help."

And silence.

"So...Penn...You normally wander around the house at four-twenty-nine in the morning carrying a loaded UZI?"

"Yeah sometimes," he said casually, still pointing the barrel straight at my head.

"Any chance of you *not* shooting me with it?"

"Oh, of course." But the gun remained trained on me.

We looked at each other blankly for a few long moments. His eyes fluttered rapidly. I could feel ice-water sweat leaking down the back of my neck. Every time he twitched a bit I wanted to dive into the pool for cover, but was sure he'd pull the trigger. Perhaps by accident. *Perhaps.* Finally he said, "Come on downstairs with me. There's something I've been wanting to show you."

He turned on his heel and headed back into the house. I followed him in, because apparently my sense of self-preservation is not as strong as it should be.

Once downstairs he lead me into what appeared to be a very small theater. The largest flat-screen TV I had ever seen covered the entire south wall. Actual old-timey theater seats lined the back. A white leather couch was positioned up front, and DeVour beckoned me to sit. He set the Carbine on a glass coffee table, upon which sat a half-empty bottle of Citron, an empty bottle of Citron, and a glass mirror with white lines cut neatly in a row.

"Want a bump?" he asked, handing me a rolled up hundred. I leaned over and snorted a fat rail off the mirror. "Go ahead, do another. You're a guest in my house." I snorted a second line, this one thinner than the first. I didn't want to be a pig, after all. I handed the roll back to him and instantly noticed that something was askew. The powder I had just hoovered into my sinuses was grittier than it should have been, and put an odd taste in the back of my throat. My heart sank (literally) as the realization came upon me. *Oh shit...This isn't coke...it's...fucking...Oxycontin...*

Any hope of a jolt buzz was dashed for good mere minutes

later, as my hypothesis was proven accurate. Everything began to soften around me as my face fell numb and my head started to bob ever so slightly, and beyond my control. My mouth lost what little moisture it had, and I felt my whole body begin to sag with additional gravity.

I wondered why Penny DeVour, who could afford the real shit, would bother with such low-rent hillbilly junk. I just couldn't imagine a guy like him sitting in his basement crushing pills like a San Bernardino trailer teen, when he could have high-grade Brown Sugar FedEx'd to him at any time. Was this his version of keeping it real? Or did he notice the lack of track marks on my arms and thought this was the best way to be hospitable?

"Sometimes I just want a cheeseburger, you know it?" he said, grinning sheepishly. Perhaps I had said something out loud and not realized it. Perhaps it was scrawled across my face.

He snorted the last line and took a swig of Citron. He handed it to me and I guzzled a mouthful. I barely tasted it.

"SHELL-ac," he enunciated. "Shellac on the attack, back in black. Man…I am all about what you guys are doing, all right. Cres and Pierre are the tightest rhythm section I have ever heard! And you and Pearl…it's like you were born to be partners. You're pretty much taking my place as the man in her life, brother."

"No I'm not."

I thought of telling him that that position was filled. Frequently.

"I started out in music, you know," he said.

"I did not."

"Late seventies. San Fran hardcore scene. Hardcore was still *punk* then. It didn't become metal 'til it reached Brooklyn."

"I know." *But thanks for the history lesson, chief.*

He reached into a leather pouch sitting on the floor and pulled out a little plastic bag of white powder.

"I've got snow," he offered. "You look like you're slipping a bit."

Although I wasn't loving the sensation of my bones liquefying just then, the idea of becoming the rope in a game of drug-of-war didn't thrill me either.

"Nah, I'm good."

"Yeah, me too. We'll save this for tonight."

"Good call."

He dropped the bag back into the leather pouch and proceeded to lick the oxy residue from the mirror.

"Yeah," he said flicking his tongue like a Gila monster, "those were fun times back then."

"What was your band called?"

"The Zero Collectors."

"What?"

"The Zero Collectors. Like, billionaires. Zero collectors. People who are so rich they make money just to collect the zeroes. They don't need it. They'll never spend it. Just collect zeroes. You know?"

"I get it."

"We had this ironic shtick, all right? We'd all go onstage in three-piece suits, and our stage names were...well, you get the picture. We had songs like *Bulldoze the Homeless,* and *God Bless You, Governor Reagan.* It was satirical, right? We were trying to really stick it to the greedheads. We broke up in eighty-two."

"Good timing."

"Yeah."

"Where are the rest of the guys today?"

"Silicon Valley. No shit. How's that for irony?"

"I've heard better."

He shrugged. "We were all upper-middle-class suburban kids, right? We had good educations. It just made sense. Well...it made sense for them. I rejected the button-down life. Wholesale. I still do. I wasn't made for it."

Nice job.

"You've done well for yourself."

"Yeah...but I miss *the fire*." He paused for a moment and took another drink. Finally, "This is what I wanted to show you. I have a...protégé, I guess you'd call him...in Reseda. I'd like to introduce you two. Maybe you can do some score work for him. Easy money."

"Yeah, okay. Score work for porno?"

He responded with a sinister chuckle.

"You'd like him I think. Young guy. He's a beast. Absolute beast. He made this." DeVour picked up a remote control and pointed it toward the TV.

And so it began...

Blank screen and some screeching, pitch-modified metallic scraping. Just the sound and nothing for nearly a minute. Then suddenly images swimming in deep, coagulated red flooded the screen. I couldn't quite tell what was going on at first. But whatever it was, I can't say I was a fan.

"What is this?" I asked.

"This..." he said, pausing dramatically, "is the future. And the end of the line."

Either my eyes began to focus more clearly, or the camera did. *Oh...that's what that is.* Bodies pumped and writhed in slo-mo, moaning and slurping in a down-pitched gurgle, squirming in meat and slop like ravenous worms, intercut with slashing and screaming, bones breaking and muscles ripping apart. Hardcore penetration, but no clearly definable human faces. All the while liquor and synthetic opiates churned in my stomach like a rat poison gumbo. I tried to pretend to watch the screen while finding somewhere else to aim my eyes. But it was not to be. The massive television covered my entire field of vision.

"Yeah..." DeVour hissed gleefully. "Van Nuys can't handle *this* stuff."

"Is...is this, um, *real*?"

"Well," DeVour said enraptured by the tableau, "The blood and the killings are all staged. Corn syrup. But the fucking and the vomit are the genuine article."

"How about that," I said as I sat there trying to concoct the best way to make a relatively polite exit. Fake a sudden kidney stone or something. But it was a no-go anyway. My legs had turned to gelatin. Just my luck.

The whole scene was rather pointless, not to mention repulsive, and I couldn't figure out why exactly DeVour felt I needed to watch it. Devil his due, though, the lighting and the camera angles were inventive.

"Let me tell you a little story, Shel."

"All right."

"You're probably too young to know this, but once upon a time there were these things known as pornographic movies."

"Okay."

"I mean they were actual *films.* Motion pictures."

"Oh yeah?"

"I crap you not a bit. People went out and watched them in theaters. Sometimes on dates! They were real fucking movies, right? They just happened to have been movies with real fucking. There were directors, producers, composers, musicians, screenwriters, script doctors, actors, location scouts, stunt coordinators, the whole package, all hired on a project-by-project basis. Just like a real film. The music was great, the cinematography was great, the direction was great, the scripts were...acceptable. They were real movies. Sometimes they were funny, sometimes they were serious and dramatic. Sometimes there were car chases and gunfights. And periodically people would ball each other."

"Uh huh. I'm with you."

I took the fact that he was talking as an opportunity to move my head away from the TV and look directly at him, but the audio on its own was actually worse. All low groaning and screeching, tearing and snapping. I wondered if I could recreate the sound on my guitar somehow, but then I'd have to borrow the DVD. *Not worth it.*

"And audiences pretty much dug it. More or less. But the trouble was, there weren't all that many films, relatively speaking. Not like today. Film stock is expensive. So in order to appeal to as large an audience as possible, most bang for the buck, the flicks had to have a little something for everybody. There'd be some straight vanilla action, some gay business, a little S & M, maybe it gets a touch rapey, what have you.

"BUT," he continued, "just like how not everybody likes the same things, *nobody* likes *all of it.* So the industry was constantly battling both the Law of Diminishing Erotic Returns, and the Law of Negative Erotic Returns. It's a fight already lost. You follow me?"

"Yes." I really didn't, though. My eyelids were getting heavy.

"But then a glorious invention fell from the heavens. Two of them, actually. Home Video, and Casio Synth. All of the sudden, where producers were making four or five flicks a month, they could do four or five *a week.* Or more! And eventually, instead of having to make prints for theaters, they could sell 'em directly to people for their own private, in-home use. Dupes were super-cheap. Like printing your own money."

"But video looks like yak shit."

"You're damn right it does! And Casio keyboards create noxious auditory drivel that pleases precisely no one. *But*...the band wasn't needed anymore. And we could cut the crew in half. And we could tailor the content of the flicks to people's individual tastes and fetishes. Cater to personal peccadilloes. Before too long we didn't need location scouts, or even script writers."

"You were making inferior product."

"Exactly! Well, technically I *always* was. I came along well after the golden age had passed. By the time I came along porn was fast, ugly, and cheap."

"And you're pleased with that?"

"Was I ever! Fast, ugly, and cheap are what I'm all about, my friend! My bread and butter. The cream in my coffee. And the great thing is...profits kept growing and growing and growing. The faster, cheaper, and uglier our output got, the more money it made. ANYTHING would sell. By this point some common-stock sow could videotape herself flying solo with various household appliances, and make nearly a hundred percent profit. Obviously the distributor takes his share, but even that model is going away now thanks to the Worldwide Web.

"Imagine that, Shel. Imagine, every time you so much as tuned up your guitar, as long as you remembered to hit 'play' on your four-track beforehand, you'd make...say, five thousand dollars. Fifty thousand dollars. *Every single time.* And your fans never complained about bum notes, or sloppy production. They never complain at all. They're just grateful that you do it. God...it's glorious."

"So people actually liked the decrease in quality?"

"No, they didn't! That's the beautiful thing! They didn't like it at all. But nobody complains about bad porn. Nobody. And they sure as shit don't return it. They assume that if they don't get off on it that means something's wrong with *them.* They think they've gone jaded. Gotten desensitized. So they seek out darker, nastier, more exotic shit. Or just bare-bones fundamentals, no fluff no frills. Something's got to do the trick, right? More often than not that doesn't cut it either. So they get more frustrated, and buy more, buy nastier, buy darker."

"And that's when you make the scene."

"And that's where Penny DeVour steps in and makes out like a fucking bandit, *mon frère.* I sell truckloads of unspeakable dreck to desperate, angry, frustrated people, and they love me for it. And, no matter what, they'll never stop dragging their dicks through the brambles and mud to gobble from this trough. My friend Joey says it's just like church. And it really is."

"Folks who don't feel the Holy Spirit think there's something wrong with them," I said. "So they fake it, and just pray harder."

"EXACTLY. It's all just masturbation, and there's always good money in that."

He paused for a moment to let that all soak in, then pointed back at the bloody fuck soup on screen. "But I'm passing the baton. I don't have the energy any more. Or the interest. If I'm just going to do it for the paycheck, then there are more interesting ways for me to do it. Pop music videos and Straight-to-DVD slasher flicks will do me just fine in my twilight years. Somebody's got to be the bottom of the barrel, Shel, the end of the line. It's not me anymore.

"But," he said, "I doff my cap to those of you who have made pushing it over the edge your life's work."

"Um...wait...huh?"

Those of you?

"Shel, when I first heard your music, without Pearl, I thought you were really on to something. Even at that early stage. It was special, don't get me wrong. But then...when I heard you all together, I said THAT'S IT! They've finally done it! They've *destroyed music*!"

"What?!"

"You have to at least *try* to destroy the thing you love, am I right? Most artists fail...but you gotta try. The Swiss Dadaists tried to destroy art. They failed, and actually *created* new art. Losers. Napalm Death tried to destroy music, but they failed spectacularly, and created new genres and countless offshoot groups instead. Worth a try, no? I tried to destroy porn, and very nearly did it. Still, I failed. But my protégé has it within his grasp. And I think Stigmata Dog may be the end of the line as well."

"Fuckin' balls."

"You GOTTA destroy your god."

"That's ridiculous."

"Eh?"

"Penn, I *make music*. I don't want to destroy it. I'm not making a...I just like this particular sound. You may not enjoy what you do, but I do. I dig the hell out of the music I make. And other people like it too."

"Sure they do, Shel," DeVour grinned conspiratorially and winked at me. "Sure they do." His head bobbed forward as the full brunt of the oxy began to settle on us both. A thin stream of drool began to spill from his bottom lip.

"Penn? Penn, are you all right?"

"I'm trying..." he mumbled. "I'm trying...to think..." and with that he was on the nod, sitting, hunched over. Lights out.

I turned off the television, and forced myself to stand up. I thought about taking the Carbine and hiding it somewhere, but I didn't know where. I noticed an Epiphone Broadway archtop sitting in the corner and picked it up. A gorgeous guitar, it appeared to have hardly been played, if it had ever been played at all. I went to tune it up and realized that I couldn't remember how to do it. I fretted a few chords to see what the tone was like at least, and totally forgot how to operate this machine. This instrument, which I had been playing religiously since I was nine years old, five hours a day every single day, was an alien apparatus in my hands.

I put the archtop down where I found it and crawled back upstairs, my muscles six hundred pounds apiece, my mouth filled with sandy cotton, a layer of jellied gauze over my eyes.

The sun was coming up. And the sun makes everything normal again.

New nightmare. *Some girl in desert fatigues slashes her lover's throat. A baby watches, sucking happily on a bottle.*

"Shel. Psssst...Shel."

I felt my hip getting tapped by the instep of a combat boot. I opened my eyes to see that I had passed out face down on the brick patio. *That's gonna leave an attractive impression.*

"What's going on? What time is it?"

"I don't know," Cres answered. "Afternoon or something. DuChamp went with Pearl and DeVour down to his editing studio to check out the footage from yesterday. Me and Annalee are gonna head to the beach. Wanna come with?"

"You two are gettin' mighty chummy, huh?"

"We just had a real good talk last night, that's all."

"Really. Was that before or after everybody got balls-out in the swimming pool? I was absent for that, alas."

"Man, come on. I never agreed to the 'hands off' policy,

you know. And I wasn't down with the group action, and neither was Annalee. No offense to nobody, but I ain't touching ANY of these broads around here."

"Whatever, cuz'n," I said, sitting up finally. I felt a puke upon me, but swallowed it back. "I don't give a shit what you all do."

"We just talked."

"Killer. Have fun."

"Cool. Oh, Pierre talked to Sally on the phone. Said everything's fine back home. 'Cept Cerberus ripped up the couch and took a shit on your bed. Fucker's neurotic."

"How does that constitute everything being fine?!"

"Well we'll see you later, all right? Take it easy."

I spent the rest of the day draining a bottle of Beam and playing DeVour's Archtop (thankfully my skills faded back in over time). Clover Honey was there most of the day as well. I never saw her eat, but she drank two full pitchers of some weird wheat grass tea shake. I didn't ask questions.

"Hey Shel," Clover said, "d'you know what's the worst thing about orgies?"

"I'm dying to find out."

"The smell."

"Ah."

"So how'd you like Amber?" she asked.

"I don't really remember."

"She is such a baby doll. She's barely been in town a year. Came in from Utah."

"Mormon?"

"That's my guess. She was so nervous when she first got here. It was so sweet. I felt kinda sorry for her, so I made her out by the pool one night. I just thought she needed a friend. Now I think she's a little hung up on me, bless her heart. She was goin' round calling herself 'Allison Chains' for a while. I talked her out of that one...then somebody else took it. She hasn't even been on camera yet."

"She's not going to do her first shoot...with *DeVour*, is

she?" For some reason the thought of the girl, *any* girl, have their first on screen go-round with Penny DeVour at the helm...well, let's just say there are some things you simply don't wish on anybody.

"I don't think so. She wants to be a contract girl, and Penny won't work with contracts. Says they're too demanding. I'm not a contract girl because I don't want to be. I make my own rules."

"Good for you."

"I'm a simple gal, after all."

"Sure."

"I like to party, I like to screw, and I like to get paid. Now you tell me, what's wrong with that?"

"Not a damn thing."

"I've got two basic rules: smack my ass and not my face, and pay me on time. And don't squirt your hot mess on my tummy. Three rules."

"Fair enough."

I saw her twitch a little out of the corner of my eye. She played it off like it didn't happen. But then she dropped a glass on the floor.

"Oh crap!"

"You okay?" I asked.

"I'm just havin' a weird muscle thingy today. No big. I just think my chakras are off or something." She went to get a dustpan and brush, and I thought of offering to help, but then opted not to.

"Careful you don't cut yourself."

"Next month Penny and I are doing our last video together. Really sending him off to retirement in style." She giggled as she swept, "He's going out with a bang." I couldn't help but sigh. It's a stupid joke, even for a porno chick.

"Let me guess...*world's biggest gangbang*, right?"

"You know it, baby! It's gonna be fuuuh-uuun."

"Good for you. But you realize, somebody else is just gonna break your record later in the year. However many dicks you take plus five."

"Don't you pee all over my good time, Sheldon Ackerlin."

"Sorry." I picked a few arpeggios on the Archtop and considered stealing it. *He'd never miss the thing,* I thought.

"I like the way you play guitar," she said. "It's really strange."

"There's something sideways about how I hear things," I said. "My ears pick up a different sound spectrum."

"Like how a Monarch sees colors?"

"Guess it has worked out for me."

"Don't hold me to this," she said in a hush, even though we were the only people in the house, "but I think my husband's planning to do a feature on y'all in his magazine."

Husband? Pony Boy? She married *that guy*?

"Oh yeah?"

"He's not really into metal, but some of his partners are. Big time."

"That'd be great," I said. "We'll take all the coverage we can get."

"I'll do what I can to make it happen," she said with a big wink. "You can owe me one."

Nice girl. Really a shame about her in the end.

Party that night in Frogtown, an industrial dead-end near the "Los Angeles River" (I don't know if it's really called that or if somebody was just yanking my chain. It is literally nothing but a dry cement canal).

It was cramped and crowded at Monroe's. The Buzzcocks were playing on the stereo all night, which is not a terrible thing, I suppose. But I can't say I'm a fan.

I tried making conversation with Amber Chestnut, but she wasn't really having it. She told me it was nothing personal, she was just "going through a thing right now" and didn't want to get attached to anyone, whatever that means. I was told later on (by Clover, "in confidence") that Amber was actually kind of creeped out by me, or specifically the fact that

I am silent and "stone cold poker-faced" during sex. Apparently it gave her a complex, and made her want to start up the old binge and purge again. *Now there's something to make a dude feel like a million and a half.*

I'll be the first to admit that I don't know jack about shit… but it would seem to me that a bulimic fluffer would be something of a liability on a porn set. Just an observation.

So after a while I slipped off to the backyard alone, to sit under a sorry little Charlie Brown palm tree with Monroe's Rickenbacker bass and a fresh bottle of Wild Turkey. I've always been a frustrated wanna-be bass player, after all. My life is a constant search for the lowest possible tone. I tuned it down to a low C (virtually imperceptible unplugged, at least for the average ear), and closed my eyes, imagining the unholy rumble splitting the fault lines, sending this whole chunk of earth out to sea…

…I find myself in a kitchen I've never seen before. A little Black toddler screams, strapped into a high chair, trapped and helpless, as a man thrashes him with a leather belt. Two women look on, passive, weeping softly. Another man, in the shadows, stands idly by, leaning on a counter and sucking down a bottle. I try to yell at the man to stop whipping the baby, but no sound comes out. I try to reach out and break the man's goddamn neck. But I am paralyzed. Blood and rice pudding everywhere…

"Shel? Shel, wake up!"

"Huh? What?"

I had apparently passed out in Monroe's backyard sometime around 2 a.m. No one had noticed that I had been gone for hours. My muscles still spasming from the dream, I felt ill, and covered in cold sweat. I had to open my eyelids with my fingers. The bottle of whiskey was nearly empty, grass and dirt was caked around the pickups of the Rickenbacker somehow.

"Where's Annalee?" Pearl asked with urgency. Despite the glistening shadow of white powder under her left nostril, I could tell that her panic was genuine, and not simply chemical.

"Um, I dun'know," I slurred. "With Cres prob'ly."

"No, Cres is with Violet Sunrise."

"Violet Sun—isn't she a *man*?"

"*Not anymore.* Look, forget it, Annalee's not with Cres. And you don't even wanna know what Pierre is doing. I need to find her."

"I think she said something earlier about not wanting to be out too late tonight. Maybe she just turned in, yeah? She's prolly back at Penn's—"

"Oh god! SHIT! No, no no...You gotta drive me up there! Right now!"

"What? You nuts?! Pearl, I can't drive now!"

"You HAVE to!" Her hands and lips started to tremble, and prickles stabbed me in the neck. I'd never seen her like this.

"What's going on h—"

"SHEL, PLEASE! You're the closest to sober of anybody here! Believe it or not. And anyway...you're the only person *in the world* I trust. *Please.*"

So against my better judgement, I finagled the van keys out of Pierre's front jeans pocket (which were actually nowhere near Pierre at the time), and we headed back up to the house on Vance.

We didn't talk once the whole ride. Pearl shivered from some inward chill. I didn't ask why. I figured I didn't want to know. I was right.

As soon as we pulled up in front she bolted from the passenger seat and tore off into the house. I jogged after her as fast as I could manage, all considered. My head felt like a bag of wet cement, and I couldn't stop squinting, despite the darkness.

She was halfway up the oak staircase by the time I was through the front door.

"Penn," she screamed desperately, "I swear to fuckin' GOD! PENN!"

As I set about the task of climbing the staircase, I could hear Pearl's screams devolve into code-red hysteria as she banged fist, foot and shoulder against the locked master bedroom door.

"Not her, Penn! PLEASE! NOT HER!"

Once upstairs I could hear it loud and clear: *Annalee.* Moaning and squealing. Getting fucked three ways from Sunday by Penny DeVour.

"Don't hurt her, Penn!" Pearl cried. "Please don't hurt her!"

I didn't know, nor did I care, what sort of dark tricks Penny DeVour was likely to get up to behind closed doors. But whatever they might be, the thought of it was enough to send his wife around the bend and back.

"PEEEEEEEEEEEEEEEEEEEENN!!!"

"It's—*huh*—it's okay, baby!" Annalee gasped from inside the master bedroom. "I w-want this! OH! OH YES! OH GOD, I WAAAANT THIS!"

Pearl collapsed to the floor, tears pouring down her cheeks, hanging by both hands from the doorknob.

"NOT HER, PENN!" she sobbed. "NOT HER!!!"

But the fucking never stopped. It got louder. And more violent. Until we heard Annalee come, hard, headboard slamming against the wall in four-four time. And I got there just in time to watch a tiny bit of Pearl Harbor's soul die, sobbing, still hanging from the bedroom doorknob.

"*Not her…P-puh*-please *not her…*"

I figured we'd be leaving LA shortly.

"You guys can stay," Pearl said as we packed up the van. "I don't want to jack up anybody's good time. I can take a bus or something." She was urgent about her business. "Seriously. No big deal." Not angry or upset. Just urgent.

"Balls to that, cuz'n," Pierre said, securing the gear inside with bungee cords. "We're a band. Whatever we do, we do together. One of us goes, we all go."

So the four of us loaded in, and in a snap, we were gone. Just like that. In the blur of it all I don't even remember saying goodbye to anyone, although I'm sure we did. There's plenty I don't remember anymore.

So long, Angel City, you great Jiffy Lube by the sea. We'll meet again some sunny day.

Interstate 10 East from LA to Baton Rouge is a punishing slog under the best of circumstances. Taken in bulk, and on the fly, it's a horror beyond all measure. Suffice it to say I'll never drive it again without stopping for shows along the way. Live and learn.

"Man," Pierre said, "I'd rather be ass-raped in church than spend one more hour in Arizona." *Agreed.*

PEARL:

I felt bad. I really did. I know for the guys this trip felt like a little sniff of the big-time. And I understand. There are plenty of good reasons to go to LA. And many more good reasons to leave. I knew I'd miss Annalee, and I wished her the best. I still do, wherever she is. I wish she would put out a new record or something, because I'd love to buy it. Maybe someday…

I didn't want the boys to be mad at me. I guess they weren't. If they ever held our abrupt departure against me, they never said as much. In fact it never came up again, at least when I was around.

I just had to go. I had to get out. My soul was still worth something back then.

As we floated along I-10 like spoiled refuse down the river

Styx, I felt the great weight of So Cal lift off my spirit for good. The night skies cleared, and for the moment so did my mind. By the time we got to El Paso, even the voices inside my head had all shut up, if only for a time. Penny DeVour, loved him though I did, was pollution for my soul. And it felt wonderful to wash him out of me. For good. I felt free. Sober even (although I wasn't). Almost virginal (certainly not). It was that same rush of hope and expectation I had the first time I made that first fateful trek down to Baton Rouge. There was fire in my feet again, and I couldn't wait to jump from the van and run straight to the studio. Finish our album, tighten it up, then unleash it like a snarling wolverine upon this poor, unsuspecting world. This was our time, and we would claim and conquer. I could not wait.

2000

Fall of '99 we finished up the final mix and master on our album. Sisyphus commissioned a buddy of ours from New York to do the cover art, and it dropped just in time for the holidaze. From there we hit the road hard and didn't look back.

I think we all felt a renewed sense of purpose and determination. Even if LA had been a bust, and it may very well have been, it narrowed our focus, served as just the bit of mental scrubbing that we needed.

There were a few rough spots coming home, no doubt. Pierre came clean on his exploits in Cali (whatever they were), and Sally freaked and moved back home to her mom and stepdad in Metairie. Down a person, we moved into a new place where the neighbors didn't like us. A late-night altercation with some old gator skinners landed Cres and I in the slammer overnight. But it all worked out. We were ready to take it up a notch.

Pearl was especially stoked and fired up. She dropped the needle and picked up *yoga*, of all things. Talked a blue streak about "soul centering" and pressure points and I-ching-a-ding or what have you. Unable as she was to do anything in half-measures, that lead straight to transcendental meditation and going full vegan as well. The rest of us, of course, did not follow suit. But hell, she was the focus on stage anyway, so she should be the most fit. We were loud, hot, tight, and armed with the best material of our career thus far.

Spring tour gave way to the summer underground festival circuit, which gave us a chance to catch up with our friends and fellows in bands from all over. We did a mini-run through the northwest with Hacksaw Abortion and Skulltower, which is a total blur to me now...which means it must have been killer.

Weeks went by, and the crowds got steadily larger. The disc was getting good buzz, and word was, apparently, getting out about us. Several indie rag ink-slingers had tagged us as "the band to watch," which we were indeed. Bit by bit shit fell into place.

Back home for a quick two-day breather in July, we got a small package in the mail. It was a DVD with a short note which read:

Hello all,

Here is the video. I hope you enjoy it and it bears fruit for you in some way. It was a pleasure working with you. Take care.

All my love,

Penny DeFleur

Had to hand it to the guy, he was one hilarious bastard.

The video looked good. I was pleased with it. Pearl called DeVour an "ass maggot," but I think she dug it too. We looked pretty badass. Pearl looked like a demon. The "live" material did indeed look like retro-thrash, which was both hella-cool and slightly embarrassing. It was kind of like having your dopiest dream come true.

Sisyphus sent the clip out to every video venue there was. MTV2 never got around to playing it on *Headbanger's Ball*, big surprise, but some independent and college channels around the country did. It got about three and a half weeks of very late night rotation...and then nothing.

And then suddenly, as if on cue, music video as a comer-cial medium disappeared forever. And it didn't really matter anyway. None of it mattered. Nothing matters. These things happen.

My nightmares had all but disappeared as well during that summer. It seemed like all of us were in a great place then, as a unit and as individuals. Pearl didn't talk about the voices anymore (she seldom did anyway), but for whatever reason—health kick, new lease on life, five hours sleep a night, whatever it was—she seemed to have put the darkness behind her. At some point she mentioned something in passing about an "official divorce," but it never came up again. It just wasn't that important.

She would periodically talk to this or that friend from LA on the phone, but more and more it caused her to pull away from them and make her double down harder on our material. The last straw was when we heard that that guy Joey had gone to prison for beating up Clover Honey while they were shooting a flick in Southern Ohio, oddly enough. *So long, fella. Have fun.*

Days and nights rocked on, and we became more and more prolific. Our music actually got more interesting because of it. We would jam twelve, fifteen hours a day, piling up new ideas that thrilled us completely (would they please an audience? No fuckin' clue. Didn't really occur to us). Pearl's lyrics, and vocals in general, strayed far from any sort of traditional structure, even by metal standards. Even by our standards. And that suited us just fine. It really did feel like we were blazing some new ground, tearing through the underbrush and making our own path.

But then again, I suppose nothing is *completely* new. It's all just a variation of what's come before. It doesn't really matter now, of course. Nothing really matters now.

It was a kind of madness, really. Collective, deliberate madness. The four of us hardly interacted with other people anymore, save our producer, and Bradley, and a couple of close friends from other bands. And even then, only when we had to. I know now that it was just a thin sliver of madness, comparatively speaking. But it felt phenomenal at the time. It was awesome to go insane for your art. So much so that when my nightmares returned, and along with them came Pearl's head voices (with a vengeance), they felt like gifts. Just more fuel for our fire. A great and killer and selfish and self-immolating fire.

"What are you writing, Pearl?"

"Anton is writing."

"Okay...what is Anton writing?"

"I'll let you know when we're done."

PEARL:

I had an hour and fifty-two minutes before the sun of dawn would break and cut through me like shards of flame, the evening prior still wrapped about my throat gurgling and squishing my jack-booted heels against the jellied asphalt river floating outside with window of the dish-rag girl scissoring step-mama for extra allowance on a beaten mattress pregnant by her own twin, as I lied in an alleyway to an old Korean man clutching own trench coats to keep our evening secret and the night time in the dark, nest of liquid corpses slipping through the cracks so thick and slow to pour we drink with a knife pouring slow and thick leading lead weights at the bottom of the river, floating outside the window of the dishrag girl...

Bang on the cellar-door screaming 'til they let you go wash the blood away, watch it dripping away into the alleyway where the rats fuck and feed outside of the windows of the ivory-tower wives biting amorous lips and devoured alive by fur coats, and old Korean men, and little dishrag girls scissoring step-mama for extra allowance...

We the scum and the trash and the filth and the holy are slipping away and dripping away devoured by the asphalt river flowing outside the windows of the ivory tower wives biting amorous lips and jilling off to our anguish as the sun of dawn breaks and cuts through us like shards of flame making liquid corpses of us all, slipping through the cracks and dripping away…

2001

I wish I could remember the exact day. I know it was July. Maybe it *was* the eleventh. We'd just gotten confirmation that we'd been booked to play a four-day heavy metal festival called *Doom Fest* in Northern Ohio somewhere. We'd probably end up going on at eleven-thirty in the morning or something, but no matter. We were pumped. A lot of our favorite bands were on the bill, and it would be crazy exposure for us.

That was the day that I found the letters. *Letters to Eva.* Written in Pearl's handwriting. Quite a day in hindsight. Here's a sample:

Dearest Eva, I was just thinking about you so I thought I'd write to catch up. The army's still icing me out and the dishonorable discharge stands, but I really don't give two shits any more. Fuck them. I've been talking to an attorney about getting the rest of my pay. Fingers crossed. I ran into Fran the other day. She says "Hey." She's got a new girlfriend, or whatever. Guess she's not exactly "new," they've been together for a while. Some skirt named Marie. She don't really look like no dyke to me, but what do I know. Seems like a cool enough girl. I'm not judging their choice of lifestyle. That's for God to do. So long as they don't try to raise up a kid or something it don't make me no nevermind. But that shit's just wrong. Fran's doing real good. Apparently Iraq didn't bother her at all. She's as happy and healthy as you please. I know a lot of folks who got sick like me out there, but it seems Fran's not one. She's all hyped up from 9/11, ready to ship off to Afghanistan or back to Iraq or whatever. Good on her, I guess. Her gal didn't seem too jazzed about it. You can relate to that, right? I know I didn't talk about it much at the time, but Desert Storm wasn't hard for me at all. It was a cakewalk. Even in combat I wasn't really scared. It wasn't till I got home that all the shit started. You know better than anyone what that was like, but over there I was fine. I don't know, maybe that poison don't affect women. Not directly, maybe. Or Fran's just tougher than me. 9/11 has kind of fucked me up. I haven't really been talking to nobody recently. I haven't been eating either. My doctor says that 9/11 has actually been "a positive" for me because it's derailed my "revenge fantasies" as he calls them. They ain't fantasies! Nothing's been derailed. I just got to re-adjust. I don't even care about what happened in New York. I mean, yeah, it's sad and boo-hoo-hoo, but fuck. That's war. It's the Pentagon that's got me up at night. Because that's EXACTLY what I was planning. It's like whoever made that attack read my mind. And I know THEY're reading my mail but I don't give a dead rat fuck. Let them come get me. I'll be a one man Waco. I really haven't been sleeping well. My stomach's fucking killing me and the dizziness is back. I think I have an ulcer.

Sorry to pour all that mess out on you, but Stephan (that's my doctor's name) says I have to be honest at all times. It's part of the "Healing." Well, that's why I don't talk so much these days. Sometimes I wonder if there'll ever be a chance for us again. Or there ever would be, in another life maybe. Do you ever think about that? How are you sleeping? Have you had any more of those dreams? I have them all the time. That's why I don't sleep. The babies won't stop crying, and then when I wake up they're gone. I never want to fall asleep again. All my love, Anton.

There was a stack of them, all along similar lines. Couldn't help but think that something was amiss.

"What's the deal here, cuz'n?" I asked her. "What is all this about?"

"I wish I knew." She shrugged. She acted like it wasn't a big deal. I sorta had to disagree.

"I mean, I get the thing about never wanting to sleep

again," I said. "I totally feel that. But...what does this all mean?"

"I'm telling you I don't know," Pearl said with a more pronounced shrug. Her voice was agitated, as if I were accusing her of something. I suppose I was. "It's gibberish," she said. "What can you do? I have no memory of writing it."

"I don't think Anton is just a voice in your head," I said. "Not anymore."

"What the shit is that supposed to mean?"

"I mean that this personality, whatever it is, is becoming its own entity. Or something. It's starting to act independent of your knowledge."

"Dude, I've looked into ALL that stuff. Okay? Read every book. Trust me. It doesn't work that way. I don't have multiple personality disorder. Multiple personalities don't talk to one another. I've had full conversations with Anton, whacked as that sounds."

"Maybe you're a new case. Scientists should study you."

"Yeah...maybe..."

I read through some more of the letters. Like the one above, it was all deranged ranting...but unnervingly specific. Like there was a full story involved somewhere. I thought, for just a moment, about setting it all to music.

But here's the thing...right around two months after the letters first fell out of Pearl's head, some real awful shit went down in New York and DC. You probably remember the day. And in a brief, horrible moment a few small questions were suddenly answered...

"Uh, Pearl?"

"*Yeah...*" she whispered, as we all sat around the TV on September the eleventh, 2001 watching the only show going, "*This was what Anton was talking about...*"

...and a lot more questions arose.

"Fucking airplanes, man," Pearl said. "Fucking airplanes."

***

It was no difficult task getting Bradley to roadie the *Doom Fest* gig for us. In fact, he offered (or, to put it another way, he begged us). Why? Because during that time he was completely clownshoes for this dogshit-terrible joke band called *Nuke The Tards* that was also on the bill. Scuttlebutt was that they were fixing to part ways with their bassist, and Bradley was planning to try to booty-shake his way into an audition or something. There's no accounting for taste. Takes all kinds, I suppose.

(Goddamn, I miss that fucking guy. I wish I could remember him...)

The concert would be tits. We were set to finish out the autumn in style. Then spend the winter fine-tuning new material and get cracking on the new platter. Sunshine on our shoulders, you know? Bluebirds and gumdrops and whatnot.

Pearl got a bad phone call the night before we hit the road. She never told us what it was, but I could tell that it was worse than normal. *Que sera sera. Ain't none of my business after all.*

Interstate 75 through Ohio is thick with big rigs, even at 2:29 a.m. It was a bob and weave all the way through Cincinnati and beyond. We finally got some relief just past Columbus. No one on the road but us, a maroon Aerostar minivan, and an old, pale blue VW bus, virtually identical to the one I grew up in, but for the hue.

Bradley was at the wheel. My job was to keep him company, and awake. We played a game to see who could list the most bands with a color in their name that wasn't black.

"Agent Orange."

"Gang Green."

"Green Jello. Later Green Jelly for legal reasons."

"Nice. Indigo Girls."

"I'll accept that. Golden Earring."

"Eh..."

"Golden's a color!"

"White Elephant."

"There's no band called White Elephant."

"Hundred bucks says there is."

Pierre, Cres and Pearl all slept more or less comfortably in the back nestled in amongst the gear. Pink Floyd's *Meddle* played on the stereo. I remember it was that song that ends with the crowd singing "*You'll never walk alone...*" I sat in the passenger seat playing along with the CD on my Ibanez GSA with the pointed headstock.

"Yellowcard."

"Pink Floyd."

"Seriously, dude? The band we're listening to right now? We said that one an hour and a half ago, along with Deep Purple, White Zombie and Blue Cheer."

"The Red Chord."

"Simply Red."

"You're simply gay."

"That don't change the fact that I'm simply right, cuz'n."

We both saw it at the same time, as I'm sure the other vehicles did too. There was nothing anyone could do about it. Going eighty-plus south bound, an eighteen wheeler flipped the median (in slow motion as I recall), and the trailer came flying down the northbound side perpendicular to the highway. It was coming straight at us. We were going straight for it. Sparks flew from the metal siding, screeching against the pavement. Bradley said:

"Aw shit."

And then nothing.

I awoke on my right side in the middle of the highway

surrounded by metal, glass and blood. Whistles screeched in my head and I vomited as the agony hit me in pulsing waves. I couldn't move my left arm at all, so I swiveled my head and waist to roll over onto my back. Piercing, shrieking pain shot through my body as I saw the headstock of my Ibanez jutting straight through my right hand, the pegs pushing through the red, pulped mess of my palm. I yanked my hand free of the headstock and blacked out once again from the pain.

I came to a second time in the same state. Somewhere in the distance, somewhere deep below the screaming whistles in my ears, I heard sirens. Ladder trucks and ambulances. I heard my heartbeat, and it was all wrong. *Lubba-dub-dub-dub-dub-dub-dub.* My left shoulder crushed and my right hand destroyed, I rolled up onto my knees and somehow managed to stand, teetering like an old-timey drunk on slightly slanted ground.

A straight row of headlights glared in the distance. None moved, likely for fear that something might burst into flames. I turned the other way to see the tractor-trailer flipped on its side longways across the highway. Our van and the Aerostar smashed up against it. The VW bus nowhere to be seen. Our windshield was gone. Bradley dangled from the front of the grill like a bloody, mangled marionette.

"*Bluh Oystuh Culd...*" I said to Bradley's corpse. Hard to believe Blue Oyster Cult had not occurred to either of us before. "*Bluh Oystuh Culd,*" I repeated, my mouth not being a team player. "Ah win, cuz'n."

Cres lay on the ground right below him in a pile. It almost looked as if he had tried to climb free. He was thoroughly dead. Pierre lay on the highway face down. Face gone. All gone. Ground flat in a straight red line across the black asphalt. They were all gone.

"Shuddup shuddup shuddup..."

I heard muffled muttering coming from the median. I could barely move my head, and each time I tried my eyes got TV static and my stomach flipped on itself. I focused on the median the best I could. There I saw Pearl wandering about aimlessly, smacking herself in the head, falling over, and getting back up. She looked like she had just been submerged in a swimming pool filled with blood.

"No time no time..." she babbled, "Shuddup no time..."

"Puurl," I said, barely able to move my jaw. "C'me 'ere ov'r 'rrre."

She shambled over, far off still, whimpering and mewling like a kitten in the rain, periodically falling over and puking. I nearly did the same. The sirens grew closer, but they were still deep in the distance. They didn't matter. Nothing mattered. Nothing matters. My friends were dead. And not just dead. Sloppy red wet mess dead. Obliterated. And there was nothing I could do about it.

I spat out a jagged chunk of broken molar.

"Not the time not the time," Pearl said to no one. "Please be quiet now..."

Thinking I saw movement in the Aerostar, I lumbered toward it like something from a Romero flick.

In the front seat a young white couple lay crumpled around one another: filthy, knotted, blood-soaked laundry in a broken washing machine.

I wondered for the moment who they were. What they were like. Who would be missing them. Where were they going. And then I just stopped thinking about it. I saw the flicker of movement again, Pearl still chattering and crying nonsensically somewhere far behind me.

"No no no no no not now not now not now..."

I moved to the back of the minivan, and there he was, pressed hard against the thick, barely cracked glass of the rear window. He was five. Maybe six. He was bloody, bashed and broken. He was alive.

"Cun you 'ear me, lil man?" I asked. He tried to smile and wave his tiny right hand. Just his first finger moved. "Imma git you out, kay. Some 'ow."

"*Hurts,*" he mouthed to me.

"I knuh it duz, buddy," I said, wrenching my jaw to make

it work, if barely. I swung my right arm up onto the back hatch, horizontal, I shoved my useless fingers into the groove of the door handle. The shredded mess throbbed, shooting bolts of lightning up my arm. "Juss hang tight fuh me, kay champ?"

He waved with his index finger again. "Hurts," he said.

"I know. I know. You gotta stay wid me, though. Stay 'wake. Juss hold on." I tried and tried to wrap my fingers around the handle, but my bones and muscles were ruined. "Puurl! Help me!!!" I looked behind me and saw her lying on the street, curled up all fetus-like, clutching her head, vomiting blood and groaning. I could not move my left arm at all. Desperately I kicked at the door handle with my boot heel.

"Sleepy," the little boy said.

"NO!" I shouted. "STAY WID ME, BUDDY! C'MON!"

I kicked harder and harder, but the door would not budge. I looked into the glass to see the boy's eyes dimming, his life light flickering out. Out. Then gone.

I got there just in time to watch his firelight flicker, fade, and die. I was there to watch him fade away and die. And then nothing. Gone.

I saw the light.

Red and blue flashes, bright white floods. That's how I realized that I had blacked out again. Both Pearl and I lay in the grass on the side of the highway, just above a brambly ditch. There I saw the VW bus, down in the brambles, flipped on its side. Orange Goblin still blasting on the stereo.

Orange Goblin...How could we have forgotten the incomparable Orange Goblin...that's another point for me, Bradley. Crushing you in this game, cuz'n. Crushing you.

A voice shouted in the distance, "More bodies over there, Ed!" The voice meant us.

Pearl continued to lay curled up, blood-soaked, banging on her skull with her fist. "Get out of my head," she whimpered. "Shut up, Anton! Please!"

And then I heard it...

A wheezing laugh, coughing and gasping for air. Then the voice, like the croak of a stroke-addled bullfrog—

"*Pearl…*"

"Outta my head!" Pearl cried into the grass. "Outta my head now, Anton!"

"*Pearl…*" it hacked and coughed. Chuckling for the insanity of it all. "*Pearl, I'm…*"

"That's not in your head, Pearl," I said. "I…hear it…I…I hear it too."

I crawled over toward the ditch, dragging my half-dead husk with my right elbow. Through the darkness, I saw the remainder of the carnage. A young blonde woman, twisted and broken. A tall, dark-skinned man laid out flat across the ground—American Indian or Mexican if I were throwing money down on it—nearly perfect, with his eyes and mouth wide open. I would have almost thought him merely stunned, but for the dark fluid dripping from his long, black hair. A pair of legs jutted out from under the bus like the witch of the East. Two pairs of legs. One set bare, thick and female, nearly covered in a dark dress. The other pair long and thin, in tight blue jeans and stack-heel boots.

And then there he lay…just beyond the broken windshield: pale, gaunt, bug-eyed, gurgling blood with every chuckle and labored breath.

"You," I said. "You're—"

"Hey!" someone shouted, as the sound of several boots came pounding toward us. "Them three are moving!"

"Anton I pr'zume huh," I said.

The creature in the ditch smiled bright red. "*I'm…y'all's… biggest…fan.*"

"Mr. Ackerlin? Mr. Ackerlin? Hello? Are we awake? Hello. Can you hear me?"

Haze. And dull pain thumping up and down both arms. Arms raised. Eyes fog. Jaw slightly off its runner.

"Hmm."

"Wonderful! It's great to see your eyes. I'll notify the doctor at once."

Dry taste in my mouth. Can't see the nurse, but her voice is pretty. And I notice a peculiar feeling in my dick. Catheter. Suddenly terrified of inadvertent hard-ons.

"Wait a sec'nd."

"Are you in pain, Mr. Ackerlin?"

"Shel. Yes. Yes I am."

"You're on a morphine drip, Shel. Is it not helping at all?"

Still can't see through the haze. Pain in my arms is constant, but not excruciating. Morphine is probably helping some.

But then it happens...My ears begin to pick up...everything. Beeping monitors. Air ducts. Creaking beds and squeaking gurneys. Crying children. Crying patients. Crying visitors. It's goddamn unbearable.

"Loudest hopital ever..." I mumble. And then I remember why I'm here...*ooooooh Christ...*"My friends...are all dead." Eyes clear like the rising sun burning off a morning mist. Nurse not as pretty as her voice. Kind of dumpy. Sudden stabbing pain in my heart surpasses pain in my ears or my arms. "I saw...my friends...dead in front of me."

"I'm very sorry, Mr. Ackerlin. You were brought in before my shift, so I don't know the details, but I—"

"My fucking friends are all dead."

"...but I will be sure to notify the doctor that you are awake finally, and I will schedule a counselor to come in to assist you."

"I saw their bodies. Crushed and rung out."

"My deepest sympathies, sir. I'm very, very sorry for your loss."

Stabbing in my heart. Screeching racket in my ears. Throbbing pain in my casted, elevated arms. And now there is a stinging in my eyes. My face is hot and wet. White rubber hospital sneakers *yeyk yeyk yeyk yeyk* up and down the goddamn tiles. Somebody fucking kill me.

***

"Hello, Shel. We weren't sure if you were ever coming back to us. It's good to see you awake."

All I can see now is that little boy dying in front of me. I close my eyes and he's there.

"*Hurts...*"

Come on, little man, you're going to be okay!

I open my eyes and he's still there.

"*Sleepy...*"

No no no, buddy, keep your eyes open!

But he fades out all the same...

I see my friends. Dead. I cannot remember their faces alive. At all. Their faces have been erased. They're just featureless corpses to me now.

"You the shrink?"

"You can call me Don. I'm a grief counselor. I'm here to help you work through this difficult time however I can."

The harder I try to remember, the more they slip away from me.

"I see. Can you get me more morphine, Don?"

"Not really."

I see the little boy. I see his mangled parents. I see the twisted, bloody, wheezing, laughing creature in the ditch. But my friends are gone for good, even from my mind.

"Tell me something, Don."

"Yes?"

"Are the air ducts in this building as loud to you as they are to me?"

I'm not, it would seem, particularly pleased to have survived this thing.

"Shel...can I call you Shel?"

"Why not."

"Shel—"

"My full name is Sheldon Ferdinand Ackerlin. The third. *Ferd* to the family, back when there was one. *Ferd the third.*"

"That's just awful. I'm terribly sorry."

"Yeah. Thanks, Mom and Dad."

Some crashes just aren't worth walking away from. Or staggering, in my case.

"You mention your parents, Shel."

"Do I?"

"You lost both of your parents at a fairly young age, am I right on that?"

"Dad for sure. Not certain about Mom, but yeah, I think she's dead too. Least they'll never have to come to my lousy funeral, eh Don?" There goes that stinging in my eyes again. "I missed their funerals, didn't I. My friends. I missed all their funerals."

Had to have been closed caskets.

"Yes, I'm afraid so. And, of course, my deepest condolences. The remains of your three friends were returned to Louisiana early last week. You've been gone for nearly fourteen days. Not so much as a peep from you."

Que sera sera...

"I wouldn't have gone anyway. I hate funerals. My dad was cremated and sprinkled about in Yosemite. Which is actually illegal come to think about it." *Wait...Hold the phone a moment...*"Did you say *three*? Three friends?"

"Yes. You and a..." he reads from his little notebook, "Ms. Yoshimoto...were the only survivors. Also a friend of yours, right? She underwent emergency surgery on arrival, and has been convalescing nicely. She's in stable condition I'm happy to say. You'll both be needing physical therapy. Perhaps you can schedule the sessions together. It certainly doesn't seem unreasonable."

The thought hits me like the truck that fucking hit me: Pearl is now my only family...my only real friend...the only person left in my life. I'm glad she's okay, all considered, but I feel a cavernous hollow inside me. Cold and empty. And I'm sure she feels it too, wherever she is.

"Can I see her? Can I see Pear—um, Katsumi? Ms. Yoshimoto?"

"Soon I'm sure. For now, I'd really like to hear how you're

feeling. I mean really feeling. You've been through a tremendous trauma, Sheldon."

I'm in no mood for this conversation.

"There was another guy," I say. "Another survivor. Family of three in a minivan, they're all dead. Cres and Pierre and Bradley, all dead. A VW bus in the ditch, there were bodies down there, I don't know how many. But I saw a guy. Alive. *Anton.* His name is probably Anton."

"How would...how would you know that, Shel?"

"Because Katsumi talked to him with her mind."

Uuuugh...

"I...see."

Crap. Nice going, ass bag. Now you look like a goddamn screwball. Maybe they'll give you more morphine now. And a lobotomy.

"I mean, I think they knew each other. Maybe. They knew each other before. We'd been on tour for a while, and she meets a lot of people."

"Katsumi and this other person knew each other? This is new information. Whom else did you all know in this other vehicle, Shel?"

"Am I in Ohio?"

"Columbus, yes. I'm curious—"

"Who was at fault? It wasn't us."

"By all accounts the driver of the semi likely fell asleep at the wheel. I don't really know too much. Now, I'm curious about your relationship to the others in this accident. I wasn't informed that you were all together."

How long before I gotta talk to the cops, I wonder...

"We weren't. We're not. It was a coincidence. Or maybe I'm just confused. Addled. Tremendous trauma, you know. I don't know what I'm saying."

"Well, okay. That's certainly understandable."

Don writes something down in his small notebook, and the sound of the graphite scratching against the paper saws into my eardrums like a dull bread knife. I wince from the sound and notice the pressure of the catheter again.

"Do you have to do that so loud?!"

"The...pencil is too loud?"

"Everything is. Why would the air ducts in a hospital rattle like that? You hear that, right? Is Ohio a fucking third world state or something? Goddamn it!"

"Well, there are budget conc—"

"I don't have anything to say about my dead friends, Don. Sorry. They're dead. Tag 'em and bag 'em. They're fucking worm food, all of them. Can you ask those people in the hallway to quiet the fuck down?!?!"

"Try to calm yourself, Shel."

"I want to talk to Pearl!"

"Pearl?"

"Pearl Bailey! I want you to resurrect Pearl fucking Bailey! Okay? Could ya do that, Don? Could ya do that for me? *It Takes Two to Tango*! She can sing us all a happy tune! Happy sounds! Everybody get fucking happy!"

"Shel, I understand you're—"

"Do ya, Don? Do ya understand? Do you see my fucking hands? You can't, can ya. Cuz they're buried in plaster. I'm a fucking musician, Don! Do you think I'll ever play guitar again? My hands are wrecked, my arms are shot, my ears have gone haywire! My bandmates are DEAD!"

"Shel—"

"DO YOU UNDERSTAND, DON!" *And the Oscar goes to...*"I WATCHED A LITTLE KID DIE! He died right in front of me, Don! AND I COULDN'T HELP HIM!!!" And now I'm crying like a little sissy girl..."I couldn't...I couldn't fucking help him..."

Cry cry cry, little pussy. You little crybaby cripple. Mommy's dead and baby's dead and all dead and everybody dead. Cry for all the poor dead people, little bitch. Boo hoo hoo. Cuz nobody cares about them and nobody cares about you. Because you don't matter and they don't matter and nobody matters and nothing matters...

Cry your little eyes out, suckerfish. Because nothing fucking matters at all.

Lights down, fade to black, curtain. Scattered applause.

PEARL:

Morphine suits me.

Good thing if you're needing your back riveted together. Two crushed discs. They had to remove my organs to get to my spine. I'm all wired back in place now. And here I was trying to get clean. Silly me, silly girl. I'm not clean now. Because morphine suits me just fine. Give me just a teensy taste, and baby, I'm yours.

But it doesn't matter now. There's no high from it now. Like a methadone fix. Just numb. And dull ache. And can't get comfortable at all. Even with the numb. Like I'm wrapped in gauze and covered in dust. My boys are dead. My friends are gone. Rock star deaths without even getting to be rock stars first. Wish I hadn't lived. Wish this numbness would eat me alive. Swallow me down forever. Drown me in an ocean of spiderwebs. I don't want to be me without them.

Hospital nightmares are often the worst nightmares. Comfort and rest come late, and they never really take.

The dream this time takes place in a bedroom. *A man and a woman. I don't know them. He's balls deep in her ass. Consensual sodomy as far as I can tell. "Fuck my pussy," she whimpers. "Fuck my pussy instead...I w-want your baby inside me..."*

Suddenly his shoulder explodes. Blast of an unseen deer rifle. He falls to the floor gushing blood and howling. I don't even try to stoop down and help. The woman runs off screaming. A figure in desert camo kicks in the door, charges after her, with a slight limp, rifle crossbar across his chest. I don't bother to chase after them. I don't really care if he catches her or not.

I wake from this dream with a steady pulse. And I drift

back to fitful, uneven slumber. Itch of the casts and disinfectant stench all around. Endless cacophony.

PEARL:

Tempted as I was that twilight, I let all the delicates shatter and scatter about the stones / leaving nothing for their books but spindled hate, a pulsating void, and envy green as the pines. I'm too high for this world. I reach to either side and balance sunrise on one hand and sunset on the other. Stretching my legs to the heavens I splash my feet in the cosmos / twirling stars on my toes / tying comet tails like ankle cuffs. When all are left drowning in an ocean of spiderwebs, I will be dancing with satellite eyes / shuddering self-satisfied. I'm too high for this world. I reach to either side and crush sunrise with one hand and sunset with the other. Stretching my legs to the heavens I splash my feet in the cosmos / twirling stars on my toes / tying comet tails like ankle cuffs. At twilight, that twilight, I let the delicates shatter and scatter about the stones. Tempting as it was to leave something for their books, there was nothing left but those left drowning in an ocean of spiderwebs. I am a woman avoiding the pulse. Shuddering, self-satisfied...

Dancing about the satellite I.

I hear sniffling, and an unmistakable voice. I don't open my eyes.

"Shel?"

"Hey Pearl. Glad you're not dead."

"Ditto."

"How you feeling?"

"Like half-squished roadkill somebody just needs to take a shovelhead to."

"That's about the long and the short. Should you be out of bed?"

"No, but I had to see you." And then a pause. "Guess you don't need to see me, huh?"

I open my eyes. She looks horrible. Sickly and stretched like yellow cellophane over a hollow skull. Her face is bruised and desperate. Her damp, red eyes as shattered and lost as I feel.

"Well that was hardly worth the effort," I say. We both laugh. And then we both wince. Laughing hurts.

"Shel, they're going to throw us out of here soon."

"I'm actually surprised we're still here, honestly."

"I put in a call to LA. I had to. Penny has been paying for all of this. For both of us. But he can't pay forever. Technically I'm still his wife, so that might be something, I don't know. But he's paying for you out of pocket because he likes you. He's really sad about what happened. I mean, as sad as he's capable of being."

"Good man, that one."

"He has his moments. But this can't go on."

"How long, you think, before they wheel us out of here and dump us on the curb?"

"Maybe a day or so. Two days tops. Then we gotta get back home somehow. Shel," she starts to break down, "what are we going to do?"

"I think you'd do well to head back to California. I mean, even if you don't wanna patch up with Penn, you've got friends out there."

And with that she cracks wide open and leaks all over. She shakes her head, tears spilling hard down her cheeks.

"No, I don't. There's no…there's nothing…I feel like I'm… being smothered, drowned, and ripped apart at the same time…"

(I come to find out that Clover Honey has offed herself. Not sure why, exactly. And her husband was murdered in that Ohio prison. I don't know which came first. Pearl has known for a while, but didn't say anything. Girl keeps a lot of pain to herself. So too, do I think, did Clover Honey.)

"What about your brother?" I ask. "Dave? He's out there somewhere."

She just cries harder.

It's a dark bit of comedy, this little tableau. Some kind of Samuel Beckett bullshit. Even if we were the comforting sort, which we're not, we can't really comfort each other now. She can barely move, I'm wired to the ceiling. So she cries, and I hang there, like a really bad outfit in the back of the closet. We are completely insignificant, and completely useless. And we are all the other has.

"How awful is that," I say out loud, continuing my inner monologue. She doesn't question it, but instead tries to dry her cheeks with the back of her hand. It's a struggle.

"Goodbye Cres," she says sniffling. "Goodbye, Pierre. Goodbye, Brad, thanks for everything. Now we can't sing. Now we can't play. Goodbye Stigmata Dog." She lays her head on my bed and sobs. And I just hang there, trying to ignore the itch under my casts.

"Goodbye LA friends," I say. *If we're doing send-offs, let's be thorough.*

I wait for the issue of Anton to come up. It doesn't. I hadn't gotten a straight answer from the grief counselor about whether there had been another survivor or not. He intimated that there hadn't. Perhaps I dreamt the whole thing. It was, after all, just like my dreams. Same basic plot.

We don't discuss it.

I do ask her this, though:

"So Pearl. How are *the voices*?"

"Well," she says, finally pulling herself together, "I have a theory."

"Okay?"

"I posit this theory now and forever, that there is no such thing as schizophrenia."

"Oh yeah?"

"Yep. It's a myth. There is no schizophrenia. Instead, there's just a million and one invisible assholes who WON'T SHUT THE HELL UP."

2002–2004

Bones heal, muscles heal, tendons heal. But they're never as good as new. There's always a fault line somewhere ready to break open again. Pearl and I made our way back to Baton Rouge. But without the guys, it wasn't home. Not anymore. We weren't sure how to pick up the pieces, if there were any pieces. We didn't really belong anywhere.

Pearl was out of her back brace in a couple of weeks. But she was far...miles...lights years from healed. She gave up yoga, because it was too painful. She gave up the organic vegan diet, because what's the point. She went back to blackout boozing and chain-smoking, cuz why the hell not. And she gobbled morphine like Now and Laters. And so did I. All day every day. *Because everything fucking hurts. All the fucking time.*

With physical therapy I finally got a bit of the strength back in my fretting hand. To celebrate I bought a cheap, no-name acoustic guitar with a bowed neck and ridiculously high action. Fretting chords was excruciating. And that's precisely why I bought the thing. Some smooth Strat or butternecked Ibanez would have felt tons better, without a doubt. And that just wouldn't do. I needed my fingers to ache, my metacarpals to throb. I needed the pain. I needed to rebuild myself. And given that my already peculiar hearing was now maddeningly hypersensitive, I had to completely rethink myself as a musician (and as a person too, I guess).

The pain from the acoustic didn't subside, but it actually got good to me over time. On some dark level I craved it. And I swore I'd never touch an electric guitar ever again.

"What, are you Blind Lemon Jefferson now?" Chuck from Sisyphus Records said. "How're you gonna sound heavy on some cheap-ass acoustic guitar, Shel? Seriously, I wanna know. You all still owe us an album. Remember? I mean, take all the time you need. We know you have gone through a lot. But we're worried, bro. We're worried."

"Oh it'll be heavy, all right," I promised him. "You've got my word on that, cuz'n."

It'll be heavy…

Tattoos aside, I'm not a needle man. I'd probably launch an air bubble straight into my heart if I tried to shoot up. So I stuck to morphine gel caps. If you slice them open before you eat them the juice hits your system pretty quick and hard. Granted, you will vomit like an overflowing sewer pipe. But hey. Good with the bad, you know.

"It's no fun when it's medicine," Pearl complained. "I'd almost rather be in pain." *Almost. But not quite.*

On the flip side, the outpouring of sympathy from fans and bands far and wide came as quite a surprise. Press about the accident gave us an expected little spike in record sales, which provided a thin cushion for a couple of months. But it wouldn't be enough. It wouldn't last. Royalties would be drying up *tout de suite.* We didn't know what to do. Despite all of the requests for bass and drum auditions, we knew we couldn't replace Cres and Pierre (and, truth be told, we were a such a collective wreck we knew no one would stay with us for very long anyway). We were a duo now, and that's how it would be.

***

PEARL:

Shel and I, we're both transients at heart. We don't need a home base. We don't even need a home. It wasn't a hard decision to make. We sold all the gear except the reel-to-reel, Shel's acoustic guitar, and a soundhole pick-up. We sold what little furniture we had that anyone might want, and the rest went in the trash. We gave Cerberus to Sally. And with the pittance we got from the insurance on the van, we bought a used Honda Civic. That was our home now. The road. We'd both lived that way before, and it's probably how we're most meant to be.

And to anyone who says the Honda Civic isn't very metal, you tell me what's more metal than hitting rock bottom, dumping your whole life on a curb in Louisiana, and driving off into oblivion packing nothing but hard dope, a guitar, and a couple of bottles of rotgut. That's what I thought.

Morbid curiosity. I'm sure that's the only reason people came out to see us initially. We kept the name Stigmata Dog, and anyone who knew who we were knew about the accident on the way to *Doom Fest.* We made no secret that there would be no rhythm section, or that we'd be playing acoustic. I think perhaps people assumed that our show would just be stripped down, unplugged versions of the material they knew already. And there was a bit of that. But it wasn't a novelty show, not by any stretch. I don't think they realized how dark and alien those songs would be now. How wandering and bottomless the new sound was. Whatever "fun" there was to be found in our music in the past, it was long gone. This was no rock concert. This was a bloodletting.

And by and large our crowd was down with it. We played to packed houses, for a while, although the venues themselves got progressively smaller. That was okay with us. I don't know that Pearl even noticed.

* * *

PEARL:

Yes, I did notice. I didn't care.

It was a completely different stage experience, no doubt about that. The relentless pain in my hands and shoulders that came from playing that cheap guitar just made me play harder, find even more twisted, dissonant chords to play. My pain, in its way, became part of "the show." So elemental did it become, that I would go medicine-free seven hours before a performance. I'd be sweating and near blackout come show time. I always fantasized that one night, right in the middle of the set, all of the clips and sutures in my hand might suddenly burst open mid-song, and I'd be a bloody, spurting, crippled mess right there in front of my audience. Literally destroyed for my art. *Metal.* I'd be an instant legend.

We lost all sight of the passage of time. Anytime I'd look about at the world around me, ever more it seemed to be nothing but a smoking, festering cauldron of diseased pig shit. Endless war, torture, ever-growing poverty, corporate scumfucks robbing the rest of us blind and skipping off scot-free. I expected no better. So I drowned myself in morphine and Demerol, bourbon and vodka, and music. Just the essentials, you know. Just the essentials.

Even with all of that, though, I never succumbed to addiction. I just don't think I'm wired for it.

Pearl is, though. Is she ever. And she gave herself over to the needle unconditionally. It was true love.

PEARL:

I had a really fine tattoo once. Right in the middle of my back, of two women with bat wings making love. After the accident and subsequent surgery, it looked like two bat-women making love whilst riddled with bullet holes. I don't know, I think it's funny.

***

"Hey, Shel?"

"Yeah?"

"I'm not sure, but I think it might be Christmas."

"Really?"

"I think so."

"Huh. You know, I actually prefer Saturnalia over Christmas. It's a better holiday all around. More sodomy and decapitation than I'm really into, but considerably less melancholy."

"Yeah. Hey Shel."

"Yo."

"Merry Christmas."

"Right back atcha, cuz'n."

Since it was just the two of us, lodging was pretty simple. You either "pay the rent," or you sleep in the car. Most nights I slept in the car. Pearl seldom did. Occasionally folks would let us crash on their couches. Ricky from Skulltower actually gave us a key to his apartment and said we could stay there any time we're in Columbus, Ohio. Much appreciated, but you'd be right in assuming that we didn't take him up on that offer very often. Fuck Columbus.

Winter of '03 was the last time I bothered attempting a post-show hook up. It wasn't worth the effort.

Dead of winter, Somewhere, Nebraska, inhumanly cold. So cold Pearl even wore shoes. I decided I wanted a warm bed to sleep in for a change. As fortune would have it, after the show, a friendly but rather worn-out looking rock chick in shiny black vinyl and stiletto pumps came up to me at the bar cooing about how much she liked "the band." We talked for a couple of minutes. Had a drink. I signed the CD for her, and then we headed back to her place. Just that easy.

We chatted for a bit more as she poured us some wine and put the disc on the stereo (which I didn't really want to listen to, honestly) and put it on shuffle. And what should come on first?

"So avert your gaze / and bury your shame /
before your Eyes Melt / and you burst into flame!"

"Romantic, eh?"

"I seen the video for this!" she squealed.

"You're one of maybe five."

"I feel so special!"

"We don't play that song anymore."

"You should. It's rad."

After about twenty minutes of *blah blah blah* about whatever, she started getting really flirty. And before I knew it, she's down on her knees with her face in my lap.

Unfortunately, the gel caps I'd snarfed down a half hour earlier were making things hard. No...wrong choice of words. They were making things *difficult.*

"What's the matter?" she said, pulling really hard on my dick like she was preparing to make balloon animals. "Don't you like me?"

"Sure I do," I said, trying not to wince in pain, shutting my eyes tight and trying to quickly conjure up some horny image in my head. *Naked Jello wrestling. Some lowlight from Penny DeVour's Greatest Hits.* Nothing. *I've always had a thing for early-1980s Grace Jones for some reason*...but even that didn't get a rise out of me. It wasn't to be.

"Jesus," she said, exasperated, "It's like a boiled noodle. What's wrong? Are you...a fag or something?"

"Um...well, I hadn't been."

That did it.

"Oh, I see. So you weren't a faggot 'til you met me, but now you are one, huh? Thanks a fuckin' lot, asshole."

I was asked to leave.

As I was zipping up and preparing to make my exit, she yanked my CD out of her stereo and stomped on it. She wasn't wearing shoes and it cut up her bare heel pretty hardcore. But she kept stomping.

"Bullshit...fuckin' bullshit..."

"Don't blame ya," I said. "The snare drum is way too high in the mix."

"Git the hell out, queer!"

No more paying the rent for me.

PEARL:

It hurt to fuck. It hurt to do anything. But you gotta do what you gotta do. I may have had to grit my teeth through most of it, having some sweaty cretin bounce up and down on top of me, but I still got mine. I come easily and I come hard. And as much as I want to. It's a gift, not a talent. I'd mix it up to keep it interesting—different folks, different strokes. But just like the morphine, it was taking more and more to satisfy me.

I told Shel that the one thing I always wanted to do that I never had done was to do a set of twins. Boys, girls, one of each, didn't matter. But they had to fuck each other too. That would be the ultimate.

"Good luck with that, cousin," he said. (Shel's a tough guy to read sometimes.) "Seems like that would have been a short order back in the DeVour days."

"Incest is Penny's one no-no. He'd talk about it, but never showed it in a video. He claimed having actual blood relations screw each other on camera could have gotten him thrown in prison, but I don't know if that's true or not."

"How come you never got in front of the camera for him?"

"I did once, just for a lark. It was an old-style loop, not very long at all. I pegged this guy's asshole with a strap-on. It was fun, but it turned out bad for him in the long run, and I felt awful about that. It pretty much wrecked the guy's career."

"What went bad?"

"The industry has a real double-standard when it comes to the gayness. At least it did back then. Girls can do whatever, but if a guy so much as brushes up against another guy on camera, he is banished to the queer ghetto forever. And people who saw the clip didn't believe I was a girl." We laughed like

hell. "I tried to get Penn to give me another shot, this time a Pearl + a set of twins threesome, but he said nyet."

"Such a lost opportunity," Shel said.

"One time," I told him, "back when I was in high school in Miami, a bunch of us were hanging out, getting stoned, just talking, you know. Sophomore year I think. Couple of guys, a couple of girls. The girl whose house it was, her brother was a senior. Track star. Reeeeeally cute. Everybody wanted a taste of his goodies. He came home from practice this particular day, and we said, Hey, join us! So we passed him the joint, and he was cool enough.

"Now, I don't remember how it came up exactly...but we started talking sex. Have you done this, would you do that. You know how high school is."

"Don't remember high school," Shel said. "I was either drunk or on mushrooms every single day."

"Well anyway...somehow, get this, I started trying to talk the girl into giving her brother head, right in front of all of us."

"What?"

"I just thought it was worth a try."

"Worth a try to talk your friend into sucking off her brother in front of you?"

"Not just me, there was a group of us there."

"How did you do that? Why *did you do that?"*

"Why not? I thought it'd be hot."

"So...what happened?"

"They said no, of course. Duh. But I stayed with it, really persistent. And after a while everyone else kinda joined in with me. Finally they both were like, 'All right, all right, if it'll get you off our backs.'"

"Jesus H. bloodshittin' Christ," Shel said. "Did it take a lot to convince them?"

"Not as much as you might think."

"That's fucked up, Pearl," he said. "That's a pretty fucked up thing."

"It was totally consensual, Shel. It's not like I held a gun to them or anything."

"That's Cool," he said. "Whatever. The whole thing just sounds a little...fundamentalist to me."

"What do you mean?"

"A little bit like those religious nuts, right? Just in reverse. You take something like, oh I don't know, fucking *for instance...that is really no big deal at all...and you inflate into something 'evil' and 'sinful' or whatever. Make it forbidden. That's what makes it 'hot.' For the fundies* and *for you. I don't see any difference."*

"There's a difference."

"Same game. Sex as a weapon, it cuts the same both ways."

"All I did, Shel, was bring light to a basic universal truth."

"And what universal truth would that be?"

"That with a few appropriately chosen words, a little persistence, and just the slightest bit of peer pressure, you can convince most people to do pretty much ANYTHING. Anything."

"Sure. Like jihad. Or the crusades. Or torture. Or genocide."

"Or semi-public incest."

"Right."

"People are sheep. Am I wrong, Shel? Am I wrong about that? People are sheep. *Is that my fault?"*

"So whatever happened to them? The brother and sister."

"We all stayed friends afterward. Nobody ever talked about it again. But apparently...one time when they were alone..."

"No way."

"They both had slipped home at lunchtime one school day..."

"No goddamn way."

"...and there they were going at it full bore in the bedroom they had shared as little kids and, well...apparently their mother came home for her lunch break. They didn't know that. Surprise!"

"Maaaaaaaaan..."

"Messed all three of them up pretty bad."

"Damn it all. You ever feel any responsibility?"

"Kind of. I still occasionally rub one out thinking about it,

though. But more than anything, it made me wonder; what could I make an audience do? Could I get them to riot? Or all spontaneously strip naked and ball each other silly? Or do the foxtrot?"

"Or commit ritual suicide?"

"How much power does a microphone really have? I mean, if you really know how to use it."

"Never too late to find out," he said. "You've got frequent access to the proverbial conch shell. See what you can do. Do a little preachifyin'. Sling some immaculate deception. Hey yeah, religions are proven money-makers, cousin. Make a bit of that holy profit. How hard could it be?"

By this time, of course, I could barely stand up on my own two feet on stage, let alone whip the congregation into a frenzy of some sort. Talk about your lost opportunities...

Portland, Oregon seemed like a good place to take a couple of days off to do some writing. We actually rented a room. Some little dump of a place, but we didn't need much. We'd been kicking around new ideas on the road for, what was it...thirteen months? Eighteen? Like I said, we had lost track of time.

We'd periodically check in with Sisyphus and they'd remind us that we needed to keep some sort of public profile. We offered to cut an EP while we worked out the new sound, but they didn't really go for it. Chuck would say something about us getting whatever it is "out of our system," and that he hoped we'd consider putting a new full band together before too long. Go back to the "classic" Stigmata Dog sound, whatever that was. *No chance, cuz'n.*

Pearl's junk habit was getting progressively worse. But at least for a while, it wasn't affecting the music too badly, apart from our now far more stationary stage presence. It wasn't only the junk. I knew just walking was painful for her. And I couldn't really talk shit about her drug use, as I was doing almost as much as she was. It just wasn't hitting me as hard. I wasn't hooked.

I *would* periodically give her static about her chain-smoking.

"You're gonna wreck your voice," I said.

"So?" she snapped. "Your hand is wrecked. Fits the program, don't you think? We're a good match."

"Okay, so then what, we're just going for the full suck now?"

"I'm sorry, Shel. I shouldn't have said that about your hand. I love your guitar playing. Probably more now than ever, somehow."

"That's excellent, because I've got big ideas. I'm buying a bass. A cheap one."

"What do you want to do with it?"

"Carve it up. Dick around with the pick-ups. Add extra machine heads and strings. Really Frankenstein it out."

"That could be cool."

"Load on the distortion, really sludgy. The sludgiest sound ever."

"Hell yes."

"I am chasing the sound of complete oblivion."

"You're a weird guy, Shel."

"I'm in good company."

Of course I didn't care if she smoked nine packs a day. I didn't care if she shot heroin into her armpits. I didn't care if she was funneling money to the Pakistani Taliban (she wasn't, as far as I know. I'm just saying). It didn't make any difference to me. It didn't matter. Nothing really mattered to me, except the music. And that bothered me. The fact that nothing mattered, it bothered me. A little.

More and more I tried to blot out the outside world as much as possible. Because every time I would check in on it, it would once again be more horrifying than the last time. Papa Doc Bush's idiot hellspawn was oiled up and squirted back into the White House. Mass murder and torture and war crimes committed in our name, it all got worse and worse. By the time the tsunami hit Thailand in '04, I was convinced that the Earth was trying to flush us all away, and it was only a matter of time before it hit the US too. *If this ain't the end of the world, it sure as balls should be.*

The war was really getting under Pearl's skin, moreso than mine. I wasn't sure why, but I'd hear her growling about it in her sleep. In Anton's voice. I was confident by that time that whatever I saw in that ditch on Interstate 71 had been a hallucination. But, no denying, it sure looked just like how Pearl sounded when "Anton" was speaking.

Her revulsion for the war was present when she was awake too.

"These neocons," she said, dragging hard on her fiftieth cigarette of the day, "they think of genocide as a cure. You know? They're the heirs of the same ball-less bastards who melted my family in Nagasaki. They want to scorch the earth clean. Set the air on fire."

"Who am I talking to now," I asked, "Pearl or Anton?"

"This is me talking," she said. *Doesn't really answer my question.* "You remember, even before 9/11, I wouldn't fly. You know how come? Because *bad things* fall out of airplanes, Shel. Bad, bad things."

"Well, as we've discovered, driving ain't exactly the teddy bears' picnic either."

"Yeah...but nobody ever sprayed people with napalm from a Honda Civic."

"Sounds like a challenge to me."

The world is flaming gasoline.
God is scarred, burned, naked in a drain pipe.
Something in the medicine is keeping us sick.
Fearless and terrified.
Another needle raping our veins
And all is quiet along the sand here tonight.

And there is just enough medicine/
to keep the disease alive…

"What do you call this song, Pearl?"

"*The Zero Collectors.*"

"No shit."

"You know we're just killing and dying to score digits for the Zero Collectors. That's all it is."

"Little homage to the old man?'

"He has his moments."

All is right with the universe
and God is scarred, burned, naked in a drain pipe.
Keep the disease alive.
Needless and terrified.
And all is quiet along the sand here tonight.
Amen.

And the plummet into hell continued unabated. Deeper and deeper still.

I remember the night: December 8, 2004. We were just stepping off stage at The Showbox in Seattle (a huge venue for us, even compared to the old days) when we got the news. One of our all-time favorite guitar players (and a personal hero of mine) had just been murdered, on stage, by a fan—a heavily armed Marine with…wait for it…paranoid schizophrenia. *Welcome home to the roost, chickens.* And where did this happen? At the Alrosa Villa…in *Columbus fucking Ohio.*

"Let's never go back to Columbus again," Pearl said. "It really is an awful place."

That's how that year ended.

"Merry Christmas, Shel."

"Right back atcha, cuz'n."

2005

Oh yeah. 2005. The dawn of the apocalypse. Long time coming, of course. But that was the year it really kicked in full throttle. I'm sure there were plenty of warning signs, but I was still trying to stay as oblivious as possible.

Our shows by that time were becoming more "intimate." That's one way to put it. More accurately, however, our audience was shrinking. Smaller and smaller. But, more devout. Whatever it was that Pearl and I were doing musically was striking some kind of chord, not with very many people, but with a passionate handful of maladjusted misfits. And that suited us. It absolutely did. It felt right.

Our new material was getting stronger all the time, but you'd have to have been as blind as a brick wall and twice as thick not to notice that Pearl's addictions were getting more severe. Much more. By early '05 she was sucking down her weight in chemicals like some sort of deranged hummingbird. I matched her dose for dose for a while, out of routine. But after a while her need for more surpassed my interest in blitzing myself into a fog. The pain from my injuries had more or less passed (or at least I'd become so accustomed to it that I hardly noticed anymore), and the damage to my nerves and muscles was more than likely permanent and fully set in by then. What can you do? You maintain. You make the best of it.

I actually thought of my crash-induced limitations as a spark for my creativity. It was cool, imagining myself in the same camp as two of my greatest guitar heroes: Tony Iommi and Django Reinhardt, two other guitarists who turned potentially devastating hand injuries into creative innovation that altered the musical landscape forever, and made the world a weirder, more awesome place to live. *Of course they're both brilliant and legendary artists and I'm homeless, broke and totally obscure...but who the hell's keeping score anyway.*

The issue with my ears was more debilitating. My hearing's not so much stronger than the average person's, but it's considerably sharper. More acute. Moreso than it had before the accident. It was as if the entire world's treble nob was now cranked too far to the right. The muttering of strangers was unbearable. It was near-crippling. But silence was worse. *Because there is no silence.* It doesn't exist. And it was getting harder and harder to find respite.

Recorded music itself became agony for me. It wasn't *just* that I didn't enjoy the sound of synthesizers or drum machines or auto-tuned vocals. No, it actually physically hurt me. And the compression of recorded digital music at large made me literally want to vomit (I could hardly even to listen to my own CDs anymore). I could hardly listen to any radio at all. I was becoming a musician with very little actual music in his life, and that's just not healthy.

Never a social person anyway, I withdrew further and further from the world. And my best friend, my only close friend, my other half, was slowly fading away.

Because of my unwanted auditory ability/handicap, I could hear what people in the audience were saying, even mid-song. They were noticing that Pearl, more and more, could barely stay awake on stage. How could they not notice? She would shoot up right before we went on, and start to nod before the opening applause had died away. She was being consumed by junk, "drowning in an ocean of spiderwebs" as she called it, and we couldn't keep it off stage any longer. I began taking over the majority of the lead vocal duties, Pearl periodically chiming in with distant harmonies. We even began throwing in a couple of Annalee's songs too, which Pearl slid into beautifully, if not consistently...

"But sometimes…I can still feel you dancing, baby…"

Pearl became a ghost on stage, haunting already cavernous music with a faint, desolate, whispering moan. And as much as it shames me to say…*I fucking loved it.* I knew she was slowly dying right in front of me. And as her friend, it pained me to watch it. But as a composer…I was enamored with what the sound of her pitiful, fading life force did for my music. And our audience, small and dwindling as they were, was taken by it too. Just as the contortions brought on by the pain in my hands had become part and parcel of our "show," so too did Pearl's wasting away. It was chilling, and it was a vibe no one else had. A horrible, repulsive energy, *but goddamn it, it was real. And I loved it.*

Anyone with a conscience would have intervened. I should have gotten angry with her. I should have shouted and raved at her, "I watched all my friends die in front of me! I'm not going to watch you die too!" But I never did. I never did. Because the sound…that gorgeous, rasping, dissonant melody of her impending death…*belonged to me.*

"Where are we, Shel?"

"Lumberton. But we're not quite there yet."

"Lumberton, Texas?"

"That'd be the one."

"Christ."

She fiddled around with the nobs for a while before finally finding a station on the car stereo playing old, tin can hillbilly music. Still a bit staticky, she turned the volume low.

"I can handle that," I said.

She lit a cigarette and stared out at outer-Lumberton flashing by. I-10 East made its own music against our rapidly balding tires as the steady rain began to grow steadily thicker.

"Shel, you ever find yourself brushing your teeth in the bathroom of a McDonalds in Macon, Georgia and wondering if maybe you fucked up somewhere along the line?"

"Nope."

"Me neither."

It had been a wet summer. It seemed everywhere we went was drenched. What can you do? Maintain. And keep your powder dry.

"What's the venue?"

"I don't know," she said. "It's written down in the back seat somewhere. Keep your eye out for 96 South I guess." She flicked the butt out the window and sighed.

"You know why my brother Dave and I don't talk?" she said.

"Tell me."

"I stole from him."

"Oh yeah? When?"

"High school. My senior year."

"Hm. Must have been something big."

"Not really." She lit another cigarette. "Living in Miami, just Dave and me and the parental units. I'm the black sheep, big shock. Two years older than my brother. And he really looked up to me. Yeah, Miami. Mom and Dad all worried that I'm a bad influence, you know. Dave's all about studying hard, and political activism and saving the world, and I'm...well, I'm me."

"Right."

"I was playing in this band at the time, and we were starting to really jump. It was getting good. And Dave was so proud of me. He wore my band's T-shirt to school, like, every day, and...I don't know. It was really great between us. We had a good relationship. But I was seeing a guy. This scabby dude. Just a real fucking crumb, you know."

"I'm astonished."

"I know, right? And he got in with some bad people, and lost some money, and they were going to rough him up bad if he didn't pay them back. Maybe even kill him. So I got it in my head that I could pawn some stuff and pay it off for him. Cuz I'm a dumb cunt."

"Indeed."

"So one night, I went into Dave's room when he's sleeping,

and I nicked his TV. I'm just about out the door and he wakes up.

"'What are you doing, Sumi?' he says, as if it wasn't obvious. 'I'm just borrowing it,' I say. But we both know it's a lie. And he didn't say another word. He just looked at me. Just shattered that I would do that to him. He never told. Never said a word. I just walked out. And I haven't seen or heard from him since."

"You pawn the TV?"

"Yep. And me and the guy ran off to Cali."

"Did the goons ever catch him?"

"I don't know. Not long after we got to LA we got in a big fight. He punched me and broke a couple of my toes with a heavy boot heel, and I threw Ajax in his eyes. End of that chapter. But I always felt horrible about my brother."

"Why don't you try to catch up with him? Say you're sorry and whatnot."

"You think I haven't tried? And anyway, I'm the one who's on tour, you know. That info's easy to get. If he ever wanted to talk to me, he would have by now. God…I wish he would. I wish he would hunt me down and curse me out and spit in my face. Something. Anything."

"What about your folks?"

"If there's a heaven, they're up there hanging out with your parents cursing us both." We laughed. Of course I got on fine with my folks, and I don't even know if my mom is dead, but point taken. "I want to go back to NOLA," she said out of nowhere.

"What?"

"We need to play a home-town show."

"Ooookay. When?"

"I don't know. Tonight. Tomorrow. I don't care, I just don't want to play Texas tonight."

"You're serious, aren't you."

"Lumberton won't miss us. Come on, you know you want to go back. We're pointed that way anyhow."

"Yeah…but it's a four and a half hour drive from here."

"Piece of cake."

"How are you on medicine?"

"Fine."

"What do you got left?"

"A quarter grain."

"Single? That enough? You start geeking out, and I'll dump you right out on the highway, I swear to Christ almighty."

"Don't worry. It'd be good. It'll be *great.*" Her face lit up like a switch had been flipped. Hadn't seen her that up in so long I'd forgotten what it looked like. She pulled out her cell phone and another cigarette and started punching digits.

"Sally?" she said into the phone. "Hey! It's Pearl! Heeeey! Good to hear your voice too, baby. So check it out—we're on our way. No, right now. Yeah! Of course Shel's here."

"Hey Sall," I said loudly, as I swerved to miss what looked like an armadillo in the road.

"She said for me to give you a kiss for her, but I ain't gonna," Pearl said.

"Thank you."

"Sall," Pearl continued into the phone, "we wanna play a show. Tonight if possible. Can you send the feelers out? We'll play with anybody anywhere. Doesn't matter." Just then the rain really started to pour. "Oh, and hey. We need a place to crash. Do your parents have a basement or anything? No, of course they don't. Duh. What the hell am I thinking." Rain hit the Civic like buckets of gravel. Cars going the opposite way began to whiz past us. No one was going our way. "What's that? No, we haven't seen a television in weeks, why? What? Katrina who? Oh. Evacuation? Come on, girlfriend, it's New Orleans in August. Of course they're calling for an evacuation. What else is new. Is anybody actually leaving? Yeah, that's what I thought. So yeah, see if anybody'll let us on the bill tonight. And I wanna swing by and see my doggie. Yes, he is still my dog."

"Actually," I interjected, "he's *my* dog." Ignored.

"All right, Sall," Pearl said. "We'll see you in about four hours. Okay. Me too. Okay. Love you too, darling. Later."

She hung up the phone and did a little dance in her seat.

"Did I hear something about a hurricane?" I asked.

"Yeah," she said, lighting up her one thousandth smoke of the day, "A Cat-2, just passing Florida."

"Heh. Who gives a shit."

"Exactly. Man, aren't you stoked, Shel? Isn't this going to be just what we need right now?"

"I guess. But you know, I've played a million shows in New Orleans. Literally a million. I've counted."

"Yeah, but this is *different.* We're a whole new thing now, and folks won't know what hit them."

I've heard that before...

"You're right," I said. "It's going to be killer."

We drove for a long time without speaking much, listening instead to the driving rain against the car, unable to get even dead hillbillies on the radio. I had to slow down for the wind and the rain, and I could tell Pearl was starting to jones. After a bit, she slipped into the back seat and got out her little magic bag. Within a minute, she was out. Fast asleep. Her breathing got heavier, and she began to mutter, in a deep, guttural drawl—

"*Come and be healed...come and be healed...*"

It was that hard, male-sounding voice. Rock salt and turpentine. Anton...

"*Come and be healed...*"

I absently tapped my left front pocket, making sure my butterfly knife was there. I figured it was only a matter of time... *minutes? Years?* Only a matter of time before something possessed her in her sleep. Something dangerous. Maybe even deadly. And I wanted to make sure I was prepared.

"*Come...come...come and be healed...*"

Hours went by: just me, the rain, and the black highway. There was a periodic rush of cars heading the other way, then nothing. Night settled in earlier than I thought it would, and I hadn't seen another set of headlights in a hundred miles.

Suddenly, down the road, I saw a dark figure caught in my beams standing right in the middle of the road. I slowed down, unsure if what I was seeing was actually there.

"Pearl," I said. "Pearl, wake up."

Groggily, she pulled herself into a sitting position.

"Huuh? Wha izzit?"

"Am I totally bugfuck, or do you see someone standing in the highway up ahead?"

She leaned in over my shoulder, her eyes wide.

"Oh god...yeah, I do. It...what? It looks like...looks like... *Blue Ida.*"

"Um, Ida is dead, Pearl."

"Yeah, no fuckin' shit, Shel. I was at her funeral too. But am I wrong? Am I?"

She wasn't. Not exactly. From that distance all we could make out were the knee-length salt and pepper dreadlocks. But as we rolled closer, the wind and rain rocking the Honda side to side, we saw that the figure was actually tall and lean. And a man. With a beard. I brought the car to a near crawl, and inched cautiously up toward him. He did not move out of the way.

"We're going to have to talk to him."

"*You* talk to him."

I slid the knife out of my pocket and flipped it open, keeping it down on my side. I rolled down the window and was blasted by rain.

"Can we help you, dread?" I called out to the figure.

He turned to look at us, eyes in the high beams hard and white like marble against his black face and the black night, shining like fog lights through the slamming rain. He walked slowly toward the car.

"Ya'll headin' to Nuh Leans?" he asked. His voice had a chill about it, loaded down with either menace or fear, I couldn't tell which.

"Yeah, we are."

"No you ain't. Ain't nobody gettin' in, ain't nobody gettin' out. Death is comin'."

"It's...it's a Cat-2," Pearl said. He did not reply.

We sat in silence for several long moments. The man was drenched, and his long, rope-like hair whipped around from the wind. But he never asked for help. Finally, not knowing what else to do, Pearl and I both said in unison:

"Get in, man."

He did.

"Much obliged, folks," he said, staring out the window into the nothing. "You gonna wanna git offa 10 when you able, find some kinda way to git to 40."

"Where you headed?"

"Same as you," he said. "North."

"We're not going north," Pearl said emphatically. "We gotta get to New Orleans. People are waiting for us."

"Give it 'bout a day's time and there won't be no Nuh Leans lef' no more," he said. "And unless they leavin' right now, e'ryone you know will be stone dead. Is that clear?"

Crystal.

So on we went. To where? No fucking clue. My heart pounded. I could feel my face burning hot, wishing we hadn't stopped, wishing we had just swerved around this guy. But something told me to listen to him. And that something must have mentioned it to Pearl as well, because she put up nary a protest.

The rain drove harder. The radio was dead. And the specter in the back seat was silent, but for a murmur under his breath only I could hear saying, "*Get away, got to get away.*"

Finally I just came right out with it—

"Got a name, mister?"

"Got several of 'em."

Great.

"Okay, so then what do they call you nearby?"

"Brown...if I 'member correct. Been quite a while. Yeah. El Brown. That was my name."

"All right, El Brown. So you...uh...You on the run there, cuz'n? I mean, besides from a tropical storm?"

"You could say that, yeah."
"Cops?"
"I wish."
"FBI?"
"I wish."
"Mafia?"
"Worse."
"Yakuza?"
"Worse."
"CIA?"
"Worse."
No further questions.

Hours went by. Traffic would thicken, then thin to nothing. Over and over. And the storm got ever worse. And we didn't talk. Pearl began to sweat and shiver, and I knew she was out of juice. *Nothing we can do about it.* I didn't know where we were going, besides Interstate 40, but I drove on.

More time crawled by, and Pearl was getting bad. Gritting her teeth and shaking.

"Gonna be sick," she said. "What are we doing…"

The man in the back spoke up—

"Just try to breathe, chile," he said. His voice suddenly less hollow, more fatherly. "You'll be a'ight. You gonna meet a girl, and she'll make e'rythang better."

"What?" Pearl said. "What girl?"

"You'll know when you meet her. She goin' make e'ry little thang all right. You gotta have faith."

We finally stopped for gas at a broke-dick little truck stop in Arkansas, the only joint with power for miles in any direction. Pearl ran off to puke somewhere, and I got out to work the pump. Without warning, our passenger grabbed my arm.

"I gotta talk to you, Sheldon," he said. I froze in my seat. I hadn't told him my name.

"How do you—"

"Listen up now. You gotta hear somethin'. I know all 'bout

this storm...cuz I may have caused it, you hear?"

"What?"

"I mighta done caused it. I try to do right, I try not to make no waves these here days. But it's too late now. I got abilities. Hear? My whole life I done had 'em. Weren't humble 'bout it neither. Been showin' my ass to the Lord since I's six years old in West Point, Mississippi. I got abilities other people ain't got. And so do you. And so does she." He pointed outward randomly, indicating Pearl in the distance.

"Dude, I seriously don't know what you're—"

"You see the future, Shel?"

"No."

"In yo' dreams?"

!!!

"What...what do you mean?"

"You see people in yo' dreams. Don'tchoo. *Don'tchoo.* Sufferin'. People in danger. And you can't help them. Am I not correct?"

What the fuck!?!?!

"How do you know that?"

"I don't just *see* the future, Sheldon. *I go there.* Body *and* spirit. I seen all kinds of things there. Things we wasn't meant to know. This is the dawn of the apocalypse, Sheldon. I have seen it. I have seen you. You ain't just a minstrel...you a shepherd. And there is another. *Dumuzid.* The king after the flood. *Follow the star.*"

"Wait a second—"

"I's a hunted man, Sheldon. Cuz I been to the future and back. Cuz I know things ain't no mortal person 'posed to know. So they huntin' me—"

"Who is?"

"*Devils.*"

"Oh."

"They wanna shut me up but good."

"That sucks, cuz'n."

"Listen now! You got to git to Columbus, Ohio. You find a girl there make e'rythang right. I hope. It ain't too late. It ain't too late. I hope. Godspeed, shepherd."

And with that he jumped out of the car and tore off into the night.

Jesus ball-swinging Christ...

Pearl came back soaking wet, shivering worse than before. She fell into the passenger seat, her eyes bloodshot from crying.

"Where'd he go?" she sniffled.

"Don't know. What's going on?"

"He's right. He's right about NOLA. The city's in lockdown. It's looking real bad. I've been trying to call in, but nothing's getting through. Seriously, did that guy just take off for no reason? Anyway, I just spent twenty of my last fifty dollars on the gas. What are we going to do?"

"Well," I said, "We've got enough..."

"Enough to do what?"

"To get us to Columbus."

"What?! Columbus, Ohio?! Are you crazy?"

"Skulltower's on tour in Europe. We can use Ricky's pad."

"Fifteen hour drive through a torrential downpour to crash in a city we hate with no money and no connections and no nothing? That's insane."

"You got a better plan? We turn around and we die. We don't have enough money to stay anywhere. You really want to try to sleep in this car, in this storm, feeling the way you do right now?"

"No."

"There's no one else we can call on anywhere around here. There's no one to help us. No one to turn to. And anyway... Columbus...that's where *the girl* is."

"*What girl?!*"

"I don't know. But I'm told that's where she is."

We finally started picking up a radio signal on Interstate 40 East through Tennessee. The situation in NOLA was worsening by the hour, as was Pearl's junk sickness. She vomited out the passenger side window, screaming out into the night—

"HOW MUCH MORE CAN YOU TAKE FROM US?!"

"Who you yelling at, Pearl?"

"God! The universe! Whatever! Whatever it is out there that hates us so much!"

"I really don't think the universe gives a shit about us one way or the other, cuz'n. Call it a hunch."

"Why..." she cried, shaking hard. "Why is this happening..."

"Cuz shit just randomly happens," I said. "That's the way it works."

But obviously I didn't believe that. I mean, I had to get to Columbus, Ohio...because why? Because some crazy old man I don't know and just met had a vision, or something.

Out of my goddamn mind...

But I've always pretty much operated this way. When you're lost, and have no idea what to do, go with whatever sounds the most like a plan. Even if it's a stupid plan. Even if it makes no sense. What do you want to bet that's exactly how Moses ended up in the desert for forty fucking years.

"Pearl. Pearl, how you holding up?"

"W-w-where are we?" she asked, teeth chattering, pouring sweat, rocking back and forth in the passenger seat. I half-expected her to fall into some sort of seizure at any moment.

"We're getting near Louisville, Kentucky."

"OH!!!" she exclaimed, throwing her head back. "Oh, thank god!" I don't suspect that's the reaction Louisville gets very often. "I forgot about Louisville!"

"You forgot?"

"There's that dude!" she said desperately. "Remember?"

"What dude?"

"The Louisville guy. Remember, we played here last year. That guy came up to us after the show. The guy! Mr. Brain Cancer, remember? Selling off his Dilaudid prescription."

"Oh yeah."

"We have to find him, Shel!"

"You think he's still alive?"

"We gotta find out. Seriously. If I don't get something in the vein soon I'm going to fucking die, and I'm not kidding."

"All right," I said, "but we better be careful. You see those headlights behind us?"

"Yeah?"

"Fucker's been following us since around Memphis."

"Oh. Jesus."

"Precisely. Can you see the driver?"

"Uh," she said looking back, "No. Can't see inside. A Tang-colored Datsun? Really? For Chrissakes. But no. The driver's just a dark shadow. Has it really been following us?"

"For at least an hour and a half."

"Fuck 'em in the eye. We gotta find Mr. Brain Cancer. Datsun Guy wants to screw with us, I'll eat his fucking face right about now."

It was eerie coming up 71 North (packing enough Dilaudid to kill three large men. No idea how Pearl was able to secure the supply from Mr. Brain Cancer. *Just sit in the car and don't ask questions*). The sun broke right as we drove through that stretch of highway where everything was destroyed four years prior.

It was there that the Orange Datsun finally disappeared off an exit ramp, all the while Pearl slept soundly, loaded to the gills, in the backseat muttering, "*See you soon…see you soon…*"

By the time we rolled into Columbus, New Orleans was fifty percent underwater. Seven and a half hours later it was eighty percent submerged. Over the course of the next few days nearly two thousand people would die. And our government pretty much let it happen, left them to die, drowning in poison. And it didn't matter. They didn't matter. Like nothing does.

We had a bit of trouble with Ricky's key at first, but we finally got in. The apartment, 3-B, was a dank basement pit. Barren, but for a couch, a TV and a good-sized card table. No matter. It was somewhere steady to lay our heads for a while.

Skulltower would be back from their tour overseas in a little over a month. We vowed to not disturb anything in the apartment (such as there was anything to disturb), and hopefully have the fridge stocked before we departed. Ricky left us a note:

Pearl and Shellac,

If you're reading this then I guess y'all decided to use the crib. Welcome. Don't worry about the neighbors, they're all cool. Word of warning, the place sometimes floods during bad rainstorms. Should you find dudes in hazmat suits kicking in the door in the middle of the night to clean up the "flood water," don't freak. You definitely *want them here, trust me. If you've brought gear, keep it up on the table or kitchen counter just in case. Otherwise have fun. We'll be back from Oslo early October. If you're still here we gotta hang out then.*

metal,
Sick Rick

"Just no escaping the flood, is there," Pearl said.

We grabbed a beer a piece, and glued ourselves to the TV, watching the nightmare back home unfold. The proverbial, theoretical, metaphorical cesspool I had been saying the world was becoming was now grossly, literally manifest right there on the screen. Our people were dying, and the media said it was their own damn fault. Their own damn fault. For being poor, or being Black, or being a general bother, or whatever. Meanwhile the president joked around with asshole country singers and partied with his asshole senator buddies as our people pleaded for help and got none. We sat and watched New Orleans drown in toxic sludge. Fade and die. What can you do? Maintain? *Whatever will be will be…*

Word began to trickle in to us from people who had survived. And we heard of the ones who didn't. Neil Stein of the band Stabbing Christ could have made it out, but he would have had to leave his invalid mother to perish alone. No way. So they both drowned in the 9th Ward together. Trumpeter Boz Nodding, the late Blue Ida's eldest son, died along with his entire band. Sally and her parents escaped on a shuttle to Houston, but they had to leave Cerberus behind. I wished I could stop thinking about how scared he must have been as the water swallowed him up. *Rest In Peace, you old stigmata dog…rest in peace.*

"Been thinking a lot about Cres and Pierre lately," Pearl said, cooking up her breakfast in a spoon over the stove.

"Yeah?" I said. "I can't remember them."

"What do you mean you can't remember them?"

"I mean I can't really remember what they looked like. When I try to remember them alive, it's just a generic, all-purpose white face on both of their heads. No detail at all. I kinda hate it."

"Cres was the cute one," she said, pushing off into the back muscle of her left tricep. "Pierre was okay. Decent enough looking, as bass players go."

"That does me absolutely no good."

"This is fucking tragic, Shel. Don't you have a picture of them anywhere?"

"I don't carry pictures."

"What about the video for *Eyes Melt*? We've got a copy, don't we?"

After much digging around, we finally found the DVD at the bottom of my gig bag. It was scratched up, but played well enough.

Watching it bothered me more than I thought it would. And that's not such a bad thing. There was a rush of memories. But also it felt more than a bit detached. Like I was watching some other band, not something I had been a part of myself. The four of us standing around looking hardcore, pretending to play in a swamp, and on stage in LA; it looked cool. I almost thought, *I gotta check this group out sometime.* I saw Cres and Pierre as they were, as they really looked. And I remembered them. But, once the clip was over, they disappeared again. Gone from my memory in an instant. My mind couldn't, or wouldn't, hold on to the picture.

It's funny, really. I think this was my brain trying to protect me somehow. It is a funny thing, how your system works. The human body is nothing more than meat, slop, calcium and electricity. But the brain is an odd muscle machine. It makes decisions independent of us, even against our conscious wishes. It can heal, or adapt, or choose to destroy itself, and we have very little say in the matter. And as I came to discover, just the right blow to the skull can force all the secrets of the universe to come spilling out all over.

Trapped in the Promised Land. With not much to do. All of our booked shows were down south, and we had no way to get back down there even if we'd wanted to. I tried to call around to reschedule, but a number of the venues were still knocked out by the hurricane. The last of our money was all but gone, and Pearl was burning through Mr. Brain Cancer's magic goodies™ at a blinding speed.

One high note during this time, such as it was; Pearl finally fulfilled her fantasy of hooking up with a pair of identical twins at the same time. Gingers at that.

"How was it?" I asked.

"Not sure," she said with a shrug. "I think I fell asleep. That Dilaudid's a mother-raper. But, whatever. Stuff's always more of a thrill in your mind than it is in real life anyway."

"Ain't it the truth."

"And besides, once you get past the initial turn-on of watching identical twins fuck each other, it's hard to get beyond just how narcissistic it looks."

One night, while we were walking home from a nearby gas station with a package of bologna and a box of Lucky Charms—aka *dinner*—Pearl stopped short, right outside the apartment complex. She shut her eyes tight, then opened them quickly with a gasp. She looked around furiously, peering into the darkness around us, at nothing.

"What is it?" I asked.

"I can see myself. I can see *us*. From the outside. When I shut my eyes, I can see us in the distance. *We're being watched.*"

"By you?"

"By somebody."

"Huh," I said. "Always an adventure with you around, Pearl."

"Right…right back atcha, cuz'n," she said.

As for myself, this was right around the time that I crawled comfortably inside a large bottle of bourbon, and settled in. The weeks on end kicking around this little chunk of Columbus, Ohio became a shapeless loop of mundanity. Pointlessly treading water. Time lost what little meaning it had left, along with everything else. And then, somewhere along the line, I lost Pearl.

Last conversation I remember having with her around this time, she said—

"You know, Shel. People talk about hearing god, or seeing god, even being touched by god. But no one ever talks about the taste of god. Or the smell. What do you think god smells like?"

"Like an old, dusty furnace," I said.

"I was thinking the exact same thing."

A true friend would have been worried. A true friend would have had some concern. But me, I didn't even notice that she was gone. Nearly four days had passed before it occurred to me that I had not seen her in quite a while. She simply vanished one day. And I hadn't even noticed. I shrugged it off and tapped the bottle. Bottoms up. Blackout…

…And that's where I saw her. Pearl. Unconscious and convulsing. On a bed with a tan cover and blue herons on the wall. Black tar spurting from her mouth like a faltering oil rig.

"Duuu…" she groans, "duuu…muuu…zeeee…"

Two unfamiliar sets of hands, one ash white and one chocolate brown, ripping her clothes off. My blade is out, I'm swinging it aimlessly around, slashing nothing but air…

BRRRRRRRIIIIIIINNNNG

The phone jarred me awake. I pulled myself up from the floor and grabbed it. The voice on the other end was nearly screaming—

"Helluh?! This Sheldon?!" It was a girl's voice, panicked and desperate.

"Yeah," I said, barely. My jaw was off the runner again, and it snapped awkwardly as I tried to work it. "Who izzis?"

"You don't know me, but this MeShayle," she said. "Min. My name Min. I's wit yo' friend here, and she in a bad, bad way."

"What's wrong? She OD'ing?"

"Maybe, but it don't really look like it. I seent overdose befo' and this ain't like what I seen. But somethin' real wrong. I wanna take her to the hospital, but she won't let me. She axin' f'you, and I fount'd yo' name on her phone. You gots to come quick! We at a little motel called the Pit-Stop Lodge. Right outside of town."

"On my way."

I screeched into the motel parking lot with less ease than what was required, trying too late not to wreck the Civic's front end on the broken pavement.

*Good god...*Even by my standards The Pit-Stop Lodge was a toilet.

I hopped out of the car and realized that I had neglected to get the room number. I called Pearl's phone. No answer. I tried to open the lobby door and it was locked tight.

"Hello?!" I shouted, pounding on the screen. "Somebody let me in! Hey! NOW, GODDAMN IT!"

The door flew open angrily, and a greasy, stumpy little man with bristly hog-jowls wearing a ripped Ohio State T-shirt pointed a threatening fried chicken leg at me. I stepped back reflexively, and noticed a Tang-powder-orange Datsun parked in the lot.

"What the hell you yellin' for?" the man grunted, his mouth packed with potato salad.

"Iss okay, Mista Runlin!" the voice from the phone hollered down the row. I looked over and saw a young Black girl standing in the doorway of room #7. "He wit me!"

I ran down toward her quickly, then suddenly stopped short.

Holy shit.

It was *her.* That girl from my dream. The silent Super-8. That girl getting the train run on her by all those drunk boys in baseball jerseys. We stared at each other for a moment before she finally said,

"Y-You comin' in?"

I found Pearl inside, lying on the bed in a bra and jean shorts, thrashing her head back and forth and moaning, upchucking vomit and coughing out black tar all over the tan bedspread.

"She runnin' a bad fever," the girl said, her voice quaking with fear. "And I been tryin' to take out the piercings in her face and ears, cuz look. They all red and pus-y."

"*Sheeel...*" Pearl wheezed. "*Need to get to...uh...black church...*"

"A what?" I asked.

"She keep saying that," the girl said, flittering her fingers nervously. "Talkin' 'bout some black church somewhere.

'Need to git to a black church.' She needin' some gospel? I don't know. Try and lif' her up, and let's take her to—"

"NOOOOO!" Pearl screamed, swinging and clawing at the air, before falling into a hoarse coughing fit. "No hospitals! *Duuuuu...Duuuumuzi...*"

"How long have you two been here?" I asked.

"*Dumuzi...*" Pearl croaked.

"Been here a minute," the girl named MeShayle said. "Bout three days or so. We done met at the club. Took me a minute 'fore I realized who she was. Friend of mine's used tuh play yo' rec'rd alla time. Thass how come I realized. Pearl and me met and we was just chillin'. All good. Jus' mellow. Kinda scar'ded me at first, a little, but she seem fine to me in a way. She real nice, and we's jus' talkin'. Then we come back here. I used tuh come here a real lot."

"You a whore?" I asked straight out. The girl didn't flinch.

"Hate that word...but yeah, guess so," she said. "Or I used tuh was. Was, am, I don't know. But it ain't like that right now."

"She can't pay you," I said. "Sorry to say."

"I don't care none 'bout that!" the girl shouted, angry and scared. "I like her!"

"Whatever."

"We just talkin' and havin' fun at firs'. After a bit she say she done run out her medicine and she hurtin', so I give her somethin' to jus' take the edge off. Ain't no thing."

"Show me what you gave her."

She handed me a small pharmacy bag. Inside I found a prescription bottle of Oxycodone tablets. And also a tube of Lidocaine jelly.

"Been a rough month," she said with a shrug, absently rubbing the backs of her thighs.

"I know it has," I said. *I know just what you've been through, little thing.* "So how many of these Oxy-whatevers, these Percocets. How many did you give her?"

"Jus' one."

"Just one?! Then *this* happened? Come on. That chick

could eat a whole crate of these and not feel it."

"It ain't happen when she took the pill. It happen after we...you know..."

"I see."

Pearl seemed to calm a little, still moaning and heaving deep breaths, saliva and dark bile glazing her bottom lip.

"It was real nice," MeShayle said. "Jus' fun and easy. She seem to like it a real lot. But then I done waked up, looked over in bed, and fount'ed her like this!"

Suddenly, Pearl's eyes shot open, rolled up white like she used to get on stage. She gasped, and said, in that deep, gravelly drawl—

"*Let me in, y'all. Ah c'n help.*"

And right at that moment there was a pounding at the door. MeShayle and I froze, still as ice. It pounded again.

"*Minnie? Shel?*" Pearl growled again. "*Let. Me. In.*"

Cautiously, I slid over to the door. I looked through the peephole, but it was black. There came a wrapping on the door again, and I slowly opened it.

Standing there in the hall was a gaunt, ashen corpse of a man, green flannel hunting jacket, red mesh Peterbilt cap with eyes to match. I stepped back, and he limped awkwardly into the room.

"*Come on, y'all,*" Pearl and the man said in unison, "*y'all cain't leave her like 'is.*"

He hobbled over to Pearl, and immediately started undoing her jean shorts. She continued to moan and cough, spitting up a bit, but did not resist him. In a flash, and without thinking, I grabbed the top of his head with my right arm, pressed his back to my chest, and held the blade of my butterfly knife to his throat.

"Cuz'n," I said, "you touch that girl's fly and I'll open you up like a Pez dispenser."

He didn't fight me. He didn't even blink. He merely said, "Say there, Min."

"I don't know you, fucka," the girl replied.

"Fair enough," he said. "But tell me somethin', Minnie.

You got pretty friendly with this girl earlier inna evenin', am I right?"

"Nunna yo' goddamn bi'ness."

"She maybe, possibly, got somethin' inner'stin' about her clit?"

Pause. Then,

"She...she done got a silver hoop through it."

For real? I didn't know that.

"It's nickel," he said. "But close enough."

"So what?" MeShayle said.

"You saw whut them rings in her ears, nose and eyebrows did. Whut do you wager that nickel hoop is doin' to her—" I let go of the man, and he limped off toward the bathroom. "Here's the thing, folks," he said, "I don't want to get into no pissin' contest 'bout who of the three of us is the one most closest to Pearl Harbor: Her best friend...her short-time lover—*cum*—savior...or the asshole inside her brain. We all got a fair case. But I'm gonna just go 'head and defer to y'all. Somebody else can tend to her delicate needs."

His vanished into the bathroom. We heard him turn on the shower, and the young Black hooker ran over to Pearl, pulled off her bra and blue jean shorts, and unhooked the aforementioned nickel ring. Pearl gave a tiny shriek of pain as the hoop unhooked, but never opened her eyes.

Instead, stark naked, Pearl turned to her side and coughed out a thick spattering of black tar across the off-white cotton pillow.

"*Who is he?*" MeShayle asked me in a whisper, absently turning the nickel clit ring over and over in her hands.

"That's...Anton," I said, in spite of myself. "I thought he was dead."

"You sho' he ain't?"

"Bring her in, Shel," Anton called from the bathroom.

I scooped Pearl up in my arms, and she grabbed a desperate hold onto my shoulders. Her skin was slathered with sweat and blazing hot. I carried her into the bathroom, MeShayle following behind. Anton opened the shower door.

"Thass freezin' cold in there!" MeShayle said, catching a bit of mist.

"It's gotta be, Minnie," said Anton. "We gotta git that fever down."

I set Pearl down on the floor of the shower stall and she screamed from the cold, clawing at me, buckling into herself, vomiting forward into the drain.

"There you go, sugar," Anton said softly. "Git alla that poison out."

"Don't leave me!" Pearl screamed, clutching at her head and shaking, and hacking more black. "Please! Help me! I'M DYING!" But Anton shut the shower door, and ushered us out.

"Is she…Is she dyin'?" MeShayle asked, still fidgeting with her fingers, her bottom lip quivering.

Anton chuckled, like sandpaper over asphalt.

"Dyin', Min? Absolutely not. She is *healing.* Her body's rejectin' all them toxins and sickness and foreign refuse she done pumped into herself over the years. And now it's all goin' down the drain." We heard Pearl scream out again, but none of us moved. I was concerned for a moment about other guests complaining, but I guess they didn't mind the bloodcurdling screams emanating from room #7. Or they didn't care.

"Fer a body as scarred and wrecked and polluted as Pearl's," Anton continued, "I'm sure it feels like an agonizin' death fer her right now. But no. She's healin' instead. Even torn muscles and fractured bones will be new again, as terr'ble as that must feel at the moment. Come sunrise, she'll be as fresh n' pure as a newborn baby."

"For fucksake," I said. "That's fuckin' clownshoes, cuz'n."

"Is it, Shel? Lookit yer arms." I looked down and saw that my forearms were a wet rainbow smear of colored ink. "It's her tattoos," he said. "Her body's gettin' rid of all of it. Everythin' alien. Her body is cleanin' house."

He limped over to the room's only chair and fell back into it with a discomforted grunt. No older than early forties, if that, but he moved like an elderly man. And I wondered if I did too. We were both in the same crash, after all.

I went to the bathroom sink to wash the ink from my forearms, deliberately avoiding a look over toward Pearl in the shower. She never spoke, but I could hear her coughing and crying. If what Anton said was true, I couldn't imagine the pain she was in.

"But...but how come?" MeShayle asked. "How come this happenin' to her?"

"Because of you, Skinny Minnie," Anton said with a dark smile. "You touched her. You healed her."

"Come on now," she said, pulling all the sheets and soiled blankets off the bed. She tossed them on the floor in the corner, and plopped down on the bare mattress. "Wittout gettin' too wrong wid it, I'll just say that I done *touched* LOTSA people. An' I ain't *never* healt'd nobody befo'."

"Well," Anton said casually, "you ain't never been pregnant before. Surprisingly enough."

"W-what?!" she said, startled. "I...I...I ain't pregnant."

Finally clean of the ink (more or less) I came back to the main room and sat on the floor.

"You wanna piss test it, Min?" Anton said with a gray, broken grin. "Have I been wrong about anythin' so far? Look, darlin'. I don't know whut it is that's growin' inside yer belly, but it's somethin' special. I do know that. And I think it has come to save us all."

"Spit it out, cuz'n," I said. "Whatever you have to say. No more games."

"This here's the dawn of the apocalypse," he said.

"So I've been told."

"When I realized that, I thought, Welp, this is it. It's the end of the line. The end of the world. Fine. Cool. I was ready to tap out anyway. Fixin' to lay down my own little 9/11, to tell the Lord's honest truth. Pretty bent on killin' myself...and as many of the bastards whut fucked me as I could, and that's no lie. I just saw this whole world fallin' straight into hell."

"No doubt," I said, just as MeShayle said—

"I know thass right."

"But now I know," he said, bloodshot eyes a-light with a peculiar joy I'd not yet seen. "Now I know the truth. The good news. The Lord has sent someone to heal this world. Someone to heal us all."

"Who?"

"Her," he said, indicating MeShayle, "and her child-to-be."

Riiiiiiiiight…

"Balls to that shit, my man," I said. "Sorry. Not buyin' it."

"You don't believe in god, Sheldon?" Anton said. "Well, it believes in you. I ain't sayin' that it will protect you from harm, cuz you know yerself and damn well that it sure as hell won't. I ain't even sayin' that it loves you. But it done *chose you.* It chose all of us. Them visions in yer head, Shel, they ain't exactly dancin' sugar plums, now are they."

He's got ya there, old boy.

"No. They're sure not."

"You think they happen fer no reason? Seein' whut you've seen now, whut you done seen tonight right before yer own eyes…you really think it's fer no reason?"

"I don't know…" I said, my doubt slowly fading, as I clung to it hard. "I don't know what I think." And I didn't. "But… okay…so why us?"

"Why not us? Why anybody? Listen. Many moons ago, when I got back home from Iraq—not the current adventure—*Daddy* Bush's war…all fucked up I was, boy howdy. Sick and poisoned. Destroyed. My marriage ruined. Dishonorably discharged. Devastated. And I was goddamn *sick.* Jeezus Christ, was I sick. So I did whut sick people do. I medicated myself. Git it in the vein, and the pain subsides. The shit works. Fer a while anyhow."

"True enough," I said.

"But then," he continued, "To top it all off, I start to hearin' voices. Just a little at first, but then…holy hell. *All the time.* They won't shut up. I push off more and more, tryin' to quiet my mind again…and they just git louder. 'What's goin' on?' I think. I'm crackin' up. I start readin' up on whut's down, writin' letters, chattin' up online tryin' to git some answers. I come to hear 'bout all these other poor sumbitches, with *Gulf War Syndrome* they call it, catchin' schizophrenia."

"I don't really think you can *catch* schizophrenia, cuz'n."

"However in hell you git it, I got it. That's whut I thought anyhow. But then...I heard y'all's music...Stigmata Dog...and I rec'nized the voice on the CD...she's one of *my* voices! *Pearl.* And I wondered...Could she hear me too?"

"I know the answer to that one."

"I started gittin' flashes too. Visions. Some of the same ones you done got, Shel. I'll bet they was. But even still, I thought I was just a loony bird. I wanted to die. I wanted this all over and done with. I was fixin' to die. Some kinda blaze of glory. Even before them Islams beat me to it."

"Yeah..."

"Then one night, my friends and me are toolin' along the highway headin' on our way to a big music concert...and a semi-truck flips, and crushes us. BAM! All my friends are squished. Dead. And I'm lyin' in a ditch, prayin' fer death to take me too. *Please please please* god...When just then, out of the nuthin' and the night sky, comes a white light floodin' all round me. And a choir of angels. Or some kinda shit. And they tell me, well...*everything.* About the comin' apocalypse, the end of the world, the start of the new world. They tell me 'bout each of y'all. Not much. Just vague little puzzle pieces I gotta click together on my own. And they tell me we all got serious work to do. A new world to build. And we need to prepare the way of the Lord." He indicated MeShayle's belly. She covered it with her hands reflexively.

And so here we are...

The three of us sat and talked until daybreak. We each told our story, how we came to be in the place we were. A lot of pain there. A lot of pain none of us could make sense of. *Until now.*

"I never did feel that I was special or nothin'," MeShayle said. "I never done felt'd like I was worth nothin' to nobody."

"Well, little girl," Anton said. "Here you are. You are a

healer. And you very well may be the mother of god. The savior is growin' inside of you as we speak. If that don't count as special, then I definitely need to git out more."

"So now what?" I said.

Just then we heard the shower water shut off finally. A minute or so later Pearl emerged from the bathroom, naked, clean…

…and as pure as the driven snow.

Her tattoos, gone. *Gone.*

Her scars, gone.

Track marks, gone.

The color streaks in her hair, gone.

The pain and rage and sorrow in her eyes entirely gone. So much so that I hardly recognized her anymore. She was some different person now. Someone I had never met. Someone no one had met. Some feather-soft alien with baby eyes, fragile as spun glass. She radiated health, and blinkered confusion.

"Somebody want to hand me some clothes?" she said.

"How do you feel?" I asked.

"Like I've been scrubbed out with steel wool," she said.

As Pearl dressed I asked the assembled once again, "So now what?"

"Whut do you think, Pearl?" Anton asked. "Do you think our bond is cut? Finally? Are we free, you and me?"

"I sure hope so," she said.

"Me too," said Anton. "We don't need to live in each other's head no more."

"Because," she said matter-of-fact, "we're going to live together. All of us."

What does that mean? I thought.

"Jesus," Pearl continued, taking deep, clean breaths, her hand pressed across her chest. "I've never felt like this before. It's really kind of scary. I can see and feel and taste and hear and smell *everything at once*. Everything. It's overwhelming. Like an assault of the senses."

"How so?" I asked.

"You know how a soft, warm blanket can comfort an

infant straight to sleep," she said, "but a bright light or a sudden noise can throw her into hysterics? That makes complete sense to me now." She sat and looked at her body, her clear, soft skin, and shook her head. She stretched her back, pain-free for the first time in years. "My feet are so soft, the sensation of this carpet against them is almost more than I can handle. If I had an orgasm right now, it would probably kill me. And believe it or not, I don't want to try it."

"You were talking about some *black church*, Pearl," I said. "What was that about?"

"I haven't got a clue," she said.

"Blackchurch is where the chosen will assemble," said Anton. "'Bout two and a half hours from here. That's where we're meant to go. It's really just a couple of blocks in a poor neighborhood. But that's where we're goin' to."

"You ever been there?" I asked.

"Once, long ago," he said. "A friend of mine lived there, before she went insane and murdered her girlfriend. No shit. The place didn't seem special to me at the time. But I was blind then. I see more clearly now."

"Me too," said Pearl, rubbing her eyes. "And it's goddamn freaky." Chuckles all around. "I never thanked you, Min," Pearl said. "Thank you for the lovely roll in the hay. No one has ever done that to me before. Forgive me if I don't want to do it ever again."

MeShayle smiled and covered her face with her hands, embarrassed, still stunned. Who wouldn't be?

"I jus' cain't believe it," MeShayle said. "I cain't believe none of this. I cain't even believe I be havin' a baby." I was a little taken aback that she was so easy to accept this, that she didn't even want to try a pregnancy test to be sure. "I couldn't even guess who the fatha could be."

"It don't matter," said Anton. "We're all gonna to help you with that child. We're all responsible. All of us in the circle. And right now our circle is only missin' one."

"Who are we missing?" asked Pearl.

"D'antre Philips," Anton said.

"Who is D'antre Philips?" I asked.

"*After the flood...*" Pearl whispered.

"What?"

"I don't know," Pearl replied.

"I don't really know him either," said Anton. "He knows we're comin'. That I do know. Saw to that m'self. But I don't know if he knows why. I don't either, fer that matter. I don't know who he is or whut he does or why he is one of us."

"Whoever *we* are," I said.

"Exactly." He continued, "I've been told his name, and that we would find him in Blackchurch. That's all. I ain't never met the man."

"I have," said MeShayle. She reached into her purse and pulled out a handwritten slip of paper holding a Cincinnati address and the name *D'antre Philips.* "Never did think I'd actually ever use this."

"Well, my friends," Anton said, "I'd say we best be on our way."

And that's how we ended up on your doorstep, cuz'n. Not a word of it a lie.

BLACKCHURCH FURNACE AND OTHER TALES

OR

For Proper Care and Maintenance of Ancient and Angry Gods

Welcome to Blackchurch

I tell you the truth, it will be more bearable for Sodom and Gomorrah on the day of judgement than for that town.

—Matthew 10:15

Blackchurch is not the sort of place where folks are inclined to be up in each other's business. Strange houseguests at a neighbor's pad are not likely to be noticed, let alone remarked upon. So on a day in early October, when two beat-up-looking crackers, a pregnant teenage whore, and a small, androgynous Japanese woman in a large-brimmed sombrero, sunglasses, and wrapped in a patchwork down comforter came to call on D'antre Philips with heads full of prophetic visions and tales of the apocalypse already in progress, nary an eye was blinked. *Shit like that just happens round here, y'heard?* And what's one more new religion to an area that matches churches to gun shops and liquor stores one-to-one. When the end times do come to Blackchurch, it'll be a day like any other day. And the next day will be too.

Shit like that just happens round here…

As for D'antre Philips himself, a saner man in a saner place and time would have questioned this. Would have thought it at least peculiar, if not thoroughly batshit. But D'antre didn't qualify as sane. Nor did Blackchurch. Or 2005. *The Portuguese said it best, onna real. Kay…sump'n sump'n. Aw'ight? Just roll widdit.*

"So, um, yeah," D'antre said to his guests. "Nice to meet y'all. This is Blackchurch. This here is THE Blackchurch. Corner of Blackstone and Churchwalk, as you can see."

"The street sign says *Desmond*," Pearl said, her voice muffled a bit by the comforter she had wrapped around her.

"Yeah," D'antre replied, "e'ryone 'round here call it Churchwalk, though."

"Oh."

"I'll show y'all inside the place in a few. There's a repair guy checkin' out the furnace downstairs and he, uh, ain't havin' a good day, y'heard?"

The five walked the perimeter of the old church building, down a side alley, through the glass-spattered gravel parking lot (Shel carrying the shoeless Pearl piggyback), past the old, empty orphanage and the half-way house. The five, together at last, for the first time. Having no clear understanding of what brought them together. Or why. Not even Anton, though his faith was strong. *God has a plan for us. God knows what it's doing.*

"Back when this was a actual church," D'antre said, "it was 'ffiliated with the orphanage and elementary school. It was a Catholic church back inna day, but I don't 'member the name. *Our Lady of Eternal Suffering*, or some shit."

"This joint looks like it should be haunted," Pearl said.

"It is," D'antre replied. "Seems to be anyway. Usually late at night, but sometimes in the middle of the afternoon, you'll sense the presence. You might-could hear the faint chatter of disembodied voices echoing all through. I ain't even playin'. But, for those of you 'customed to hearin' voices, don't 'spect to hear nothin' worthwhile, knamsayin?"

"Used to that," Pearl and Anton said in unison.

"All they be doin' is prayin', complainin', and axin' god for shit. Now, f'real, if they prayers wasn't answered in life, I don't know what they think they be accomplishin' now, knahmean? Word. Straight *irritating*. But they don't hurt nothin'."

"Thass good to hear," said Min, shoulders tense and squared.

"A coupla friendly neighborhood baseheads been gatherin' mattresses for the past coupla weeks for folks—*y'all*, I guess—to sleep on. Don't worry, I scrubbed 'em out. There some in the balcony, some in the old sacristy. Aw'ight? Speakin' on that subject, there's a group of 'em squattin' down in the cellar. Keep to they own selfs, mostly. I don't really know how many, but they cool. Dirty as fuck, and stank as all hell, but good people overall, knahmean?"

"Stank and dirty?!" Anton said, his heavy eyes suddenly bright and alive. "Petey Wheatstraw!"

"Ummm...yeah," D'antre said, more startled than he probably should have been, all things considered. "How you know 'bout Petey?"

"Same as I know about all y'all," Anton replied, tapping his forehead. "He's a prophet, I'm told."

"Oracle actually," D'antre said. "Got a business card and e'rything."

"Is he around?" Anton asked. "I need to talk with—"

No sooner did the question leave Anton's mouth, when out old Petey came, through a thick oak door which lead straight to the church cellar. On cue. With an air of pious serenity, like Moses wrapped in a plastic trash bag.

"Yeah son," D'antre replied. "S'yah lucky day, y'heard?"

"Welcome, weary travelers," said Petey with a great smile and grand salute, ragged and bedraggled, yet with incongruously perfect white teeth. "Greetings, you who are highly favored, for the Lord is with you. Welcome seers and saints and speakers of the Good Word. Welcome to the Castle of River Sam!"

They all looked over to D'antre with questioning eyes (all sans Anton, who appeared to understand perfectly). D'antre gave them a nod and a look back that said, *I'll explain later.*

Petey walked over toward Min, but did not touch her. When he spoke again, his voice was tender. "Welcome, Me-Shayle Ida Nodding. Child of light, mother of salvation. May you find safety and comfort here, amongst friends."

"A'ight," Min said with a nervous smile. "Thanks. A real lot."

"And how are you feeling now, Ms. Yoshimoto?" Petey asked, turning toward Pearl. "How does it feel to be healed?

To be pure before god?"

"It's taking some getting used to," Pearl replied, removing her sombrero and sunglasses, squinting in the mild mid-day sun. "We'll see how it goes."

"Indeed we will, my dear. Indeed we will." Pause. "So," Petey continued to the assembled. "Here we are. Here we are, standing at the epicenter of the new beginning. Mark Twain's famous, though likely apocryphal, quip about being in Cincinnati during the end of the world now seems ironically prophetic, yes? HA!" Petey laughed heartily, deep from his chest, as did Anton. Everyone else chuckled. Only D'antre actually caught the reference. Petey turned to Anton with a military salute. "Corporal Anton Poole. Brother Anton, welcome at last."

"Thank you, brother," Anton replied. They embraced forcefully, Anton not at all squeamish about the filthy state of his fellow prophet. "Good to meet you finally, Ol' Pete. God, it's weird as shit to be back here. I ain't been to this place since my friend—"

"Slashed her lover's throat," Petey said, somber but direct. "And the boys in blue had to take her down like an animal. Such a waste. Such a beautiful lady. Both of them. Tragic, tragic day."

"I saw that," Shel said. "In my mind. In my dreams. Or some version of it. But…I don't know…"

"How much can we trust dreams and visions, right Sheldon?" Petey said with a sympathetic nod. "I don't really know either. I wish I had an answer. We just need to put our trust in god."

"That's right," Anton said. "Sometimes you just gotta have faith."

"The Lord has given us these gifts for a reason, friends," said Petey. "We have to believe in that."

"What happened to the baby?" Min asked. "Anton's homegirl done killt'd the baby mama. What happened to him?"

"Ward of the state, I believe." Petey replied. "If I'm not mistaken, they eventually found a next of kin. I don't know anything else. But I have a feeling *we may hear from that boy yet.*"

It was not uncharacteristic of Petey Wheatstraw to toss off cryptic statements like this without explanation. In fact, it was pretty common. But this particular line drew up a chill that shot through everyone. And yet no one asked what he meant.

"Brother Pete," Anton said finally. "I think me and you, we got some shit to discuss."

"That we do, my friend," Petey replied. "Come with me to the catacombs. I'm not a drinking man normally, but we do have plenty of wine down here. I have much to share. And, I would imagine, much to learn."

The two departed, down through the doors to the cellar, furnace clanging and redneck cursing emanated from the bowels of the Church. Awkward silence was left in their wake. Finally D'antre turned to the remaining three and said, "Y'all wanna peep the hood a minute?"

D'antre felt a peculiar, and thoroughly unexpected, sense of pride creeping up on him as he showed his new friends around the Blackchurch area, and beyond, through Madisonville proper. The condemned buildings, the boarded up store fronts and empty commercial spaces, the vacant, bulldozed lots where viable warehouses and apartments once stood, now felt, not hollow and abandoned, but oddly imbued with promise and potential. A brighter sun seemed to shine down that day. The more they walked, the more D'antre's spirit lifted, more than it had for so long he could scarcely remember. He practically beamed as he talked about how a handful of dedicated local Mad-ville residents had finagled some "weed and seed" money from the government to renovate and renew some particularly troubled spots. Or at least try to. He pointed out some of the new Jimmy Carter houses, and a newly refurbished playground for children, and talked of (hopefully) more to come. All chimed in with individual enthusiasm.

"Blackchurch, son," D'antre said, his voice crackling with a new-found joy, "we ain't playin', right?"

"Well cuz'n," Shel said quite sincerely, "any place where shopkeepers advertise bootleg DVDs on their sandwich boards out on the sidewalk, *and* you can buy fried chicken at the gas station, that's a place I can definitely call home."

"You gotta know somethin', D'antre," Min said emphatic-cally. "I ain't no moocher, and I know my partners here ain't either. We ain't squattin' at yo' crib like them folks inna basement you done mentioned, god love 'em. We gonna throw in our share of rent and alla that, hear?"

"That's right," said Shel.

"Absolutely," Pearl chimed in.

"Cool, y'all," D'antre said with a shrug. "I'm widdit, ya heard? I might-could prolly help with findin' some decent work for whoever be lookin'. I know people here and there."

With no small bit of surprise, D'antre found himself exceedingly glad that these strange people had arrived. He felt that, in some abstract way, he had known them already. That they were somehow meant to come together. That they had some collective purpose, whatever it may be, that was larger than any of them individually.

"Shel," D'antre said. "It is Shel, right?"

"Yep," Shel replied.

"Sheldon Ackerlin?"

"Unfortunately."

"I been gettin' packages witcho' name on it for a minute, dog. Since 2000 at least. From Reseda, California."

"I'm almost afraid to ask."

"DVDs. Tried to watcha a couple of 'em. That shit is wrong, son. *Wrong.* Is a nigga s'posed to yank off to that mess?"

"Business opportunity I let slide. Sorry about that, though."

"I still got 'em if you want 'em."

"No thanks."

"I'll take them," Pearl said.

"Shel," D'antre said, "you mentioned befo' the shit you be seein' in your head. Visions? Dreams?"

"Yeah," Shel replied.

"You said that you saw the murder that happened here. Francine Voight-sex, *whatthafuckever*, you saw in yo' mind what she done did."

"That's right. I've seen lots of shit, cuz'n. And I've seen some of it come true."

"Can you write it all out for me? Much as you can? Imma be keepin' records. A Blackchurch archive. I want *everything*. Not just visions. As much of the whole story as I can get."

"I'll try, dude," Shel said. "But I'm a songwriter. I'm not much of a *writer* writer."

"Just do whatchoo can, son. I'll make it work, ya heard?"

They got back to the Church to find Will Fanon, the furnace service technician, sitting on the side of the building, flushed, flustered, and streaked with dirt. An air of defeat hung about him (and a slight shaking in his fingers told D'antre what was *really* the problem).

"I'm sorry, D'antre," Will Fanon said. "I just can't find it. By the way, there's some dirty old bum hangin' out down there. I was gonna call the police, but I thought he might be an uncle or somethin'."

"Yeah, we all look the same, right?"

"Absolutely."

"Don't worry 'bout'm. He cool."

"Anyhow," Will continued, "I thought for sure that that squealing sound was a slipped blower belt. But no, that's fine. I oiled the shaft bearings, but...hell 'n goddamn, I just don't know."

"The squealing's not an issue," Shel chimed in unsolicited. He shut his eyes and cocked his head to the left, his stronger ear toward the open cellar door. "Either that or you fixed it. That deep-pitched rumble is the bigger problem."

"What?" Will Fanon said. "I didn't hear no rumble."

"It's there," said Shel. "Dirty gas burners maybe?"

"The burners are off, buddy."

"Hmmm," Shel said, opening his eyes and walking into the

cellar. A moment later he shouted from deep inside, "It's right here then!"

Will Fanon gave D'antre a quizzical look. D'antre shrugged. Will wandered in after Shel.

"Well I'll be damned!" they all heard Will Fanon say. Shel returned from the cellar with a look of casual satisfaction about him, Will not long behind him.

"It was just the pilot light," Will said to D'antre. "Needed a bit of adjusting. Easy enough fix. Didn't even think of it...and I sure as shit couldn't hear it!" He turned to Shel in amazement. "You got quite an ear, boy."

"It's a gift, I guess," Shel said. "One decent hand and two crazy ears."

"You ever think of tryin' that one decent hand at HVAC?"

A New and Everlasting Covenant

The three fundamental factors which affect the operation of a furnace are temperature, atmosphere, and pressure.

—Matthew H. Mawhinney,
Practical Industrial Furnace Design (1928)

The four new arrivals in Blackchurch settled in with relative ease. In a rash move (he later regretted) D'antre broke all of the locks on every door leading into The Church, declaring it an open space for all who wished to come. Petey Wheatstraw applauded the move saying, "All who have been called are welcome." And so began the coming together of the New Tribe.

The first time Pearl and Sheldon set foot inside the Church itself was instant rapture.

"The acoustics! Oh my fuck, Shel, the acoustics!"

"D'antre," Shel asked, practically spilling over with joy as he and Pearl clapped, stomped their heels, and snapped their fingers inside the main Church hall, testing out the sonic capabilities. "You ever give any thought to turning this place into a performance venue? Maybe even a recording studio too?"

"We should talk, son," D'antre replied. And they would.

Before long Shel made a critical discovery about the furnace in the basement, the very one he had diagnosed his first day in Blackchurch—

"It is, bar none, hands down, the most spectacular percussion instrument I've ever heard," he said breathlessly. "You pound that thing in the basement and mic all of the ducts in the building...my god...my god..." At the risk of putting too fine a point on it, it was *a revelation.*

Shel took Will Fanon up on his offer, and began working in furnace repair with him, while also taking up something of an unofficial apprenticeship as a freelance boiler operator under Fanon's tutelage.

He took to the machines with a passion, particularly taken was he with their intrinsic ambient, even musical, qualities: clanging, rumbling, thumping, roaring, hissing, all glorious to Shel's ravenous ears.

For Fanon, it was Shel's uncanny ability to audibly perceive and locate flaws in the systems, not to mention the additional hand he could provide, that made him such an asset to the operation (This is to saying nothing of Shel's ability to be a thoroughly functional drunk, which no doubt endeared him to the older man on a personal level).

Pearl picked up a position slinging steaming hot joe right around the corner at a family-owned, self-described "Christian coffee shop" called *Jefferson Beans N' Cream* ("These are Holy Grounds!").

Proprietors Malachi and Shonda Jefferson were quite enamored of Pearl right from the start, particularly tickled were they to discover that she was a professional musician (although, admittedly, they were unfamiliar with her work). They offered the shop's modest stage as a place for her and Shel to perform acoustic music whenever they would like, provided they kept the "bad swears" to a minimum. They also insisted that she wear at least flip flops while working the counter, for safety reasons. Agreed.

D'antre was able to directly secure gainful employment for both Anton and Min. The Liquid Container factory in Mason, Ohio where D'antre worked full-time was serendipitously in need of a first-shift forklift driver, a job with which Anton had a good amount of experience from his days knocking around Tennessee. Anton and D'antre would greet each other during shift change with a "See ya at home!" thus prompting a number of line workers to ask D'antre on several occasions—

"Y'all fags er sumthin'?"

To which D'antre would only reply, "Quit tryin' to oppress me!"

D'antre also successfully convinced the Madisonville Branch public library to give his shelving position to Min, her bookstore experience a definite plus (and no one need know of her pregnancy yet).

She enjoyed this work very much, and felt right at home in Madisonville...although she did feel an awkward twinge she couldn't quite make sense of whenever someone checked out a copy of *Princess Africa Jones*. She knew full well that, if she wanted to, she could tell them, "That's me! I modeled for that book!" But that might bring about many questions she did not want to have to answer. So she kept silent, and obscure, and anonymous.

Petey Wheatstraw continued his habit of bringing his drafting paper and dark pencils into the library, drawing away in his spot in the back corner, next to the microfiche machine. If there were other people around he would mutter to himself about Jesus masturbating to child pornography or whatever it was, until someone complained to the Head Librarian and she threatened to toss him out (at which point he would mutter the exact same things, only quieter). But the second it was only he and Min in the vicinity, the act shifted.

"You have nothing to be ashamed of, my dear," he'd say, "and every cause for pride. God has chosen you, Min, and you and your precious child-to-be will heal this wretched Earth. You are beautiful, you are holy, and you are loved. And your family grows by the day. Never despair, my child. Never despair."

She laughed this language off at first, attempting to dismiss it with an eye-roll and a "Wha'evah."

"You'll see what I mean in time," he said with a kind and knowing smile. "You'll see. You are most favored by The One Most High."

"Lotta muhfuckas pretty goddamn high up in Blackchurch, I know that much. Don't know that I could pick the *most high*, hear?"

Petey would just laugh. "You don't even realize how important you are, child. But you will."

"Psssht, nigga please. I ain't nobody's *magical Negro*, a'ight? Fuck ALLA dat. And somebody say this bitch got a heart of gold? Somebody done tol' ya wrong, old nigga."

But, eventually, and perhaps inevitably, his soft, grandfatherly voice and warm, tender eyes won her over in the end.

Then someone would walk by, and he'd whistle like a parrot and say, "Dip dip dip. Oh green machine, lean on my bean, toot toot." And she would giggle. And he would wink and tap his nose.

One afternoon she happened to snatch a glimpse of what he was drawing: a detailed schematic of a line of row houses... branching off left and right, with The Church on the corner of Blackstone and Desmond at the center. A caption written in the top left corner read: *For the Disciples*. Min simply walked away. She never asked questions.

Days turned to weeks, and The Church became, in its own way, downright domestic. Min, Shel, D'antre, Pearl and Anton would talk, hour upon hour, sharing their past lives, periodically searching for—and often finding—common threads connecting them to each other. They would frequently have a meal together, usually around two-thirty in the morning when D'antre got home from the factory. More and more they related to one another as friends, as family, strictly in "real world" terms. Hardly ever did they refer to the seemingly supernatural forces that had brought them together, and what said forces might ultimately want from them.

Such discussions were instead the domain of Anton and Petey Wheatstraw, which seemed to suit everyone just fine.

Often, after the shared meal, and they had finished cleaning up, Anton would venture down to the catacombs to meet with Petey. Pearl and Shel would proceed to work on their music either in the main hall or up in the balcony (moving gradually down into the furnace room in the cellar), periodically asking someone to come for a listen or even to join in. Some level of incessant sound (and more than occasional full-blown cacophony) was *de rigueur* in The Church, music (of a sort) melding with faint, chattering voices...all slathered with dull, ethereal static (as Shel pointed out, the ghost whispers were actually coming through the heating vents, a distinction he felt was a crucial one). It was never silent there. Ever. Even in those rare moments when it was completely empty.

At first there was little interaction between "Upper Church" (D'antre, Pearl, Shel, Min, and Anton as the go-between) and "Lower Church" (the squatters in the cellar). This was not due to any open hostility on anyone's part. Petey Wheatstraw, and his long-time companion Loraina (known throughout Blackchurch as Loraina the Tweak) simply felt that "his children," as they called them, weren't quite ready to officially meet the new arrivals...especially Min. All this would come in proper time. Anton, acting as liaison and representative of Upper Church, agreed wholeheartedly. The four who dwelled mostly in Upper Church seldom went down to the cellar, except (at Shel's behest) to sing, scream, and pound on the furnace with rag-tied mallets.

Anton, of course, thoroughly supported these endeavors, as he remained Shel and Pearl's #1 fan (whether they were still Stigmata Dog or not). Petey applauded and encouraged these clattering musical ventures as well, seeing this sound as he did, as the sacred works of the new world to come.

"This, my friends, is truly a joyful noise."

Songs of Love and Praise

And I heard a sound from heaven like the roar of rushing waters and like a loud peal of thunder.

—Revelation 14:2

"Man, D, whut's with yer movies, bud?"

An early-autumn storm rattled the loose panes of The Church windows as Shel and Pearl worked through the night and into the morning composing their new masterpiece down in the main Church hall. They had discovered, and subsequently re-tubed, an old Hammond organ that had been buried in the back of an overfull storage room, and with it a beat-up PA speaker that Shel repaired to run his new modified electric bass guitar monstrosity through. Played with a metal slide, the bass, in tandem with the organ, sounded roughly like a military aircraft warming its engines somewhere inside The Church.

Meanwhile, Anton, Min and D'antre sat up in D'antre's apartment talking, and assembling baby furniture. Although they had set up a special place for Min in the old sacristy—certainly the coziest, most comfortable spot in the building—she often spent most of her time up in D'antre's place.

After several hours of frustration and near-failure, the baby's bed was finally built, and they could relax at last. Anton perused D'antre's video collection, quite bemused.

"*Roxanne? Legal Eagles? Clan of the Cave Bear*? Whut the fuck is this crap?"

"Maaan, you just don't know," D'antre replied, "*Clan of the Cave Bear* is a adaptation of a literary classic, dog! You ain't hip to that shit? I'll put it on and you tell me it ain't the goods."

"*Dancing at the Blue Iguana*?" Anton continued. "*Casa de los babys*?!?! Whut the hell is that?!"

"I ain't buy that," D'antre lied. "It was a present or sump'n. But look! I got *Blade Runner* up in'is place, and *Kill Bill*. You KNOW that shit is good, son."

"Yeah..." Anton said suspiciously, "I guess so. But you ain't got no Bruce Lee. No *Death Mask of the Ninja*. No *Scarface*. No *Scarface?*! And yer a rapper?! Ain't it against code fer you to not even own a copy of *Scarface*?"

"Aw, I got that shit, kid," D'antre lied again. "Iss in there. Keep lookin'."

Just then a transformer blew outside, and all went dark. And, for a very short moment, silent. Then, in no time at all, they could hear the sound of Shel's acoustic guitar wafting up through the vents, faint but undeterred. Hearing this, Anton laughed out loud, and slapped his hand across his knee.

"No shit! HA! I LOVE that song! It's an old Stigmata Dog cut! *This Whole Side of Town*. Hell yes. But they're...singing new lyrics, though. Sounds like...it's about Blackchurch now. How 'bout that."

"They say they writin' songs 'bout all us," Min said, lighting some candles around the small kitchen.

"Well," D'antre said with a shrug, "it is sacred music, right? And we *are* the chosen ones n' shit. Makes sense." He did not sound convincing. Or convinced. Anton grinned.

"I don't know how 'sacred' you could call them old Stigmata Dog songs," Anton said, "but I'm glad to hear 'em again, I'll tell you whut."

"They usta play at my grammama's joint in New Orleans 'parently," Min said. "Ain't that crazy? How we all tied together."

"It ain't crazy, Min," Anton said in all earnest. "It is god's will."

There was a lot of talk about "god's will" around The Church. Most of the time D'antre left it alone. But every once in a while, he felt it necessary to chime in.

"Was it god's will all the terr'ble shit that done happened to this little girl?" D'antre said, indicating Min. "Was it god's will all that happened to you, dog?"

"I suppose so," Anton replied. "Yeah, I 'spect it was. It has to be."

"Thass a punk-ass god right there for ya."

"The Lord's people always suffer, D," Anton said. "That's part of the gig. Look through all the great holy books; nothin' but severely jacked up people. Across the board, full-on fucked. And hey, we're all damaged, no doubt. Min, and me, and Shel and Pearl. And them folks down in the basement, don't even git me started on them. BUT, although we're all different, all unique, we are all damaged in a lot of similar ways. You know whut I mean?"

"Seems to be true," D'antre said.

"What about you, D?" Min asked. "We ain't heard a real lot of yo' story yet."

"I'm aw'ight," D'antre replied. "Nuh'in too wrong here, knahmean."

"I don't believe you," Anton said.

You right to not believe it, son, D'antre thought. But he said nothing.

"Guess it's how you use it, huh?" Min said. "The *damage.*"

"You gotta offer it up," Anton said. "And know in your heart when it feels right."

"Heard that shit my whole life," D'antre said. "And it ain't never made sense to me."

"It feel right now," Min said, candlelight dancing across her soft, mahogany face. "But I been wrong befo'. I really felt right in Columbus. Not when I was hoin', you know, but at Mike and Marsia's. Alla they friends, who became my friends, they all so cool to me. And e'rybody accept me. Ain't nobody judge me. Or feel sorry for me. We was just all real good together. I belonged'd there. Or so I thought...Show what I know, huh."

"What happened?" D'antre asked. "What went wrong?"

"Well..." Min said...

Marsia and Mike, they like to think of theyselfs as real...I don't know...edgy and shit. Diff'rent from "normal" people, whatever those are. But turn'd out they wasn't so diff'rent after all...

A lotta the folks who been crashin' at they crib had been headin' out. Goin' on back to school and shit. After while it was just five of us left...kinda like now! Ha! And we was all just gettin' real...just real close, the five of us. Mike and Marsia had been kinda-half-jokin' that we should all just git it overwit and git our freak on group-style. But we all be just laughin' it off. We be drinkin' a real lot, and shit just gits said, you know. Can't take it too serious. But I could tell it wasn't really a alla-way joke. They was layin' down a vibe that they was wantin' to bring a third party into they bedroom mix, ain't no matter if it was a guy or a girl, you know? But of the three poss'ble contenders it was pretty clear who it WUD'NT gonna be.

"Who?" Anton asked.

"Them other two besides me," Min answered with a chuckle. "Dalton and Chen, these two queer boys inna house."

"How come not one of them?"

"Cuz them two's IN LOOOVE. Deep, crazy in love. I mean, Mikal and Marsia, they was in love wid each other too...still are I 'spect...I hope...but them two gay boys...goddamn...I ain't never seen two people so genuinely locked in to each other. And only each other. You know that old song, *I only have eyes for youuuuuu shoo-bop shoo-bop*? Thass them two. Ain't no way either them gonna git in bed wit a straight couple, no matter how much they got love for 'em. So... well..."

It was way more awkward at first than I ever woulda thought it'da been. I mean, I ain't know what to do to git the ball rollin'. So to speak. If somebody ain't droppin' bills and tellin' me 'xactly what they want, I don't know whass what, you know? And Mike and Marsia, they ain't know either. They new to it same as me.

So Chen and Dalton was away fo' the weekend, and it was just us three up inna crib. We all knew it was the time now to do it, if ever…but how's it s'ppose to start? I guess we was all too nervous to make the first move.

Marsia try her best to git it goin', talkin' flirty, dancin' round in her underthangs. But wudn't nothin' really makin' it. Finally, it was real late, and we finally had nuff wine I guess, and we all just start kissin'. Like outta nowhere. It was real weird.

At first, Marisa ain't want Mikal and me to touch each other. But, I guess it got hot to her at some point, and she was really all 'bout it.

"Go ahead, baby, touch her," she coo in his ear, "Kiss her nipples, rub her clitty," alla that, really gettin' it, playin' with herself and all. 'Fore I know it, Mikal right above me, and his wife guidin' his dick wit her fingers, slidin' it right up into my stuff. Just right up in it, workin' it. It was…a'ight, I guess. This what e'rybody wanted, you know? Wha'evah. So we doin' it, and Marsia kissin' me, then kissin' Mikal, and he pumpin' away inside me. Slow at first, but gettin' more intense… pumpin' harder…and harder…

And then…it happen.

He on toppa me, we lock in together, and he look me straight inna eyes fo' the first time since we done started…and I saw somethin'. Somethin' in the way he lookin' at me. It was diff'rent now. This wudn't just some kinda-kinky fun 'tween friends no more. It was serious. I done got to him. It wudn't just my pussy, either. It was alla me. It was clear. I don't know if it was…I don't know if he fell in love wit me…I don't know nothin' 'BOUT love…but there's too much sadness in his eyes…too much wantin'…Too much for it to be just 'bout a quick nut, hear? Our eyes met, him deep up in me, I hook my feet right above his ass and arch my lower back just a little… and that was it.

And then we all got real still. Cuz it just got real.

"You weren't supposed to come inside her!" Marsia cry. "You're supposed to only come in me!!!" She broke out in hard tears, and ran out the room.

Mikal roll offa me, pale as a sheet. Even more paler than

normal, an' thass pretty fuckin' pale. He slowly stand up, and walk on out the bedroom, never once lookin' back at me. And I just lay there, confused as all hell, wit his cold mess leakin' out my pussy. And I knew somebody was gonna hafta go.

Marisa sob and beg me not to go away. Sayin' she love me and I ain't got to leave out. She say she sorry for gettin' upset, and it just startled her and all, but e'rything okay now.

But Mikal...he just stare away. Off inna cold distance. Never sayin' nothin'. Couldn't even look at me no more.

Thass how he done threw me out. Widdout no word spoken.

I was hurt, hear? Believe. I was so goddamn hurt. And scared. I ain't know where to go, or what to do. So I, you know, just fell back into it. Back into the only thing I really did know...

"You talked to them since?" D'antre asked.

"Nuh," Min said. "Ain't talk to nobody. Dalton and Chen was blowin' up my phone for a minute. But I lost my cell service 'fore I could ever holla back. I ditch my phone, and alla my contact info. 'Cept yours, D'antre."

"I wouldn't leave that shit hang, girl," D'antre said. "Fuck loose ends, knahmean? Thass some bullshit."

Ironic, coming from him.

"I gotta axe you somethin', D," Min said. "You still got a agent for yo' books?"

"Far as I know."

"You think, if I give you a copy of Mikal's book, you might-could pass it along to yo' man? It would sure help him out a real lot. He ain't got no connections inna book world."

D'antre blinked in astonishment. Anton simply smiled. Further proof, as if he needed any more, of why god had chosen Min as the mother of the new savior. *Purity of heart... purity of heart...*

"Well..." D'antre said, "I ain't holla'd at my boy Sal in a minute. But I...uh...for real?"

"Am I angry?" Min said, "Yes. Is my heart broke that he

done kicked me out? Yes. But he still my friend. I still care 'bout him. And want the best for botha them. Help him. Please, D. If you can."

"I'll...I'll try my best."

The rain outside eased up just a bit. For a moment the lights flickered on, but then went out again. Not too far in the distance they heard gunshots and wailing sirens.

"What do y'all wanna bet," Anton said, "Shel's downstairs beatin' his own ass right now cuz he cain't record that?"

They all laughed.

"Hey, this is Blackchurch," D'antre said. "Plenty more where that came from, y'heard?"

A loud crash of thunder exploded right outside the window, and Anton jerked hard reflexively. He shuddered for a moment, eyes tight. Then he was fine.

"You a'ight, A?" Min asked.

Anton smiled, embarrassed.

"Still git a bit of the war shakes from time to time," he said. "Funny thing is, I was the one in the tank, so a lotta time the thunder was my doin'!"

I joined up at the start of 1989. I had just got married to Evangeline McDonald, girl I was sweet on since elementary school. My family was so proud of me, especially my old man. I come from Army people. Did basic at Fort Jackson, moved around a bit from there, then headed off to Germany. Third Armored Division, that was us. Met Schwarzkopf and ever'thing. We was sent to Saudi Arabia fer the grand openin' of Operation: Desert Shield. Then off to Iraq fer the real party.

Saw a lot of bad shit there. Did a lot of bad shit there too. But I made some good friends there, among them Sergeant Frannie Woyzeck, the chick who...used to live here. Great lady. Great soldier. Ever'body called her the "secret dyke," which was funny cuz it wasn't much of a secret. She was cool, though. Couldn't nothin' rattle her cage...or so I thought. When Baby Bush decided to invade Iraq, Frannie was first in line to re-up. Me, not so much. The shit was different by then.

By 1991 I had done my time, and I was headin' home. I

thought, except fer a bit of blisterin' on my forearms, that I'd made it through Desert Storm more or less without a scratch.

I was wrong. Boy howdy, was I wrong.

And I shoulda seen it comin'. I just knew somethin' was weird about the color of the sand in Zakhu…

Got home in August of '91. Went back to work at the printin' factory, settled into a nice house in Sweetwater with Eva, and was ready to really start my life. Yeah…it was good. It was real good.

Christmas day that year we found out Eva was pregnant. Hella-excited. Our families was beyond thrilled. Eva'd been wantin' a baby fer as long as I'd known her. Happiest time of my life. Hands down, the happiest.

Over the next coupla months, though, I started gettin' bad headaches. And dizzy spells. Docs all said I was fine. Hey, just suck it up, right? But it was gettin' worse. And some of my friends were having problems too.

The DoD put out a report about "Gulf War Syndrome," particularly the effects of depleted uranium that may or may not have been in play on the field of battle. They concluded that small traces could linger in the kidneys, but there was no real need for concern. Okay then, case closed.

A year to the day that I returned home from Iraq, Eva's water broke. She'd had a rough pregnancy, and was on bed rest the last two months. But she was feelin' great that day. We drove to the hospital excited and nervous, but cool. We was ready. Everything would be just fine…

I'll never forget when the doctor pulled it out of her. That thing. My baby. The nurses all gasped and went white at the sight of it. Never seen nothin' like it. Like somethin' from yer darkest nightmare. Thank god it was dead, I woulda had to have…just thank god. We was devastated…but Eva, she was undeterred. She would be a mama if it killed her. I was worried that it just might. She didn't care.

We tried again. This time she was pregnant for several good months before that one came out in the shower. Like a large tequila worm with hind legs.

"No more," I said. "No more of this. It ain't worth it."

But there was one more. Saw it all the way through to the delivery room again. It lived, but I sure wish it hadn't. I sat next to that hot glass box they kept it in fer the whole three days it was alive. Singin' lullabies. They told me I couldn't do that, but no one really tried to stop me. It was my baby, after all. My little brainless baby. How could it live with no brain? It died on a Thursday morning, praise the Lord. Eva never saw it alive. She had to be wheeled out into emergency care straight from the delivery room, and into isolation. Yeah. It died on a Thursday morning. Eva left me not long after that. Said she didn't blame me...but come on now.

I sought some kinda restitution from Uncle Sam. Funny, right? Hey, I was young. Their docs tested me and said I was tip top. All in my head. Right. Mutant offspring was somehow a product of whut, my imagination?

I banded together with some other vets who was havin' similar problems. We started diggin' round, and found out that, as bad as we got it, the Iraqis got it worse. Birth defects, cancer rates, through the fuckin' roof. One thousand percent, three thousand percent. How is that possible?! And yet the official word was "inconclusive." Me and a coupla guys decided we was gonna take on the brass head on. Not smart. Not smart at all.

"Sump'n you oughta know 'bout y'wife, son," D'antre said.

"Whut's 'at?" Anton asked.

"She ain't gettin' yo' letters."

Thin chuckles all around.

"Shit was bad with my family too," Anton said. "My folks couldn't handle whut I was turnin' into. Pops and me, we had a big fight about my sudden 'lack of patriotism.' They just wouldn't believe that my country, my gov'ment, my military, done whut they done to us. Just not possible! After the dishonorable discharge they both shunned me for good. And they both died still not speakin' to me. Eva got a restrainin' order on me sometime soon after."

"Whass she up to these days, A?" Min asked.

"Gettin' boned by her sister's husband. Howzat fer a how-do-you-do. Her sister Micki just gave birth not long ago to a healthy baby boy. Handsome lil nipper. And Eva obviously thought, 'Hey, Jason's sperm is clean. He'll do.'" Anton laughed bitterly, then caught himself. "It's fer the best," he said quickly, refusing to succumb to despair. "It brung me here after all, which is where I'm meant to be. All's well whut ends well."

"*Que sera sera*," said Min.

"Yup, that's a good cliché too."

The rain outside died away, and the electricity kicked back on. D'antre went to fetch himself and Anton each a forty-ounce from the fridge, and a glass of cranberry juice for Min.

"Iss about 5:30 a.m.," D'antre said. "Sun should be comin' up 'fore too long."

"Imma hafta git to work here in a bit," Anton said, waving off the malt liquor D'antre offered him.

"Anton?" Min said.

"Yeah?"

"I got somethin' to say to you."

"Okay shoot."

"I think you need to come down to the sacristy wit me befo' you head off to work."

"Whut?"

"You should come on down. If I really do got a healin' touch, and Pearl wudn't just some fluke...I mean, then...you know. I ain't got a great track record fo' gettin' wit friends, but..."

"Oooooh..."

"Course, if it goes right, you be prolly needin' to call in sick."

"True enough."

"There's a reason why you and Pearl, why yo' brains was linked up," said Min. "Right? *You both sick*. And you sicker than she was! If I could heal her, I might-could heal you too, you know?"

"She got a point, dog," D'antre offered, pulling a deep swig from his forty.

"Thank you, Skinny Minnie," Anton said with a sad but genuinely grateful smile. "Thank you fer the offer. But I cain't."

"But you might-could be dyin'!"

"Darlin'," Anton said, "I am loaded brain to balls with *depleted uranium trioxide.* I am a chemical weapon on two legs. I cain't risk the harm to you. Or yer precious cargo." He laid his hand softly on her still mostly-flat belly. Then he quickly pulled his hand away, as if his external touch alone might be toxic. "And besides," he continued, running his fingers through his greasy mullet, "the poison and the pain, the blows to my cranium, the shocks to my system, the temporal lobe sensitivity, that's the shit whut opened me up, sweetheart. Opened wide my channel straight to god. That's why I'm a seer now, you unnerstan'? And I can guide the people...and do some good...fer the first time in my life. Without my cracked head and dirty blood, I'm just another angry, junk-gobblin' redneck. Dyin' er not, I prefer to be a poisoned prophet, right with god. And if I'm dyin, baby, I'm dyin' free."

When All The World is Palestine

It is something of an oversimplification to say that noise is an unwanted or unpleasant sound.

—Robert D. Reed,
Furnace Operations (1981)

"D'antre? Psst! Wake up."

"Meh? Huh? Eh? Whass goin' on?"

It was three-thirty in the morning. It was Pearl. It was, apparently, urgent.

"Wake up, D. We need some rhymes downstairs."

"What? Rhymes?"

D'antre looked over to check the clock. Sure enough, 3:30 a.m.

"We're recording in the basement," Pearl said, swaying a bit from a bit of a wine buzz. She had only had a few sips this evening, but she just couldn't drink like she used to. "Great, creepy acoustics down there, D. Fucking nice. I can't believe you've never taped down there before. We laid down a scratch track of some crazy-heavy furnace percussion, and Min and I put down some *oooooo*s and what-all. You were right about Min! You give that girl some mallets and some sheet metal, and she's got some beat! But Shel said, 'We need D'antre on this.' So he sent me up to collect you."

D'antre yawned and sat up, staring blankly ahead, attempting to gather his wits about him. "It's your own fault, dude," Pearl continued, "You never should have given him that *Bomb Droppas* record. He's obsessed with it now. He can even stomach the drum loops."

"Aw'ight," D'antre said, rubbing his eyes. "Let me grab my notebook, and I'll be down."

D'antre shuffled sleepily into the cellar's dusty furnace room to discover a multitude of dynamic microphones hanging from the beams overhead, a free-standing ambient mic in the middle of the room, and Shel looking very much the mad scientist rigging up a large diaphragm condenser mic and pop screen for vocals precariously close to the furnace itself. Sitting on the floor along the southwest wall was Min, Anton, and Pearl, Min drinking from a plastic bottle of orange juice, and Pearl and Anton passing a large jug of Jesus blood between them.

"Just the man I need," Shel said, amped and grinning wide. "You just wake up, cuz'n?"

"Yup."

"Perfect. Your voice is probably a good step and a half deeper than it normally is when it's warm. Maybe more!"

"What is it you lookin' for, dog?"

"Just some, you know, mad rhymes. Old style. From the street."

"Um. Aw'ight," D'antre said, scratching the back of his nappy head. "What you mean by 'old' exactly? Are we talkin' Big Daddy Kane old? Last Poets old? Langston Hughes old? Whass the score here?"

"Well...not really rap, I guess. Let's try some of that Afro-and-power-fist sorta action. sixties, early seventies. Can you swing that?"

"I can try."

"You three," Shel said, looking toward Pearl, Anton and Min, "Don't be shy about shouting out or interjecting. We need some energy. D'antre, do you want to hear the scratch beat?"

"F'sho."

Shel handed D'antre a pair of headphones. What D'antre heard being pumped into his ears was like something to haunt a junkman's fever dreams. Clanging, distorted sheet metal slamming against a thudding bass grind underneath. Over top, the faintest dark moaning of two girl phantasms cooing out a double dose of seduction and doom. Shel had managed, D'antre thought, to capture some dark essence of The Church with eerie precision. *Nice job, homie. Shit's workin'.*

"Yeah," D'antre said. "I'm feelin' this."

"Whenever you're ready," said Shel, his finger on the button. D'antre nodded, and it was a go.

"*I am a Black man/ I am THE Black man/ I am original man/ Warrior of the Motherland/ Keeper of the flame/ Redefining the game/ The white man can not oppress me...*"

"YEAH!"

"A'ight now!"

"Ha HAAAAA!"

"I am THE Black man/ Original man/ Flying fast/ The sharpened flint at the end of the spear/ Lacerating your heart and compounding your fear/ Your white sheets do not distress me..."

"Go 'head now!"

"Tell it, brother!"

"*I am original man/ Black warrior of the Motherland/ Breaking chains and staking my claim / Taking pains and overtaking the game/ Your White House does not impress me...*"

"Aw Hell!"

"That's what I'M talkin' 'bout!"

"*I am a Black man/ I am THE Black man/ Other and lover of the THE Black woman/ Original woman/ Mother of the Earth/ Her eyes bright starlight against the Black face of eternity/ Your white skin does not entice me...*"

"OOOOOOOOOOOOOOOOOOOOOOOOOOOOOHHH SHIT!"

"PREACH, NIGGA, PREACH!"

"*I am a Black man/ I am THE Black man/ I am original man/ I am man...I am. I. AM. I am.*"

The track ended, and Shel hit pause, smiling ear to ear. Pearl, Min and Anton whooped and cheered. Petey Wheatstraw and Loraina the Tweak entered from the catacombs to see about the hub bub.

"Imma dedicate that one to my old man," D'antre said, catching his breath. "Even though I hate that dead muhfucka."

Petey smiled and nodded to D'antre, giving him the thumbs up.

"That was several kinds of all right for a warm up, D," said Shel. "Now I wanna try something new. We need something for the ages. Okay? Lay down your place in history, cuz'n."

"Something for Blackchurch," said Anton.

"A record for the new world on the other side," Petey interjected. Anton nodded agreement.

"Aw'ight, no pressure, y'all," D'antre laughed, flipping through his notebook. Sketches and scattered thoughts and blunted nonsense from late nights lost in the nothing. *Maybe thass where the truth lies, y'heard?*

"You the right man for the job, D," Min said. "Go 'head now."

Indeed, as the chosen scribe for a misfit clan of rootless psychotics, he was well qualified. *From each, according to his talents...*

"We're going with a new track," Shel said, switching up the reels. "We need to go deeper here."

It was on.

Someone switched off the one naked light swinging above in the windowless cellar. No shadow cast now. Pitch black.

And D'antre said:

I must have been high...
Higher than Jesus when I called you "brother and sister."
Twist the spit, get lit and forget it.
None to forgive.
Give nothing but a twist of the dial
and a blood stained smile
burning highways like flies on fire
burning down the sky and light my fuse on the stars.

I must have been high
when I thought we could unite behind a common cause
because the clause was writ large—
The people in charge are heavy hands molesting
and pressing steel boots on our collective neck.
But you're a minstrel show
tap dancing in camo
letting the Devil laugh.
And pass "Go"
and collect his cut
(something to the tune of one hundred percent).
I've got a cut for him
a slash for him across his soft gullet
feeding bullets to dark babies
and unleash us on each other like starved rats in cages.
And I know the sound of the thrasher machine.
Harvesting bodies for fossil fuel.
I know the sound of metal
grinding metal
grinding bone.
Dance to that jackhammer beat.
Someone somewhere is singing for her baby in pieces.

I must have been high, false rebels,
higher than Allah,
when I thought you could learn
to turn your burning rages
against those who destroy us all
and garnish our wages
for bombs
to kill more dark babies and mothers.
Someone somewhere is singing for her child
in two or more tiny graves.

Run for cover, brother,
it's the other man whose plan has got us licking crumbs from his hand.

They keep you petty,
and you "pretty please" to oblige,
you adore
and glorify
and whore for the warmonger,
just stoked to be stroking him off.
Just shucking and
joking and
choking the breath from your own.
Your devotion is scoring your promotion.
But once more I'm causing commotion.
I feel like a psychopath circling through a constant cycle of repeated history
which leaves us
not-so discrete
pleading in the street
beat and defeated,
bleeding and cheated.
Embracing the taste of disgrace as I hate
starting again at square one with a clean slate
and nil for the babies
but carpet bombs
and empty plates.
I'm forever your carrion?
Carry on!
CARRY ON!
I can no longer carry on
with these thoughts all to myself.
I gotta vent them.
There are voices in my head
and I harass and bully and haunt and torment them.
In my cage—
no ventilation
and desperation's breeding mutilation.
Am I facing east?
Someone somewhere is singing to her god
while a voice in my head says—

"Throw your body on the gears of the machine."
The machine.
Keeping yourselves
and your cells
clean for the machine.

I must have been higher than Lucifer—
the harbinger of light.
I must have been high
when I called you "brother and sister."
Brother and sister.
Killing and dying for holy land and dust and sand.
Feed your bones to the fossil fuel machine
draining blood and uranium from holy sand.
Are you high there?
I'm higher here.
Let me die here.
Let me die here or let me die nearby here.
Desperation's breeding hallucination...
And someone
somewhere
is singing...

New Testament?

Men will faint from terror, apprehensive of what is coming on the world, for the heavenly bodies will be shaken.

—Luke 21:26

D'antre and Petey Wheatstraw sat out on The Church's front stoop, looking out across the neighborhood as the bite of mid-autumn began to set its teeth in Blackchurch. There would be no more patrol cars rolling down Blackstone Street for the night, and D'antre was confident enough of this that he comfortably sparked up a blunt right there out in the open. They wouldn't be catching so much as a glimpse of the boys in blue again until sunrise, barring some unforeseen violence. *And even then...*

"So here we are, Brother D'antre," Petey said.

"Yup yup," D'antre replied, a plume of white smoke seeping through his teeth. There was something different about Petey Whatstraw this evening, and at first D'antre could not quite put his finger on it. Then he realized that something was obviously missing: *that iconic Wheatstraw stench.* Petey Wheatstraw was clean, actually *clean*, for the first time in... several decades at least. Longer than D'antre could remember. Possibly longer than D'antre had been alive. It must have taken hours to scrub the years of grime and fifth (and whatever else) from his body. His clothes were clean as well. Ragged and ancient still, but laundered. D'antre thought he noticed the faintest hint of Irish Spring about the old man. And maybe... Old Spice?

"Do you remember MOVE, young D?"

"That group in Philly who had beef with Rizzo's pigs?"

"The very same."

"They still round, ain't they?"

"In some form I'm sure."

"I was just startin' out high school when I heard some shit went down out there. I 'member hearin' 'bout it, but wudn't really keepin' up, knahmean?"

"They actually had two *major* confrontations," Petey said, "among frequent altercations here and there. There was the shoot-out in seventy-six when the police stormed in and stomped the three-week-old baby to death—"

"Allegedly."

"No, they did it. They did it all right. The Philly police had made general practice of attacking MOVE women and beating them into miscarriage."

"Goddamn."

"Indeed."

"I was only five when that shit went down."

"The MOVE members who weren't arrested, or killed, relocated to a different house. The neighbors there complained about the noise and general ruckus, and the police flew a helicopter over the house on May 13, 1985 and dropped a bomb on them. Set fire to most of the surrounding houses as well. In America."

"Heh. Yeah. You act like you s'prised, ol' son."

"Aren't you?"

"*Am I surprised*...that the po-lice in America dropped a bomb on a buncha niggas, in America, and blew 'em up? In America? Ha ha. Nope, I sho' ain't. I be s'prised when they *don't* do that."

"But why?"

"*Cuz they niggas*, ya heard?"

"Not all of them. John Africa believed that—"

"Oh yes," D'antre said, shaking his head. "Yes they was, Petey. Just cuz some of them was white, don't mean they wudn't all *niggas*. Anyway, history's fun. Whass on y'mind, Mr. Wellson?"

"I was just thinking...if it could happen to John Africa and his people..."

"What, that it might-could happen to us?"

"Maybe."

"Naw."

"Why do you say that? You're the cynical one after all."

"Look, dog, MOVE was *tryin'* to cause a ruckus, ya heard? I know they was on the side of righteousness, 'bout *everything*, and what happen to them is a straight up tragedy. And a buncha bullshit on top. But thass how America deals wit niggas who act up. Feel me? Standard operatin' procedure. But as for us, hey. We just chillin', you know."

"We are preparing the way of the Lord, D'antre. Once the savior comes, we will have the plan for building the new world. We were chosen with a holy task."

"Cool, son. I don't think nobody gonna bomb us for that, knahmean? The surveillance cameras is up on Madison and Whetsel. Just a lil puppet show fo' the voters, you feel me? But I'm pretty sure you can do jus' 'bout *anything* on Blackstone and Churchwalk."

"Perhaps," Petey sighed. "We'll see. I'm applying for tax-exempt status, by the way. Just thought you should know."

"Thass on you, dog. I don't know nothin' 'bout *status*, I just know how to play them hoes, you know what I'm sayin'?"

"Fair enough. On a completely unrelated topic, you lot in Upper Church need to see about taking Min to a doctor. She needs frequent prenatal check-ups, vitamins, the whole kaboodle. You've got experience in that arena, so that's a good thing."

"Yeah. Been a minute."

"Fourteen years, yes?"

"Comin' up soon. December."

"Not to worry. It's like riding a bicycle."

"Never understood that phrase. Bet I done forgot how to ride a bike by now."

"Whatever the cost, I have it covered," said Petey. "Don't be concerned about that."

"Whass wit the sudden flush of cheese, ol' son? I don't know too many niggas who can be homeless for forty years, then alla sudden got bills to spare."

"I've been keeping my savings liquid since the 1960s. Stored away in secret lockboxes all over Blackchurch. I figured I would need it someday. Call it fate. Call it good planning."

"I'll git her in to see a doctor next week f'sho."

"I think you should be in the delivery room with her when the time comes, D'antre," Petey said. "She's very fond of you, you know."

"Yeah..."

They sat in silence for a few moments as D'antre finished his smoke. Finally,

"You ready?" D'antre asked.

"Ready Freddy," Petey replied, stroking his newly scrubbed but still unkempt beard.

"You know whatchoo gonna say to 'em?"

"It's all in the plan," Petey replied with a bright white grin. D'antre stood and helped the older man to stand. "Here's to destiny, young D."

"Here's to it."

They entered The Church proper to find all of the congregation together in one place for the first time, gathered and seated in the dusty, abandoned old pews. From those who sleep in the balcony to those up from the catacombs, all were in attendance. They had spent the time waiting for Petey and D'antre to enter making awkward introductions, facilitated by Anton to the best of his abilities. The residents of Lower Church, also known informally as the *Followers of River Sam*, were particularly nervous to meet Min for the first time. Several of them broke out in tears at the mere sight of her. Two fainted on the spot.

For their part, Pearl, Min and Shel were surprised at how young Lower Church was. They had assumed that the people in the catacombs must all be filthy old hobos like Petey Wheatstraw and Loraina the Tweak. But in actuality, many of them were as young as Min. Some even younger. A motley assortment of tweakers, drifters, baseheads, and runaways, they were just the sort Min knew well from the streets in Columbus, and who hung around the alleys near Blue Ida's in NOLA. Little doubt that more than a few of them had on occasion offered up their own bodies as payment for a fix or an evening's shelter. In another time they would have been Stigmata Dog's main fan base. The ones who sneaked into every show, and sold bootlegged CDs for crank money. The kids Shel once referred to as, "The only people who have ever really understood me."

Though it went largely unstated, it was something of a forgone conclusion that Min would try to heal whomever needed or desired such a thing. If the thought of letting a crowd of hollow-eyed derelicts run a train on her bothered Min at all, she never gave any indication of it. *Whatever be god's will…*

D'antre sauntered over in slo-mo to sit with Pearl, Min, and Shel, thoroughly blazed. Anton sat in front, alone and deep in thought. Eyes closed and head down. He needed the time to formulate his thoughts. D'antre looked at Pearl and wondered if, even now that they were in the same room, she could still hear Anton echoing deep in the back of her mind somewhere. She said that she no longer could, but who could know for sure.

Petey walked over to Loraina, gave her a quick peck on her pale, blotchy cheek, and stepped on up to where the alter once stood. He sat down on the step leading up to the raked, stage-like platform, and shut his eyes tight. He sat for nearly half a minute before he finally spoke. Everyone watched him with breathless anticipation.

Finally—

"Three hundred and twenty years ago, when the nation was new and the land was raw, many of the ancestors of the people in this very room were the property of other human beings. For others of us, our forbearers were indentured servants. Not much more than property. Others may have been on reservetions, or trapped on prison farms."

He stood and began to pace, not nervously, but deliberately. As if he very much needed to get some place, and that place was right over there. And then back again.

"The *civilized* of the society thought nothing wrong or peculiar about any of this. Good business after all. Good for the economy, their only true god. And their god is a ravenous god, always wanting more. Its hunger is never appeased. These *civilized* people, they were the ones who wrote the history books. And the ones who taught the lies from those same books. Their progeny continue this tradition of lies.

"But *our history is so much wilder.* So much messier than the pabulum the civilized will offer. Or allow. So thoroughly vast and thrilling in scope and design is our history, that some of it would be well worth repeating. I speak, of course, to the grand tradition of the *maroon state.*"

The bulk of the crowd leaned in *en masse* with great attention. They had made practice of hanging on to Petey Wheatstraw's every word. He had rescued many of them from the streets after all, or from the horrors of Washington Park and other desolate waste pits of human failure. And he was, to date, never, *ever* wrong.

"Founded mostly by runaway slaves, comprised of escaped white and Indian convicts, bandits and gypsies of every shade and hue, dialect and religion, the maroon states were the true face of America at its greatest. Those people who took fierce control of their own freedom. Owned it. Gripped it with force and conviction. Those people who refused to be chained, refused to be imprisoned or contained in fences. Or municipalities. No surprise that they were hunted down like dogs. Many were killed. They were too early, you see. Too far ahead of their time. A shame and a loss to be sure. But their blood was spilled for us."

Petey paused for a moment and dabbed at his brow with a graying handkerchief. D'antre chuckled lightly to himself. He had seen so many preachers in his time pull the exact same maneuver. Hell, D'antre had done it himself on occasion. For emphasis.

"When I look out at this congregation tonight," Petey continued, "at this beautiful collection of god's chosen hobos, I see the progeny of that last and greatest of the maroon states.

"The Ben Ishmael Tribe founded this land right here. From the mountains of West Virginia, through Kentucky and Indiana, and settling in what we now call Cincinnati, this Tribe, by then several thousand strong, created and cultivated the gypsy hobo's paradise right here on earth. Some claim that the Ben Ishmaels were Judeo-Christian at their center. Others say pagan. Still more claim Islam was at their core...but the Ishmael's knew, as we all here know, that there is no need for the artificial infrastructure of pre-existing dogma when your god will speak *directly to you.*"

"That's right!" some kid shouted. "Fuck the greedy charlatan ministers!" Someone else shouted. "Fuck the baby raping priests and phony monks and cardinals!" "Fuck all of them!"

"Yes," Petey said with a broad smile. "Fuck all of them indeed."

"Brother Pete!" a young female voice shouted, "What became of the Ben Ishmael Tribe?"

"Well, sister," Petey replied, running his fingers through his wild shock of silver hair pointing out in all directions like a large pile of steel wool, "that's really two questions: what became of them then...and where are they today. When Cincinnati was finally 'settled,' by those same so-called civilized people whose false god gave them the go-ahead for slavery and genocide, they ran off, and killed off, most of the Ben Ishmaels. Most. *Not all.* Plenty of them survived, and hunkered down in their river camps not far from where we stand right now. 'We will not be moved,' they said, and sure enough they wouldn't be. They held out for much longer than anyone thought they would. Or could. But eventually, they died away and wove into the fabric of this then-bustling pig town, and disappeared...but their spirit lives. The spirit lives on. When nomads and hobos unite...they carry the spirit of the Ishmaels. When drifters and the so-called 'homeless' refuse to succumb to despair, and instead find their joy despite all, they carry with them the spirit of the Ishmaels. When god's chosen people open their eyes to their own visions, yes? When they are wise enough to listen to and pay heed to the angels who walk among us, when they honor and follow our beloved River Sam, they carry on the spirit of the Ishmael's."

At the mention of River Sam a great cheer filled the cavernous Church hall. Min, Pearl and Shel all instinctively looked over toward D'antre. He was stoic, but his eyes seemed pinched with an inscrutable pain. It was Pearl who first observed that any passing talk of "River Sam" caused D'antre to tense. D'antre was a closed man, though, and they knew that he would simply shrug off any inquiries. Even still, truths have a way of revealing themselves in due time...

"Brother Anton?" Petey said, offering the floor to Anton. Petey went to sit in a pew with Loraina, who squeezed his thigh and took his hand.

"Thank you, Brother Pete," Anton said standing, a bit nervous and less showy in front of a crowd than his partner in prophecy. "Thanks to all y'all. Brother Pete mentioned despair, and how the spirit lives and thrives when we refuse to allow despair to swalluh us up. And I think ever'body in this place tonight knows how hard a job that can be." Heads nodded all around. "I came through this state in 2001 a suicidal, near homicidal, wreck. A disaster of a man if ever there was one. Ever'one I'd loved had turned from me. The country that I loved and fought fer, spilled blood fer, nearly died fer, tossed me out like a sack of garbage. Come this time, I was more despair than man." A light, sympathetic chuckle filled the hall. "It was gonna take a pretty sound ass beatin' to knock all that rage outta me. A real sound ass beatin'. And that's just whut I done got.

"Laid up in a hospital bed fer weeks straight, I couldn't move. And in that time I got a hellacious dose of god's word. And believe me, I ain't want it at first. I resisted. But the stakes were just too high, and the way and the truth and the light came upon me with a firey vengeance. I seen the path I was headed down, and there weren't no future there. I knew I had to change my path. I knew I had to open myself up to the word. I knew I couldn't do whut some of my friends had gone and done. I was on a terr'ble path, and I needed to seek a new way 'fore it was too late."

Anton stopped and looked around absently, finally fixing his eyes on the ceiling of The Church. Suddenly he shouted out, toward D'antre's apartment,

"YOU HEAR ME, FRANNIE?!?! DO YOU HEAR? You listenin'?! I'm right here, right where you done it! I'm here, where you surrendered to yer despair! I AIN'T GONNA DO WHUT YOU DONE, FRAN!!! I'm free! I AM FREE!!!" Anton looked back toward the startled crowd, breathing hard and wild-eyed. He caught himself and smiled at them, humble and grateful. "We are all free people now, y'all. Ever' single one of us. We're free. Ever'one here done suffered loss. Brother Pete lost his Olivia. We done all lost our families. We know the sharp sting of rejection. And violence. We wouldn't be here, I don't think, if we hadn't. We all done had pain. We all, or a good lot of us anyhow, have had to deal with *the snakes in our bellies*, as Sister Loraina says. But we ain't gonna be prisoners to sickness and despair no more. No sir. Never again. Come, and be healed, brothers and sisters. Come, and be healed. Come and be healed..." Anton trailed off, looking absently around again, as if something from the shadows might jump out and grab him.

"Brother Anton," a young man asked, "Were you lead here by River Sam?"

"Um...well..."

Petey stood and walked forward, joining Anton on the stage floor.

"God has brought us all together via many paths, young brother," Petey said. "Brother Anton is an oracle, like myself, but we've been spoken to in different ways." Anton nodded, clearly relieved to no longer be the focus of attention. Petey touched his shoulder warmly, and Anton limped back to his seat. "I think god has lead us all in our own unique fashions. Some have received visions, great and terrible I'm told. Some among us have connected to one another with our minds. For a time. All a part of what has brought us together. As for me, I am visited by angels. Even now I meet them from time to time. Friends they are to me, walking and talking like men and women of the world. But they're dangerous and wild. They're not bound by the trappings of linear time. They are servants of god, ancient and angry, carrying messages to its conduits on Earth. I believe Brother Shel and Sister Pearl met one of my friends right outside the hurricane, before the great flood. They walk to the past, and they walk to the future, and they've told me what's to come. Much of it will be horrible. Brother Anton will attest to as much, for he has seen it in visions, as has Brother Sheldon." Anton and Shel both nodded reflexively. "But know this, brothers and sisters, know this. Someday, that horror will pass. And we will build anew. And our savior, whom Sister Min now carries in her sacred womb, and has already begun to heal us, will lead us to a glorious new future." Everyone cast their eyes toward Pearl who gave a startled, awkward smile. "I give you my word on this, my children," Petey continued, "The word that god's angels on Earth have given to me. Have faith in that. Have faith."

"Brother Pete," asked a very skinny, very young woman sitting toward the rear, "were the Ben Ishmael Tribe god's chosen people too?"

"Of course they were, sister," Petey chuckled. "Of course."

"But they were killed off! They're all dead now! And any true progeny of theirs are scattered to the far winds. How do we know that won't happen to us too?!"

"Dead?!" Petey said, his eyes alight, arms raised to his shoulders and spread wide like a great embrace of the entire room. "Oh, sister, The Ben Ishmael Tribe is not dead."

"Their spirit lives within us?"

"No. It is not just their spirit, child. It is not just the spirit that lives. WE ARE THE BEN ISHMAELS."

***

Later that evening, as the newly united Tribe split for the night and went their separate ways, departing with pronouncements of love and fidelity to all others, D'antre cornered Anton in the stairwell alone.

"Axe you sump'n, kid."

"Whut's up, D?"

"Whass the word on yo' old lady?"

Anton chuckled dryly. "She got her thing, I got mine. Whut more can be said." D'antre just looked at him. Clearly this was not a sufficient answer. "When we split," Anton continued, "we sold the house and split it fifty/fifty. Even though I paid fer it all. Whatever. *Que sera.* We done sold it to her uncle, fer less than we coulda got on the market, but we just wanted to git it over with. Eva moved up to Canton, Ohio fer a spell, to stay with some friends. Then, after a while, she moved back down to Sweetwater, and her uncle *gave her the house back.* Fer free. *My house.* And I ain't seen a bit of that money. Could let it bother me, I guess, but I don't."

"Cuz god done had a whole 'nother plan for you."

"That's right, amigo."

"So tell me 'bout yo' latest visions."

Anton blanched a bit (even more than normal). He looked down somberly.

"They're bad, bro. Real bad. The shit's gonna get a whole fuckuvalot worse before it gits any better. We may be safe here all together, but outside...it's gonna be a hell like you cain't imagine."

"But *you* can."

"Unfortunately, yes. I can. I seen it."

"Spit that shit, son."

"The earth is gonna shake and rip right open. Hundreds of thousands of people—good, decent, innocent people—crushed like soft fruit. Torn to shreds. Men and women and little ones all. It breaks me up to see it, and I cain't make it stop. God needs me to see it all."

"How come izzat?"

"I...I don't know. So I can warn ever'body when the time is right? It ain't right now, though, I don't think."

"Who is it you see? Who gettin' crushed in yo' mind?"

"Just...people," Anton fidgeted nervously. "You know. Just regular folk."

"Uh huh. And would these regular folk happen to be *colored* folk?"

Anton swallowed hard. He couldn't look D'antre in the eyes. "Um. Well. Um. Yes. Yes they would."

"All of 'em?"

"So far."

"Now why you s'pose that could be?"

"I don't know, D. God's plannin' to wipe ever'body out. That's all I can figger."

"And god just happen to decide to take out all the niggas first."

"I don't unner'stan' it all. I just know whut I see. We'll know when Min's baby comes. We gotta trust in god's plan," Anton said looking up finally. His eyes met D'antre's, a pleading need to believe (and to share that belief) slathered thick across them. "We all're here fer a purp'se. We're preparin' the way of the Lord. Min's baby is gonna make ever'thin' okay again. You know that, D'antre. We gotta believe in that. Why would all this have happened if that wasn't whut's goin' down? The savior will come, and heal this broken world. But it's gonna git real bad first. And I gotta say..."

"What?"

"I don't know...Nuthin'."

"Spit it out, nigga."

"From whut I seen up in this ol' melon of mine...without Min's baby...It ain't gonna be a world worth survivin' into. Min's baby's opposite, the *anti*, done already made his presence known in this here Church."

"What you seen, son?"

"The whole godfersaken world...desolate and hot. Dust storms and endless sand and dry rock. Tent cities and armed checkpoints. *Total oppression.* Just like...whut's it called... Palestine. The whole world will be Palestine."

"Except for us."

"Yeah. We're free."

"And this ALL be god's plan, huh. Thass what you sayin'."

"I'm sayin' yes, it's all god's plan. I ain't sayin' it's a *good* plan."

Come and Be Healed
or
The Sound of Two Churches

The limitations upon almost all types of furnaces lie in the limitations of refractory materials which are available.

—Charles F. Burgess,
Applied Electrochemistry (1917)

The tiny stage of *Jefferson Beans N' Cream* was the venue where Pearl and Shel would make their Blackchurch debut. They had played Cincinnati before many years ago, before the crash, before LA even, at some little dive called *Top Cats.* Although Cincinnati left little impression on them otherwise at the time, Pearl never forgot the night, for she swore on her very life that she had seen her brother Dave in the audience there, somewhere toward the edge of the bar. He never materialized afterward, though, and the sighting was shrugged off, attributed to the usual cocktail of unsavory treats that Stigmata Dog were all dumping into their systems at the time. Pearl reluctantly dismissed it as well, but in the back of her mind she always wondered. *Always wondered...*

Fast-forward eight years or so, and the surviving half of Stigmata Dog took to the tiny stage of the modest coffee house before an over-capacity crowd (forty people at least), made up in large part by the New Ben Ishmael Tribe. Though comprised, with few exceptions, of wayward drifters and jobless runaways, the crowd managed to drink the establishment utterly dry of coffee (due entirely to their leader and spiritual father Petey Wheatstraw's sudden and inexplicably deep pockets). And of course, this crowd were no strangers to chemical stimulants in large quantities.

Whatever the case, Malachi and Shonda Jefferson were overjoyed for the business, and said that this shifty, unwashed rabble of troubled and troublesome heretics was welcome in their establishment at any time. They also happily forgave the bad swears rolling off the stage at frequent intervals.

"Thank you all for coming out to the first, but hopefully not last, music night here at Madisonville's own *Beans N Cream*," Pearl said into the microphone, kicking off her flip-flops and sitting cross-legged on a stool next to Shel. The crowd cheered and clapped. "These good folks here are my bosses, so please don't fuck up the joint."

Everyone laughed.

Shel and Pearl proceeded to play a two and a half hour set comprised of old and new material, a couple of odd cover songs, and a selection of experimental pieces they called their "sacred works." What made them sacred it would seem, was their oblique references to The Church, which brought knowing nods from those assembled who were in the loop, but would have been (and was) thoroughly lost on anyone else. A large cheer went up when Min was invited to the stage to sing harmony on a couple of numbers.

Anton, unsurprisingly, whooped and hollered the loudest when they busted out the old, though modified, Stigmata Dog cuts—

Alone here.
I'm well-known here.
Among the glass and the stone here I am home.
Roam here.
To the beat of the chrome here.
Rips meat from the bone here.
I am home.
I'm busted and rusted, just out now

Cussed out and maladjusted.
The power's out
and dark's devoured
this whole side of town.
But my heart's still blacker than this night.
Fuck this world—You ain't stayin', right?
Blackchurch, son—We ain't playin', right?
You picked a hard time to bleed me, Lucille!!!
(And the crowd got loud, like the old crowds of yore.)
Alone here.
I'm well known here.
Among the glass and the stone here I am home.
Roam here.
To the beat of the chrome here.
Rips meat from the bone here. I am home.
And I've come to watch the firelight
in your eyes flicker fade and die—
I'VE COME TO WATCH YOU FADE AWAY AND DIIIIIIE!!!

D'antre stood in the back and smiled. He hadn't realized how much he had wanted something like this, whatever it was. Not just for himself, or his life, but for his hood. Church or no Church, this odd assortment of characters could be just the force needed to pump new life into his old stamping grounds, an area that has forever languished far beneath its potential. He was hopeful, and unaccustomed to the feeling. This might soon just be a place, after all, that he could bring his daughter to without shame. *Soon and very soon.*

Shonda and Malachi Jefferson, meanwhile, watched the show with their heads cocked slightly, puzzled and perplexed. They finally just shrugged, and continued serving up steaming hot mugs of deep black salvation. *All shapes and sizes, you know…*

"Interesting stuff, sugar," Shonda said to Pearl afterward. "When can y'all play again?"

***

Later that evening…

D'antre sat in his bedroom alone, smoking what he thought would be his last Camel of the night, drinking a glass of Rosé and listening to his mother's old vinyl records on his small Crosley turntable. He hadn't played this stuff in decades, and couldn't figure why he had the urge to listen to it now…

I was standin' by my window
On a cold and cloudy day
When I saw a hearse come a-rollin'
O, to carry my mother away…
Will the circle be unbroken
By and by, Lord?
By and by?
There's a better home a-waitin'
In the sky, Lord
In the sky…

A knock came at the door, and Pearl peeked her head in.

"Hey D, mind if I come in?"

He quickly stubbed out the cigarette.

"F'sho. Sorry for the smoke."

She gave her watery eyes a quick rub as she walked in. He went to open a window, but she stopped him short.

"No, don't. It's fine. It's so weird," she said, inhaling through her nose. "It hurts my eyes and my lungs…but it smells so good to me. I still crave the hell out of them. Old habits, right?"

"Hear that," D'antre said, sitting back down on the edge of his small bed. "Y'all sounded real tight tonight. Real tight. I was diggin' it."

"I appreciate that. Hey, is this the Staple Singers?"

"You know it."

"God, they're magic. Love them. The lyrics never meant much to me, but the music is so amazing. That reverb guitar, the harmonies…wow."

"Right there witcha, girl. Talkin' 'bout weird, I just had the urge to listen to this shit tonight from outta nowhere. Been just sittin' here reminiscin' on my moms, ya heard? Don't know why really."

"Who can figure these things?" Pearl said, sitting next to D'antre on the bed. "Just go with it. I know how it is. I think about my parents sometimes too. Or...I used to."

"Me and moms actually went to this here church for a minute back inna day," D'antre said. "After she and pops split finally. She dated around a bit, and was seein' this cat fo' a stretch who was Catholic. I's 'bout seven when they met. He came to this joint for mass, so we did too, along wit my cousin Terell. He's 'bout seven too then, prolly. Eight maybe. You ever been to a Catholic service?"

"A wedding once. OH! And a funeral too."

"Shit's freaky, innit?"

"It was. Kinda metal, actually. All this chanting and smoke and minor keys. I wished it would have been in Latin, you know, that pre-Vatican II shit. But alas, no luck."

"My cousin and me had Sunday school from nine to ten. Actual mass ain't start 'til eleven. So inna meanwhile, we sneak into the sacristy when the choir was doin' they warm up, and steal gulps of wine and fistfuls of them little Christ cakes. At first we was real nervous 'bout it, y'heard? And pretty rev'rent too. We'd do the whole ceremony 'fore gobblin' that shit down, you know: 'As supper was ended he took the cup, again he gave thanks and praise, gave the cup to his disciples and said, *Take this all of you and drink it. It is the cup of my blood. The blood of the new and everlasting covenant. It has been shed for you and for all and so on.*

"Well any old way, we go through the whole blessin' rigmarole thinkin', 'Fuck,' you know? One-a these little biscuits will save you from Satan, then a whole box of 'em just might-could build up some kinda devil-proof force field round you and shit!"

"Makes perfect sense to me."

"After while, it was old hat for us, y'heard? Ritual. Just like mass itself. We slip in, guzzle guzzle guzzle, grab a box of holy wafers, and out we go. No one was ever the wiser. No punishment. No repercussions. No lesson learned. Presumably no magical devil blocker either, but time will tell on that one I s'pose."

"You might just be immune to the apocalypse!"

"You know! Ha ha. Yeah...that was a long time ago. These days my cousin servin' time in the state pen. Guess he never lost his taste fo' larceny. And I never lost my taste fo' cheap red wine."

He took a long drink from his glass. He offered her some, but she declined.

"You don't mind me in here, do you D'antre? I mean, on your bed and all."

"Ain't never kick nobody out befo', knamsayin?" he said with a cheesy smile. She smiled back. "So, what can I do for you, Pearl Harbor?"

"Well..." she said with a grand sigh. "Let's see...how to say it...how to say it...Would you like me to say that I'm dying from horniness, and that I ache to have your cock inside me?"

D'antre blinked, startled for the forthrightness.

"Um...well...whass the alternative?"

"The truth."

"Ah. Aw'ight. Let's go with that."

"Truth is...I just don't feel like *me* anymore. Do you know what I mean? I just don't. And I'd like to feel...at least a little bit of myself again. If only for just a short while. This clean, virginal girl...she's just not me. Not the real Pearl Harbor. Not that Pearl Harbor is a real person anyway..."

"Word."

"I'd just like to be an adult again. Right? A grown woman. And, not to be a bitch, because I love everybody here...but honestly, you're the only man in this whole place who I don't find, well, kinda repellant physically. Now how's that for a compliment!"

"I'll take it."

She leaned over and kissed him. They looked at one another

closely, and smiled. She kissed him again. *Cool*, D'antre though, *I can roll with this.*

They took it slow at first, moving gradually ever closer. Then, it was on with the quickness.

He instinctively reached for her breasts, and finding not much there, he lightly traced his fingers around her nipples… one, then the other…

She lay back and pulled him on top of her. He reached over her head and grabbed his last condom from the drawer of the bedside table.

"What are you trying to do, sweetheart," she teased, "*live*?"

"I jus' ain't tryin' to *multiply* no more, knamsayin?"

"Yes," she said. "Absolutely. Kiss me." He did. "Now fuck me hard."

"F'real?"

"Fuck me as hard as you can."

"Um…"

"Don't worry. I'll be fine."

So yeah…'cept for the pussy, it really was actually kinda like fuckin' a teenage boy. A fine lookin' boy, though, don't git it twisted. Whatever. I'm easy, ya heard? And besides, this IS a old Catholic church after all. Shit like that just happens round here…

Later…

They lay naked together on the twin mattress, covered by nothing but a gauze-thin sheet, Mavis Staples singing softly about salvation on the spinning platter beside them.

"So dig," D'antre said. "My baby girl birthday comin' up here pretty soon."

"Are you going to go up to Wisconsin to see her?"

"Hell yeah I am."

"And you trust this lot to be left here unsupervised?" They laughed. "Seriously, though, that's great. Give her a big squeeze for me."

"Yeah, will do," D'antre said. "But here's the thing,

though. I ain't got the first clue what to git her."

"Wow," Pearl laughed. "You're asking *me* for advice on a present for your fourteen-year-old daughter? *Me?*"

"I woulda axed Min, but I KNOW where she was at at fourteen, knahmean?"

"Sad to say, I'm probably an even worse source of advice on the subject. Unless you think your little girl might secretly be a Napalm Death fan."

"Hmmm...I'm thinkin' not. Aw'ight I'll come up wit sump'n."

"You could always give her a CD by this little band called Stigmata Dog. It might jar her at first, give her a nightmare or two. But I'll bet she'd come around eventually."

"I don't think CDs still exist as a commercial medium anymore, ya heard?"

"Apparently I hadn't."

"That shit's out wit the steam shovel."

"Just my luck."

"Mine too," D'antre said. "Mine too." He paused. Then, "Quieter up in here than normal."

"Cuz I'm up here with you instead of down there with Shel."

"Word."

"Right now," Pearl said, "Min is down in the catacombs with some of the Ishmaels. Laying *healing hands* on them."

"Yeah? Aw'ight. Cool. Just...hands?"

"Anton felt that anything else could endanger the baby." She proceeded to give an eerily spot-on Anton impersonation, "'We gotta have faith that her touch alone will heal,' he said. But, and this is on the down-low, Petey had pulled Min aside and asked her to give a little 'extra' attention to Loraina. I don't know what 'extra' means exactly...but that's what I heard."

"Huh. Always pays to be tight wit a nigga onna mainline, you feel me?"

"I certainly do."

"Old girl *is* in a bad way, though. Has been fo' LONG

time. He prolly just worried for her and wanna make sure, if she *can* git better, that she will git better. Them kids down there ain't been at it like she been."

"Oh, I'm not so sure about that," Pearl said. "I've talked with a number of them this evening, and there is some *serious* damage going on here. I talked to one girl after the show who told me she was raised by some older relatives because she never knew her parents. 'All I knew was that they were crack addicts,' she said. 'Both of them. When I hit my own skids later on, I hit them hard. Ended up sleeping in Washington Park for close to a year. Some months ago,' this is what she said straight up, 'Some months ago, I fucked my own dad in Washington Park. I didn't realize he was my dad until it was too late.'"

"How did she find it out?"

"Didn't say."

"Goddamn...that is hard..."

"She was going to kill herself. But one night, she said, she saw a shadow who told her to *Follow...follow...*"

"The *River Sam* routine, huh," D'antre chuckled bitterly.

"I guess. It brought her here, and to Petey Wheatstraw, who took her in. Took care of her. Have you seen what they've done to the catacombs? It's actually pretty nice down there. As windowless concrete cellars go." Pearl noticed that D'antre was still looking off, a tightness to his face, and a distant anger.

"What is it with you and this River Sam story?" she asked.

"Iss just some ol' bullshit," he said quietly.

"Okay then. So anyway, do you think it'll work? Minnie's magic touch? It sure worked on me...but there was quite a bit of a lot more going on than just *laying hands*. If you know what I mean."

"Nope, I sho' don't."

"So what do you think?"

"Prolly it will work. Cuz they *believe* in it. It'll work f'while. But they'll relapse. Bets on it right now."

"That'd be awfully sad if they did. I hope you're wrong."

"Addiction ain't leprosy, ya heard? You gotta *wanna* be healed. You gotta maintain."

"Hmm...yeah..." she murmured contemplatively. "Hey, you mind if I have one of those Camels, D?"

"Aw yeah." He pulled two cigarettes out of the pack enthusiastically, one for each of them. He lit them both in his mouth and handed one to her.

"Thank you. I apologize ahead of time if this makes me sick. I haven't smoked a single one since..."

"You wanna spark up a joint instead? Better for y'health."

"Maybe later. I'm craving one of these right now."

"Whatever's good witcha, girl."

She took a drag, shut her eyes tight, and coughed out the smoke.

"*Whoa...good god...*"

"You aw'ight?" he asked.

"Hurts," she coughed sharply, eyes red and cheeks splotchy. "A lot. But that's okay. So did the sex. And thank you for that too."

"We aim to please."

She continued to cough and clear her throat, as if she had never smoked before. After a moment, though, her breath and composure returned.

"I just wanted to tell you, D'antre, that I've been writing too. Thought you should know, in case, whatever. In case you're interested."

"Say what now?"

"You had asked Shel to write for you. From his dreams. And his life. Our life. Get everything down. For the archives, or whatever you're doing."

"Yup?"

"Well, I've been writing too. Ever since we got here."

"Thass good! I'll take whatever you got!"

"Heh heh, well...you think you're going to have a job cleaning up what Shel's been writing, just wait 'til you see my pages. Best of luck with them."

"I'll make it work, don't worry. Glad to have 'em."

"I've got to be really fast about it," she said. "Get it down while it's still in my brain. It's like...there have been two different Pearls at this point. Like I've had two completely different lives: *Previous to Min*, and *After Min*. And my P.T.M. life is fading away fast. It's almost gone from my memory."

"What do you mean?" D'antre said, enunciating more clearly than he had been. His attention was entirely on her.

"I mean, whatever Min did to me, for me, it wasn't an all-at-once thing it seems. I've been cleansed, body and spirit. I guess. And now my mind is washing clean too. My past is fading away from me. And I have to get it all down on paper before...before...before it's all gone."

A thin, lonely tear suddenly spilled down her cheek. D'antre wiped it away with his thumb.

"Are you all right, Pearl?"

She sniffled, and smiled with closed lips.

"I mean, it's not that I'm not grateful. Right? I am. *I am.* I'm happy to not be a junkie anymore. I'm happy my back doesn't hurt me anymore. It's wonderful. It's just...I don't know...Fuck me for an ungrateful miracle, right?"

"When you had your surgery, they clamped your spine together with titanium clips, right?"

"Yes."

"What happened to them? When Min healed you, what happened to the titanium clips?"

Silence. She did not answer.

"So what was it like?" D'antre asked moving on, maintaining his clearer diction. "When she...when the two of you got together. Could you tell that something different had gone down? Did you feel a change right away?"

"Well...it was the best sex I've ever had. I never came so hard in my life. No offense."

"Not at all."

"It was incredible. I'm not kidding. It was like every orgasm I had ever had came flooding down on me all at once. It was... frightening, kind of. And I tend to not frighten easily. I completely lost control. Almost knocked me unconscious. I guess it did, actually."

"Damn."

"Right? Hey, you think, when Jesus healed the lepers, they all creamed in their dirty rags?"

They laughed.

"Girl," D'antre said, "I don't even know if there *was* a Jesus."

"What do you mean by that?"

"So much of the Jesus story...it's just bits of old, recycled Jewish folklore."

"Really?"

"Really."

"Still...good story, though."

"Yeah. But it's a story."

"Everything's just a story when you get down to it."

"Yeah. Deep."

"So D'antre, are you aware that your voice...? I don't know. It's different now somehow. It takes on different tones sometimes. Almost different personas. Is it a conscious thing? Are you aware of it?"

"I've been told that I do that, but I don't hear it myself."

"Min's the one who pointed it out to me. She said her white friend Mikal who used to live around here, he did the same thing. It must be a Blackchurch phenomenon."

"There's an assumption around these parts, and it's a correct one, that you can't 'act Blackchurch' outside of here. You'll be treated poorly if you do. It's like a handicap. So we tend to develop multiple personalities. Or at least a dual consciousness."

"Well, you won't have to any longer once the end comes."

"I'm still a bit unclear on all of that. Who and what exactly is going to survive the apocalypse? Will it be just *us*? Just Blackchurch? Because we're really only talking about four city blocks tops. Will it be all of Madisonville? Still a pretty small neighborhood in the grand scheme of things. Cincinnati? Most of Southern Ohio? What's the score here?"

"Fuck if I know. I doubt even Petey and Anton could answer that. But, you know, you gotta—"

"Have faith. Yeah. I know. I know. Thanks, but I'll leave that shit for the true believers."

"So you're both our scribe *and* our resident skeptic, huh?" She chuckled.

"Guess so. Good thing too. You look at the other scribes of all the other holy books throughout history, and goddamn. Just a bunch of drunks, psychotics, and lonely perverts."

"Yeah," Pearl said grinning wryly, "I suppose we lucked out."

"It's the community that I'm all about. Right? That's what matters to me. The family. The ones we're born into may be bullshit, but the families we choose for ourselves, that's where it's at."

"Yeah…But…god chose *this* family for *us*, D'antre."

"Yeah…that's good too."

"I figured you weren't fully convinced about any of this, because if you were you would have gone and snatched up your daughter and brought her back here."

"If shit actually starts gettin' raw Imma do just that," he said, the ghetto essence sliding back into his diction. "Prolly her mama too, to be straight up widdit."

"That's sweet," she said, and kissed him on the cheek.

"Wha' 'bout Shel? He strikes me as a skeptic."

"Oh, Shel's a true believer, don't doubt that. It might not be in Anton's and Petey's god maybe, but he's got his god. And nothing else really matters to him in the end."

"Even you?"

"*Especially* me. But that's okay. I share his god. I share *everyone's* god I think. I've been touched by many powers. I mean, I came and was healed."

"Word."

"It's just…damn, you know? Why do I have to lose it all? Couldn't I be just *partially* purified?"

"I think that would pretty much blow the whole 'purity' concept, y'know? That shit can't be *partial* by definition."

"Yeah...I guess." She took a very light pull from her cigarette and quickly released the smoke. "After the accident, Shel couldn't remember our friends' faces anymore. Our band-mates. But I could! I could back then. But now...now I can't remember them either. At all. How sad is that, that neither of us can remember them. It's like they never existed. I can barely remember my parents, my brother, my husband...ex-husband...it's all leaving me. Dribbling out, like murky water from a storm drain. I look at the pages I've written so far, and it's like I'm reading someone else's words. Shel's frustrated with me because he has to teach me our songs again. Even stuff I wrote!"

"Thass hard, girl," D'antre said. "My grammama went through that, knamsayin? But you WAY too young for that shit. Way too young."

"That's not even the worst of it. It's not just the chemicals and sickness, the injuries and scars. I'm glad to have that gone from me. Obviously. But it's not even just the memories that I'm missing either. It's that...*my fire* has gone out."

"I don't know 'bout alla that, girl. You seemed pretty on it tonight. You got stage presence, y'heard?"

"You should have seen me before. I was a demon back then. Possessed. Not now. I just don't feel the rage anymore. Or the passion. Or any kind of real intensity. I'm just...pretty happy for the most part...and kinda sad. And that's just not metal."

"Word."

"Soft, clean, and empty. That's not who I'm supposed to be. I mean, okay, you know? Give me soft feet and clean veins. Thank you for the latter definitely. But please...please let me keep my memories. And my fire." The ash grew on her cigarette as it was her turn to look off in the distance. He handed her the ashtray, and she stubbed out her Camel. "Some of it was bad, I know. A lot of it was painful. But it was mine! I don't regret my life! I'm not ashamed! I'm sorry for hurting anyone else that I might have, but I'm not sorry for hurting myself. That's my business. There was a lot of *shit*...okay...but there was a lot of joy too. A lot of wild nights. And anyway, it was mine to do whatever the hell I wanted with it! Or so I thought."

"You know what they say, right? You gotta offer it all up to the Lord. Whatever that means."

"Soon it'll all be gone. I'm holding on as much as I can."

"So…thass why there's a bag of opiates and syringes in the back of my fridge?"

She smiled apologetically.

"I hope you don't mind."

"Whatever you need, y'heard?" He shrugged, glancing at the veins in the crook of her arm surreptitiously.

"I don't plan to ever shoot up again," she said. "I really don't want to. And I won't. But it goes against every junkie impulse to throw smack away. It's just not done. Stupid, I guess."

"Yeah. Kinda. But I feel you. I ain't never shot the shit, but I done smoked my share of OPM. That shit's nice, onna real."

"That it is," she said wistfully. "That it is." She nibbled on her thumbnail absently. "Is this what it means to be a pure woman of god?" She said with a humorless laugh. "To be a blank little nothing? An empty vessel just waiting to be filled up?"

D'antre looked down and noticed a few dots of blood on his sheets. *Ain't took nobody's virginity in a long, long time,* he thought.

"Yup," he said, "Thass pretty much it so far as I can tell."

Despite what was coming out if his mouth, inside D'antre had to concede that his lack of faith was certainly being tested. Things were happening around him that he simply could not explain.

"Great," she said, resigned. They lay back, and she rested her head on his bare chest. "So be it. Do whatever you must, god. Whatever be your will." She sighed. "It does kind of suck, though, to lose three thousand dollars' worth of tattoos."

D'antre looked at the vast, sprawling web of colored ink that covered Pearl's body and wondered which tattoos she could have possibly lost. How could there have been three thousand dollars' worth more than this?

Suddenly there was a knock at the door.

"D'antre?" It was Shel.

"Whass good, dog?"

Shel entered quickly, with that caffeine gleam in his eye that stated he was on a creative roll, and probably a White Cross high. Thanks to Shel's associates in the furnace-and-boiler business, his overall productivity and output had increased exponentially. And he had never been fond of sleeping anyway.

"Good!" Shel said, seeing Pearl in bed with D'antre. "I'm glad you're both in here, cuz I wanted to talk to both of you anyway. Hey! Staple Singers!"

"You know it, son. So whass the word?"

"Johannesburg."

"Thass what I'M talkin' 'bout. Howz it goin' inna catacombs?"

"Swimmingly, I guess," Shel said, fidgeting absently with a compartment ring on his left hand. "There's already kids puking in the alley."

"Let the healing begin," said Pearl.

"You all need to get dressed," Shel said. "There's something I need to show you. The alley's actually where we're going."

Pearl and D'antre sighed, separated from one another, and rolled out of their naked, comfortable stasis. They rummaged on the floor for clothes as Shel paced, chattering excitedly.

"So D," he said, "that church across the alley, is it currently in use? Do they have services and whatnot?"

"Far as I know. Them two house-lookin' Baptist churches across Blackstone Street definitely are. But I ain't awake when nonna them likely to be havin' service, knamsayin?"

"The one across the alley, they're Seventh Day Adventists?"

"I think so."

"What I thought." Shel spotted a roach in D'antre's ashtray. He looked to D'antre who gave him a thumbs-up. Shel fished it from the tray and sparked it up. "Fun fact about those folks," Shel said taking a toke, "Seventh Day Adventists. They were founded by a lady named Ellen White, who started having prophetic visions of spirits and saints after a severe head injury that left her in a coma for three weeks. She suffered from temporal lobe epilepsy, which causes, besides vivid hallucinations, seizures which resemble possession by the Holy Spirit—"

"You ramblin', dog."

"Anyway, to the issue at hand, there's this outside vent shaft coming up from the furnace facing that church over there across the alleyway that I want you guys to—" he stopped short, distracted by the sight of Pearl's bare back as she pulled on her blue jeans. Clear and perfect, to his eyes, like the skin of a newborn. He was so used to seeing her wide array of injected artwork, that he was still not used to seeing her skin empty, devoid of any marking. "Sorry," he said. "I was just remembering your ink, Pearl. The two scissoring bat-girls? Man, that was such a great piece. It woulda made a great album cover. Shame you had to lose it."

"I know, right?" Pearl said, clipping on her bra, and looking at her own back in a full-sized mirror propped against the wall, clear to her eyes as well. "I miss that one so much. And it wasn't cheap."

Listening to the two of them, D'antre felt an uncomfortable prickle on the back of his neck. *What the fuck they talkin' 'bout?* He was looking at Pearl's back as well, and there was no missing that, among a great multitude of others, she very clearly had a tattoo of two naked, bat-winged women with their legs intertwined, marred slightly by several dime-sized surgery scars near her spine. How they could not see this at all was beyond his comprehension. He said nothing about it, though, and they all exited.

Outside in the alleyway, they found two jittery young cellar-dwellers retching into rusted out tin garbage cans. Their faith and Min's healing caress had obviously done the job.

"Y'all aw'ight?" D'antre asked. "Need anythang?"

"We're good, Brother D'antre," one of them answered, keeping his eyes lowered, reverently acknowledging D'antre's station in The Church, as well as his being Master of the House. "We're doing better already. Praise god and River Sam. And god bless Sister Min for what she's done for us." He proceeded to vomit painfully into the can once again.

"No doubt," D'antre said with a close-lipped smile. "Well, y'all take care. Drink plenty of water tonight. You don't wanna dehydrate now, y'heard?"

They thanked him, then shuffled queasily off back inside, and downstairs. It was going to be a rough night for the newly purified.

"At least they're conscious and mobile," Pearl observed. "Better than I was."

"They're probably not as loaded as you were," Shel said. "And they weren't *touched as deeply.*"

"True enough."

"So look..." Shel said, pointing to a mesh-covered vent on the side of the building. "I noticed this after we came back from the show tonight. This vent shaft leads directly down to the furnace in nearly a straight shot. The acoustics inside it are *intense.* I was down recording my Frankenstein bass in the furnace room earlier tonight, and I could hear—faint but distinct—outside sound carrying through the shaft, which also carries straight off to the main hall. It might very well bleed through the entire Church!"

"We could baffle it," Pearl said.

"No fuckin' way!"

"Thass cool, son, I guess," D'antre said with a shrug. "But whass that got to do wit me and Pearl?"

"The sound I was hearing," Shel said, "I think, was coming from inside the Seventh Day Adventist church."

"Oh...yeah?"

"I'm pretty sure. And the sound was...Look at this," he said, pointing to the side of the opposing church in question. There it was, another vent shaft leading inside that building as well. "It works kinda like those old tin horns they used to use for recording back in the early 1900s. The sound is *other-fucking-worldly*. What I would like to do if we can swing it, and Will told me it's possible with minimal damage to the ducts if we're careful, is run a dynamic mic up through the shaft, and record the two of you inside the *other* church laying down some heavy-as-balls vocals! Screaming, rhyming, testifying, what have you. What do y'all think?"

"I think you done lost yo' damn mind, dog."

"Probably!" Shel agreed.

"But yeah," D'antre said. "I'll ask 'em. See if they'll let us come in and do it. Aw'ight?"

"This is it," Shel said, fists clenched triumphantly. "This is the sound I've been hunting for my whole life. I can't believe it's taken this long to find it, cuz it seems so obvious now. The sound caught between two churches. The sound of *total annihilation.*"

"If we're going to record the soundtrack to the end of the world," Pearl said, just as bent and gleeful as her partner, "we sure as hell better get it right. We should set up an actual drum kit in there. Record some blast beats. Old-school thrash."

"It was meant to be," Shel said assuredly. "Fate has brought us here at just this time."

D'antre nodded, but he felt that nagging prickle on the back of his neck again. Though he had heard plenty of voices himself back in druggier days, he wasn't one for visions or prophesies. And he had nothing at all for talk of fate. *F'sho, though*, he thought, *a muhfucka's got to listen to his gut onna real.* And something inside was telling him that shit around here just might be teetering a bit out of control.

In the Castle of River Sam

A sacred play in one act

by

Peter James Wellson

If you belonged to this world, it would love you as its own. As it is, you do not belong to this world, but I have chosen you out of this world. That is why the world hates you.

—John 15:23

Cast of Characters:

The Kid
Loraina the Tweak
Petey Wheatstraw

(*Dim lights rise on the main hall of an old, broken down Catholic church. PETEY WHEATSTRAW and LORAINA THE TWEAK sit on the floor on large, maroon seat cushions that have been ripped from their chairs. The two old hobos enjoy steaming mugs of coffee and bowls of piping hot cream of wheat. Outside, thunder booms and winter rain and wind slam against the rickety windowpanes. The sound of a large door creaking open is heard…*)

KID (OS): Hey! Somebody in here?

LORAINA: If you comin' in come on and do it cuz you lettin' all the cold and wet in! (*Enter THE KID, shivering from the cold and junk sickness.*) So what brings you to our home tonight?

KID: Home? Did you say home?

PETEY: Must be the echo in here.

LORAINA: Home, boy. Home. And you home now too, if you means ta be.

KID: Well I don't know what the hell you're talking about, but I'm glad to be out of that shit out there.

(*Petey hands him a mug of coffee.*)

PETEY: I know this isn't what you want, but it's what you need. (*Kid nods a quick "thanks" and gulps the coffee without even blowing first. Kid sits on a spare cushion*). So answer the lady's question.

KID (*cryptic*): I was brung here.

PETEY: Is that right? (*Petey and Loraina share a smile and a wink. Loraina twitches slightly*). Aw'right, let's hear it.

KID: Who are you people?

LORAINA: What's eatin' ya, boy?

KID: Nothing. Nothing's eating me. Nothing at all. I'm just sick, that's all. I got this bad stomach thing. It might be kidney stones or ulcers or something. I need medicine for it, but I—

PETEY: You don't have to make excuses here.

KID: I'm not making excuses. And I'm not a junkie, if that's what you're getting at. Look, I didn't come here to be judged by two old drunks.

PETEY(chuckling): 'Raina's really more of a speed freak.

LORAINA: Hello. We all got snakes in our bellies here, sugar. (*Twitches*).

KID: What is this place?

PETEY: This is The Castle. That's what we call it.

KID: Why have I never heard of it? How many people are here?

PETEY: Couldn't say. Don't really know. We're all nomads, am I right? But everybody got here the same way you did I'm sure. More or less.

LORAINA: So let's hear it.

KID: Well...I don't really know what to say. Earlier I was downtown. I was nodding. Had made a real clean score and I was trying to find a warm enough spot to sleep. I found a decent place right back from the river wall. So there I am. I'm drifting off, and I see all this graffiti painted on the brick there—"Here Lies—

KID, LORAINA, & PETEY (*in unison*): "River Sam."

(*Kid is startled*)

KID: Yeah. Yeah, that's right. And a bunch of other things around it too. "Loving father..."

LORAINA: "War hero..."

PETEY: "Quick with a laugh."

KID: Yeah. What's going on?

LORAINA: Keep on with your story now.

KID: Well, I have no idea who this River Sam character is. But I'm thinking it's pretty interesting that this wall down by the river is, like, a monument to him or something. I'm reading all the things people had wrote, and I'm starting to feel better cuz the juice is kicking in nicely. So I decide to add a little something to the wall myself. I took a broken corner of brick and scraped in, "free man." I don't know why. I just wanted to be a part of it I guess. Maybe I meant myself. Like I'm a free man. Or this Sam guy, if he's dead like I assume he is, well, does it get much freer than that?

PETEY: True.

KID: So, don't you know just then I see them red and blue rolling lights coming from the landing above. I hear these pigs and their dogs slobbering up there, "Who's down there? Don't fuggin' move!" And I'm panicking, you know, cuz they test me right now and I'm finished. (*Barking like a cop.*) "Call it in, I'm going down." I'm so screwed, because there's nothing but prison in front of me, and nothing but the river behind. (Beat.) But then…I see…something. Something rustling in the trees by the riverbank…

(*Silhouette of a figure appears.)*

FIGURE (*monotone*): Follow me.

KID: "Who is it?" I wonder. But I don't really have room or time to argue or ask questions.

FIGURE: Follow me.

KID: So I did. Through the pitch black. Through the blinding rain and the wind. With those pigs screeching behind me. I walked and walked for hours, through the mud along the river, sometimes wondering if there even was anybody there.

FIGURE: Follow me.

KID: But I'd catch enough of a glimpse to keep going. And my juice is wearing off. Fast. I double over in pain.

FIGURE: Quarter G.

(*The figure fades away.*)

KID: Sure enough, it was right! I checked my pocket and I had a quarter grain tab I didn't even know about. I threw my coat over my head, cooked it up, pushed off, and when I pulled my head back out, I saw this here church across the street. I'd never seen it before...and I've been down this road plenty. (*Loraina and Petey laugh.*) So yeah, I'm crazy, right? Piss off.

LORAINA: You ain't crazy, boy. You home. Have some supper.

(*She dishes out some cream of wheat.*)

KID: There's...a...stove?

PETEY: Stove. Sink. Water closet. Cellar full of wine, if that's your bag at all. Everything works.

LORAINA: And no pigs. Ever. (*Twitch.*)

PETEY: No pigs, no college boys, no nothing but us. And everything works.

KID: It's a church. It's a Catholic church.

PETEY: Used to be.

KID: Yours and yours.

LORAINA: And yours. And Chief's. And Henry's. And D'antre's. And that girl everybody calls Goosey. Everybody's.

KID: Why? How?

(Petey and Loraina are silent and reflective. Finally…)

LORAINA: I didn't know Sam. Petey ain't know'd him none either, but I ain't never even spoke to the man. (Twitch.)

PETEY: Sam was a quiet one. Kept to himself most of the time. Friendly enough, but not really needing much in the way of friends, if you get my meaning. Hung out down by the riverside all the time. So we got to calling him River Sam, and he seemed to like that just fine. Well, you know how we do it. A body wants to be left alone, we leave them alone.

LORAINA: That's right.

PETEY: So anyway, I got to sticking with that Navajo everyone calls Chief. Big, strong bastard. Good man to have in a tight corner. You know that city hall…they mean to run us all out of town. Just like the original Ben Ishmaels. They've been on that kick for some years now. Plays well with the electorate. They say we're an embarrassment, a blight on the city. And so, that pretty much makes it open season on hobos.

LORAINA: I was staying under the Viaduct when I heard the news that there was roaming gangs of college boys going 'round attacking us. This was two summers ago. And ole Mista Mayor ain't got boo to say about it. It was a nasty night that night. Them boys…and don't think the pigs wasn't party to this…they had some wild hairs on them that night and they was bashing people this and that-a-way.

(Sounds of screaming and bloody violence are heard...)

LORAINA: Next morning was like a hobo convention, I'll tell you what. Folks I never did spoke with before was all comin' up sayin', "Is you all right? Something I can do?" We did come to find that everybody made it through the night alive. Almost...*(Masked people appear. They are the college boys. They carry baseball bats and blackjacks. The silhouette of the figure appears as well. The college boys cackle.)*

FIGURE: Y'all just let me be, ya hear?

COLLEGE BOY 1: Shut the fuck up, you fucking bum.

COLLEGE BOY 2: Worthless goddamn trash. Why don't you just fucking die.

FIGURE: Just leave me alone, now.

(The boys proceed to beat the figure to death. They disappear laughing.)

PETEY: I didn't really know the man. I know that he fought in the Vietnam War. I know that he drank.

LORAINA: Somebody said he got a daughter in Pittsburgh he ain't seen in twenty years.

PETEY: But nobody knew River Sam. Nobody knew him. But...it just all...it just got to us. Do you understand? It got to us. Here he was, this man, this human being, beaten to death. And there was nobody to care about it. What were THEY going to do? Just burn him up or throw him on a pile?

LORAINA: Put tags on his toes and call him "John Doe?" We all felt it. Fifteen of us standing around. Old timers. Feeling the same thing. They do him like that, they do ALL us like that. And we can't have it. So everybody start to poolin' together what change we got. Money folks was gonna spend on food or drink or whatever they was needin' all went into the pool. And we scrounged up enough that we all marched down to that hardware store downtown what's going out of business and we bought us a shovel and a can of black spray paint. No telling what folks was thinking on that when they seen us all marching there! (*They laugh.*)

PETEY: We went back. And we took turns digging a nice, big hole down by the riverside. Up far enough so that it wouldn't all just rush away down stream. And we painted on that wall everything we could think of. "Here Lies River Sam. The World is poorer without him here." And we buried him. And we had a funeral as if old Sam had been a millionaire. It was right. It was right for us to do.

LORAINA: Then...it started to happen. People started seeing...shadows.

FIGURE: Follow me, Pete.

PETEY: One by one, those of us whom had been there started seeing just what you saw, my boy.

FIGURE: Follow me, 'Raina.

LORAINA: Winter was comin' on by the time the last of us followed. Followed him right here to this big ole empty church. First weeks we just waited. For the bum's rush, as they say, heh heh. But it never come.

FIGURE: Home...now...(*fades away.*)

LORAINA: We don't know who owns it. Young man upstairs payin' the rent. We stay outta his way much as possible. But more's comin'. Lots more. Young 'uns like you. Folks what slipped through the cracks.

KID: Slipped through the cracks.

LORAINA: Slipped right through the cracks.

KID: Just like us.

PETEY: That's right. And we come here to work out our demons.

LORAINA: Get the snakes outta our bellies. (*Twitch.*) Or not.

PETEY: When hobos mark the river wall, just like you did, River Sam thanks them for their kindness and leads them here.

LORAINA: This is our castle.

KID: Ours.

PETEY: Our castle.

LORAINA: And we's ALL Lords and Ladies here.

Ancient and Angry Gods

There are many different kinds of pushers, and each installation is different, but the principles are always alike. The first step in the design of a pusher is to determine the force necessary to move the material to be pushed.

—Matthew H. Mawhinney,
Practical Industrial Furnace Design (1928)

After a solid week of high fevers, nausea and a collective 'bout of "the shakes," the newly healed Lower Church Ishmaels emerged from the catacombs, wobbly, but energized and invigorated.

Queries as to the whereabouts of Petey Wheatstraw and Loraina the former Tweak went unanswered with any satisfaction, as they had not been seen by anyone in several days. This was of little concern. People disappearing for days or weeks at a time was common around The Church. The assumption was always that they would be back eventually, which was often (though not always) the case.

With Petey MIA, the younger River-Samites looked to Anton for wisdom and guidance, however temporary. Taken by surprise, and a bit drunk, he proceeded to fill their heads with horrific tales of military black ops and secret US torture programs being carried out all over the globe that made the worst that had already been exposed by the mainstream news media sound like a sissy girl pillow fight. So much for wisdom or guidance, but asses were certainly perched at seats' edge.

It was periodically remarked upon that no one outside of The Church, even still, given all that had happened, seemed to notice that the end of the world was eminent. But then this observation was quickly dismissed. *Of course they're noticing. The Earth itself is falling apart at the seams (or trying to shed us from it), people are slaughtering one another at a fantastic rate, dogmatic fundamentalist religions are all the rage these days, and are dictating the world's collective social policy...* Really it was textbook, boilerplate Armageddon. But how is one to react to the slow grind of the apocalypse? Panicking and screaming and running about? How long can that sort of hysteria be maintained? How long before you eventually just go back to laying down the day-to-day routines you're accustomed to? Everyone knew. Everyone knows. *End of the world. Fine. Que sera sera.* If anything, it just made the society as a whole more numb to the atrocities being committed around them (and by them, by proxy). American professionals overseas, at the behest of their "elected" leaders, had taken a fancy to the practice of raping small children in front of their parents. "For information." And hunting brown people like they were wild game. Just good sport. And folks back home, by and large, were cool with that (excluding the residents of The Blackchurch, of course).

"If there some knowledge out there I can only acquire by ass-fuckin' a six-year-old in fronta his mama," D'antre said to no one in particular, "thass some shit I don't really need to know, ya feel me?"

Pearl listened in on Anton's rambling, booze-addled lecture as well, and felt a jolt of rage that she hadn't in a very long time. It inspired her to write some "real metal" again, which Shel was quite happy to hear.

For his part, Shel was equally glad to have a solid number of the cellar dwellers up and around. He proceeded to recruit quite a few of them, give them all mallets and drum sticks, and asked,

"Any of y'all know about Art Blakey? How about John Bonham?"

He (with Min's assistance) taught them some basic drum patterns, and positioned them at different sections along the Blackchurch furnace's sprawling steel and aluminum ductwork, into which he had already snaked several dynamic microphones. Come what may, Shel was hell-bent on not only capturing the acoustic possibilities of the ambient space at large, but of using the entire Church itself as one, massive musical instrument.

After forty-odd minutes of rehearsal, Shel counted off the beat and the banging commenced in, more or less, proper time. Subsequent takes yielded progressively faster, tighter, louder results. Malachi and Shonda Jefferson later said that they could hear it all the way from the coffee shop.

"What in hell y'all doin' to that beautiful unit down there?" Will Fanon grumbled indignantly as he walked in on the twelfth, and hardest, take of the recording.

"It's called a blast beat, cuz'n," Shel said, oddly pleased with the interruption. So pleased, in fact, that he decided to keep it on the final released version of the cut.

"I gotta borrow yer man for a little while, Lydia," Will said to Pearl. "Hope that's okay." Will Fanon never quite grasped the nature of Shel and Pearl's relationship, and assumed, despite all evidence to the contrary, that they must be a couple. (On the flipside, Pearl and Shel could never figure out why Will Fanon insisted on calling her "Lydia." D'antre told them it was a Groucho Marx reference, but they still didn't get it, and he opted not to explain.)

In addition to paying his share of the rent, Shel had been amassing, over the previous few months, a sizable arsenal of analog recording equipment and bargain-bin instruments to tear apart and re-shape. So as a result, he and Will Fanon had been taking on a larger workload to cover the costs. Win-win all around, as it got Will out of the house more, in addition to providing him more opportunities to get drunk after work.

"Okay, Mr. Fanon," Pearl said, trying to keep her eyes from rolling out of her skull. "Just not too late now."

Much later that evening, the Upper Church Five had their late-late-night meal together. It would actually have been a *Thanks-*

giving dinner, had any of them bothered to check the date. As it was, the meal was entirely vegan, unable as Pearl's delicate system was to handle any meat products (rough going for carnivores like Anton and D'antre, but they made do).

"You know, Shel," Anton said, "if yer lookin' to capture the sound of a giant heavy metal beast-machine, you really outta come out to the factory with me or D'antre some night and record the bottle press. Course that shit'll destroy them supersonic ears of yers if you ain't careful. I'm goin' 'bout deaf from it already. But it makes a helluva lotta badass racket."

"True, son, true," D'antre said. "I be settin' all kindsa rhymes to the beat of that machine."

"I may just do that, cuz'n," Shel said. "Will took me out to see that massive boiler they got down under University Hospital. Goddamn, what a glorious monstrosity that fucker is. Dante didn't dream that shit up."

"Ol' boy is crazy fo' that stuff onna real," D'antre said. "But hey. Gotta do whatcha love, knahmean? Thass what I'm sayin'."

"It's funny," said Shel. "I meant to tell y'all this before. Will came to pick me up one day last week and he goes, 'So... are y'all...like a cult here or something?'" They all laughed. Shel continued, "I told him, joking of course, that he should join up with us, and he said, not a word of it a lie, 'No sir. I have my own gods, thank you very much.'"

"Please tell me he wasn't talking about furnaces," Pearl said.

"Pressure boilers, yeah."

"Jesus."

"You gotta understand," Shel said, "Those guys...they're fundamentalists. Radical fundamentalists. HVAC is their religion, and furnace units and pressure boilers really are their gods. And Will is far from the most zealous of them. By a long shot. He rolls with a gang of boiler operators who are...they're *jihadists.* They are actually plotting a holy war against the Ohio Special."

"What's the Ohio Special?" Pearl asked.

"Automatic pressure boiler," D'antre interjected. "Totally unmanned. Requires no operator."

"It's sacrilege," Shel said nodding his head. "Heresy."

"All shapes and sizes," Anton said with a shrug. "No dumber, I guess, than thinkin' god created you in its image."

"You tell him I'm stealin' his book title?" D'antre asked Shel.

"Yeah," Shel said. "He had no idea what you're talking about. No memory whatsoever. I think you're in the clear."

"Cool."

"I don't like that mothafucka," Min said with a scowl, getting up to take her plate to the sink. "He a mean, racist old drunk."

"Aw come on, girl," D'antre said, "he ain't *that* old. White dudes just don't age that well, knamsayin?"

"Hello," said Anton pointing at his own ravaged face. "I'm only thirty-eight."

"Good god, cuz'n," Shel said, nearly choking on his wine. "For real?"

"Look at yer future, amigo," Anton replied with a sinister, rasping cackle. "*There ain't no escape.*"

"You're not a fair example, Anton," Pearl said. "You've been through the ringer harder than the average honky."

"True enough."

"ANYWAY," Min said, "it ain't that he old. I don't like him cuz he used to beat up his wife and son and pull guns on 'em when he drunk."

"How on earth do you know that?" Pearl asked.

"*I just know,*" Min answered cryptically.

"Mother of the unborn savior got access to all kinda inside info," D'antre said. "Ya heard?" And he wasn't sure if he was serious or not.

"You read Mikal's manuscript yet?" Min asked D'antre. "You might-could find it s'prisin'."

"Not yet, but I will," D'antre said. "I promise. And Imma send it to my boy Sal in New York right after."

"A'ight."

"So D," Pearl said, "You've been chatting with your ex a lot on the phone lately."

"Gooda you to notice," D'antre replied.

"Are you trying to rekindle the old spark or something?" she asked with a sly grin.

"Naaaaw, that ship done LONG since sailed, you feel me? We just gettin' along better now. I think she finally openin' up to the idea of me and Meka havin' a real kinda relationship. TJ got full custody cuz of my record, and I get that, knahmean? Thass why I ain't had no recourse when she done took my baby girl outta state. But iss gittin' good now. I think she aw'ight wit seein' me when I head up there in a coupla weeks. Maybe not. I don't really care, though, I just wanna see my daughter, ya heard?"

"That's good, bro," Anton said, knocking on the table in affirmation. "You got somethin' special there, and you ought not let it slip away from you."

Anton looked up at Min. They shared a quick smile that no one else saw (or so they thought. D'antre saw it. And he understood. Min's baby-to-be meant more than life itself to Anton… and even if she hadn't been pregnant with the messiah, he would have felt the same. Anymore, helping shepherd that precious child through the barbs and jags of this wretched Earth was truly Anton's abiding…in fact *only*…concern. His every egg rested in that basket). Just as quickly, they each looked away again.

For a brief moment no one spoke, and they all caught a quick listen to the gunshots providing a bit of soundtrack somewhere not too far in the distance.

"Somethin' stank up in here, D'antre," Min said.

"F'real?" he replied. "I don't smell nothin.'"

"I do," Pearl said. "It's real faint, but I smell it. Like a dead animal maybe."

"There might-could be a raccoon or sump'n that got trapped up inna steeple," D'antre said. "Iss happen befo'."

"Whose responsibility is that?"

"Prolly mine," D'antre answered with a sigh as they all set

about clearing the table. "I'll climb up and check inna mornin'."

The following day Anton held the ladder for D'antre as he climbed up into the Church steeple searching for the source of the offending aroma, which grew steadily more apparent by the hour. Finding nothing out of the ordinary, D'antre climbed back down just in time to see an unfamiliar figure stride briskly through the front double doors and into the main hall. From D'antre's vantage point, the dapper stranger cut the unmistakable shape of a generic Black TV preacher: Double-breasted lavender suit. Salmon necktie. Head shaved, black and shiny, to match a spit-polished pair of Paxton loafers.

"Yo, TD Jakes," D'antre called down from the Church loft, "can I help you, sir?"

The figure looked up toward the loft, and D'antre nearly tipped over the railing. *Mothafuck. Naaaaw...Naaaaaaaaaaaaaaw...*

D'antre ran down the steps, nearly tripping, and into the main hall.

"Hello D'antre," Petey said, cool and detached. He looked around The Church, absently tracing his perfectly chiseled, pencil-thin salt-and-pepper van dyke with his thumb and index finger, appraising the space as if he had been gone for several months, instead of the week or so that it had been. "How are my children feeling? Have you seen them?"

"They doin' good from what I seen," D'antre said, still more than a bit dumbstruck. "A lot better now than they first was. Shel been teachin' 'em how to play...uh...the furnace."

Petey chuckled and nodded.

"I see."

"So...whass good witchoo, nigga?"

Petey gave D'antre a sour glance and said, "Enough with the colloquial patter, D'antre. It is beneath a man of your intelligence."

"Um...aw'ight." D'antre scratched the back of his head.

Several of the younger members of the Tribe emerged into the main hall, caught sight of Petey and gasped, then ran off to gather the others. "Where y'been at, dog? *Where have you been?*"

"Here and there, "Petey replied. "Hither and yon. My principle task, of course, concerned looking into filing a 501c3."

"How come?" Anton said, hobbling down the steps from the loft and out into the hall, looking Petey up and down, clearly unnerved by the man's sudden change in appearance and demeanor. "Whut's that about, brother?" Anton limped closer toward Petey and D'antre, a palpable edge of suspicion about him.

"Just a smart precaution, brother," Petey replied with a bland smile. "That's all."

"Precaution fer whut?" Anton asked. "Whut's tax exemption gonna mean when the apocalypse comes? Whut's 'at got to do with buildin' the new world after? Huh?"

"I simply think it best to cross every *T*," Petey said. "We all know the end is coming. Of course we know that. It's clear. It has been foretold. But when? Have you seen when for sure?"

"Soon, brother," Anton said, squaring his jaw. "Soon and very soon."

"Of course," Petey said. "Absolutely. But until that day comes, we have the reality of *this* world with which to contend. You understand."

Anton stepped back, stunned, affronted by Petey's words.

"Yeah?" Anton said. "Huh. That don't sound too much like faith to me. Brother."

The main Church hall began to fill with young Ishmaels just in time to witness the battle of the hobo prophets begin. They gathered in a wide circle around Petey and Anton as they stood set across from each other, D'antre back a few paces.

"Interesting observation, Brother Anton," Petey said. "Particularly coming from you."

Resentments had apparently been brewing deep inside the two of them for some time, and no one had been aware. There was certainly no mystery now.

"What's 'at mean?" Anton growled. "You questionin' MY faith? I done spoke with the angels of the Lord! Just like you done! I seen visions of all that was and alla whut's yet to come. Have you?! I been blessed, or cursed, with god's ev'ry holy afflicttion, from telepathy to second sight. It's all packed tight into my head, *brother*, whether I want it or not. And I done used it all to praise god and do its will. Whut YOU got, brother, besides a shiny new suit, a buncha confused kids follerin' you round like the pied fuckin' piper...oh, and *River Sam*?"

An alarmed murmur filled the hall at Anton's sarcastic dismissal of their guiding spirit. Shel entered from Min's sacristy (Min and Pearl being both away at work), a pair of headphones around his neck and an unplugged eight-string bass guitar in hand, drawn away from his craft and obsession by the sound of raised voices.

"Do you think I'm envious of your *hallucinations*, Anton?" Petey said, with a mocking chuckle. "Do you think I'm trying to take some sort of control over The Tribe?" That was, in fact, precisely what Anton thought. "Do you actually think I am threatened by your gifts? Dear Lord, brother. Nothing could be further from the truth. I am open to *all* that god have given us...not just *your* particular brand of damaged neurotheology." Anton raised his left eyebrow and cocked his head to the side, clearly not sure of what Petey was saying. He was not alone. "But you, Anton, you're always closed off to other possibilities. You've just never been able to open your heart to River Sam." D'antre opened his mouth to interject, but then did not. "Because you've never been a true gypsy have you," Petey continued. "Never *really* been a hobo. It's a damn shame. Your loss, brother, and I'm sad for you. So full of rage, Anton, even now. And regret. And so full of nagging doubt."

"Ain't got no doubt at all. No sir. I believe in whut I can actu'lly see, Pete," Anton hissed through his gray, crooked teeth, tapping himself hard on the forehead.

"The very definition of *lack of faith*, Anton," Petey said.

"By the way, I no longer answer to that name. Call me BEN ISHMAEL."

The Church fell, for perhaps the first time ever, utterly silent. No static, no voices, no outside Blackchurch noise. Not even the subharmonic ambient hum of empty space. Nothing. The pure, undiluted silence stabbed straight into Shel's ear canals like two flat blade screwdrivers, and he fell to the floor clutching his ears in agony. No one noticed him.

Finally, Anton broke the oppressive silence with a meager, "Okay then, Ben Ishmael. Okay then." He continued, in nothing much but a baffled, rasping whisper, "You still ain't said... whut exactly you bringin' to rebuild the world when the time does come."

"Quite obviously," the new Ben Ishmael replied, "I am not just an oracle or a prophet. *I am an architect.*"

Suddenly two young cellar dwellers, a boy and a girl, came flying into the hall, hysterical and screaming, tears pouring down their cheeks—

"COME NOW! FURNACE ROOM! NOW! IT'S LORAINA!!!"

Everyone followed quickly down into the cellar.

And there, wedged in a dark stone corner behind the Church furnace, a broken, cloudy lightbulb in one hand, a cheap plastic lighter in the other, they found Loraina the former Tweak. Staring eyes wide and devoid of light. Hollow. Mouth wide and hollow. All hollow.

To the Sleeping Church

Satan himself masquerades as an angel of light.

—2 Corinthians 11:14

"WE'VE GOT TO GET HER OUT OF HERE!"

Wrapped in a black cotton bedsheet, Loraina was carried out of The Church and on back across the gravel lot behind the empty orphanage. Someone was sent to the library to fetch Min, and someone else thought to go collect Pearl from the coffee shop as well.

Min arrived minutes later to find the Tribe gathered there between the building and the dumpster, far more conspicuous than they should have been, but for the moment caution was not top priority. There she found the nameless man who was once called Petey Wheatstraw, but who would soon be cuffed and booked as Peter Wellson, on the ground and on his knees in a fine lavender suit, cradling the body of his longtime companion in his arms.

"Save her, Minnie," he whispered, "please...save her..."

Seeing Loraina there dead in her old lover's arms Min burst into tears, her pregnant hormones beating her senseless from the inside. Not because she knew the woman (in fact no one from Upper Church except Anton could recall ever even hearing Loraina speak), but because her first thought was, *This my fault!!!*

"Please Min...please...she's my queen here...You have to bring her back..."

"I-I don't know if I can, Petey!"

"Please try..."

"How?!"

"Please...*please...*"

Min got down on the ground and took Loraina into her arms. She caressed the deceased woman's stringy blonde hair, kissed her discolored face softly, as tears spilled heavy down her own.

Everyone else stood around dumbly, hoping against hope that they would witness a miracle there in the gravel lot, some already writing their own Lazarus gospel in their heads, should this actually work.

Only D'antre thought to himself, *She already startin' to swell and stiffen. Don't nobody come back from that shit. Stop this madness now. Stop this madness. Now.*

After what felt like an eternity for everyone, Min finally gave up.

"I'm s-so sorry, Petey," Min sobbed. "I don't know w-w-what to do!"

He took Loraina back gingerly into his arms.

"I just thought that maybe..." he whispered. "Thank you for trying, honey-child."

"I'm so s-s-s-sorry...I'm so sorry..."

Tears began to flow throughout the gathered crowd. Anton and D'antre bowed their heads solemnly, offering shoulders to cry on. Pearl and Shel retreated quietly to the furthest edge of the group, unsure of how to react or behave.

Finally Pearl felt that she had to say something.

"What...what can we do for you, Pete?"

"Someone," he replied, quietly, but direct and official, "anyone other than D'antre, needs to go down to the pay phone on Whetsel Avenue in front of the *Down South Fish Fry* and call the police. Tell them that Loraina and I are back here behind the orphanage. Do NOT give your name or any other information.

"Everyone else, go back to The Church. And *hide.* Do not go all at once. Do not draw attention to The Church. There is no way to keep anyone out, remember? The locks are all gone. If the police come to investigate for any reason, D'antre will be evicted and the rest of you will be hunted down and caged like wild dogs. Do not give them a reason to do that."

"What are you going to tell the police when they come?" someone asked.

"The truth," he replied. "That Loraina and I have been squatting here in the old orphanage, and she overdosed on Desoxyn and Adderall."

"Nobody's going to believe you're a hobo wearing that suit, cuz'n," Shel said.

"They have no choice but to believe me. Now you people need to get away from here. RIGHT NOW."

Everybody turned around and went slowly in a variety of opposing directions, each that would eventually lead back to The Blackchurch.

Once all backs were turned and some distance had been achieved, those still furthest back heard a sound that absolutely everyone hates to hear: the sound of a grown man crying.

"They've got him in handcuffs," Shel said peeking out of the westward side door of The Church toward the orphanage. "And they're loading Loraina into an ambulance. What the fuck good is that now?"

"Gonna be a long night for ol' son," D'antre to no one in particular. He pulled a bent, off-white business card out of his pocket and said, "He ain't got no ID in his wallet 'cept fo' one-a these." The card read simply:

ORACLE.

Shel continued to peek out the slightly cracked door, hoping to remain unnoticed by the police across the lot as they stuffed the former Peter Wellson into the back of a cruiser. Shel wrapped his right knuckles lightly against the door, just enough to keep the piercing silence from returning. From the compartment ring on his left hand he would periodically snort a bit of white powder, sniffing surreptitiously with a quick grimace, and shudder it off.

For their part, the young Ben Ishmaels looked at the dusty

Church floor, lost and confused.

"She was healed…she was clean…" someone would periodically mumble. It went unanswered.

An hour went by. And then two. And more. The only sound after a while being Shel tapping rhythmically on any object within his reach.

Suddenly, and utterly out of the blue, a scrawny girl with a black knit skullcap pulled tightly down over her ears stood up and walked over to where Anton sat on a front pew, deep in thought. She stood in front of him solidly for several long moments not saying a word.

"Can I help you, little sister?" Anton said finally.

"Brother Anton," she said, pointing an accusing finger at him. "You have brought this upon us. This is your fault. You are the reason Sister Loraina relapsed. It is your doing that she died."

"What'n god's black hell…?" Anton replied, taken aback. "Howzit my fault?!"

"It was your lack of faith. Yes. Your cold dismissal of the guiding spirit of the New Ben Ishmael Tribe. Your denial of River Sam that has so angered god. It is punishing us because of you."

Several of the girl's fellows looked up at this pronouncement. Their collective look stated that this hypothesis made good sense to them.

"Come on," Pearl said. "That is plain bullshit right there. Your River Sam clearly does not come for everyone. It hasn't come for…all of us. And that's okay."

"*Our* River Sam, Sister Pearl?" the girl said pointedly. "I thought River Sam was for *all of us*. But I catch your meaning. I sure do. Go ahead and say it, sister. Go ahead and say that he didn't appear for Upper Church because…you didn't *need* him to. You all think you're better than us, right? That you simply don't need the grace and guiding power of River Sam, because you're all so mighty and high. Interesting isn't it, Sister Pearl, that both you and Brother Sheldon conveniently lost your voices and your visions, shed them like so much old skin, once Brother Anton could assume them all for you. I think this man," the girl said indicating Anton, "is a false prophet come to deceive us and lead us astray."

"On the contrary," Anton said with a dark smile, standing painfully to face the girl down, his bum leg clearly hurting him, "I reckon you, ALL y'all little whelps, done been sold a billa goods on this River Sam nonsense. River Sam ain't nothin' but a folktale to me. Just a cheesy old grateful dead story gussied up fer today. I ain't never seen a sadder case of propped-up false idol worship in all my days."

"More slander!" the girl spat, shouting out to The Church at large. Several of her contemporaries stood angrily, and began slowly advancing toward Anton. Instinctively he held up his dukes like a nineteenth-century bare-knuckled brawler. "More lies! How much longer must we tolerate this heresy?!"

"YOU DUMB LITTLE HONKY BITCH!" D'antre snarled from out of nowhere, "SIT YO' FATHA-FUCKIN' ASS DOOOOOWN!!!" The girl instantly plopped to the floor Indian-style, staring up at D'antre startled, eyes like rattling saucers. The rest of them sat as well. Even Anton did, and Shel walked over cautiously from the west side door, grabbing a quick toot from his ring in the process. "Y'all wanna know 'bout River Sam? Huh?! Do you?! PAY ATTENTION. I'm fittin' to drop it real up in this piece."

D'antre, now up on the elevated stage, proceeded to pace the proscenium, not like a preacher, but a panther. He glared out at them all, breathing heavy through clenched teeth.

"First off…first off…Anton got it wrong. Feel me? So-called River Sam might-could be false, and he might-could be a phantom, but he sho' ain't no fuckin' folk story. Aw'ight? I KNOWS that nigga. I *knew* him. And he wudn't no saint in life. I don't know how death coulda scrubbed his ass clean." D'antre wiped a shaking hand across his sweaty brow, and continued, "Lamont Samuel Lincoln, oh yes. He my old man's best good friend. *Inseparable.* Like real brothas, aw'ight?

Fought side by side durin' the raid on Dong Xai in 1965."

"*Special forces*," Anton whispered to himself.

"Drove the Vietcong out all on they own," D'antre said, "to hear them two niggas tell it. *Uncle* Lamont, thass what I done called him...even though he wudn't my real uncle, his oldest son Terell and me both born right 'bout six years after that raid. Had three other kids a bit later, Tremaine, Arnold and then Shaniqua. And he ain't paid none of them no mind. At all. Ain' never raise one finger to help raise them up. Too busy drinkin' and runnin' round on they mama. Drive 'Aunt' Tessa alla way crazy. Knamsayin? But them four kids, they got off light. Ya heard? They ain't had MY old man to contend wit.

"That muhfucka...that pile of human trash...I don't know what got into his ass in Vietnam, but it musta been *my* fault. Somehow. Even though I ain't exist yet. Cuz he started beatin' my ass befo' I couldn't even hardly walk. I reach up for him, to pick me up, and instead he throw me to the ground. Hard. Knamsayin?! Look!" D'antre pulled up his right pant leg to reveal a web of raised scars spread across his calf. "Lookit what he done to me! Scalded me wit boilin' water! Fo' spillin' fuckin' Cheerios! Or he strap me into a baby chair and whup me half to death wit a leather belt...fo' any old thing. I WAS TWO YEARS OLD!"

"I saw that!" Shel said, standing up, mouth agape. "I saw it, D'antre! In my mind! That was you?!"

"I was jus' a baby," D'antre growled, trembling with rage. "*Just a goddamn baby*. And that nigga tryin' to kill me. And mama don't do nothin', can't do nothin', cuz he give it to her worser if she do. But who should be there aaaaalways standin' by jus' watchin'? Y'boy *River Sam*, ya heard? Uncle fuckin' Lamont. Not doin' nothin' but standin' there watchin' a baby git beat bloody and half dead. Thass yo' saint, aw'ight? He just as guilty. All he ever done did is stand by lettin' that shit happen. His wife couldn't take it no more, she leave out, and his daughter run off to Philly, and all three a' his boys end up inna pen, and he don't do nothin' but stand there, drinkin' hisself homeless. And that piece of shit gonna *guide* y'all? From beyond his unmarked grave? He couldn't guide his own ass to the shit house. Fuck that muhfucka. Word. Fuck *botha* them bitch-niggas. I wish they wudn't dead...I wish they wudn't...so I could pump rounds into BOTH they sorry asses. Buk buk buk! Believe that. *Die, daddy, die...*Shit. I was...*I was just... just a goddamn baby.*"

Pearl walked slowly toward D'antre, arms outstretched to him, her eyes wet and red-rimmed.

"D'antre..."

"*I was just a baby...*"

She wrapped her arms around him. He did not return the embrace, but stood there still, a pillar of seething rage.

"*Please, D'antre,*" she whispered to him, crying, "*Please let Min heal you. Let her wash that all away.*"

"Just a baby..."

"*They're dead. Okay? They're all dead. They can't hurt you now. Don't let them hurt you anymore.*"

"Just a...fuck...FUCK!"

"*Min can take it away for you. Wash it out. For good. All the memories. All the pain. All the ugliness. You don't need it. Please let her heal you.*"

D'antre snapped back to reality. Back to the present. The eyes of The Church all dead fixed upon him. Pearl softly let go of him, and he stepped back away from her.

"No," he said, shaking his head. "I ain't lettin' that shit go. None of it. It's mine. It's all mine. *My hatred belongs to me.*"

"Brother D'antre," a young, mohawked Chicano said standing up, "with all due deference to you and your station... can you not see that, whatever his trespass in life, god has redeemed River Sam in death? That so favored was he that god has entrusted in him a sacred task? Can you not see that, or are you so blinded by your anger? Of all of us here, brother, you are the *only one* who has not been touched by god's light: by the sight of god, or the voice of god, or even a single one of god's angels on Earth. You have experienced none of it. You're closed off to it. Only you. Perhaps you are not chosen after all.

Perhaps you are meant to leave this place."

D'antre laughed bitterly. "Y'all gonna try to force ME out? Me? Onna real?! Thass some funny-ass shit right there. I'm the only nigga who got a LEASE up in here!"

"No one is leaving," a voice said, from over by the oak double doors. Into the dim light of The Church stepped a now familiar figure in a fine lavender suit, now looking worn out and weary. Ragged at the knees. "No one. LEAST of all that man there." He pointed toward D'antre.

Anton limped over to the new arrival. They looked at one another for several long seconds. Finally they embraced.

"I'm so sorry fer yer loss, brother," Anton said.

The older man looked Anton in the eyes. "Why couldn't you see it, brother?" He looked over toward Shel. "Or you? Why did your second sight not tell you about Loraina?" There was nothing accusatory in his tone. It was simply a question, one for which he desperately desired an answer. He patted Anton on the shoulder and walked out into the front center of the main hall. "Of all the angels who have visited me, could none who have seen the future, been to the future, could none of them have noticed that she was no longer in it? Was so she insignificant to god that it felt that she didn't warrant so much as a mention? Nothing at all? Well hell...she was special to me. *She was special to me...*" he trailed off, tracing a half-moon in the dust of the Church floor with the tip of his scuffed Paxton loafer. "She was my..."

"*Ereshkigal...*" D'antre whispered to himself.

"She was special to me."

"Whass the word, ol' son," D'antre said to the man in lavender, still shaking slightly from the adrenaline draining from his system.

"*Que sera sera*, young D. That's three words, isn't it. How about *ventricular tachycardia*. That's one less word. Wordy word word. No real surprises there."

"Thass what did her?" D'antre asked. "How you know? Ain't no way they done the autopsy and toxicology test that quick."

"You don't need to be a forensic pathologist to diagnose that one, young Master Philips. Or an oracle."

"Aw'ight. But what abou'choo?"

"They have nothing on me," he replied. "What's the punishment for squatting; a night in a free bed? They know I didn't kill her, and even if I had...they wouldn't care."

The older man walked slowly toward the cellar door, a droop in his shoulders never seen before by the kids who had followed him. It disturbed them all, so accustomed were they to his confidence and pride. His assuredness. Many stood to join him in the catacombs, but several others did not.

"Brother Ishmael," Anton called out before the man in lavender reached the cellar door. "Whut do you suggest we do now?"

"Be a family," the older man said over his shoulder as he disappeared down the stairs. "Stay a family. Look out for each other. When the end of everything else comes, we will be all that we have. And, as always, prepare ye the way of the Lord."

Blackchurch Furnace

The Earth died screaming, while I lay dreaming of you.
—Tom Waits

In the wake of Loraina the Tweak's passing, there were noticeably fewer Lower Church Ishmaels around than there had been. Speculation was that several of them had departed, possibly to try to piece together some semblance of a "normal life" before it was too late. A less charitable theory went that they had all gone off in search of isolation so they could relapse in peace, without interference. If anyone were to have known for sure it would have been their spiritual father down in the catacombs, but he was temporarily out if service, tucked away in his bed in a dark corner, sleeping for days on end. The young ones who were still about stayed largely out of sight.

In the meantime, the Upper Church Five went about their business much as they had been. A Paxton shoebox marked *prenatal* and filled with cash was found on D'antre's kitchen table, and he, Pearl, Anton, and Shel all accompanied Min to the doctor's office for a check-up and ultrasound.

"MeShayle?" a sweet-voiced older nurse called into the waiting room. "MeShayle Nodding?"

"Right here," Min said standing.

"Wonderful!" the kindly lady said with a bright smile. "You can come on back with me, dear. Is, by chance, the father with you?" Anton, Shel, D'antre and Pearl all raised their hands. The nurse furrowed her brow for a moment, then shrugged. "Very well. You all can come on back too."

The four huddled around the monitor as the nurse ran the

camera across Min's bare, jelly-coated belly. Her stomach remained mostly flat as yet, although a slight bump was starting to show.

"Nope...nope..." the nurse said, trying to locate a heartbeat. "Oh, here we are!" There on the monitor they could all see, clear as day, the tiny hummingbird heart beating rapidly. A collective smile shot across every face in the room. Min beamed at the sight of it, as a few small tears of joy escaped from her bright, shining eyes. "Congratulations, mama," the nurse said, patting Min's small hand. "That's a perfectly healthy little heartbeat you got in there. You're both fit as too little fiddles."

Out of the corner of his eye, D'antre noticed Anton mouthing silently to himself, his eyes transfixed on the screen, *Yer gonna save us...Yer gonna save us...*

"Can you see the sex?" Min asked. "Can you tell?"

"It's a bit early yet, sweetheart," the nurse replied. "Come back in a couple of weeks and we'll know then."

"I will! I sho nuff will! We got enough money to come back, D'antre?"

"Yup," he replied. "The shoebox done got it covered, ya heard?"

The nurse raised her right eyebrow and twisted her lips to the side, clearly not sure of what to make of this lot. But she kept mum, and simply went about the business of wiping the jelly from Min's belly. Some questions, after all, are best left unasked.

This week everyone picked up extra hours at their respective places of employment. They all wanted to contribute to the shoebox as well. Additionally, D'antre wanted to pack in a bit of overtime as he would be taking a five-day holiday to Madison, Wisconsin for his daughter's birthday party. He bought her an iPod, including a handful of songs that he considered essential for her library...the X Clan...the Pharcyde... Stigmata Dog...D'antre and Tijuana Smalls spoke on the phone every day that week, ostensibly to nail down last minute plans, but in actuality there wasn't that much more to plan.

"So I's thinkin', D."

"Yeah?"

"You think you...might-could cancel your hotel reservetion?"

"Uh...prolly. Whass up?"

"Well, if it's too late, than nev'mind. But if you can, why don't you stay wit us? Meka been campaignin' hard for it for weeks. The house is pretty big here, and we do actually got a guest room. No sense spendin' that money, you know?"

"I won't be inna way, ya heard? You know I ain't tryin' to trip."

"It's...I don't know. It's kinda crazy. I am actually kinda sorta maybe almost lookin' forward to seein' you, D'antre."

"Me too, Boo. Me too."

The day of the party D'antre worked a half-day morning shift. Driving home early from the factory was a peculiar experience. He was not used to coming home in the daylight, and it was somewhat disorienting, even though this particular day was dark and overcast. Just knowing the sun was up there somewhere threw off his rhythms.

He was eager to get home and pack a bag for the drive up to Madison. *Fourteen. Could she really be fourteen...*He was excited to see Dameka. *Baby girl.* It had been quite a while, and maybe he was a bit nervous as well.

Even though their numbers were down, there was still usually somebody at home, somewhere in The Church knocking around. Everyone was fine by then, all more or less forgiven, but D'antre still hoped beyond hope that he'd have at least a little time all to himself for a short bit. To unwind, to collect his thoughts.

Once home, the joint seemed downright *cave-like,* barren and hollow. No one about at all. He stuck his head into The Church proper and shouted out, "Hellooo!" Nothing. "Anybody up in this piece?" Not a word. No voices, no banging or thumping in the basement, not a sound.

He was just about to turn and head on up to the crib, fire one up, grab some food and get ready to hit the road, when he heard a bit of crying echoing from somewhere…

"Somebody here?" he asked. He was so used to hearing random creaks and voices and various noises throughout The Church that he nearly ignored it and went on about his business. But he heard it again. No mistaking.

The sound got louder the closer he stepped toward the old ladies washroom that he didn't think anyone even used anymore. He heard the crying again, louder still, and he recognized the voice.

"Min?" D'antre said. "Min? That you in there, girl?"

Could she still be upset 'bout Loraina? D'antre wondered to himself. *Or just a hormone thing?* He heard a whimper and a squeak from her that wasn't in character at all.

"Somethin' wrong," she cried softly. "Somethin' real wrong."

He opened the door, and *Oh my god…*

Blood.

So much blood. In the sink, on the tiles, dripping from the edge of the toilet. Min sat in the middle of the floor, rocking, arms wrapped around her shins, blood on her hands and thighs. "Somethin' wrong, D," she whispered, tears pouring down her cheeks.

Without another word D'antre reached down and scooped her up from the floor, and was set to sprint out of there to the car and head straight to the hospital—

"NO!" she screamed, and jerked free of his grasp, plummeting to the floor with a wet thump. "Not yet!!"

She clutched the blood-smeared bowl of the toilet, sobbing.

"Girl, come on!" D'antre said, his voice shaking. "We gotta git you to a doctor right now!"

"I kn-know," she said, with deep heaving breaths. "I know it. I jus'—*sob*—I jus' w-wanna say g'night first." She started sing-talking straight into the toilet bowl—

"*Ni-night, baby. Go seepy now. Go seepy now...*"

Poor Min
Poor Min
Poooooor Miiiiiiiiiiin...

...I picked her up again and carried her off through The Church proper. She gripped tight to my neck and I could feel the warm blood oozing from within her thighs into the crook of my left arm...

From under The Church the furnace gurgled and growled, angry, bilious, ready to purge and punish.

The vents in the walls suddenly began to vomit blood and black tar, filling the broken pews with hot sludge. It got deep fast. Harder and harder it was to move, the more my heart pumped, the more Min would hemorrhage all over me. She moaned low, catatonic, still singing lullabies to the baby who was gone...

...I kicked open the door of The Church and headed outside to see the streets every which way filling thick with blood, ash and afterbirth spat out from the mouth of the furnace underground. The whole of the hood was nothing now but a churning quagmire of blood and meat, tiny arms and mutilated, miscarried torsos floated past my knees. Sky was gray and damaged over Blackchurch, like the film stock of a 1920s movie. In the distance Shel and Pearl crawled, mangled and misshapen, from the wreckage of their beat little tour van. Their dead friends hanging red and dripping from broken windows, swinging in the breeze like saturated scarecrows. Shel fell to his knees, impaled on an electric guitar. Pearl wandered about in a daze, coated thick with blood, stumbling and banging her head with her fist—

"No no, not the time, not the time..."

Anton marched through the crimson swamp in full desert

camo, rifle across his chest. "There's a live one, Sarge!" he shouted, and unloaded his bullets into a floating patch of little pomegranate heads. Babies cried, cheap and distorted on an old reel-to-reel somewhere, and Anton fired again.

"Daddy please." MeShayle clutched my neck tighter and sobbed, "Help me, Daddy. Help me, please..."

"I ain't your daddy, little girl," I said, and let go of her. She fell straight into the rising blood swamp below, sank deep and quick, and disappeared. "I'm sorry. I can't help you..."

Daddy...
Daddy...

"Daddy...Daddy...C'mon, Daddy, pleeeeeeeeease..."

I feel a weight on my chest and a small hand pushing on my cheek. A pointy little fingernail jabbing like a dull sewing needle.

"What the," I mumble, half-dazed. "Girl, what time is it?"

I open my eyes to see that it's clearly morning, but still too early just yet to be getting up.

"Thass yo' daughter the early riser," TJ mutters next to me, still half-asleep, hogging up all the covers. "Folks sleep late on my side of the family."

"I need me some breffiss, Daddy," Dameka says, sitting on my belly Indian-style.

"Breakfast, eh?" I sigh and stretch, awake and committed by that time. "Aw'ight, Boo. Whatchoo wanna eat?"

"Appazoz."

"Apple sauce?! Girl, you gonna wake me up at six inna morning for apple sauce?"

TJ laughs lazily and rolls over. "Y'all enjoy."

"Wif cimmamin," Meka clarifies.

"Oh," I say. "Well why ain't you say so? I can see that." I stretch one last time. "Aw'ight baby girl, let's get us some eats." I sit up and she climbs onto my back.

She cackles like a maniac and holds my neck tighter as I try to bounce her off my back, sliding in my tube socks, dancing the herky-jerk all the way down the hall to the kitchen.

It's six in the morning.

I'm on two hours sleep.

My head is slamming with a vodka hangover.

And I'm the happiest motherfucker alive.

I fix us up two bowls of cinnamon apple sauce, whole wheat toast with peanut butter, and some one percent milk. Pretty goddamn tasty, actually. Good vitamins and fiber for her, not too heavy on my boozy stomach.

TJ pads into the kitchen finally, and heads straight for the coffee pot. "You 'member it's the first day of pre-school, right?" she says. I look over at her. She's getting rounder in the booty. She lookin' fiiiiiine, my queen.

"I remember," I say. And I do remember. Now.

"And you takin' her, right? I got to go see Mama 'fore I head to the club."

"Course I'm takin' her," I say. "Wouldn't miss it. You excited for your first day of school, baby girl?"

"YEAH!" Dameka exclaims, throwing her hands up, and in the process flinging cinnamon applesauce off her spoon and onto the floor. Our fat, dumbass Pit bull Iceberg Slim scampers over to lick it up. "Sorry," Meka says. TJ and I just laugh. Meka finishes her food and runs off to get dressed.

"Keyz called last night when you was out with Mao," TJ says pouring herself a cup of joe. "Y'all's singles is pressed and ready. He done played me the final mix of *Straight Clockin'* over the phone. It sound dope, D. Real dope. Even on the phone."

"Nice of you to say, Boo."

"Nigga please. You know I wouldn't bullshit you. I think it sounds on time. F'real. And I think it might just make you. No lie."

"Thanks, baby. Mean that."

"If you want, I might-could pump it at the club tonight. Exposure, you know?"

"See," I say. "Thass why I love you, Tijuana Smalls." I pull her close to me. She giggles. I reach under her nightgown and cup her bare ass with both hands. Round and soft and gorgeous. I'd get with her right this second, right here in the kitchen. She gives my bottom lip a quick nibble, and saunters away, coffee in hand.

"Later," she whispers over her shoulder. I can only laugh.

Dameka is dressed for her first day of pre-school, brand new backpack on, watching cartoons in the living room. Phone rings. TJ answers.

"Helluh? Who dis? What? *Who is this*? Huh? He ain't here right now." Click.

Uh oh.

I turn slowly around to look at her. Not too happy.

"Who was it?" I ask.

"Some bitch," she answers, laying the stink eye on me, but says nothing else.

Phone rings again.

"*Ah fuck...*"

She answers, sharp and pointed. "Hello?!"

"Gimme the phone, TJ."

She slams the receiver down instead.

"Who *Pearl*?"

A cold chill shoots through my chest, but I don't know why.

"I don't know nobody named Pearl," I say. And I don't. "Thass the truth."

Long silence. Finally, "I believe you." But she doesn't.

Phone rings again. It's louder this time. Super loud. It hurts my ears.

"Just unplug it," I say. She picks up the receiver and slams it down again.

"Daddy!" Dameka calls from the next room. "There some Chinese lady on TV sayin' she need to talk to you!"

"She ain't Chinese, baby girl, she Japanese."

What are you talking about, D'antre?!?!

I run into the living room. The face on TV is crying and saying my name. I kick the TV off with my heel. Dameka is not there.

"Dameka!"

"In here, Daddy," she says from the hallway. "Got to get to school."

"Wait for me, Boo!"

I run to the hallway, and she's not there.

"MEKA!"

No answer.

"No, baby," I say, "don't leave out just yet! Don't leave without me!" Silence. "TJ!" No answer. "TJ, she with you?!" Nothing. I see the door to the house is open, but the light is too bright, and I can't see out. I walk quickly toward the door, but cannot seem to make it there. "Dameka, wait! Don't leave without me! DON'T LEAVE WITHOUT ME!!!"

Stuck in the hallway. Look over to the living room. The TV comes back on. On its own. The face on TV is sobbing. "She lost it, D'antre." I look down at my forearms. They are caked with blood.

"I'm sorry, baby girl," I call out the door. "I'm sorry I couldn't come. I'm sorry I missed your party. I had to take my friend to the hospital. I'm sorry."

"It's a'ight, Daddy," her voice says, much older, and very, very far away. "It's cool. It don't matter. Wha'evah, you know? It's cool."

And the TV sobs—

"Gone. Just gone. Just like that. She lost it, D'antre. She lost the baby."

Where's Your God Now or The Immaculate Deception

Because reaction to noise is so much a matter of individual tolerance, the psychological problems become almost infinite.

—Robert D. Reed,
Furnace Operations (1981)

D'antre awoke in the hospital waiting room, on his back, wedged awkwardly into two blue vinyl seats. Neck wrenched and sore. His cellphone was flipped open in his hand, but there was no one on the line.

"How're you feeling, cuz'n?" Shel asked, in a similar state. His eyes were red and heavy, like he hadn't slept in years, but he smiled weakly to his friend.

"Done seen the end o' days, son," D'antre said with a stale yawn. "It was really sump'n."

"Was I there?"

"Yeah. Wudn't pretty, though."

"What was it like?"

"Uh, you know who Rev'rend Tim LaHaye is?"

"That sheepfucker who writes those *Left Behind* books?"

"Thass the one."

"Yeah?"

"He don't know shit," D'antre said, sitting up, cracking his neck. "Fuck that bitch straight up his asshole. Wit sump'n sharp."

"Well, I'll see what I can do."

D'antre noticed Shel's empty left hand.

"What happen to yo' ring, son?"

"Eh," Shel replied. "Got rid of it." He sniffed absently. "I'm done recording for now. I'd like to actually sleep sometime soon."

"So..." D'antre sighed. "How bad is it?"

"It's good you came home when you did, man," Shel said. "She lost quite a bit of blood, but you got her here just in time. You saved her life, D. They say she's going to be fine now. Physically, anyway."

D'antre shook his head. Saw that his cellphone was dead. Flipped it shut and stuck it into his pocket.

"Goddamn...Goddamn..."

"You talked to your daughter, cuz'n?"

"Yeah. Told her alla what happen."

"Was she upset with you that you couldn't come?"

"I wish. I wish she was upset. She act like she ain't really even care at all. Her mama gonna shoot me inna dick if I ever come round again, though. Believe that."

"You saved Min's life, D. Don't forget that."

"Yeah..."

"I wonder if we can go back there," Shel said looking past the reception desk, more to himself than to D'antre. "See how she's doing. Pearl's back with her."

"Where Anton at?"

"He's gone, cuz'n. He freaked when he heard. Do you remember calling him?"

"Nope."

"Yeah, he took off into the night. You know how he was. That little bundle of cells in Min's womb was the only thing keeping him together. The only hope he had left."

"Hope is fuckin' stupid, y'heard?"

"Yeah. It really is."

"You know, iss funny," D'antre said. "Thinkin' 'bout Blackchurch. 'Bout Mad-ville proper, really. You walk into any church inna hood on any Sunday, and up front playin' in the church band will be somebody who used to be *somebody.*

LOTSA old members of Parliament Funkadelic. Lots of 'em. You know that old security guard at the library?"

"Uh huh."

"Used to play drums fo' James Brown. No shit. Blackchurch...iss like a graveyard...fo' people who ain't dead yet."

A muscular white orderly with a long red ponytail wheeled Min out in a wheelchair. She looked drained. She was drained. She held Pearl's right hand tightly, who softly caressed Min's kinky hair with her left. They both looked beaten to hell. Shel and D'antre stood up and walked over toward them. D'antre crouched down on his knees in front of Min, and she fell into him, sobbing into his shoulder.

"*Shhhhh...shhhhh...*Aw'ight, girl...iss okay...iss okay..."

"I'm gonna get the car," Shel said, and walked out.

"Aw'ight now," D'antre said to Min, rubbing her back in a circular pattern. "Iss gon' be okay...*shhhhh...*Iss okay..."

Once outside, Min slowly stood up. Pearl thanked the orderly, who pushed the wheelchair back inside. D'antre opened the door for Min, who simply remained standing. She shivered, and her breath steamed in the crisp December air, but her mind was lost and wandering somewhere far away.

"Come on, sweetheart," Pearl coaxed, "I'll sit in back with you. Come on. Let's go home."

Suddenly Min threw her head back and screamed at the heavens—

"This all you got f'me? HUH?! This all you got!?! You cain't fade me, muhfucka! You *ain't* fadin' me! YOU HEAR?! This ain't loud! It ain't loud at all. This ain't loud ENOUGH, ya heard!?!! TURN THIS FUCKER UP!!!" Her face wrenched in devastation and grief, head bobbing back and forth, eyes shut tight, squeezing out scalding tears that scorched like acid down her soft brown cheeks. Pearl and D'antre both put their arms around her, holding her tight, not knowing what else to do. "Don't y'all git it?" she cried. "Huh? Don'tchoo git it? Widdout...my baby...widdout my baby...I'm just a *whore.*"

***

Back at The Church, the four of them rolled up to discover the seven remaining Lower Church Ishmaels huddled together, standing out in the side lot eyeing their spiritual father with alarm as he scooped down jauntily, picking up cold handfuls of dirt and smearing them all over his lavender suit jacket, muttering wildly to himself.

"Brother Ishmael!" they pleaded. "Brother Ishmael, please! What are you doing?!"

"Flippity dip dip dip dip dip!" he replied. "Jack off Jesus, slurp his juice, drive the nails and tie the noose! HOO HOO!"

Pearl, Min, Shel and D'antre walked cautiously over to this grotesque bit of street theatre.

"Brother D'antre!" a young girl said, spotting them. "Please! Please, can you make him stop?!"

"Ladies and gennl'men," D'antre said with a broad sweep of his hand, "I'd like to introduce y'all...to *Petey Wheatstraw.*"

"Young D Philips!" the old man exclaimed pointing an index finger excitedly toward D'antre. "Spare a trash bag, young brother?"

"I'll check, ol' son."

"So how's your mama?"

"My mama dead, Petey. And you know this."

"Tell her I said hello."

"Yup. Will do."

"Oh god..." The kids all covered their faces. The old man slid around in his ruined Paxton loafers, laying down a beatless electric slide right there in the gravel. "What do we do?" they groaned. "What do we do now?"

"Now listen, y'all," D'antre said. They came over closer, partly to hear better, but mostly to get further away from the boogie-down derelict shaking his tail feathers on the south side of the lot. "This is good. Ya heard? This is a good thing right here. Trust me, iss all good." They listened, attentive, but unsure. "No mo' leaders. Knahmean? No mo' heroes. No mo' prophets or messiahs. Or anti-messiahs. No mo' Jesus, or Mohammad, or Moses, or Abraham, or Buddha, or Ben Ishmael...

this one here *or* the first one."

"Jesus was just a man," one of the young ones said, "Just a man fighting and losing the class war."

"They all just men. Be done widd'm. Have done widdit. All of it. Aw'ight? F'ever. No mo' gods no more. Be y'own god, if you can hack it. If you can't do that...then choose wisely at least. And keep yo' options loose. Ya heard?"

They looked at him, scared, but understanding. He smiled at them, as did Shel, Min and Pearl. They nodded, smiling sadly at Min. She nodded. *It'll be okay...*

"Okay...Okay..."

They all slowly started to walk away.

"One mo' thang, y'all," D'antre said. "Don't you be relapsin' now. If you do, Imma come an' kick alla y'all's asses. Aw'ight?"

And with that, they were gone.

Once the young former Ishmaels were out of sight, Petey Wheatstraw ceased cutting a rug, dropped his routine and walked over to the Upper Church four.

"Well played, D'antre."

"Thanks."

"I believe that they'll be okay now," he said. "I have faith in that."

"No doubt."

"I'm so sorry, Min," Petey said turning toward her, grandfatherly, clear and calm. "I am so sorry for your loss, child. It's a loss for the Earth. But understand this; you are the light of the world. *You* are. And you always will be, no matter what."

"I'm jus' a...I'm jus' a girl, Petey," she said.

He smiled, lifting his hand to touch her, then noticing how dirty he was. He put his hand back down to his side.

"That's enough. That's good enough." He turned to walk away.

"Hey Pete," Shel said. "So, is the end of the world really coming, dude? Or what?"

"Oh yes it is, Sheldon. Yes, it most definitely is. But, it's still going to be a bit. Eleven or twelve years yet, I'd say. I wouldn't quit flossing or anything."

"I's thinkin'," Min said, "laying in that hospital bed, and Pearl and me was talkin' 'bout it. The only one-a us who really got it right, I think, outta all, was that drunk-ass bigot Shel work wit. He done got it correct. Him and all them boiler people. They gods, they god, that might really could be the only *true* god, you know?"

"The furnace," Petey said with a smile and a nod. "Of course. It has no plan. No thoughts. No spite. No grand design. It doesn't love, or hate. It simply keeps us alive with its heat in the winter. And its cool in the summer. If we tamper with it, misuse it, or just get too close to it, it might kill us. Not out of anger…it has no feelings. It's a machine, and a perfectly serviceable god. When it's broken, we fix it. Or call someone who can."

"So much for the creator, huh?" Pearl said. "Man in god's image and all."

"That was always a dumb story anyhow," D'antre said. "Jus' a fairy tale, and not a good one even."

"Some say that man created god in *his* image," Petey said. "But that's just as ridiculous. No, man created god to satisfy a basic need for survival. In a more temperate climate, we wouldn't need a god at all."

"This Blackchurch furnace is, at best, a lesser god," Shel interjected. "The large pressure boiler, now THAT is the real deal. It is the pinnacle of human invention, and is most definitely god for all who need it…and we are all going to need it someday."

"Some sooner'n othas," Min said.

"It will run for infinity," Shel continued, "so long as there are operators on duty at all times to maintain it."

"If you're looking for a deity to worship," Petey said, "it's certainly a superior choice over some vengeful, intergalactic Santa Claus."

And with that, he tapped his nose and whistled high and low, just like Harpo Marx. He turned on his heel once again, and began heading off.

"Take care of y'self, ol' son," D'antre said. "I'll see ya round."

Petey whistled in reply. And then he stopped. Without turning around he said, "I still miss her, you know. After all this time, I still miss her every single day."

"Loraina?" Min asked.

"Well…" Petey said, shuffling away. "Yes. Her too." Over his shoulder he shouted, "Do something worthwhile with yourselves, you beautiful children! For the hell of it!"

And with that, the new Ben Ishmael disappeared down a dingy Blackchurch alley, and into oblivion. And so did old Peter Wellson.

"I done lef' my car at the hospital," D'antre said to no one in particular.

Upstairs in D'antre's pad they found four shoeboxes sitting on the kitchen table. Upon each was written:

ALL THE REST OF IT—do something worthwhile

Each contained one thousand five hundred dollars, packed tightly in clean, pressed bundles.

From each, according to his talents…

God Dismantled

Only in his hometown and in his own house is a prophet without honor.

—Matthew 13:57

"So you really gonna fly?" D'antre asked Pearl as she, Min and Shel gathered up their things. "I mean, like, in a actual airplane?"

"Sure," she replied with a shrug, "What's the worst that could happen?"

"You could crash and die."

"Yeah, but what else?"

Min, Pearl and Shel had decided to use the money from Petey Wheatstraw to move back down to New Orleans.

"Figured," Shel said, "if we were going to try to rebuild the world anyway, what better place to start?"

"Feel that," D'antre said. "Iss a solid plan, y'heard?"

They had been in touch with a number of relief organizations down there that they would connect with as soon as they were settled in. It seemed, in every possible way, to be the most worthwhile thing to do.

"Plus," Shel said, "With the money I got from selling the Honda, I'm getting myself a new electric guitar. Gibson SG, flat, square headstock. Just in case. Scrubbin' oil and mold off houses all day, layin' down nasty riffs all night. That's how it's gonna be, you know?"

"I'm widdit," D'antre said.

"I got a fever for some dirty swamp thrash."

"Work that shit, nigga. Can't wait to hear it. Is yo' hand up to it, though?"

"Only one way to know."

"Word."

"I don't know what happened to me," said Shel, "but I slept last night. Actually slept. No nightmares, no visions. I slept straight through the night. Ten freakin' hours. And now, jesus, the world has more color today. It's not so desolate anymore. Does it look like this normally? For everybody?"

"It should, knahmean?"

"I'm not quite sure I dig it. Anyway, if you see Will Fanon, D, and he's lucid, tell him I said *take'r easy.*"

"No doubt, dog. No doubt."

Shel and D'antre man-hugged with gusto, and Shel grabbed his and Min's bags from the floor.

"Door's always open, cuz'n. Right? We'd love to have you anytime. Don't forget that."

"We'll see how it go," D'antre replied.

Shel threw the bags over his shoulder and headed out of The Church to the cab waiting outside.

Min kissed D'antre on the cheek.

"Thank you for e'rything, D," she said. "Imma miss you."

"Just wish I coulda done more, baby girl."

"Did you read Mikal's book?"

"Sent it off to New York this mornin'. Fingers crossed."

"Be sho' to say g'bye to old Manfred the security guard at the library fo' me."

"Gotcha covered, Boo."

She smiled, and departed right behind Shel.

Pearl and D'antre stood in silence for nearly a minute. Finally she said,

"Come with us, D'antre."

"I might," he said. "F'real. I might catch up witchall after while. Believe that." She didn't. "I jus' got some shit I gotta take care of up in here first. Then we'll see."

"Yeah? Like what?"

"Just some shit, knahmean?"

"Okay. Fine. Well, be sure to—"

"Shonda and Malachi, I gotcha."

"Thanks." Pause. "They're not coming back, D'antre. You know that, right?"

"Say what?"

"They're not coming back. Okay? They're *never* coming back. Your daughter, your wife, they're not coming back to you. Ever."

"Girl, don't even trip."

"It's less than a nine-hour drive to, or from, Wisconsin. If you were ever going to be a happy little family again, it certainly would have happened by now. Come on. Come with us. You can mail a child support check from anywhere."

"Look, I ain't playin'. Aw'ight? I jus' got me a coupla thangs I gotta iron out round here. Affairs in order, ducks in a row. You know what I'm sayin'. But after that, then I'm all about maybe hookin' up witchall down in Louisiana. Although, I heard niggas be drinkin' cough syrup outta big Styrofoam cups down there, and I just don't roll that way."

"It's more suggested than strictly enforced."

"Well then there you go. Hey, I'm f'real here. I really like the music we all made together. I'm all 'bout doin' that again, feel me? So hey. I'll be seein' you. Onna real."

She leaned up and kissed him on the lips, soft and long.

"Take care of yourself, D'antre Philips."

"Right back atcha, Katsumi Yoshimoto."

And like that, she was gone.

D'antre was only somewhat surprised at how easily he slipped back into his old rhythms. His old routines. His patterns, well worn and only slightly too tight, like an old pair of Adidas with no laces that'd been buried in a cupboard since '87.

He worked long hours, wrote rhymes on the line he'd likely never use, got blunted on the drive home, ate dinner alone, beat off to Daryl Hannah (*and Kathy Bates. She a good actress!*), and drank himself to sleep on cheap red jug wine. *So it be, so shall it always be.*

On the rare occasion that he broke free from the normal grind, it didn't go well.

One night, for old, old time's sake, he scored a nice chunk of black tar OPM, and smoked it in a bowl of seedy stank weed. Instead of easing into a dim, fuzzy stupor, his mind flooded with voices from all directions. Pushy, chattering, boring as hell. Some woman yelling in Castilian Spanish. Somebody praying to his god for some hot Wall Street action. Some gay white boy arguing with his Chinese boyfriend. *What, a nigga can't even be by hisself inside his own damn head?*

Apparently not.

He turned on the radio to a local station, and the vanilla voice said that several "maintenance people" had been arrested for attempting to rig up homemade explosives to a number of new-model pressure boilers. Police were looking into possible motives. He switched to NPR and heard some croony girl singer playing a Stigmata Dog song on piano.

God is scarred, burned, naked in a drain pipe.

Keep the disease alive / Needless and terrified…

D'antre wondered if Pearl and Shel would ever see a dime from it. *Not likely.*

Several days after, a letter arrived addressed to Oscar Pederson Montgomery. It read:

Picked up a cassette tape of The Bomb Droppas in a little used record store in Memphis. It is hella-good, partner, and I don't even like rap. You should really consider getting back together with DJ Mao Mao and MC Keyz. I think the world is ready for a new one.

Take care, brother,

A

"Might just do that," D'antre said to no one in particular. In fact, to no one at all.

***

Periodically D'antre would run into Petey Wheatstraw out on the street. D'antre would try to talk with him, but all he ever got in reply was whistling and hooting, or some blathering nonsense about Jesus molesting small fat children on video for profit.

"But it's a *false profit*, young D Philips. Tiddle biddle biddle. Obscene in the bean. It's a green scene."

Try though he did, D'antre never met or heard from Ben Ishmael ever again, nor for that matter from Peter James Wellson. Only the jabbering derelict remained.

Que sera sera…

Sometime in mid-February, the furnace shut down entirely. Conked out with a loud thud. And then nothing.

ring ring ring ring

"Yello? This is Fanon."

"Will. Iss D'antre."

"Who?"

"D'antre Philips."

"Who?"

"From The Church, goddamn it. Blackstone and Desmond."

"Oh! Hey there, D'antre! How are ya?"

"Cold!"

"Is Sheldon around? I ain't seen him in a coon's age. No offense."

"You drunk-ass, cracka muthafucka, he done lef' out for New Orleans almost two months ago!"

"Ohhhh…right. Well, what can I do ya for?"

"The furnace done went out, knahmsayin? I mean totally. Out."

"Rats. I was afraid of that. I think I know what might be the problem, but I'm gonna hafta completely rip that sumbitch apart. It could take a while."

"Gaaahhhh..."

"Too bad Shel's not around, he'd be able to hear the trouble spots right away."

"He gone for good, son."

"Took off with Lydia the Tattooed lady, huh?"

"You could see Pearl's tattoos?"

"See 'em?! Goddamn, boy, the girl was coated with 'em!"

"Word."

See?! I am NOT the crazy one.

"Tell ya what, D'antre, I'll be over in a little while." *You just need to sober up a little?* "I just need to sober up a little. Shitballs. I didn't mean to say that out loud."

"Iss aw'ight, man. Jus' come when you can, aw'ight? It ain't locked up, so if I ain't here jus' come on in. I'll be at the *Soul Lounge* tryin' to not freeze my dick off, y'heard? You can meet me there and tell me whass the prognosis n' shit."

"Hmm, yeah, well I'm afraid I'm no longer welc—Never mind. Okay. I'll see ya in a bit."

"Cool. Peace, nigga."

"What?"

And so went D'antre's life in much the same way. He'd periodically put a call in to Madison, Wisconsin, and if Dameka answered, they would chat a bit. If she didn't, he was greeted only by the sound of a cold click and a dial tone. One evening he called and the line opened up, but there was no greeting at all. Instead all he heard was the sound of Tijuana Smalls getting the old jolly roger by some unknown cat. Maybe Ramon. Maybe somebody else. D'antre listened for about a minute, then hung up.

Don't mean nothin' to me. It don't matter. Nothin' matters.

Sometime in late March, and just because, D'antre started receiving letters to Eva again. Same deal as it had been: Canton, Ohio, yellow forwarding label, *return to sender.*

The first batch was fairly mundane. *Dear Eva, how are you,*

I'm fine, how's your family, blah blah blah.

Then, one day, there were seven of them. All at the same time.

Dear Eva,
So does Micki know? How do you think she feels?
love 4-ever,
A

Dearest Eva,
It is Tuesday. That is all.
See you in my dreams,
A

Eva,

Do you know about Lucifer? Of course you do, good little church girl, you. Lucifer was god's right hand. The light giver. Cast out for betrayal. Makes you think, huh?

Sleep tight, Evangeline, I'll see you in my dreams,
A

Eva. Please help me. Please make it stop. Anton

Eva,
My Eva, My bringer of light
I always did love you, we always did fight
I am always near you, though just out of sight
Eva, my Eva, my bringer of light

Eva,
Time's up, darling thing. Time's up for everyone.
Sleep tight, Evangeline, I'll be there in your dreams,
Corporal Anton Poole

And finally,

To My Darling Lucifer,
All Is Forgiven.

And D'antre thought, as much as he hated to do it, that it might just be time to pay a little visit to the boys in blue.

All Is Forgiven

Stay away from all peep holes while the furnace is upset.

—Robert D. Reed,
Furnace Operations (1981)

Last call had come sooner than D'antre expected. He stumbled home from the Soul Lounge late one Thursday night. *A Black-church kinda evening-slash-morning f'sho*—Bass thumpin somewhere in the distance, twelve-year-olds hanging on the corner on a school night, somebody nearby taking in some late-night target practice (one would hope), and all was steady in D'antre's world. *As it be, so shall it always be…*

Fishing for his keys as he walked up Blackstone, D'antre saw a vehicle parked out in the old gravel lot. It happens. A rare occurrence, perhaps, but not unheard of. Nonetheless, he decided to grab a quick peek.

Datsun. A goddamn Datsun, of all things. Tang-powder orange, rusted at the wheel wells, and rocking Tennessee plates. Not a good sign. He moved closer to see the driver side door wide open, and a dark shadow cast on the ground beside it. He moved in a bit more, and his throat went dry as he saw a sheen and glisten in the light of the street lamps. *What's up with that shadow? Shadows don't shimmer. That ain't no mothafuckin' shadow, is it…*

Worst fears realized as he headed up to his apartment door, and saw that it was open. With no small bit of reluctance, he pushed it wide to find just what he had expected: a trail of blood leading straight up the staircase and up into his crib.

I s'ppose I shoulda been scared. But scared of what? With this much blood loss, whatever's up there could be easily subdued by a light push...if it's alive at all.

Walking into the kitchen, D'antre flipped on the light, and stepped right into an expanding pond of bright red. Jittering fluorescent light danced across its surface. In the center of the pond, curled up on the tiles, just as bent and bone white as the Reaper's cock, was Anton.

"Sorry 'bout the mess here, chief," he said in that rasping twang of his, a thin, quivering grin spread weakly across his pale lips. "I was gonna...look fer a mop 'fore...I 'membered you ain't...got one."

"'Sall good, son," D'antre said, trying to maintain a steady, casual tone.

"Wasn't even bleedin' too bad...on the outside...fer a while," Anton said with a quick shiver. "This hardcore spillage...is a new twist."

"Yup, that'd be a hemorrhage right there. How 'bout we go 'head and call you a ambulance, cool?"

"No point, amigo. No point. Been drivin' nearly four hours...with my stomach leakin' battery fluid somethin' awful. And that's good. Cuz the hospital would just...turn me over... to the police. And I...cain't go back to jail, D. You know how that is. I...gotta...die free, you know? I gotta die free."

And D'antre just came right out with it—

"You done kill't yo' wife, didn't you. Just like yo' friend. It was inevitable. And shit."

Anton tried to laugh, but just wheezed and spat up, black, dark green and deep red. "You think it's the Blackchurch... curse, my man?"

"I think you done lost yo' shit in Iraq, son. Or Tennessee or some kinda bullshit place. And somebody done you wrong. And now you done *real* wrong cuz of it. Thass what I think."

Anton coughed, and squeezed hard against his wounded stomach, wrapped tight in a ripped flannel shirt.

"I saw 'em in bed together," he said. "It's a hot night,

yeah? Been hot...all day. Weird for this...time of year. And they had the...w-window open. My window. MY bedroom window. In the bed that...I bought and paid fer. Her ankles was up...on his shoulders...and he was balls deep up her ass. Just plowin' away. Really goin' to town. '*I want you in...my pussy,*' she says. '*I want your baby. Please put...put your baby inside me.*' So he slides it on out...her back door...peels off the rubber...and is just about to take...the holy plunge, when goddamn it...if my .243 Winchester don't just up and go off. Straight through the window. Bullet hits his right bicep... explodes...and throws him...off the bed, wailin', 'I'm hit! I'm hit!' She screams and...takes off bare-ass naked...through the house as I kick in the door...and go runnin' on after her."

"Don't make me no accessory after the fact, Anton. F'real, dog. I ain't havin' it."

"Just listen...okay?"

"So you done kill't yo' brother-in-law then?"

"He ain't dead. He's a...big boy. If I'da wanted to kill him...I woulda done it. I hate the sunuvawhore...but that don't mean I don't...still love him. And anyway, I...I was there fer *her*. Not him."

"Right."

"'DON'T KILL ME, ANTON!' She cries...runnin' hysterical through the house...with no real plan. 'Please don't kill me! PLEASE!' Fuckin'...funny, really. I'm laughin'. 'C'mon, Eva'...I shout at her...'Think clear 'bout this now!' But she's runnin'...and squawkin' around...like a headless chicken."

"How can a headless chicken squawk?"

"*Where the fuck's she think...she's goin'*? I think to myself. Finally...I just tell her...'It's in the...den, Eva!' I yell, 'It's in the...goddamn den!' What, I gotta draw her...a map? She's still beggin' me...not to kill her, and I shout, 'Godsake, woman...there's a loaded fuckin' subnose...in the stupid roll-top desk!'"

At that he started really laughing. Hard. Cackling. And coughing. Wet.

"You wanted her to shoot *you*?"

"It's only right...don't you think? Somebody had to...and I sure ain't gonna...do myself. One of us had to go...might as well be me."

"Huh..."

"She's such a...bad shot, though. Took out two lamps... and the TV...'fore she finally nicked me...in the gut." He laughed even harder at this, spitting up more in the process. "Well, I *thought* it was a nick. Seems a bit...deeper, don't it."

"Sho' nuff."

The pool got slowly wider, spreading toward the fridge and stove. The look of clenched, quaking agony in Anton's eyes made D'antre sick. And, as terrible as it was to think, D'antre wished he would just die already.

"You know..." Anton said, "they always say...the worst thing 'bout gettin' shot...is the fear. But that...ain't really true."

"What is the worst thang?"

"The big, burnin' hole...rippin' through yer body."

"Feel that."

"Shit don't tickle."

"I hope you ain't 'spectin' me to finish you off, son. I ain't gettin' locked up cuz of this, knahmean?"

"You got the letters...right?"

"Yup."

"You turned 'em over...to the pigs, right?"

"You know I did."

He smiled. "Noticed the all-points...in Sweetwater."

I felt like I musta been crazy, standin' there conversatin' in my kitchen at 2:45 in the a.m. with a man whose blood I'm 'bout ankle-deep in.

But there they were.

"Why come back up in here, son?" D'antre asked. "Why Blackchurch?"

"Blackchurch is the only...place I ever...felt free, bud. And I gotta...die free."

He started to glaze a bit, and D'antre thought, *Finally, he might-could go kinda peaceful right now.* But he didn't. He kept hanging on, even though he clearly no longer wanted to hang on. D'antre could tell that Anton wanted it over with once and for all, and he was thoroughly at a loss about what to do.

"Yer a good friend, D'antre. Whatever it's worth to ya, yer a good friend."

"Friendship's temp'rary, dog. Like family. And marriage. And e'rything."

"Yeah, I heard that," Anton wheezed. "Nothin' matters, you know? Nothin' at all. 'Cept the *nothing*. Now that shit matters, all right.—*cough*—Man alive. Sure would like...to take the...edge off." He coughed again. "Really don't feel too good."

The thought crossed D'antre's mind (briefly) to maybe just push the fridge over on his head.

Then I r'membered...

"Hold up, son."

D'antre reached deep into the refrigerator, and sure enough, in the back, behind year-old fried rice and other spoiled odds and ends, was Pearl's old bag of magic goodies. Near frozen. And one brittle syringe left. D'antre looked on the side—*use once and destroy.*

"You gotta fix me, brother," Anton said, barely. "I'm more than a bit useless at the moment. Sorry I cain't be more help."

"I'll do what I can, y'heard?"

The bag was packed to the top with ten-milligram ampoules of liquid morphine. D'antre set the bag down on the small Formica and aluminum kitchen table, and tried to open the syringe packet carefully...but the needle snapped off still in the wrap.

"Mothafuck!"

"C-Can you just...just..." Anton looked at D'antre with desperate eyes, teeth gritted, red and dark. He rolled on his back, made like a baby bird.

Saying *fuck it all*, D'antre pulled out a glass vial from the bag, snapped its neck, and dumped the contents into Anton's open mouth. He gagged a bit on the solution, but swallowed it down in a pained gulp. Anton opened his mouth again, and D'antre snapped another ampoule and poured it down his dying friend's waiting throat, dropping the empty vials into Anton's bloody left hand. Anton gripped them as tightly as he could, smearing them with his scarlet fingerprints, before letting them slip from his fingers into the glistening red pond. D'antre snapped another, and another, feeding each to Anton, on and on, vial after vial. Until they were all gone. *No turnin' back now.* There would be no last minute call to 9-1-1.

It didn't take long for the pain to begin to drain from Anton's bloodshot eyes like the steady leak of a cracked clay jug. His gaunt, haggard face grew ever more serene and dull. Tension slacked. Misery gave way to relief. Acceptance. And then finally to a whispering peace.

"One last thing. My man." Anton said, clipped and halting. D'antre, already kneeling beside him, bent his head lower to hear. "Gotta say. To you. I got a gift. I don't know if. It was from god that I got it. Or whut. Maybe so. Maybe it's the. Uranium in me. Or the. Cracked little bones behind my eyes. But I...see things. Visions. And my visions. Are right. Always. Right. You know this. And I wanna. Give you. Tell you. My. My last one. I don't always under. Stand whut I see. But the things. They're always right. You know it. And you. Gotta know...whut I seen." His body released from the fetal grip it had been in, and he slid slowly into a state of hollow grace. "I...seen you, D. In my mind. I seen you with. Yer old lady. And yer little...little girl. I seen you. Together again. Three of you. It. Ain't. Perfect. Never gonna be. Perfect. But you. Will be. Together. And it. Will be. *Boring.* Promise you. Life is at... its best. When it's borin'. Right? And yer gonna...be borin' again. Someday. My friend. Borin' and. Happy. I. Promise. You. I promise." His lights dimmed. "Tell 'em I died free, D. Scratch it on. My stone. Tell the world I died free..."

He gasped hard. And then he went out. For good. Gone.

D'antre gave himself a moment. Then he headed over to the

phone. And he braced himself for the long morning of questions to come.

Much to D'antre's surprise, the police were more or less satisfied with his story. Given Ex-Corporal Anton Poole's history of erratic behavior and mental illness, coupled with his very recent acts of violence in Sweetwater, Tennessee, his suicide seemed not only plausible, but sadly inevitable. Details about how Messrs. Poole and Philips had become friends, co-workers and house mates were sketchy at best, but ultimately the issue was not pressed. Madisonville is known for its misfits and rejects, after all, and the Blackchurch section all the more so.

Anton's body was shipped back to Knoxville. D'antre did not attend his funeral. He notified his friends in New Orleans of the news, and they were devastated...but not surprised. They didn't come up for the funeral either. However, the four surviving members of Upper Church swore to one another that they would get together, and soon, which may very well happen someday.

Or not.

All charges against Ms. Evangeline McDonald regarding the death of her ex-husband were subsequently dropped. The case was on her side to begin with, but the letters Anton had been sending her, a few of which had ended up in D'antre's possession, clinched it solidly in her favor. When word of this got to D'antre, he was glad to hear it. He sent her sympathy flowers, with no return address. Somehow she sent a reply, which said in total:

Thank you for what you done for him.

D'antre decided not to ponder what she could have meant.

Not long after, D'antre received a package from New Orleans.

Dear D'antre,

Hope all is well in Cincinnati. We're still totally wrecked here, as we imagine you are too. There are no words that will lessen the pain of what a tragic loss this is for us all, so let's just say that we will always miss him, and we hope that he has finally found his peace. May we all find peace by and by. But whatever will be will be.

We have plenty keeping us busy down here. The 9th Ward is still in horrific disarray, but signs of progress are finally starting to appear. NOLA has a long way to go, but we're coming back with a vengeance, have no doubt about it. You should see for yourself.

Enclosed in this package you will find two CDs. The first is the final mix and master of the recording we all made in Blackchurch. We hope you enjoy it. We've sent it to our record label, and provided they accept it, you can look forward to sporadic and miniscule royalty checks occasionally darkening your mailbox. Livin' the dream, cuz'n. In a just world your performance on this disc would make you a legend. It might just do that, but no guarantees. Thank you for your spectacular work on that, and thank you beyond words for everything.

The invitation to come here and be with us still stands, as it always will. We miss you, brother, and we hope to see you soon. Take care of yourself.

Love always and forever,

Skinny Minnie, Pearl Harbor, and Shellac

D'antre popped the first CD into his stereo. And he had to laugh. It was far and away the clangiest, noisiest, strangest, most atonal thing he had ever heard, much less had a hand in creating. He liked it a lot, and thought he'd like to make more of its kind.

The second disc contained just one song. It featured Shel only, on vocals and accompanied by a single, spare acoustic guitar. The song told of a soldier who has come home from war, and has brought the war back home.

I guess it's way too late, my love, this time / for "I'm sorry" again / so I'll just lay right here beside you / and we'll both just wait for them to barge on in / it is cold in your arms / you are cold in my arms...

D'antre enjoyed it very much. And he never, ever listened to it again.

Back in The Church, D'antre had his own personal 9th Ward to tend to. He had gone out to the nearest big-box megastore and bought several gallons of industrial strength cleaning supplies. And then he went back and bought some more. He had, after all, quite a bit to clean up. It was going to take time. Time was what he had plenty of. But he didn't mind so much. He appreciated the time alone. It gave him time to think...

I had wanted so much for Blackchurch to be a gathering place. Whether it was chosen by god or chose by people ain't matter. I wanted it to be somewhere to come for people to create and think and get it together. I looked around and saw so much here that could be done. So much potential to really catch a bright fire, if it just had the right spark.

But it don't work that way, ya heard? It don't work that way round here. It just ain't meant to be for most folks. When the end times do finally come, and everything is destroyed and dark, barren and covered with a blanket of ash, Blackchurch won't even notice the difference. It's Irkalla, for me at least. Land of no return. F'real.

It ain't nothing but a graveyard up in here. Mean that. Blackchurch is where hopes and dreams and the best of intentions come to be buried for good. You plant whatever it is you wanna cultivate here, whatever it is that brings you joy and a reason to live, and you water it, and you nurture it, and you give it light...and deep in the hard ground is where it will stay. And if, by chance, something was to sprout, you better recognize that it's just gonna die on the vine.

This goes for everybody. Everybody. Don't matter how good. Don't matter how smart. Don't matter how creative or strong. Don't matter how holy or sacred. Don't matter who you are. Everybody's hopes and dreams die here.

*Everybody's...*except mine...

I am the exception. Ya heard? Don't get it twisted. Ain't nothing but joy in this man's heart, believe that. Nothing but pure and simple joy. Because I am right where I belong. Roam here, to the beat of the chrome here, among the glass and the stone here...I am home. Right where I am meant to be. Right now. And good things coming my way. It has been prophesied. It has been spoken. All I got to do is sit tight and keep straight and get my house in order. I got scrubbing to do. But I got time. And time on my side. I'll be waiting, and I'll be ready, and I know in my heart that the day is coming. The one true prophet gave me his word. His last, dying word. I know, for sure, without a single doubt in my mind, that my girls will be coming home soon. They coming home to me. And my house will be ready when they do. The heat will be working, and the cool will be working, and they will find comfort here.

It's like something these motherfuckers told me once—

"Sometimes, you just gotta have faith."

THE END

For Inanna's Daughter (With Notes)

PRINCESS AFRICA JONES
BY D'antRE PHILIPS
HEDGEHOG PRESS, 2002

(A note on the illustrations: It is important to contrast the very real life Princess lives in versus the fantasy world in which she also inhabits. The urban streets where we see her should be stark, gray, crumbling, and decrepit. We should see shadowy figures sitting defeated and/or drunk on front steps, girls playing double-dutch in parking lots, boys shooting hoops in broken down looking areas. Contrast that with the explosions of color when we see imps, fairies, ogres, Princess's giant Falcon, which we should see her riding high in the sky. [editor's note*: we cannot afford color at this time.*] She should be seen in medieval situations involving knights and battles, fantasy situations with dragons and sprites, outer space situations with aliens, African folk tale situations *a la* Anansie and the like, also historical situations—particularly from the African American perspective. As we do in the Jeff M. original sketches, we should see her dressed like Harriet Tubman leading her people to freedom. We should see her dressed like a Black Panther and sitting in the African wicker throne *a la* Huey Newton In these historical poses the color scheme could be more subtle and 'real,' but still richer than the 'real world.' [ed: *see previous.*] The apartment we see where Princess lives with her momma and "auntie" Benita should be cozy, but very very small. Perhaps just one room with a fold-out couch/bed and a kitchenette. Her cat Stubby should be a round and bedraggled looking gray tom cat with a bent ear, scraggly pointed teeth, and eyes completely whited out with cataracts. Momma and "auntie" Benita should actually appear to be a couple—we could see them doing some mundane domestic activity together like washing dishes.)

1.

"Princess Africa Jones got no daddy," the other girls liked to say when she walked by. But Princess Africa Jones paid them no mind. Her momma had given her all three names, and everybody called her by all three. "Princess," so everyone in the world would have to address her with respect. "Africa," the Motherland, where all of us came from. "Jones," her daddy's name, even though she'd never met him, and probably never would.

2.

"Princess Africa Jones got no daddy, and her momma got no money," the other kids would taunt and laugh. But Princess Africa Jones paid them no mind. She had a policy about dealing with mean people. "I ignore them," she'd say. "It's really that simple." Princess Africa Jones could hold her head high, because she had a secret. She had a secret that she would never tell.

3.

"Princess Africa Jones? Pull your head out of the clouds and join the real world!" her teacher Miss Laurie Pritchett would say. But Princess Africa Jones paid her no mind. She had a policy about dealing with mean people. And she would *not* be pulling her head out of the clouds. "That's where my head is comfortable!" she'd say. "It's really that simple." And she would *not* be joining the real world. She had a policy about dealing with a world so nasty and mean.

"I ignore it," she'd say.

4.

Princess Africa Jones held her head high, because she had a secret that she would never tell...

5.

Princess Africa Jones seemed like a shy little girl. She lived on Sixth Street with her momma and auntie Benita. She didn't make noise, and she didn't talk back, and she did her homework right after school, and she went to bed at nine-thirty sharp. You probably wouldn't even notice Princess Africa Jones, unless you were looking for her. And if you were looking for her you'd probably wonder how she could walk right on by when the other girls laughed, and the other kids pointed, and the grown-ups all clucked their tongues and shook their heads and said, "What is wrong with that Princess Africa Jones?"

6.

Princess Africa Jones could tell you how she's able to ignore all the meanness, and meanosity, and meanitude. But she won't. It's her secret.

7.

But it's not MY secret, so I will tell you. You see...it's like this. Princess Africa Jones isn't really from here...

8.

She's not really from the "real" world. And she doesn't really live here either. She only visits for a short time each day, and then she goes back. She goes back to where she's from. Where she's from, she really IS a princess. But that's not all. Oh heavens no! That's not all at all. She's also a warrior and a sorceress and a great solver of mysteries. She cracks codes and frees slaves and defends the weak and battles evil tyrants all night long. She has important business in Nairobi, and on Jupiter, and a thousand wonderful places. No wonder she doesn't care about long division. She has her kingdom to defend! She doesn't need to play double-dutch with a bunch of silly girls. Not when she could be riding her giant falcon over The Black Sea!

9.

"Princess Africa Jones got no friends," the other girls would say. "We all decided we don't like you, Princess Africa Jones." But Princess Africa Jones paid them no mind. She had no time for hopscotch or make up. "It's really that simple." She had clouds to dance in. "That's where I'm most comfortable." She had books to climb inside of. That's where she belonged. In Books. In EVERY book. She lived inside every book she could find. Everything from demons and dragons to The Underground Railroad. And she was a hero. She was ALWAYS the hero. She was powerful. She belonged.

10.

Princess Africa Jones wished she could stay in her books. She wished she never had to come back to the boring, mean "real" world with its boring mean people, who spend all their boring meantime being boring and mean to her. She wished she could find a book from which she COULDN'T escape...

11.

And then one day, her wish came true...

12.

Princess Africa Jones stopped in the library one day, that one day, the day her wish came true. She stopped in the library most days after school, so it made sense that she'd stop in that day.

13.

"How are you today, Princess Africa Jones?" I asked as she walked by.

"I have important business in Egypt, and on Alpha Centauri, and a kerzillion wonderful places," she replied in a hurry.

"Well you'd best to scurry and get to it then," I said. "It's really that simple."

14.

Princess Africa Jones was away for quite awhile. Away in the books, in EVERY book, right where she belonged. Away in books, riding her giant falcon high in the sky with her head right in the clouds (which is where she finds it's most comfortable). But after a while, a shorter while than usual, Princess Africa Jones came on back to the "real" world. The library was short on mean people just then, and there weren't too many boring people around. But even if there had been, it wouldn't really matter. Princess Africa Jones would pay them no mind.

15.

"How are things going, Princess Africa Jones?" I asked as she shuffled by.

"Oh, fine just now. Really just fine." But the rest of her face, it seemed, didn't quite agree with her mouth.

"Have you been dancing with dragons?"

"Uh huh."

"Have you been defending your people, m'lady?"

"Yep."

"Have you been casting spells on evil tyrants and turning them into lumpy toadstools all covered in snot?"

"Well of COURSE I have. It's really quite simple."

"Then why does your face not agree with your mouth when your mouth says things are really just fine?"

"Well…I'm nervous to say, but it seems that today my wish has finally come true. I found a book, one book, THE book, from which I can't escape. See?"

16.

And she held up that book to me. It was called…PRINCESS AFRICA JONES.

17.

Princess Africa Jones and I paged through that book that day, and sure enough, she was there on every page. And there she was on every page battling demons, and ogres, and the Ku Klux Klan, and a thousand horrible monsters. But also, right there on page three, was her teacher Miss Laurie Pritchett. And there were bullying boys, and mean little girls, and boring tongue cluckers galore.

18.

"Why are THEY in my book?" asked Princess Africa Jones. "Why are *they* in my book saying I got no daddy and no friends and Momma got no money? Why are *they* allowed in my book to be mean to me and tell me to pull my head out of the clouds like it's wrong for my head to be there?"

19.

"Because *they* are a part of your story too, Princess Africa Jones. And look," I said, pointing to page five which showed her momma and auntie Benita and her chubby cat Stubby who has diabetes and cloudy eyes. "If you're going to live in a book from which you can't escape, surely you want *them* to be in there too."

"There's my chubby gray Stubby!" said Princess Africa Jones. "And his cat racks, er...cata...uh...with his cloudy eyes. And here's US right now!"

20.

And sure enough, there we were, Princess Africa Jones and I, on page twenty reading the part in PRINCESS AFRICA JONES when we're reading PRINCESS AFRICA JONES on page twenty.

21.

Princess Africa Jones flipped to page one and read aloud to herself. "*'Princess,'*" she mumbled, *"so everyone in the world would have to address her with respect. 'Africa,' the Mother-*

land, where all of us came from. 'Jones,' her daddy's name, even though she'd never met him, and probably never would." But I'm nervous about the *last* page. On the last page it always says, The End. The end? But this book is so short! That *can't* be all. Oh heavens no! That can't be all at all!"

22.

So I flipped to the back of PRINCESS AFRICA JONES to see if it said The End. It did *not* say The End. It didn't even *have* an end. It only said: "this is just the beginning."

23.

"You know, Princess Africa Jones, the library has a policy about not returning borrowed books. And writing in the books that you borrow."

"Not allowed," said Princess Africa Jones. "It's really that simple."

"But I think," I said further, "in the case of PRINCESS AFRICA JONES we'll make an exception. This is *your* story, and it's up to you to keep writing it. And you can write it in any way *you* choose. It's up to you, and it's just *that* simple. But you have to share it with the people you love a lot. And even the people you love just a little."

24.

So Princess Africa Jones headed home with her head held high. High in the clouds: which is a mighty fine place for a head to be. She headed home to Sixth Street where the other girls might have laughed, and the other kids may very well have pointed, and all the grown-ups could very possibly have clucked their tongues and shook their heads and said, "What is wrong with that Princess Africa Jones?" But Princess Africa Jones paid them no mind. For she had a story. A story she was eager to tell. A story she was eager to share. But first, she had a story to write. And she knew that the last page couldn't say The End because it was no longer The End or even *the last page.* This isn't all. Oh, heavens no. This isn't all at all. For Princess Africa Jones,

25.

This is just the beginning…

(Additional notes on the illustrations for the last few pages: We should see Princess leaving the library with her head held high as she walks out into the bleak urban landscape, but off in the distance we should see her falcon in the sky. Also, peeping around corners and stoops we can see little beasties and fairies, conspicuous by their bright colors. Next we should see Princess riding her falcon back home to Sixth Street above the city below. The falcon drops her off right in front of her apartment building and Princess and the falcon bow courteously to each other. Next we see Princess in her apartment—Momma and "auntie" Benita both kiss her as she walks in, Stubby rubs against her leg. Princess shows them the book PRINCESS AFRICA JONES and they're both flabbergasted. The second to last page should be the three of them cuddled on the fold out bed, Princess snuggled between Momma and "auntie" Benita while they read PRINCESS AFRICA JONES together and eat popcorn and drink chocolate milk. Stubby can be curled up asleep at the foot of the bed. From out the window there should be trolls and winged alligators or what have you trying to peer in to read the book. The very last page should be almost completely white with Princess herself drawing/painting what will be a colorful bit of scenery. [ed: *sorry, D'antre, no color.*] There should be one completely white page at the very end.)

Dedication:
For Dameka. Daddy loves you baby girl.

About the author:
D'antre Philips lives in Cincinnati, Ohio.
This is his first book for children.

D'antre would like to thank:
Sal Willis, Yishai Seidman,
Eric Campbell, Lance Wright,
BL and Jeff M. for the dope visuals,
and all his fam and friends for their support.

APOCRYPHA

The Killer Whispers and Prays...or Like a Sledgehammer to the Ribcage

I don't think he's being forthright with us, Sergeant...

"No, I don't think he is. Are you getting excited, fella? Is this turning you on? Do you think this is a game?"

This isn't a game. This is war. Somebody told him wrong.

"Somebody told you wrong, Habib. Oh, and he whispers and prays. The killers all whisper and pray. But you see, Achmed...I'm sweet and nice. It's the *corporals* who are mean and tough. And the corporals have your little baby boy in the other room. And they have garden shears and a long, hard mag-light. Do you know what those shears will do to his little toes? Do you know what that rod will do in his little bottom? Shhh shhhh shhhhhhhhhhhhh...none of that now."

Is all that screaming going to help him, Woyzeck?

"The screaming's not helping you, Haji. Pose for your glamour shot."

Smile and say Jihad...

"Just like the sheep at the slaughterhouse back home."

Tell us all about it, Frannie.

"Hang them by a chain, alive and terrified, by their back feet. They roll in one after the other. Slit one throat, slit the next. It all drains into a bucket."

Message coming in, Sergeant. OPEN FIRE!

When Frannie came marchin' home again / Hurrah! Hurrah! / She was pale, gaunt, vacant and thin / Hurrah! Hurrah!

***

I was discharged. And given special duty. There are terrorists and rogue agents operating on our very soil. I had to work under cover of midnight. Equipped with a customized rifle I would shoot diamonds into their throats. No trace. No serial numbers. Just hard cut diamonds right to the throat. I walled them up in the paneling at the neighborhood grocery store. The walls are packed with them now. Sometimes they weren't fully dead, and I'd hear them trying to scream as I walled up another. But they couldn't scream. Not really. Not with diamonds in their throats. There are hundreds. You can smell them rotting when you shop for produce. Special Ops. Not sanctioned. If I'd been caught I'd have been on my own. The pay was slimmer than I thought it would be. But I'm a proud soldier. I serve one master only. The one most high. I used to pretend that there was no God. But I'm not blind. Even in the roaring midnight I'm not blind. Oh Lord, make me an instrument of your justice...And a channel for your righteous genocide. Wind. And rain. They've put out the sun. I could love this cellar life. Where spiderlets devour their own mothers... Twilight is my cloak and salvation. And the killer whispers and prays. I am still. Centered. My head is gravel, my teeth are arrowheads, my eyes are sand packed tight pounded clear and sharp into brittle liquid windows into your forever nothing. I am where chaos goes to die, dragged kicking and wailing, baffled and grief-struck into its own annihilation. I suffer neither the fools nor the wise.

I don't suffer at all.

"So today's the big day, huh?"

Second lieutenant J. Rogers packed his duffel with the few personal items he'd left lying about. He was an intruder in this the meager efficiency and he knew it. He liked the feeling. Pulling a Camel Red out of his shirt pocket, he watched Marie pace about, shoeless, plain and simple, as she straightened second-hand lamps resting on cut-rate end tables. *No smoking around the baby, idiot.* He dropped the cigarette back into his pocket.

"Not the time," Marie said distracted, furiously tossing odds and ends into available drawers: pens, lighters, loose change, an old, worn copy of *The Unfinished Works of Georg Buchner.* "Not the time not the time." With a slight shudder-breath, she bent over and picked a piece of condom wrapper out of the stained carpet. She slid a cleaning bucket under the dining table.

"She's my friend too," said J.

"Come on, J. Please."

"We're probably closer, in fact. We were in combat—"

"You know what? That's great and that's awesome and I'm all about it...but not today."

"I'm gonna be around, you know."

"Hey, fantastic—"

"So what? Do we meet for the first time next week? How we working this?"

"Oh god..."

"Well?"

"Please!!!"

"I just want to do this right. That's all." Quite to his own surprise, J found himself filled with the sudden urge to go into the bedroom, pick up the baby and tickle him. Kiss him one last time. And at once, he was not so keen to leave after all. "Marie...look...You've got to realize...she's not the person you know any more. That person is gone forever."

"You don't know," Marie replied. The finality of his tone chilled her, and she absently gritted her teeth. "You didn't know her before."

"No, but I know her NOW, and you don't."

"You don't know." *Ohhh yes...*"Stop it."

"What?"

"I said stop." *Up a little higher.* "You can't touch me like that anymore."

"You don't like it?"

"I didn't say that." *Just a little lower.* "I said *don't.* Let go."

"All right. I'm out." But he stood still. "Can I just see Christian for a moment?"

"Why? He's not your son."

"HE'S NOT HER'S EITHER!!!"

Get a grip, soldier!

"Okay," she said, cool and direct, "Do you really want to have that talk with me now?"

"No."

"What I thought."

Say something, you fuck! Don't let her slip away this easy!

"You're not going to have any sort of...safety net, you know. No protection. No benefits. And she's not going to be able to take care of you."

"I can take care of myself."

"Yeah, and that's another thing. Does she know about that? Does she know how you've been *getting by* in her absence? What do you think she'll think? Huh? Will she be as understanding? Or forgiving?"

"Oooooh, you've got some big brass balls throwing *that* in my face. You wanna talk about dirty money? How've YOU been earning a paycheck the past couple of years, lieutenant? Let me see your hands; is that blood? Yeah. *Honorable.*"

"You're not going to tell her, are you?" He laughed. Cold.

"Why would I?"

"It's just going to be our little secret." *Our little secret.* "Well...yours, mine, and every miserable pathetic hunchback in town who's got the itch and the scratch, right?"

"Fuck."

"I'm leaving. It's been real nice. How much do I owe you?"

"Goddamn..."

Asshole!

"I'm sorry, Marie. That was wrong and I didn't mean it. I didn't mean to hurt you."

"I didn't mean to hurt *you.*"

"So…I guess…I'll meet you, or whatever, in a week or two."

"Can't wait." And as he left, she whispered, "Goodbye."

And Frannie sings:

Run away, run away, run away, run away from me. Run away, run away, run away, run away from me. I don't trust myself when I'm like this. I don't like myself when I'm like this. Run away, run away, run away, run away from me.

Master Sergeant Francine Woyzeck entered her own apartment as if she'd never been there before. Tossing her satchel onto the couch, she surveyed the scene scanning for a trigger of tangible memory. *A little.* She sat down and opened the satchel, more out of habit than necessity just then. She pulled out her medicine kit and bag of toiletries. A few magazines. A butterfly knife, some length of rope, and a couple of black burlap hood sacks—*OH FUCK!* Those last items quickly went back into to bag and zipped up twice. She scanned the room again. *Nothing much.* No less alien than the barracks from which she just came. *Ahhhhhhh…Blackchurch…home again home again…*

"Fran?"

From out of the adjacent bedroom Marie walked with naked feather footsteps. This moment she'd waited for for so many months was now here…and at once she secretly prayed for *just one more dress rehearsal, Dear God.* No dice.

"Hm."

Fran stood before her still and on display. Same pretty girl, love of Marie's life. Auburn hair and hazel eyes like cool, shimmering lakes. Funny and silly and ticklish around her calves and heels…now strangely hard like pewter. Angular and pointed.

"Hey baby…Wow…um…So…"

"Yeah. Hey there you."

They hugged. Stiff. They stopped.

"Doing...good?"

"How's...stuff?"

"Stuff is...yeah. Feeling well?"

"It's...you know."

"Totally. Anton called."

"Crazy bastard."

"It's been a..."

"Couple. Maybe...a while. A little."

"So...it's good to..."

"It's...it is. Yeah. God, you know, I thought it was going to be a little tough, and I THINK it is a bit rough but, but, but I think that, yeah, you know, it's quite a thing, right? Isn't it? Don't you think so? Yeah? Sure. I mean, how often are you just like FUCK, you know? It's crazy, uh huh, all the things that can happen in such a short time and, you know, things pass through your head that are *really* over here and then there's this OTHER stuff and you're thinking HOLY SHIT, you know. It's just such a different scene but all in all it's good, right. Things are great and it's all pretty great. Great. Yeah. Good stuff. Good...stuff..."

"Yeah..."

"Fran?"

"Yep."

"Was it...lonely?"

"Little chilly here."

"Fran?"

"Yup."

"Wake up now."

"I should...uh...maybe this isn't the right time."

"Oooooh no you don't. Not again."

"You're free to go on, Marie."

"You're free to stop now."

As Fran turned toward the door, Marie grabbed her arms with both hands.

"Let go, goddamn it."

"No."

"Marie!"

Instinctively Fran raised her fist and Marie screamed, "Don't you DARE hit me!" Like a lioness, Marie jumped onto Fran's back and sunk her teeth hard into her lover's neck. Fran howled in pain and they both tumbled to the floor in a heap. "See," Marie chuckled, wiping her wet lips across the back of her hand, "you're not dead after all."

"Aggggh, let me go!!!"

"Not a chance."

"I changed my mind," Fran spat. "I don't want you anymore."

"Tough shit."

"LET GO OF ME!"

"Not happening."

"You're fucking hideous!" snarled Fran. "You make me sick!"

"Bummer for you." Marie, grabbing the upper hand, pinned Fran to the floor at both wrists. With her knees she forced Fran's legs open and slid between them.

"Get away from me!"

"Nope."

"I put a bullet through a baby's heart!" Fran growled, thrashing, gnashing her teeth, her watery eyes so red her tears resembled blood.

"Sure you did." Without thinking Marie began to slowly grind her pelvic bone into Fran's.

"Collected, fuckin', eyeballs...and teeth!"

"F...fuh...fascinating."

"AAAAARGHHH!" Fran's aggressive thrashing gradually transformed into a futile squirm, and Marie pressed and pushed and rubbed harder between her thighs.

"You're wasting...your energy."

"FUUUUUUCK!!!" Fran screamed, absently joining in on the grind as the two of them began to slither and pulse against one another.

"Yessss ma'am..."

Just as Marie thought she might climax, Fran crumbled and collapsed inward, sobbing. Marie cradled her tightly in her arms, *shushing* and rocking like only a skilled mama can.

"I d-d-don't…want, *sob*, want to hurt you!"

"Shhhhhhh. You won't, sweetie. You won't."

"I was…afraid…I'd, I'd, *sob*, lose you."

Marie smiled and brushed a few rebel strands of hair from Fran's damp checks.

"But you're the beautifulest girl I know."

"Marie, I'm…"

"Shhhhh. I know, sweetheart. I know."

"It's just like…yeah…"

"Yeah…"

"Just…"

"Now, missy, howzbout you tell me the *truth*."

"It was…boring and lame and no big deal and I missed you every day."

"See, that wasn't so hard, was it." They giggled softly. They kissed. Warm and familiar. Marie held Fran's head to her breast and mouthed silently, *Love you…love you forever'nd-ever.*

"Say somethin'?"

"Nah."

"Okay…" Fran exhaled deeply and looked Marie directly in the eyes. "I'm ready now. I want to meet him."

"Really? Are…are you sure?"

"Y…Yes."

"I don't think you are."

"I AM. I'm ready."

"'Kay."

Fran remained sitting Indian-style on the floor as Marie exited to the bedroom. She returned with a cooing gurgling bundle swaddled in a thin, aqua-colored wrap.

"This…." Marie said by way of a grand introduction, "is Christian. Here, hold him."

"Oh, I don't know."

"C'mon. You're his mommy too."

Marie handed the bundle to Fran. Fran could not help but be startled at how light and shapeless the baby was. Without much to go on, Fran had been imagining this child as the round, rosy cherubic infants one is likely to see on television commercials hawking fruit juices and rash salves. But this *Christian* here, with his ashen skin and skeletal, claw-like little fingers slashing randomly about, was nothing like those creatures. His tight, thin lips snapped aimlessly, like a vulture chick hungrily awaiting mother's vomit. At once the baby's head fell backward and his mouth gaped open, his eyes blank like a rag doll's corpse.

"OH NO!" Fran panicked. "OH GOD!"

"It's all right! It's okay. See?" Marie instantly righted the small boy's head in the crook of Fran's arm and he returned to his gurgling and lip-smacking. "See? He's alive. See?"

"Jesus..."

"Yeah."

"Tiny."

"Wave for Mommy, Christian."

"Does he breathe okay?"

"It'll get better. See? That's better already. I've been waiting for this for so long."

A metallic bang and clunking rumble startled both Fran and the baby.

"Jesus!"

"It's okay, sweetie," Marie giggled. "It's just the furnace."

"Fuckin' raising a baby in a creepy-ass church," Fran said, shaking her head.

"Don't you just love him?"

"He's got your mouth."

"He loves you already. He loves you already."

My head is a thousand pounds of gravel. I walk spiders on a leash. I cast a shadow at midnight in pitch black with screaming indigo splashing across emerald eyes overflowing. I leave the quick wailing in my wake. Baffled and grief-struck. Tear ducts like choking deserts. Ducking shrapnel tearing throats coated with mother's dust and blood. I have no fear. I have no shame. I'm not proud of what I do but...I'm proud to do what I can.

"Woyzeck?"

"Huh?"

Second lieutenant J. Rogers entered the squalid upstairs apartment of the old, converted church bold and unannounced, without so much as a knock. Fran had, just moments prior, been rooting through the couch cushions in desperate search for spare change or at least a loose cigarette. No dice.

"At ease, sergeant."

"Well HOLY SH—"

"Shhhhhhh...Baby's sleeping." Indeed he was, in a thrift store pumpkin seat next to a small but mighty space heater.

"Right right. How you been, Rogers?" They embraced forcefully. "With your big ole head start. Fucknut."

"Eh, you know. What'd I miss?"

"Sand."

"Goddamn, I miss that sand."

"Love it."

"I brought some home. I store it in my jockeys."

"For safe-keeping."

"Totally. Right next to my ass. Only way I can sleep." Fran nodded, smiling. "Look at you F.W. You and your little family. Settling in I see. Nice."

They went on to catch up about the state of the war in bland, businesslike terms, never discussing anything beyond day to day soldier grunt work. The subject of their commanding officers came up briefly which quickly devolved into language such as "necro-pederast," "cretin rat fuck" and "jizz mop," followed by a round of hearty laughter.

"So, F. Tell me straight. Holding up okay?"

"Like a steel rod."

"That's what she said."

"Dude...that doesn't even...make any sort of sense." Thunder crashed hard right outside the window. "Fucking hell!"

"Rain's been killing me," J said. "Like needles out of a cannon. For weeks. And I'm out there at the docks drowning in it. I've heard there's hail coming. Greaaaaat."

"So you're working these days."

"I'm solid. Doing well. Money in my pocket. Money to burn."

"I'm a little concerned."

"You're not working? You've been back for a while now."

"I can't...get it together."

"Huh. No problem for me."

"Sooooo...what are you saying?"

"I'm just saying, you know. Maybe I could help—"

"NO."

"Well, you'd better hop to it, F. You got these angels to look after. They're counting on you."

"I'm not...at my best. But I'm good."

"How does labor suit you?"

"What? Oh..."

"Huh?"

"Labor. Never mind. I thought...never mind...Labor. Yeah, I'm fine for lifting and shit."

"You'll be good, Ef Dub. You're pretty strong. For a woman."

"Yeah..."

Another thunder crash and Christian began to fuss and whimper, never actually waking. J looked over to him with a warmth that betrayed his *official story.*

"Cute kid ya got there. I love babies," J whispered to no one in particular. "They suit me."

"Yeah..." Fran replied. "Me too."

"I could at least make some calls for you."

"That'd...be great."

"Hey, I'm not trying to—"

"You're not stepping on my toes. Got a cigarette?"

He pointed at the sleeping baby with a disapproving scowl.

"Right," said Fran resigned. "Thanksamil."

"Anything I can do to help. Call on me tomorrow. Or I'll call on you."

Suddenly the baby let out a shriek, and Marie came running in from the bedroom wearing nothing but an oversized flannel shirt. She picked him up in one swoop and began bouncing him to the beat of a song no one else heard.

"Shhhh shhhh shhh shhhhh...It's okay..."

"Marie." J said stiffly. "Hello. Again."

"Hi. Uh..."

"You've met, right?" Fran interjected.

"Well..." Marie squinted. "Maybe..."

"Yeah, cuz, remember," J stammered. "I brought you the thing? *The thing*?"

"Oh...yeah."

"Yeah. Remember Fran? I was heading back home and you weren't sure when you'd be, well anyway, you gave me, the, the package—"

"The anklet." Marie *remembered.*

"The anklet. Right."

"Uh huh," said Fran.

"Right. You asked me to bring the anklet, and give it, yeah, that one there."

Marie held up her leg to show off the anklet in question and J pointed at it as if it wasn't plainly visible. Fran stood quietly, perplexed by their behavior.

"So...yeah."

"Right," J smiled, relieved. "Good to see you again."

"Ditto," Marie replied.

"I've heard so much."

"Yeah..."

"Oh, and this must be Christian, yes? How doin' there, buddy? Huh? How doing? He's adorable." The baby cooed and chortled. J looked up at Fran and said, "Yours?" And the silence was radioactive. Finally he continued, "So I'll see you tomorrow, Fran. Marie, my pleasure."

"All mine," Marie said as J made his exit. Marie kissed the baby's belly. "All mine," she said again and the infant giggled and belched. Marie placed him back in his pumpkin seat, and he nodded off immediately. Marie wrapped her arms around Fran. "Aaaaaall mine. Chilly?"

"Little."

"Feel my feet."

"They're cold."

"They're soft. They haven't touched anything but this floor in a million years."

"That's a long time. Well, get dressed. Go have fun. I'll watch him."

"Um...No...that's okay honey. I'm fine here. Hungry?"

"Nah."

"Tired maybe? Need to lie down a bit?"

"Uh uh. You've got to be freezing."

"You should warm me up."

"Yeah. GAAAAAA! God, your toes are ice!"

Marie giggled, "You're gonna wake him."

"Don't want to scare him."

"Don't worry."

"He should be fatter. He's not fat enough."

"He's happy, Fran. He's really happy."

"Are you happy, Marie?"

"I love you."

"I'm sorry."

"I *love* you."

"There's a draft."

"It's warmer now."

And with that, they fell to the couch and made love.

"Marie...I...love...you...back."

"Oh...oh...OH GOD!"

"Shhhhhhhh! You're so loud."

"I can't...help it! You make me crazy. Oh sweet Jesus...My my my lordy..."

Naked and sweat-drenched, the rest of the world dissolved around them. As if flashed back in time, Fran was, briefly, once again herself.

"Marie...oh...yes..."

"Don't p-penetrate me. All I need is...oh yes, *riiiiiiiiight there...*"

All at once Marie came to a shuddering, bucking orgasm and squealed with delight.

"Shhhhh..." Fran giggled, covering Marie's mouth with her hand.

"Too long" Marie gasped. "It's been...too damn long..."

"Hey, how do you think *I* feel?"

"You feel pretty good to me."

"You're silly."

"Be silly with me."

They lay together, silently, breathing hard and listening to the leaden rain smash against the asphalt outside. "You think you're hard," Marie said finally. "But you're not. I think you're as soft and sweet as hot butterscotch."

"'Kay."

"I'll bet you didn't hurt anyone at all."

"You got me."

"Damn right I do. Wanna go outside?"

"It's raining! Real hard!"

"Let's go be naked in the rain."

"Oh Christ."

"It'll be good stuff. We'll splash our bare feet in icy puddles. We'll freeze our asses numb."

"Freeze our assets?"

"Then we'll come in and get warm again."

"Sheesh."

"Aw, whaddaya 'fraid of, soldier?"

"You are too crazy."

"I'm just crazy enough."

"Goddamn...you're so pretty when your cheeks are flushed."

"Honey dripper."

"I could live in your smile. I could swim in your eyes."

"See? You're why I'm crazy."

"I'm addicted to your skin."

"Oh my..."

"You're my heroin."

"You're mine. You're *my* heroine, Soldier girl."

"Do you understand how bad I—"

Marie suddenly burst into tears

"If you ever, *sob,* leave again I'm going to…"

"I'm home now, sugar," Fran said, soothing. "I'm home for good."

"Tell me how it was," Marie cried. "Please."

"You got my letters, yeah?"

"Oh. Yeah. *Wish you were here.*"

"Heh heh heh."

"Too crazy…" she sniffled.

"Home now. For good."

"I'm thinking of cutting all my hair off."

"Don't do that."

"Maybe I should grow it out long."

"No, I like it like it is."

"I need a change. I want a ball gown."

"Yuck!"

"And a sparkly neck-thing."

"Necklace."

"If you insist."

"What, and a pumpkin coach? And glass slippers too?"

"Nope. No shoes. Never. Rings are good, though. *A-hem.*"

"For your toes?"

"Toes OR *fingers. A-HEM.*"

"Subtle."

"I'm so sleepy."

"You're gonna drive me poor. More so."

"Not even, *yawn,* a plastic ring?" With that Marie fell deep into sleep. Fran covered her with an old, knotty afghan and walked over to the window to watch the storm. The hail had begun. Tennis ball sized, they pummeled the poor unfortunates caught out in it, and crashed through windshields, setting off car alarms for blocks. The wail of sirens increased as more and more lethal chunks of ice made their destructive descent. Fran turned back to find the baby wide-awake in his seat, eyeing at her with sharp, calculated appraisal.

"You need a plan, soldier," the baby said matter-of-fact. "We're hungry."

"Um...well...I could mercenary," Fran replied. "I don't know much, but I know how to kill."

"Plan plan plan, Fran."

Fran instantly felt awkward standing naked before an infant boy and quickly slid into a pair of jeans and a T-shirt.

"Nobody will fucking hire me."

"Tell us about it, Frannie."

"I do get sick on occasion. And dizzy. And I'm falling."

"Your feet are flat on the ground."

"But I'm still falling."

"All scooped out?"

"Hollow. Like a stone cave."

"Poison in the sand. It creeps up inside."

"Sand. Air. Sky."

"Do tell. Tell us about *over there.*"

"Pretty boring. Nothing much to say."

"Tell us all about it."

"Lots of sitting around. Meet the locals. Rebuild. Good things."

"Tell us about the *torture*, Frannie-belle."

"There are lies in the spires and the magic lies. All the magic lies. All of it. All my magic lies. All my magic lies...every one of them. This is where all my magic lies. This is where you will find all my magic lies..."

"Tell us a little story about the *torture.*"

"There was no torture."

"Tell us about the dogs."

"There was no torture."

"Pigs and dogs sniffing on the mezzanine. Pigs and dogs sniffing on the mezzanine. Thump, what was that? They're not coming, are they? Thump thump thump."

"All of it...lies...still..."

"Tells us about the black burlap hoods, Frannie-belle. The rape and the dogs and beatings and the torture and we laughed

laughed laughed laughed laughed, didn't we laugh at the blood and the sodomy, Frannie-belle? Didn't we laugh at all the burning babies?"

Fran giggled, "Some corpses keep hard-ons..." She put her face in her hands, horrified with herself. But she laughed again at the notion.

"No one blames you."

"Do they blame that brain-dead fascist who sent us down there?!?!"

"Nope. Him neither."

"It'll make us murder. It'll make us meat. Make us monsters all..."

"Buck up, sergeant."

"The past has passed. It's gone now. Gone."

"Are you home now, love?"

"I gotta be pretty for her now. And strong. And strong for you. The past is the past and I'm hanging it on a nail in the hallway."

"You'll take care of us then? Strong and tough and all of that?"

"And all of that."

"Not like a *daddy* I hope."

"NO."

And once again the baby let out a shriek. Instant rage, the little figure shook and turned a deep shade of crimson, forcing out a scream to push his tiny lungs to their splitting point. Marie awoke with a sigh.

"Ohhh, will he never sleep?!?!"

"Why's he so loud?" Fran asked, gripping her head in agony.

"Jesus, Fran. Could you take him for a while?"

The baby fixed its razor wire eyes on Fran and hissed, "Take us with you, Frannie-belle. Teach us how you work. Should we follow the turkey buzzards?"

Marie bounced him shushing, oblivious.

"I...can...take him," Fran offered.

"Never mind."

"Marie...We're gonna do better than this. I promise."

"I know."

"You yourself could sell, Frannie," the baby hissed again. "Bodies do sell we've learned. Hungry."

"I think he's just hungry," Marie said, squeezing her left nipple to express a bit of milk.

"Hungry," the child continued. "And we sleep and live in shit. You're still a pretty little kitty, Fran, and boys pay top dollar for sweet meat. Poor girls whore, love."

Fran paced, considering the infant's proposition. "I don't know if..."

"He's just fussy," Marie said.

"I need a physical," said Fran. "But I'm good to work. I'm seeing a doctor tomorrow, then I'm good. I'll make you happy, Marie."

"I...am. Already."

"You're good," the baby taunted. "You'll *make* her."

"It's too fucking loud in here. I gotta step out for a cigarette."

"We don't have any more."

"Somebody does."

"MOMMA!" the baby cried out, reaching for Fran. Fran backed away slowly toward the door.

"He doesn't want you to leave," Marie said, small.

"I'll be right back."

"Hush, now, baby you don't have to cry / I'm here and I'll always be by / Hush, now, you'll always be in my arms / Safe, warm, protected from all harm / My love / My baby my love / My love / My baby my love..."

Marie sang as she changed Christian's diaper and wrapped him up tight in his receiving blanket. J entered the flat quietly and stood watching and listening. He smiled and thought to himself, *this could be your life*. And a shot of anger jolted through his body. Finally,

"Beautiful," he said interrupting the song.

"OH! J," Marie turned with a start. "Hi. Thanks for coming. I wasn't sure if you would."

"Hey, I'm always happy to help a damsel in distress. Especially if I can help her out of *dis dress.*" There was an excruciatingly long pause until Marie realized it was a joke. "Um, just kidding." She giggled obligatorily and set Christian in his seat. "Soooo...how was the big welcome home?"

"No big deal."

"Yeah?"

"Oh yeah. You know. She rode in on a white horse, lifted me off my feet, carried me off into a green field and we made mad passionate love in the tall grass."

"No shit."

"All day long in the warm sunshine."

"Well I'll be damned."

"Yes you will."

"But see, I don't remember the sun shining for a month of Sundays."

"Well it did. And she's aces with Christian too. Like a pro."

"Good. Good to hear. So where *is* the missus?"

"Out."

"Thank heaven for tiny miracles."

Another horrible pause, and J thought that maybe he should just stop talking altogether.

"She's just out...you know...doctor and job and alla that."

"That's a full bill. I walked that road already. I'm clean now, and healthy. And working. Frannie will too I'm sure."

"Of course."

"Fran's one of my favorite people, you know." Marie nodded absently. J continued, "She's who I want in my corner. But I wouldn't want to cross her."

"Yeah. Look, let's cut the *happily ever after* bullshit."

"What? It's not great?"

"It's...not."

"It's not all roses and soft music and long walks in the moonlight?"

"It ain't Paris. It's just not. I mean...we're good, but..."

"But..."

"So, just 'but.' Dot dot dot."

"So what can I do to make it better?"

"What can you do?"

"I want to help you."

"I couldn't ask—"

"You called. I came. I want to be here for you. So name it."

"I just wanted to...talk to you. I miss talking to you."

"That's it?"

"Yeah."

"Quit playing." He simply couldn't take this stupid two-step any longer. Urgently he said, "She's not well, Marie. Let's be honest. She's not going to be able to come through. You're gonna starve. *He's* gonna starve."

"I don't think—"

"Somebody's gonna have to work. Cuz she won't. She can't."

"Maybe this isn't the time."

"I love Fran. You know that. But I just don't think Fran—"

"Fran Fran Fran. She's all over your lips." He moved in quickly to kiss her. "Don't!"

"Okay, fine. Maybe this was a mistake."

"Wait. I miss you. I...care about you."

"But you LOVE her!" He seethed.

"I do. Oh god, do I love her. Like a deep cut."

"Like a sledgehammer to the fuckin' ribcage."

"It's fatal."

"Goddamn..."

"I'm being honest, J. Do you want me to lie?"

"Maybe a little," he replied small.

"And you're right. If she can't take...Well, maybe it's about me taking care of *her*. So I will take care of her. If she can't provide for me...for *us*, then I have to. Somehow."

"So it would seem."

"I just need a quick bit of cash to get us on sturdier feet. Fran doesn't have to know. She *can't*. Then we'll be good from there."

"So," he said coldly. "Go make that money. You know what to do."

"I'm innocent."

"Uh huh. I'll take that bet."

"You want to wreck my innocence?"

"No games, for Chrissakes."

"Just keep it quiet..."

"Everybody's got needs..."

"Business..."

"Sure. If you say so."

"Just a fine bit of business."

"Just fine."

"Nobody's hurt."

"Everybody wins."

"You shouldn't...touch me like that."

"You want me to stop? Tell me to stop."

"Sssssssssssssssssssss..."

"Tell me to leave and I'll leave. Go on, Marie. Tell me to leave." Without warning she lunged, biting deep into his chest. He yelped like a dog as the pain shot through him, and he picked her up and threw her hard against the couch. Tearing each other's clothes away, they fucked fucked fucked fucked FUCKED FUCKED FUCKED. *FUCKED.* Hard, rough, deep. Savage.

"Don't you miss this? Huh? You miss this cock?"

"I don't...I..."

"Shit...slow down..."

"No. OOOHHH!!! DEEP! Deeper than that! YESSSS!!"

Marie climaxed wildly. The soldier did not. They fucked harder.

"Come on," he panted. "Wait for me."

"No."

"Baby watching?"

"Shut up. OOOOOOOOOOH YES!"

"Not...working for me."

"Yes! Works for me."

"Goddamn it. I'm trying—"

"Try HARDER. Oh Jesus! HARDER! OH GOD!"

"Here, turn around."

"NO!"

"Turn around!"

Frustrated, J flipped her over onto her stomach and began pounding into her from behind.

"NO! Don't fuck me like that! I'M NOT A BOY!"

Marie buried her face in the cushions wailing as J continued to slam into her, finally grunting out a brutish orgasm.

"YES!!! Oh yeah...Holy...fucking...Jesus . . "He rolled over panting. Marie refused to remove her face from the cushions, treating J instead only to the sounds of wrenching sobs. "Hey. What's wrong? Don't cry. Come on, Marie. Stop crying!" No response. He stood up, fidgety and nervous. He quickly began to throw his clothes back on, never once having the nerve to look over at the silent infant watching it all. "You're not going to...tell anybody, are you? ARE YOU?!" He grabbed her hair roughly and she let out a shriek of pain. "Sorry! Sorry! Come on. You hear me?! Sorry. I'm sorry. You won't tell anybody. You're not going to. I know you won't. Come on, please don't cry. I wanted to help you. Come on. Shhhhhhh. Shhhh. Please stop crying. Here." He pulled out his wallet and began raining down bills all around her. No response. Just the sobbing. "Come on. Take it. I just want to help you! Take the money, Marie. Here, take it all. Take the goddamn money."

After dumping all the cash from his wallet, J fled the apartment in a panic. Silence followed. Finally, Marie lifted up her head. Not sobbing. Not a bit weepy. Not even blotchy. Perfectly fine. She smiled, self-satisfied, counted the money happily, and sang to herself...

"Hush now / baby you don't have to cry..."

It's hard to see in this light just how glum and dreary all those faces are. Drones and worker ants marching off to feed and gang fuck the queen bee. Clomping down the sidewalk with granite feet. It's a pity. What? No, I don't do that sort of work anymore. Yes, I'm desperate, but the answer is no. What? Speak up, you're cutting out. What's that? Come on, do I have to walk you through it? You tie 'em tight behind his back, push him to his knees, put the hood over his head, and slit a wide smile from earlobe to earlobe. Then just let him drain out into the tub. Easy as cherry cordial. There's no mess if you do it right. Well, get clean.

Fran entered freezing and soaked. No employment found today. The storm outside had gotten ever more severe. Winds up to one hundred and three miles per hour. Piercing rain. And hail grown to thick daggers of ice. Fran herself watched a man's face lacerated open by such a jagged chunk as this, his cheek ripped asunder exposing his white teeth like a bloody, wailing skull. She thought to tell Marie about it, but decided instead not to say a word, lest it upset her.

Once inside Fran found only the baby, alone in his pumpkin seat. His talon-esque little hands waving absently in the air as if conducting an unseen and unheard orchestra.

"She whored while you were gone, you know," he said. "Babies need bottles, Frannie. She let strangers do all sorts of things to her. In your bed. In her hair. Poor girls only serve one purpose, my dear."

"The past is behind us now, baby-love. Sunny days on the horizon."

"Not the past. Today! They ate her skin right off her bones. She swallowed their poison. Babies get hungry and poor girls *get by somehow.*"

"Get bi?"

"And get bought."

"It's...all passing away into nothing. I'll have forgotten it all soon. Bright times ahead. But..."

"But?"

"It's always cold here. Goddamn furnace."

"Are you sleeping, Fran? Wake up. They're dripping with

her as we speak. Sopping. *Drenched.* RIGHT NOW. On your best day you'll NEVER be the mercenary she is. We'll eat now. We may be just fine. There are some women in this house who know how to work."

"No."

"How are things today, Fran?"

"Not true."

"Going well?"

"Wrong."

"She points her feet toward the heavens and earns her daily bread."

"You're wrong. The past is...hanging...in the hallway."

"What has *he* got that you haven't, huh?"

"He? Nothing. Nothing good."

"Oh but what a busy little beaver she can be."

"She's all I have."

"And not even yours."

"SHE'S ALL I HAVE!!!"

"You've got talents. Gifts."

"I don't know much...but..."

"Skills. Training. Expertise. *Experience.*"

"I'm falling. Odd sky today. Imperial violet."

"Lamb's blood."

"Even the sun is cold. Everything's cold here. She's all I have. I can't stop falling! There's even a damp chill about the sun. SHE'S All I...!"

"Hang them on a chain. One right after the other. Slit and spill. Slit and spill."

"Not true. Not real. Everything's fine."

She ran from the flat, down the stairs, outside the crumbling church, into the screaming wind. The storm had eased slightly just there, but Fran knew there were corpses not but a mile from home crushed by falling hail the size of Volkswagens. Heading into a blind run, she ran smack into Second lieutenant J. Rogers.

"Rogers..."

J stepped back, unsure as yet of what she knew or didn't.

She appeared distracted and upset, but not particularly *at him.* He offered her a Camel and a light. She took it and breathed in the smoke hungrily.

"Say there, Ef Dub. Uh...Fit as a fiddle?"

"Fit to be tied."

"Odd sky today. Hepatitis yellow."

"Thank God I'm not a sailor. Have you seen the hail?"

"No."

"Impossible."

"Hey F, if you're a little low—"

"Can't even afford a plastic..." she mumbled to herself.

"Fran?"

"I like your ring."

"Huh? Oh. Yeah."

"How much for it?"

"It was my great-grandfathers."

"She's got tiny fingers," Fran mumbled again to herself. "I could have it cut smaller, though."

"Not for sale."

"Everyone's for sale."

"Huh?!"

"Every*thing.* I mean every*thing.*"

"So...uh...How's the old doc then?"

"Bearing glad tidings of course."

"Ill news?"

"I got no love for uncertainty."

"Dizzy? Vertigo."

"Devoured alive from the inside out. I'm rotting."

"You can still work. I work."

"Poison. In my blood like sludge in a river. In my tears. In my..."

"It was all in the sand and the air, Woyzeck. I have it too."

"At least I can't pass it to *her.*"

"Oh..." *Shit.* "Yeah...well you can still work."

"Sure. Sunny days ahead."

Standing out in the cold and the wet, J felt his nervousness subside. Replaced with a burning rage.

"Or maybe...you...can't. Maybe you haven't got what it takes."

"What?"

"Maybe you're lacking the necessaries."

"Say again?"

"Maybe you're *under-equipped.*"

"Fuck you." Fran flicked her lit cigarette at his chest.

"Would you even know how?"

"I...I'm..."

"Oh, I know you're tough like a cheap steak. I know what went down over there in the dust. I heard the screaming. Poor little babies. They suit you, huh? I know what you did. Or rather, what you *let happen.*"

"I...need a moment—"

"Cuz when you can't do the job, F, there's always someone waiting in the wings to finish it off for you."

"Your hands are just as bloody—"

"Hey, I'm just the trigger man, darlin'. The boy with the *gun.* It's the bullets' fault, not mine."

"It's just—"

"You can toss and turn all you like. I sleep like a newborn all night."

"You've got a lot of fucking nerve—" Suddenly J grabbed Fran's wrist and twisted it behind her back. "AAAAGH!!!"

"You've got a lot of what you don't deserve," he growled through clenched teeth. Hot spit spraying out against her cheek. "A lot of what you can't handle. A lot of what rightly belongs to one better suited. You cunt."

"Don's sleep, maggot," she hissed. "I live in the pitch-black."

"Stop by any time, sergeant. We'll have a drink. Compare notes." He twisted her arm higher between her shoulder blades. She winced in pain, but was determined not to cry out. With his free hand, J began to run his fingertips over her nipples, and trail down her stomach. "Don't you just love it, Woyzeck? Don't you just love the way she claws your back when you hit that sweet spot just right? Don't you love how she always wants it deeper, deeper, *deeper*? Or...did you not know about that." He let go and she fell to the cement kneecaps first, rubbing her sore shoulder, refusing to look anywhere but down. "Take it easy, Fran. I'll be seeing you. Again and again. Some sunny day."

And away he strolled.

Fran lay on the cold paved ground feeling it throb with the violence and death that surely was taking place not but a few miles away. The sharpened, pointed metallic rain began afresh, and she felt the little pin pricks slashing tiny cuts into her face.

"No." she said to no one at all. "I won't. I can't." She put her hand to her ear. "Shut up. I said shut up!" She began smacking herself in the head as hard as she could, desperately trying to *chase it away*. "SHUT UP!!!" She began to sing. "Run away, run away, run away, run away from me...I don't like myself when I'm like this. Run away from me..."

As Fran crawled back upstairs and into the apartment, she was greeted by the sound of Marie singing,

"Hush, now, I'll always be here for you / I love who you are and not what you do / Hush now, and know if ever you're scared in the night / just look and I'll be your bright light, my love / My baby my love . ."

Christian sat still in his little chair, sucking happily on a bottle of milk. Under the table upon which the baby and his pumpkin seat rested was Fran's satchel: her special compartment opened. Unzipped twice. The baby gave Fran a tiny wink and resumed sucking away.

Marie entered, radiant. Gorgeous and feminine in a brand new dress, make-up, jewelry.

"Still in your bare feet though, I see," said Fran.

"Of course," Marie chirped.

"You can get to hell without shoes."

"Am I a bad girl, my love? Am I as lovely as sin?"

"Do you hate me? Is that what it is?"

"What? You're the beautifulest girl I know. I LOVE you."

"Yeah...Still need a ring? Or what?"

"Everything I do is for you."

"For me..."

"For us. I want what's best for *us.* And I do what I can."

"DO YOU THINK I'M AN IDIOT!?"

"NO!!! But...I know you're not well, Fran. You hear things that aren't there. You think things that aren't true. Your eyes play tricks."

"But I'm not blind."

"Sweetheart, I—"

"Even in the roaring midnight I'm not blind. Do you hear a snare drum? Cannons?"

"It's just the rain. And the furnace. Fran, please think for just—"

"I'm done thinking. My head is a thousand pounds of gravel. I walk spiders on a leash. I cast a shadow at midnight. In pitch black. With screaming indigo splashing across emerald eyes overflowing...my love."

"Fran—"

"I leave the quick wailing in my wake. Baffled and grief-struck. Tear ducts like choking deserts." Fran slid her satchel out from under the table with the tip of her boot. "There are lies in the spires. And all my magic lies."

"Fran, don't look at me like that. Oh god..."

"Ducking shrapnel, tearing throats coated with mother's dust and blood."

"I love you, Fran. Please—"

"No fear. No shame." Grabbing Marie's wrist she said, "I whisper and pray—"

"OW! Fran, PLEASE! Let go! You're HURTING me!"

"Oh Lord, make me an instrument of your justice."

Fran forced Marie to her knees. She reached into the satchel and grabbed the rope and butterfly knife.

"Oh god, NO! PUT THAT AWAY!"

"It's only kind of sharp."

"Oh god...no...think of the baby, Fran!"

"Cold in here, darling?" Fran asked as she slid a black

burlap hood over her lover's head.

"Please don't put that on me! Fran please!!! Take it off!!!"

"And dark? Wind and rain have put out the sun. Stay on your knees. I could love this cellar life. Where spiderlets devour their own mothers." Marie thrashed and screamed, muffled by the hood. Fran tied her wrists tight behind her back. "Be quiet," said Fran, irritated. The baby looked on intently as Fran slid the cleaning bucket from under the table. "Twilight is my cloak and salvation." In one clean slash Fran slit a half-moon from Marie's left ear to her right. "Oops. I think I penetrated you, hon." The body slumped forward, gushing and spilling right into the bucket. "I am still. Centered. And all that hot blood drains out."

Fran stood up, silently crying. Yanking off her boots, she began to sweat and shake. "God, it's so hot in here. And sticky. Need to scrub clean." She peeled off her shirt and pants. "It's getting worse!" She tore off her undergarments. "Boiling! Wash clean. I'm boiling alive!" From there she fell to her bruised, gashed knees and, using her shirt as a rag, soaked up Marie's blood, *washing* herself with it all over her body. "Wash...clean..."

"Fran?" J said as he entered the apartment, his boldness his undoing. "Marie?"

The baby laughed.

"My head is gravel," said Fran.

"Fr—" Catching the scene, J stopped short in horror. "Oh Jesus..."

"You're free to stop right now," Fran said, pointing the butterfly knife directly at him. "You think I won't catch you? You think I won't eat your skin right off your bones? My teeth are arrowheads, my eyes are sand packed tight pounded clear and sharp into brittle liquid windows. Into your forever nothing."

"Fran, I can—"

"I am where chaos goes to die, dragged kicking and wailing, baffled and grief-struck into its own annihilation. I suffer neither the fools nor the wise. I don't suffer at all. Come here and you live."

"Wait—"

"COME HERE NOW AND YOU'LL LIVE."

"Is that...Marie's? Oh my god, Fran. It's all over you. You're dripping with her."

"I'm drowning."

"You're drenched in her. MARIE! NO!"

"You pumped your poison into her. You put your disease in her. But we're going to get clean. Thump. Do you hear that? Are they up on the roof? In the steeple? Thump thump."

"It's not real. No no no..."

"They're not coming, are they? Up the stairs? Pigs and dogs sniffing on the mezzanine. Pigs and dogs sniffing on the mezzanine. Thump, what was that? They're coming for us. Thump thump thump. They're coming for us both."

"Fran, it isn't real. It isn't real!"

"Take you shirt off."

"It isn't real!"

"TAKE IT ALL OFF!" Crying, J peeled off all of his clothes down to his tube socks. Fran muttered, "All the magic lies. Make us murder. Make us meat."

"Make us monsters all," whimpered J. "God, god, please god..."

"We're washing clean."

Dabbing the rag into the bucket again, Fran smeared blood all over J's skin.

"AGH!" he groaned. "It's freezing cold!"

"Boiling. This is where all the magic lies. This is where you will find all the magic lies. Put your hands out in front. We're just the same," she said as she pulled his arms forward and tied a bit of rope around his wrists. "Don't squirm! You squirm they burn your wrists. You know that. We're just the same. Soldiers. It's all we know. Kneel down. We're praying and scrubbing clean."

"Oh god...oh god!"

"Quiet. Whisper. Keeps your prayers quiet. Hold out your

arms." Fran removed Christian from his seat without so much as a peep, and lay him across the soldier's out-stretched arms. "Take him. Hold him, like a big, strong man."

"I can't! I can't hold him like this!"

"I don't think he's being forthright with us, Sergeant," the baby said with a smirk.

"No, I don't think he is."

"Take him back!" J screamed, his armed quaking in agony.

"Don't drop him. Don't wake him."

"He's awake now!"

He began to sob as she covered his head with another black burlap hood.

"Buy the kid a hobbyhorse, Daddy."

"I can't breathe!"

"It'll get better. It's better already." The storm continued to rage outside as snow mixed with rain and hail. Bullet shots were heard as hoarding and looting had begun. Such is the end of things. Such is the end of all things. It gave Fran a great familiar comfort. But the messages trying to get through to her from her commanding officers were muffled, and loaded with static.

"Woyzeck? Sergeant Woyzeck? Do you read?"

Master Sergeant Francine Woyzeck, naked and drenched in blood, simply resumed her duties like a good soldier, following the last command given. Should any more terrorists or rogue agents be delivered she had more hoods, more rope, her knack for improvisation, plenty of hard-cut diamonds ready to be shot.

"What's the word, lieutenant?" She asked the baby as he rested steadily upon the soldier's shaking outstretched arms. The soldier's moaning muffled by the burlap.

"They're coming, Woyzeck," he replied solemnly. "Pigs and dogs. Thump thump. They're on their way."

"I await your word, sir," she said, reaching for her specialized rifle, eyeing the door.

"The time is now, soldier," the infant bellowed, "OPEN FIRE!"

Nathan Singer is a novelist, playwright, composer, and experimental performing artist. He is also the lead vocalist and guitarist for award-winning "ultra-blues" band The Whiskey Shambles. His published novels are the controversial and critically-acclaimed *A Prayer for Dawn*, *Chasing the Wolf*, *In the Light of You*, *The Song in the Squall*, and *Transorbital.* He currently lives in Cincinnati, Ohio where he is working on a multitude of new projects.

On the following pages are a few
more great titles from the
Down & Out Books publishing family.

For a complete list of books and to
sign up for our newsletter,
go to DownAndOutBooks.com.

Life During Wartime
and Other Stories by Thomas Pluck

Down & Out Books
January 2018
978-1-946502-39-1

Take a ride on the neuter scooter, follow a mountain man who's not what he seems, dine at the most exclusive restaurant in New York, where "Eat the Rich" takes on a whole new meaning, and meet Denny the Dent, a hulking 350 pounds of muscle who wouldn't harm a fly…but who'll glad crush a bully's skull.

A blackjack 21 of stories of people caught up in crime, facing bleak horrors, or spun in the whirlpool of human absurdity, this collects the best stories of Thomas Pluck.

Through the Ant Farm
Robert Leland Taylor

ABC Group Documentation,
an imprint of Down & Out Books
July 2017
978-1-943402-94-6

I'm not really retarded, as far as I know, but I suppose some of the other inmates around here might think so. Not because I killed my daddy, but because of the social thing—I'm just not very good at it…

And it's a shame, too, because I know God would've been very proud of me, saving his little creatures and all. There's not a doubt in my mind.

Selena
Book 1 of the Selena Series
Greg Barth

All Due Respect, an imprint of
Down & Out Books
December 2017
978-1-946502-79-7

Selena is living the dream on her terms—carefree and sloppy and all in the pursuit of pleasure. When a careless act of petty theft puts her in the crosshairs of a violent crime syndicate, her choices are clear—either curl up and die, or tear down the whole damned organization one bloody shotgun blast at a time.

Nothing will satisfy her but savage retribution. Nothing can stop her. Get ready.

Blacky Jaguar Against the Cool Clux Cult
Angel Luis Colón

Shotgun Honey, an imprint of
Down & Out Books
June 2017
978-1-943402-86-1

After painting the Cross Bronx Expressway red—literally—and losing his beloved car Polly to his ex, Linda Chen (who isn't returning his calls because she's not a complete idiot), Blacky decides his time is running short and has tasked himself with one last stop before tossing hands up and surrendering: Graceland.

Of course, nothing Blacky Jaguar sets his mind to ends up being simple. Contacted by an old frenemy, Blacky finds himself strong-armed into an online cabal known as The Cool Clux Cult and their shadowy internet tough-guy leader, neilDATASStyson.